MISSION GREEN

THINGS ARE GETTING OUT OF HAND.....

**A NOVEL
BY WALLY G. REIDE**

FIRST EDITION

MISSION CREEP

Wally G Reide
Abridged, edited and published by Ecovril Publishing ©
All rights Ecovril Ltd 2021
Copyright the property of Ecovril Ltd 2021
ecovril@gmail.com

ISBN 978-1-8383954-1-4

MISSION CREEP

World English dictionary
Origin approx. 1993
"The gradual process by which a campaign or mission's
objectives change over time with undesirable consequences"

OR

"The expansion of a project beyond its original goals often after
initial successes.
Mission creep is usually considered undesirable due to the
dangerous path of each success breeding more ambitious
attempts, only stopping when a final, often catastrophic failure
occurs"

Author's note

This is my version of events to put the record straight in the best way I can. Others involved would tell it in a different way. When I was present, my recollection may be flawed but the narrative will reflect what I remember to have occurred.
Where I was not present the story I tell is my best guess at what happened. I do not wish to be contacted to debate or explain or justify myself and I have taken steps to ensure that this is my epitaph. This manuscript will remain hidden until I am gone.

N.B.
*All the characters in this book are fictional, sometimes a fictionalised amalgam of aspects of more than one real person, but not intended to represent anyone who ever did or still exists. All the events described here are fictional or at worst a fictionalised version of events portrayed in the wrong order, attributed to different people, locations or timelines. Any resemblance to real people or events, are coincidental.
Wally G. Reide
North Herts. UK 2015

**'You have to say all that don't you?' - W
'Yes'- Ed

Publisher's note

This publication was made possible after a manuscript discovered
in a pine chest in an abandoned and remote woodland building in
Hertfordshire during the course of restoration work was identified
as belonging to the former deer keeper of an estate nearby.
After some considerable difficulty he was contacted and legal
documents were signed to enable us to take ownership and
publish.
The person in question demanded a five year embargo and
anonymity. He used those five years to vanish without trace. All
attempts to trace him to invite him to participate in interviews or
provide copy to coincide with the publication of this book, from
Nottingham to Lincolnshire via North Herts, Yorkshire,
Cambridge and back have failed. His legal representative died
unexpectedly in 2019.
He has been un-contactable since 2016

Ecovril Publishing
Fishing Cottage
Jan 2021

Contents

1 Reluctant Servants

Bradford, Feb 2004.

A green neon sign depicting the bowl of Hygeia enveloped by a serpent partaking of a mystical healing liquid dominates the cracked display window, crudely repaired with cardboard and gaffer tape. Illuminating the drenched and slippery stone flagged pavement outside is a lone beacon of waxy, feeble light offering the hope of a cure or soporific anaesthetic from this corner shop Pharmacy. Here the possibility of survival for the weak, damaged and infirm is liberally dispensed without question, along with chemicals which enable the sentient to endure life in a dismal, cold, defeated and forgotten northern city.

It's 9.15am and should be daylight, but endless drizzle sparkles in car headlights and the sky is laden with a relentless supply of freezing rain and dark northern winter grey. Without the lame illumination of the shop sign, which is vanquished only feet away by darkness and shadow, the cold unwelcoming hillside, clad entirely in Yorkshire sandstone flags, kerbs and cobbles would be in darkness still.

On this harsh morning, as ever, the small independent medical enterprise offers only at best the hope of survival through another joyless Bradford winter's day. No permanent cure for the dull pain of living here is offered, just something to numb the senses.

The shop, on the end of a row of identically decaying mill workers dwellings is surrounded and shadowed permanently by the tall stone walls of the redundant Victorian textile sheds and warehouses. William Blake's dark satanic mills are said to have been inspired by the shell of the burnt out Albion Mill in Southwark near his home in London. Anyone who has walked the narrow streets between the derelict stone mills and warehouses off Thornton Road or in Little Germany will appreciate how that phrase came to represent the towering monolithic workhouses of the northern industrial revolution, now abandoned and unloved.

The sorry streets here are overlooked with aloof majesty by the towering Italianate masterpiece of golden sandstone that funnelled the fetid breath of industry from Lister's Mill into the damp air far above the city. The mill and its spectacular chimney are, like Salt's three miles up the road, magnificent monuments to thrusting Victorian self-confidence and icons of the 19th century global textile trade, now lonely reminders of great fortune and dominance.

'I absolutely hate this shit hole. Get out of the fucking way you total moron!'

Roberto Antonelli is a locum pharmacist. In his early 40's, a man of some style, or so he imagines. He has a slightly olive skinned Mediterranean countenance, inherited from a Puglian or perhaps Ligerian father. He knows not from where he came.

'No! No, stay green! Stay green you *bastard*!' he screams at the tenth traffic light to disobey him as he roars across the city from the North. His anger management issues betray his efforts to portray a suave exterior.

'You might have all fucking day but I'm late! Move, move! Get out of the way. NOW!'

His exotic black sports car, incongruous in this neighbourhood, roars out of Manningham Lane on to Bowland Street taking a short cut to Lumb Lane. Finding it blocked by a van, he reverses into an arched swerve and skids broadside, out of control on the wet road. Pausing for a moment and cursing as he searches for first gear, he changes a CD flinging 'Rumours' to the floor and poking home Muse's 'Absolution' to better suit his mood, before barging back out into traffic on the main road, steering with one hand whilst opening a can of Red Bull with the other.

His car flies sideways, the hump of a mini roundabout launching it from the surface as its huge tyres fight to transfer power from a roaring V10 motor onto the slippery tarmac.

'AAgghhhhh! Bollocks!' he shouts to no one as he loses all traction and the car clips a kerb, the impact luckily correcting its trajectory. After barely a mouthful he lets go of the can out of the driver's door window on to the street and deploys both hands to grapple with the steering wheel.

He arrives twenty minutes late, skidding to a halt on the loose gravel of a small car park, spraying pebbles at the dustbins and parked cars. The waste ground parking area lies at the side of the tiny shop. He bursts inside to find a small queue of quiet and compliant, but slightly impatient, customers muttering inaudibly to themselves and exchanging raised eyebrows at each other as the English do when inconvenienced. He briefly meets the sharp judgemental glance of a disgruntled colleague.

'Hello! Hello! Yes I get it. Sorry I'm late. Good morning to you all.'

He addresses the customers and his female colleague with the same breezy, cheerfully dismissive welcome as he grabs a clipboard from the counter and immediately begins to prepare prescriptions.

Roberto is in charge today to cover temporarily for the owner who, drained by the relentless obligations and travails of a beleaguered sole proprietor, has become depressed and increasingly reluctant to continue without abusing his own products.

Roberto has worked here more frequently than he would like of late as the owner's life comes apart and he increasingly takes the easy option of putting a temp in post.

The struggling patron is doing his best to keep hold of his shop. He is doomed by chemical addictions that he shares with many of his customers. For now his meltdown is postponed by employing the expensive last minute services of a 'Rentapharm' locum to keep the hoards at bay and a finger in the dyke when the pressure gets too much.

'Coffee please.'

'In a moment Mr Antonelli, I'm busy as you can see.'

'Cheers love, no sugar. Leave that stuff would you? The quicker I get my numskulls out of bed and functioning, the quicker we will get rid of this lot.'

'What did your last slave die of?' she mutters just loud enough for him to hear.

'By the way it's Rob as you well know,' he replies unmoved by her rebellion.

In the kitchen drowned out by the kettle she tells him out loud what she thinks of him before returning with a smile, banging his drink on the counter.

He says nothing but responds with a cold hard look that goes on far too long for comfort as he sips the coffee, giving up the pretence of helping with the work as quickly as he took it up. After this entrance a deep frost descends between them which is only thawed by the accelerating workload.

Antonelli is no surname for a Yorkshire man. His name and appearance has, since his 1970's school days in a Northern English community, set him slightly apart from his contemporaries.

His mother, a shambolic bohemian artist known to be a trifle too fond for her own good; who, in the late 1950's and 60's enjoyed with gusto all the exotic fruits available to an attractive libertine in her prime. She may well, as she claimed, have randomly met an Italian stallion one crazy night in Rome and brought Roberto to life but he will never know for sure.

In his early twenties, for a short while a curiosity about the identity of his father became an all-consuming but mercifully temporary obsession. Using papers and photographs he found amongst his late mother's personal effects, he did get close enough to the truth to discover that a feisty Ligerian firebrand who she certainly met whilst blowing her mind and parent's budget on an extended student holiday in Italy could have been responsible. Letters found amongst her possessions seemed to confirm the dates and suggested something more than a pen pal from an enigmatic letter with the address of what turned out to be a Ramalia Barracks signed simply 'M'.

So perhaps not a Spanish conceptual artist from Andalucía whom she encountered at a party in London as she also fancifully claimed; or a Portuguese chef she met in Sheffield.

In later life her memory let her down and her stories changed by each retelling. It was never easy to tell when his mother was in the room or off somewhere on a dreamy romantic adventure entirely within her head. Her grasp of detail was deliberately random at best. Her weed-addled memory and propensity to confuse reality with a yearn for excitement and mystery was not to be relied upon when searching for comfort in the truth.

In his late teens, assuming incorrectly that a superb local chef, known for his uncompromising attitude toward unhappy customers and wives had aggrandised himself to great success, becoming Marco by simply dropping an '-o' on to the end of his pedestrian Anglo Saxon Christian name and swaggering down to London to awe the glitterati.

Inspired by that urban myth he jettisoned the parochial Robert Peckitt his mother had given him and elected to go forth as Roberto Antonelli after noting a passing ice-cream van.

He had a disconcerting habit of drifting into a trance-like state and causing discomfort to others in the process which was deployed repeatedly this morning. His dilated pupils remained motionless and he became momentarily unaware of his surroundings. His colleagues were used to it but today's logjam of customers, exacerbated by his late arrival, made it worse than the usual inconvenience.

Maybe it was detached boredom or simply a way of buying time to think. Whatever it was, he became aware of the power of this affliction (or attribute) after it prompted transformative reactions. During negotiations, it was mistaken for the calculated pause of a gambler unwilling to show his hand. Helpfully it was also the kind of cool detachment that some women found irresistible, mistaking it for 'depth'.

'Mr Antonelli would you *please* help me!'

He hears her but it's like a voice in a dream until she breaks into his trance by slamming a large tray of prescriptions down leaving them spilling over his shoes.

He looks down at the mess at his feet and shoves it aside without comment.

Scarred and impoverished by divorce and business failure, but resilient enough to maintain a relatively enviable standard of living, he found himself working lucratively as an emergency locum pharmacist. He sold his skills temporarily to small independent outlets in and around unsavoury neighbourhoods in Bradford and other down-at-heel Northern towns.

He nurtured and cultivated a desire to remain self-reliant, be resilient and unbowed by failure or rejection and enjoyed the challenge of reinvention and renewal that calamitous changes in his circumstances regularly brought forth. By creating a relentless flow of cliff edge dramas and adventures he left no space for analytical contemplation.

Right now in the time of New Labour optimism, he had also carefully acquired and lost a small portfolio of stone terrace houses and three or four flats in the courageous Urban Splash Lister's Mill development which boosted an already comfortable income and offered places to go and play out, away from prying eyes.

Having expensive and oft dangerous tastes and an angry ex-wife, the nous to develop alternative income streams and live multiple separate lives was a vital attribute.

He had lost his own pharmacy business when the lease expired in the same month as his wife filed for divorce. The unexplained death of one of his customers had led to an investigation into his competence by the General Pharmaceutical Council. Despite some difficult interviews and awkward questions, no criminal charges came his way and professional censure was narrowly avoided. He was eventually cleared to continue, cowed but unbroken by the experience.

His unforgiving bank lost faith during this time and forced him to liquidate his company. He hung on to two flats initially, but later in the eye of the storm sold one before his wife could get her share. After the tempest subsided he fulfilled a lifelong dream and quickly pumped the proceeds of the house sale and some other funds that unexpectedly came his way into a car. He chose carefully, knowing that the right one could be as rewarding as an investment in the property market - its mobility and value represented ready cash in a crisis.

He had quickly adapted to a nomadic life following the collapse of his business and marriage. He learnt to play on his availability and the desperate need of owners of small businesses to keep the doors open and hang on to regular trade in times of illness and family commitment.

And so here he was, standing in a small Bradford shop, like everyone else there wishing it were not so.

Regular work at the three nationwide pharmacies or behind the desk at a supermarket's in-store chemist was easily the most comfortable option for someone in his position, but he avoided opportunities in that entry level market unless it was an emergency that would enable him to negotiate his day rate upwards. To build his premium service in an increasingly crowded market, he made himself available to go wherever asked without notice and to take all the weekend and bank holiday duty cover where sudden staff incapacitation left the owners with no choice.

Often he could improve his daily rate simply by ignoring his phone until the evening. If he picked up in the morning, his booker had time to shop around. He found it more rewarding to stay aloof until the last minute, even if he missed the odd day's work. He could pick up a full day's cash for an afternoon's work if a chemist had fallen ill during their shift. Occasionally with only an hour or two left until closing time, he would leap into action and show up with a false smile and an invoice. His long silences on the phone, an extension of his disinterested stare ploy, often gained him a pecuniary advantage. The longer he paused before replying to a request for emergency cover, the greater the chance that the offer increased.

Today was no different. He had been begged by the proprietor and was pocketing almost twice the going rate.

He was widely regarded as a cold fish, a moody and contrary oddball. He knew that the shortage of qualified pharmacists was coming to an end. Rates were falling as many new graduates came through the system and in from Europe. The work was often tedious, and in deprived urban areas, occasionally confrontational.

Regular visits from self- appointed 'community leaders' and health professionals, who he suspected of over prescribing and trading in prescription drugs caused him to ask grave questions about the system he was fronting at the counter.

To thaw the frosty atmosphere he attempts a dialogue with his colleague.

'Surely this was not the idea when the National Health Service was established. The intention was not to provide cheap medication for greedy middle men to export to their homelands, neither was presumably facilitating a free service to assist in the proliferation of appalling lifestyle choices for recreational drug users and self-inflicted illnesses of the obese,' he offers *sotto voce* whilst nodding towards an example.

His colleague hissed back 'Not now.'

He had not endeared himself to his assistant by arriving late and did nothing to improve on a poor start by offering her the benefit of his holistic view. He knows he has some work to do to erase the memory of his unprofessional arrival and can sense that he is being unhelpful so he tries approachable, chatty, patronising patter instead.

'What have you done to your hair it looks so much more erm... I don't know, err vibrant today.'

This is certainly never going to work on a middle aged Bradford mother of four whose husband had left her with a house full of disrespectful greedy teenagers and no funds to feed them. Consequently she hadn't visited a hairdresser in three years, cutting her own hair in front of her bathroom mirror.

Quickly giving that up, he changes tack again to give the benefit of some more of his philosophical musings.

'You know what Alison, in most urban areas of the UK, one of the unintended consequences of a health service free at the point of delivery to a largely bovine and suicidal, self-indulgent populous has been to provide a free sweetshop to dispense pretty much anything a lazy addict or despicable chancer could want.'

'Oh Mr Antonelli, please could you focus on the prescriptions for heaven's sake. They are not deaf. Have another coffee and leave them alone!'

'Particularly when they're on benefits, have a corrupt or lazy GP or are a member of the ever increasing living dead, ' he continues.

'...Irritating endless line of customers who all seem incapable of looking after their own welfare, relentlessly and impatiently thrusting undeserved prescriptions at me.'

'Oh come on, that is why we're here. To serve them, not to be rude.'

His gargantuan throbbing hangover was not helpful either. He could be an unpleasant man to work with at the best of times, but today his muttered condemnation of all around him reached a new low.

The appalling weather had conspired to ramp up his usual cynical vituperative attitude to an increasingly bitter and openly unforgiving anger towards everyone round him.

'Worse still, the vast swarm of those with no intention of making the slightest contribution to anything beyond their own selfish needs from birth to coffin seem to arrive relentlessly like a zombie army seeking the chemicals they need to keep them on the march.'

'I know what you mean, Roberto, but we must crack on otherwise we will have an overcrowding situation in here.' His tired no-nonsense assistant replies, simply wanting to get through the day and back to her family.

'Life at the sharp end of this can be extremely tiresome and very stressful for someone like myself who cares about quality of service and pride in their work,' he whinges dishonestly. He doesn't really care at all.

'Their GP's have got them off their backs by scribbling hasty prescriptions…'

'I know, I know but this is definitely *not* an appropriate conversation to have in front of our customers,' she replies with finality, catching his eye and cutting him off whilst pointing angrily towards the now packed shop.

He doesn't care about any of these people and becomes enraged by the position he is in despite it being of his own making.

Once he had pretended to have a moral compass and even a desire to change the world for the better but the fashionable urge to present himself as someone who gave a toss had gradually abandoned him as he approached middle age.

He can see that sharing the depth of his disgust isn't getting any traction, so he stays mostly silent for the rest of the morning with a volcano erupting in his brain.

His hatred for the world around him and feelings of toxic harm within his veins from the last evening's reverie ferment wild ideas of revenge and violence.

The day takes an unexpected turn when an almost comical bare knuckle fight breaks out following his refusal to hand out a repeat prescription to an addict. On a normal day he would have dealt with it by deploying detached good humour, but with a black dog barking inside his brain, his calm exterior is now hiding a brewing storm.

A tiny, thin and hirsute dishevelled Scot, a regular customer known to Roberto, refuses to accept casual rejection of his demands.

'Ye have to give it to me; ye have to its yer job man. I know you... I know youse don't I pal?' The deranged wreck of a man takes his chemically fuelled rage and fear of supply chain difficulties out on the nearest person in the queue by falling into him and being roughly pushed away.

'He has to fecking give it to me,' says the addict as he falls to the floor.

Luckily, the next person turns out to be a man Roberto believes to be a crook with a fake prescription, a regular visitor, wielding notes almost daily from his GP, who oddly shares his surname. Roberto is minded to begin to question his customers more rigorously.

'More heart trouble,' claims the customer handing over a prescription, whilst batting off the swinging arms of the Scottish addict.

So why do you need a drug that is known to be addictive and mostly used for unrelated complaints? Roberto thinks to himself. *And why every couple of days in such a large quantity?*

'No, I don't care about your cravings Mr Err,' he addresses the tramp absent-mindedly, whilst pretending to flick through some papers.

'I can't find your prescription at the moment, but perhaps if you come back this afternoon, we may be able to help you. I'll phone your GP for a chat first. We may not be helping you by simply doing your bidding. There are some inconsistencies in your prescription here. It appears to be a crudely produced photocopy.'

Roberto's call to the GP never happens. It would have made no difference. In Bradford challenges to questionable behaviour could be brushed aside with the threat of investigation fermenting already difficult community tensions.

In addition to the less troublesome majority of customers there are addicts who shuffle around the derelict mill sites and hang around outside the pharmacy that he would rather weren't making the place untidy, but there were social and operational constraints which held Roberto back from dealing with them in the way he would prefer. Unnerved by the fact that he couldn't see his car from the shop and imagining what unknown heathens may be doing to it he stared at the ceiling whilst the two men in front of him began pushing, shoving and arguing in his peripheral vision.

Ever present sensitivity around the possibility of being branded a racist brought too much caution to the proceedings for Roberto's liking. Too often theft, benefit fraud, malfeasance and corruption were swept under the carpet for fear of unsettling the community, thus creating a dysfunctional system where despicable behaviour of very many kinds too regularly went unchallenged. He had heard many stories about a trade in prescribed medication being spirited out of the country. His only evidence was the same faces calling in far too regularly. Customers, whose prescriptions suggested that they were suffering ailments dire enough to incapacitate them, were skipping off with medication sufficient to keep a modestly large and distant village healthy.

He was no paragon of virtue either and had been known to abuse the broken and overused system to enrich himself too; never one to let the hypocrisy of his position get in the way. He would often observe with disdain apparently unconnected groups of people arrive in the same car and pretend not to know each other when in the shop.

It gets so busy that the easiest thing was to turn a blind eye. He spots a young girl making the most of the congestion and noise by slipping some boxes of toothpaste into her pocket and decides to ignore it.

This is surely not what the NHS was created for? To perpetuate this carnival of unchecked waste and abuse; I can stand this no longer!

The police station nearby had given them an extension number they could call which would get an instant response and they used it several times a week. Although less than a ten minute walk away, it could be half an hour or several days before they got a response. A 999 call would get a more focussed and speedy reaction, but most often troublemakers had disappeared before the police arrived.

Of late he had simply been turning up for the cash. If they had found a way to turn a profit why should he be concerned?

Everyone is on the make so fair-play to them, right?

No! Sort it out Rob. Why don't you knock both of them out of the game? His evil hung-over shoulder monkey whispers.

Whilst he ruminates in his own world, the fracas turned uglier still. After carefully pushing the Scot away several times, the recipient of his violence, forgetting his age and lack of fitness, snaps and fights back, shoving the tramp to the floor once more.

'Ahhh! So you want some do youse? Eh? Cammman then! Ave some of that!' yells the belligerent elf as he leaps from the floor and smashes his fist into the older man's face, who responds with violence and persistence that somewhat alters Roberto's opinion of who is the victim and who the perpetrator.

The tramp is a lost cause, but the other appears of sound mind and is venting his anger from choice rather than chemical necessity and his response is beyond self-defence.

As they knock the living daylights out of each other, terrorising unlucky bystanders and destroying the interior of the shop, Roberto watches impassively.

He formulates a special prescription for both of them in his mind and wonders if he can dispense with both of them in one go. Before moving an inch, he has rehearsed every moment of what is about to happen.

'We should do something about this, shall I call the police?' screams the assistant as she cowers at the rear of the shop.

He ignores her and continues to examine the ceiling, transported elsewhere, waiting for it all to stop.

The itinerant drug addict continues to swing at the bloated prescription fiddler, who shouts, 'I was here before you. Don't you dare push in front of me'

'Cam and have some ye bastard 'all tek ye ARLL on!' Slurring as he rotates randomly and ineffectively with raised fists, offering to shadow-box imaginary assailants. The remaining customers are pushing each other aside in order to flee into the street.

Neither can be described as anywhere near fighting fit. They are doing some minor harm to each other, but the fixtures and fittings are suffering more.

The shelves and display stands are taking a substantial hit as bottles rain down from the shelves and liquids burst onto the floor.

Customers are clearly alarmed by the violence and he can't continue to do his job in a madhouse. It is an opportunity to try out something he has considered for many years. A keen student of the history of forensic pharmacy, Roberto had knowledge of long forgotten poisons and recipes for potions that many modern pharmacists would never know.

An enthusiastic collector, he had amassed an extensive library of research papers and publications from Victorian practitioners and academics and had spent many hours in university libraries and museums, imagining that life would have been more interesting in research and product development rather than toiling at the delivery end of the service.

His appetite for wine, women, song and passion for all manner of sport and sports cars put the career he wanted and felt he deserved beyond his reach. Without a long period of study and penury, elevation to a more cerebral vocation would remain unattainable. He had no social status or family connections to assist his ascent. His voracious and wanton appetite for hedonistic exploration won the day, but he did retain a keen interest in the academic side of his chosen profession.

He had, for years, been carrying out his own simple experiments on animals and then, emboldened by interesting outcomes, had become more cavalier. His oblivious friends and family were included in his research. He quite fancied a professorship. Somewhere he could have taught and tinkered around in the laboratories and with the students, or maybe held a senior research scientist posting for a multinational drug company. He would never achieve the academic qualifications to reach that level, but being a freelance alchemist beyond censure or peer review had its own attractions

He had noticed some weeks earlier that the cellar of this particular pharmacy, like many other small independent ones he had worked in recently, still had mysterious jars in cupboards which should have been cleared out carefully and put beyond reach but were not. Astonishingly, littered around the store rooms, attics and cellars of buildings of small independent chemists, extraordinary quantities of lethal chemicals still remain - bottles, jars, and unopened pill boxes, many without labels leftover from a less regulated age.

His colleague is terrified and pleads for action.

'Get me ma fucking Skript, u ponce before I come round there an tek youse out aam telling u now.' The addict continues with this tirade until his nemesis smashes a mobile display of foot repair creams and intimate crevice remedies over his head, rendering him temporarily incapacitated.

Revved up to the point of explosion, Roberto eventually releases his handbrake.

'Hold the fort a moment please,' says Roberto calmly as he dashes down the stairs to the cellar, grasping the medical notes of the two men from his desk as he passes it.

'Don't leave me alone in here with these crazy people!' the assistant shouts down the stairs. 'I'm not paid to provide security. I think we should call the police.'

'No need! Back in a moment,' he calls over his shoulder.

From their notes, he first satisfies himself that they are both under the care of their GPs and in a flash snaps out of his benign torpor. He becomes energised, focused and excited. After finding and quickly mixing the extra chemicals required, he emerges two or three minutes later and discreetly re-seals some packages behind the counter. He thrusts their contaminated prescriptions into their hands and shoos them towards the door.

'Right! Out of here now chaps. You've had your fun! You have what you came for. Go… go, out you go!' he shouts.

With help from a large construction worker who had called in for a bandage, he manages to restore order and bundle them out of the shop into the rain. The addict falls over in the sodden gutter and before he returns to his post and behind the back of the man who helped clear the shop, Roberto kicks the wreck whilst he is down. Twice, in his face.

'You don't know me you fucking waste of space and you never will!' he spits.

'Thank you so much for your help and I apologise for the disturbance,' he calls to the back of the retreating building worker.

During this episode his terrified assistant had indeed called the police.

'They're sending someone immediately,' she tells him.

'Yeah right they are!' replies Roberto, not even slightly concerned.

'What happened to civility and decorum? I'm going for a drink. Close the shop.'

Before she has the chance to protest, he's out of the door leaving it swinging in the wind. He strides purposefully down the hill and hops over floating debris in a flooded, litter-strewn underpass to emerge at the Jacob's Well Pub where he waits for the attention of the balding, overweight barman.

His pulse is slowing but he needs a drink to soothe his tormented brain to try and match it to his calm exterior.

The pub is empty except for a middle aged couple who seem very keen to leave.

'Thank you very much for the history lesson,' the woman says as they pass behind Roberto.

'Hurry up before he starts again,' hisses her partner as he holds open the door.

'Something you said?' asks Roberto whilst grabbing a dog eared newspaper from a rack. 'Jack Daniels and a Thirkell's pie please, double.'

His drink disappears in a flash and he orders another immediately. The pie fails to materialise. Gazing around the empty pub he wonders how it can continue.

'What went wrong here, where are your punters?'

'Well you might ask. Bratfud is on its knees, pal. It's a city wi' no reason to be here since wool trade went away and all them who came to work in't mills are still here with nowt to do.'

Roberto takes his drink and finds a chair facing away from the bar sensing correctly that the bar keeper with no customers might seek to engage him further to keep him company.

Roberto gazes at the newspaper but before he can focus, the man has left his post and joins him at the table.

'Aye, I'm studying 'istry of Bratfud as it 'appens, it were once one of t'biggest cities in the country wi' tens of thousands working in t' mills and -'

'Just the fucking pie please, I could do with some space too if you don't mind, I have a lot on my mind just now.'

'Oh I see. You asked me now you don't want know eh?' challenges the barman.

Roberto snaps; he jumps up and pushes the man against the wall, seething an inch from his face. 'Just a pie that's all I want, and some peace and quiet. Is that too much for you to compute? If you want to know why this place is empty, maybe take look in the mirror.' Roberto pushes him over and starts to leave.

He gets as far as the door and suddenly turns back to where the man is cowering on the floor as if used to being kicked and offering himself compliantly to the kicker.

Telling himself that his visit is best be as low key as possible, Roberto says 'Look, I am so sorry, I've had a difficult morning and I'm not feeling too well, but that's no excuse for my behaviour.'

Roberto helps him up and asks for another drink which he sips quietly. Throwing a twenty pound note on the bar, he says 'Keep the change and get yourself a drink.'

Roberto sits for an hour or more, downing three more drinks, plotting and planning to unleash mayhem in Bradford if he is ever forced to return. Gradually aided by the drink, his mood calms.

Despite being on the receiving end of a violent outburst the landlord senses Roberto's more relaxed mood and can't help himself but continue to share his knowledge of the city.

'I think it's suffered rather than prospered from its proximity to Leeds, which 'as pulled its socks up way more successfully. This pub is one of the oldest in t' town and it used to be the very 'art of t'place. If you came in here in 1890 right up to 1980 there would 'ave been three or four hundred in every night. Saltaire were a pioneering social experiment where workforce were looked after from cradle to grave (Provided they put in t'hours in t'mill of course!) Bratfud was 'ome of one of t' most successful of early such industrial experiments. Textile trade were quite simply enormous. This were the 'art of it, right 'ere. No, I'm telling you!

'...All I get in here these days unless the football is on is the dregs and the cops. There's two coming in now as it 'appens.'

By their dress and demeanour Roberto can tell immediately that these two were the latter.

The two incoming detectives give Roberto the motivation and opportunity he needs to escape. They carry the slow and deliberate countenance of two weary soldiers returning to the safety of their camp, throwing off their weapons and relaxing by a fire to compare stories of the battle.

'Jeez it's fucking wet,' one says as he shakes raindrops from his jacket.

They share Roberto's hatred of the city and like him, yearn to be elsewhere.

'Your turn. I recommend ear-defenders or a shotgun to shut that boring twat up. There's a pie behind the bar with my name on it, be my guest if you can get him to do his fucking job,' Roberto says to them as he leaves by the back door and heads back to the pharmacy to collect his car.

'Eh?' The shorter stockier of the coppers turns to see who had spoken.

The other taller and thinner one stands at the bar. 'What are you having, Pete? Pete! Wake up mate.'

'Err... Pint, Adrian. I know him from somewhere,' says DC Peter Manford with a puzzled expression, watching Roberto walk away towards the underpass taking his phone out of his pocket.

'Usual 'drain?' says the barman. I was just telling that gentleman there about....'

'Yes, yes we fucking know.....!' they cry in unison as they pull their chairs away facing out from the bar as if to huddle and warm by a fire, although the fire isn't lit, so they just face a nicotine-stained wall away from the barman.

'I don't know how long I can carry on in the job you know,' says DC Manford. 'The days get longer, the back-up no longer there...'

'Get that down, you moaning git!'

The pie stays on the bar beneath a glass cover decaying for another week before it is thrown on the fire.

This will my last day in Bradford. Roberto promises himself as he walks back up the hill dodging windblown litter, dog shit, dejected pedestrians and traffic.

Working here always lowers his spirit.

Just as spending time with positive people raises the game, working in a depressing environment lowers it. Dealing with the self-inflicted problems of people for whom he has no empathy gives succour to increasingly dark thoughts.

As he crosses Great Horton Road, his ex-wife calls to berate him over his latest act of selfish disregard for their children and her finances.

'Rob, you arsehole, how can I feed, clothe and educate your kids if you keep missing payment dates. For fuck's sake sort your life out and grow a pair. They only have one shot at it you know'

'Yes, yes I hear you perhaps you could spend less of it in 'Shiny Leather' or wherever it is you shop?'

'Put that cash you owe me in my account by the morning you wanker, or I will drop them off at yours and fuck off to Barbados!'

'With that gardener? There's some lucrative hoeing he could do out there is there? Maybe some celebrity weeding or lawn mowing? I bet you could blow his monthly income in one deft swipe of a credit card,' he sneers.

'Fuck off you evil shit. Murray is a landscape designer not a gardener and you know it. You have always been an uncaring, cold hearted, selfish, ungrateful, jealous and ice-cold total evil SHIT!' she screams as she throws her phone at the wall.

Who decides what is evil? It's subjective, Roberto ponders. *Am I evil to feel such anger towards this place and the people I meet, or is it through a fog of personal disappointment that I project such hatred upon them? Can deeds, considered evil by some, be justified in the context of a better outcome for all? …What a crappy world I inhabit. It's time for a change here. Perhaps I can be a catalyst …Can I function happily untroubled by the rule of law? Am I capable of remaining aloof from moral constraints, above legal restraints?*

Lacking in empathy and becoming more like an observer of conventional society rather than participant, he muses: *If pushed, could I be content on the outside. Without membership, am I beyond censure?*

He feels minded to remove any blockages on the rocky path to happiness. The road to nirvana would be eased firstly by getting his ex-wife off his back he thinks.

On returning to his car, he discovers that it has been scratched and a wing mirror partly detached.

'BASTARDS!' he yells out loud into the foggy dank evening. *'BASTAAARDS!'*

It's not clear whether this is the work of a careless delivery van driver without the decency to own up, a passing vandal or an enemy. It doesn't matter who. It's the final straw. He curses his bad fortune to have to breathe the same air as someone who would do something so pointless.

I will never return to this shit hole. I will no longer tolerate anyone who makes the ugly world even more so.

He notices the pharmacy owner's car had arrived and the right thing to do would be to call in and make peace or say farewell. Instead he quietly removes the damaged wing mirror, throws it on the passenger seat and roars away, knowing they would hear the engine.

Having sunk several whiskys, only a crazy man would drive. But he is not minded to leave the car to be preyed upon further so blasts through the dark and foreboding streets as irresponsibly as he arrived this morning, scattering pedestrians.

2 Nice Work If You Can Get It

The following day after an un-tormented sleep Roberto takes his coffee onto the balcony of his flat overlooking Middleton Woods and the River Wharfe beyond. He calls the Filton Kensington HQ to arrange to repair the damage to his car and get it serviced and chases up some work contacts to plan how to fund the now inevitable invoices.

He enjoys some rare winter sun and takes a call from the Bradford Pharmacy.

'Roberto, what on earth is going on? You left us in a complete mess and Alison has handed in her notice. I pay you twice the going rate and you disappeared for the whole afternoon. I was supposed to be on leave until the weekend but I've had to come back in and my wife is in hospital. Hello, are you there Roberto?'

After a long silence Roberto replies quietly.

'Sorry it's not safe there, you are on your own.'

'Please come back and help me, I am completely at the end, I'm prepared to forget this if you come tomorrow. Hello? ...Hello?'

'I said no.'

'Well thanks for nothing. I trust you will return the money I sent to you for the afternoon... Hello?'

'I'll think about it,' he eventually whispers as he puts the phone down.

'Fuck you,' he says to the handset.

Usually in addition to direct contacts he has developed over the years, he finds work through specialist agencies who provide health service professionals. They provide staff to cover holiday or sickness for overworked pharmacists. Many of the chemists now cut out the agents and call him directly. Sole traders in small shops who fall ill or have a family crisis must have qualified staff behind the dispensing counter and are easy prey for his selfish demands. It is rare for him to work in one pharmacy for long, often finding himself covering three or four locations in a fortnight.

Roberto can earn more in a busy three-month period than a whole year toiling for the NHS. As a locum he can still find time to enjoy a day's pheasant shooting or deer-stalking and to occasionally dabble with his amateur motor racing hobby. Although unable to complete a full season due to the random nature of his employment, he has managed to turn out and compete once; racing a hand built British G33 in the Ginetta class.

A complex human with a great many contradictions in his life, he also owns a tiny cabin deep in a wood in Hertfordshire which he rarely uses but keeps as a base from which to hit London and return with the Sunday papers on the last train to relax among the bluebells, watching deer. Latterly, only there does the rage inside his head - which is disgusted by disorder, retreat enough to enable him to find peace.

He recently joined a local shoot and keeps shotguns in a steel floor box under the bed but when questions about his personal life persisted, he eventually declined social invitations.

He bought the wood very cheaply from the widowed mother of a former girlfriend and had an oak framed shack built on an articulated wagon trailer to avoid planning issues. He placed it out of sight in a chalk pit surrounded by bramble, nettles and self-sown hornbeam. Some years after careful planting of hawthorn mixed with yew, rhododendron and holly, it is invisible all year round.

His ex-wife assumed that he stayed in Central London where they enjoyed many weekend trips when times were good.

Today as he looked across the valley towards Ilkley Moor, he is excited by the thought that he may have got away with his own personal filtration of society.

Some conversations can only be held inside one's head.

By the time the consequences of a dodgy prescription or an overdose of the wrong powder, liquid or pill come to pass, it's unlikely anyone would remember the quiet bloke, the temp who was there for a couple of days. Especially if someone dies unexpectedly but has seen their GP within the past fortnight. Unless they met a violent or unusual death, an autopsy would be unlikely.

A cool breeze sends him inside where he sits and stares at the wall deep in thought. His evil voice begins the battle to rationalise the unforgivable to his rational voice.

The dose of pain control drug for those suffering cancer can be increased to end a life. Far more carefully regulated today, most health service professionals at some time or another, until the turn of the century have tweaked a dose to end someone's relentless and incurable pain. Witnessing the painful and terminal decline of a frightened and suffering patient, how many if forced to honestly disclose could say that they had never in a faux absent-minded or even caring and benevolent way, been a trifle generous with the methadone? He asks himself.

In the dead of night in hospital wards all over the country, chemicals are administered but sometimes never measured or questioned. It is the unspoken truth of the nurse, the doctor and the pharmacist.

'You all know who you are!' He calls out to the ether. *They all accept this as de- rigueur, but they will never speak of it. Those who did lost a good and honest career as a result. Often the repercussions after honest disclosure from health care professionals around the issue of end-of-life care resulted in loss of liberty.*

I would never condemn them for it. On the contrary, I would contend that those placed in that unenviable position should be supported. Apart from the deserving unwell there are the deliberate degenerates, the lazy and the sneaks who take without contributing.

Roberto works over in his mind his own version of ethical considerations around his potentially transformative mission. He considers himself a reluctant public servant put in harm's way by an ungrateful master, who may have found an alternative way to serve. Thus far it was mostly just a philosophical, theoretical proposal he was considering internally, just an exciting idea. But one that just refused to go away. He can see himself providing the same kind of service that a marksman shooting a hostage-taking madman with the skill of a keyhole surgeon removing a tumour does. Precision strikes at targets he chooses, when he chooses. Who would ever trace the assassin?

The idea enlivens him. He can give it a go and stop if it becomes too risky. Perhaps he has already dealt with a couple of social problems this way. One with a 'defective heart', who he is sure is involved in a prescription drug scam and one who is taking methadone to 'help' with his state-funded heroin addiction and insulin for diabetes, but both a drain on public resources. If he has done his work well, neither will trouble the overburdened pill shop or anywhere else again.

The fate of his two troublesome customers are now beyond his control. All he can do is to wait for the outcome. Like walking onto a frozen lake not knowing if the ice will hold or jumping out of a plane hoping the chute opens.

Dramatic consequences? Or none at all? Only time will tell.

He tries to focus on other things over the next few days expecting some kind of outcome, but he hears nothing.

Meanwhile back in Bradford another weary public servant, an unappreciated but vital link in the thin blue line is having yet again, a terrible day.

He rings the nick from his car.

'Hi Sam. Did you get that address for me? I'm in Shipley and I have to be back in ten minutes to attend to some diversity bollocks. I want to be away by six. I'm putting on the Aardvarks at the Dungeon this evening.'

Peter Manford, is a stocky and cocky detective constable in the West Yorkshire police. Aged 42, divorced, underpaid, undervalued and overworked, still finds time to indulge in a side-line as an occasional stand-up comic and promoter of local rock gigs. Without these distractions which take up all of his spare time and more, he would have left the force years ago. Most of his colleagues want out too.

His direct approach is a mixture of expedience in the line of fire and innate no-nonsense northern DNA.

It is a popular myth that the police career structure includes benefits such as early retirement on a healthy pension to make up for the danger, abuse, insane hours and endless pointless paperwork. It doesn't. He can retire after thirty years, but the shit he has to deal with to get there is nowhere near worth it. Most of the people of quality have given up trying to make a difference.

The Home Office view now is that long serving officers are expensive, require an expensive retirement package and are far less biddable than youngsters on a 10 to 15 year average churn. It doesn't require the vision of Da Vinci to see that with that policy comes incompetence, inexperience and lack of guidance. Local knowledge and wisdom cascading through the ranks has kept the quality of service intact. That is now irreparably changing.

DC Manford will in time get around to dealing with a disturbance in a pharmacy which has been piled upon his already overfull schedule for the day. A PC has been assigned to look at it but asked for his overview.

He has been tasked to join a team investigating a murder, an unprovoked attack on a pensioner in her own home and a fire in drugs den. He has already been on duty for 8 hours.

The already overstretched team are 2 short due to the resignation of yet another colleague and the long term sickness of another. His team were promised reinforcements as a result of a reorganisation. A super division was created and his team should have become 12 strong. It never happened.

They are lucky if they can count five at any one time covering a vast urban area. Many times it is far fewer. Proactive policing is impossible; they rarely have the numbers on duty to react successfully.

'No chance of a sneaky curry in the Karaachi this evening then?' enquires his favourite workmate.

'No chance today Sam, I'm up to my neck in it.'

The last perk of his job is the chance occasionally to grab a quick bite in one of the many superb Asian restaurants in and around the city. The removal of police HQ canteens gives them moral justification. They have to eat and they all keep their radios on in case anything serious kicks off, which it often does.

Not today though. He will be lucky to find time for a cup of tea. The calls are filtered by the office team, but once instructed by the daily 8am briefing he has to do his own prioritising as emergencies jump the queue when he is out and about. There is no other way for just two detectives to cover this city and the surrounding towns. His DS is his immediate superior, but as a seasoned detective, he is trusted to work out what needs doing and when within the overall priorities.

A female PC is partnered with him for a month as part of her training.

'Pete.'

'Hi, what's occurring?'

'The Thornton Street Pharmacy: there's been another incident up there. This time a fight and some property damage.'

'We should have a PC working from there; it would save a load of time. Whatsup?'

'I wanted to interview a guy who works there or worked there, but he left that day in the middle of it and didn't come back, the owner is mightily peeved about him and he's not answering his phone.'

'Do you think he was involved?'

'Well no not really, but he was at least a witness and by all accounts a bit odd.'

'Do we know him?'

'Roberto Antonelli.'

'That rings a bell from somewhere… Any previous?'

'No nothing. He's hard to pin down, I don't think that's his birth name and he's not Italian.'

'Let me have a quick look at it, I think I know him. It's a strange thing, I bought a car from him a few years back, I know where he lives and strangely I saw him yesterday out of the blue.'

When Pete does eventually pop round for a chat with the pharmacy owner, it seems like there is nothing much he can do. The poor man looks defeated and haunted.

'Nothing is missing; no one was hurt, but look at the damage! We *are* insured but I don't know how much longer I can deal with this. It's the fourth time in the past twelve months. The main troublemaker is well known to you lot, but hasn't been seen around his usual haunts since. So I assume he'll just turn up again in a week or two when he's forgotten all about it and expect us to serve him again and we'll have to.

I'm unwell. So is my wife and I have to work in the shop. The last locum we had won't come back. He walked out after the violence and didn't finish the day. I can't get a replacement and he's ignoring the phone.'

'Yes, about him... Robert? Roberto Antonelli? Did you know him? Did he work for you often?'

'Quite a lot last year, yes. I don't know where he's from, but he always struck me as Mediterranean and the name is a clue I suppose; but he doesn't have an accent. My staff can usually extract every detail of someone's life with relentless questioning with tea and biscuits but they got nothing out of him at all, not a thing. Strange man and very expensive but we can't be choosy. No one who has a choice would work here. I doubt he will work for us again and I can't blame him. Apparently when it all kicked off, he hid in the cellar; then walked out on his colleague, leaving us with no prescription cover. Totally unprofessional, not to say cruel towards his co-worker.'

'Well, I hope the insurance comes good for you,' says Pete as he examines the shop window 'If there is anything I can do, let me know. And give me a call if your favourite customer returns. We'll see if we can pick him up, but you know there is little we can do about him don't you? He has a string of convictions already and is oblivious to any sanction. He'll just disappear unless we can hold him for something.'

With that DC Manford drives to Little Germany and parks on some waste ground. He hangs up his supermarket-bought suit jacket and shirt on a hook in the back, exposing the Embrace T-shirt beneath and is in The Dungeon with a pint in his hand in a moment.

When they eventually get themselves organised The Aardvarks are a surreal sight. A high-energy five piece band, they blast out soul and funk in pubs and clubs around West Yorkshire. A middle aged balding lead guitarist, teacher by day, Alvin Lee by night, a horn section of one lunatic who's puffed up cheeks when blowing Dixie uses all the spare flesh and blood in his emaciated frame, revealing blue popping veins through gossamer skin on his forehead making him look like a starving puffer fish with his eyelids super glued shut when his lips are welded to the trumpet. They have a bearded drummer and reclusive fossilised bass player with haunted eyes who fights and fails to keep up with the manic slightly fey Caribbean lead singer Macdonald. He looks like he has landed in the wrong band from planet Camp but the whole thing kind of works due to their collective sense of humour. The CD their roadie tries to sell to all thirty in the crowd -'Always Be First in the Phone Book' doesn't tempt many.

As so often, DC Manford deosn't see the evening out before retiring exhausted.

He forgets all about the pharmacy until several weeks later, when it comes up again at a team briefing. There has been a robbery and the intel includes the fact that the men fighting in the shop are now both dead. One was found in the street, a suspected overdose and the other of a heart attack at home, both on the same day.

Bit odd that, Pete thinks. *One, I wouldn't question - but two in such a short time, that has to be against the odds even for this City.*

He remembers why he knows the locum who was working there and who he bumped into the same day in the pub, when you would expect that he would have been preoccupied tidying up after the fight and completing his day's work.

He could have spent time listening to a lecture on Bradford history any other day, so why was he at Jacob's Well for so long that day? The incident happened before noon and he was still there at 3pm. Did he go somewhere else before he went to the pub? Anyway might be nothing, but interesting.

They had met briefly at a track day racing Ginetta sports cars and Pete bought one from him having answered a small ad for a 1992 G33. It was eight grand he didn't have, but Pete was trying to avoid being just a boring DC with worn out shoes and a Ford Fiesta and he thought wrongly that he could spot a bargain.

He was assured by people who said they knew about these things that it was a snip. He sorted the car's shortcomings out over the years, as it didn't live up to the condition promised by the vendor. The cost of upgrading it, making it reliable and running it had prevented him from improving his wardrobe, going on holiday or completing the home improvements on his modest terrace house.

This was a sleek little car with some grunt that he could race and he saw himself using it every day like Bergerac or Morse, but it required more regular TLC to keep it reliable than he was prepared for, more down to the way it had been treated by its previous owner than any inherent flaws.

He recalls shaking hands on the deal with a wealthy looking flash guy with very strange staring eyes when they met outside the Cow and Calf Hotel on Ilkley Moor one summer evening. He had swapped a thick handful of notes for the car and its paperwork and lived to rue the day every time it let him down. Roberto had arrived at the brow of the steep hill from the town centre at the Cow and Calf car park long after his approach had been announced by the howling engine which could be heard all across the Wharfe Valley as he gave it one last blast up the side of the moor. After a quick pint Pete had dropped the guy off at the fancy flats on the sunny side of the valley where they rooted out some spares and some track tyres from the back of his garage.

They had not met since that day but he remembers a twinge of resentment at the strange man's lifestyle and had wondered what he did for a living. Pete had him marked as a money market bloke or maybe a lawyer or surgeon.

Antonelli was not a local name and the man had not come up on his radar at work. Pete didn't know *everyone* in Ilkley but having grown up in the small, prosperous town and being around the same age with a common interest in sports cars, it surprised him that he had never come across the man.

Finding that he was handing out prescriptions up a dismal street in Bradford is a surprise. His behaviour that day seems very odd too. Pete has a hundred more urgent issues to deal with but makes a mental note to sniff him out sometime soon for a chat about what went on that day.

He is an ambitious man ready to move up the food chain in the force and is known for spotting incongruous behaviours which often hide interesting character traits. It niggles DC Manford that the man can have so much going on, yet work in the worst place imaginable. Something about him doesn't add up.

3 Escape to the Northern Dales

After the debacle in Bradford and a lack of offers, Roberto takes the car to London to be serviced at the only outlet of the Filton Car Company on Kensington High Street.

An appointment is only possible due to a cancellation, and it takes a ridiculous four days. The car has to be delivered from there to Chiswick to have the work done then returned to the showroom for a final check and clean before being returned. He is told that he is not allowed to deliver it himself. It is not company policy to receive customers at the service centre.

He probably could have had it done in Otley by Colin Peckitt, as the best old vehicle restoration man in the country and depending who was telling it, could be his mother's brother. He never checked this with Colin, who welcomed him as 'lad' as he did everyone else. Colin regularly worked on Rolls Royces, Bentleys and all manner of exotic and rare vehicles.

The value of Roberto's car, which is appreciating spectacularly and the sublime thrill of opening it up on a lonely country road makes the trip south bearable. To have an up-to-date service history authenticated by the manufacturer maintains its value. It also affords opportunity for some leisure time in London and a pitstop at his woodland idyll.

After dropping off the car, parting with enough money to spend a fortnight in The Ritz, and wondering *Who pays up front for a service? ...and how do they know what the extent of the work will be before it comes in?* Roberto strolls along Holland Walk and checks into the Ravina Goranga; a down-at-heel bed and breakfast joint owned by the Balkan Orthodox church and run by refugees from the former Yugoslav Republic.

The Ravina Goranga's prime location on Holland Park Avenue belies its seedy interior. The shell is badly decaying and the rooms are small and ill-equipped. The soft furnishings are cheap and worn and the staff and clientele suspicious and guarded.

Very basic but well placed for Notting Hill or Kensington High Street. It is an area he knows well. He nips into the Churchill Arms for a pint and a Thai meal. Gerry O'Brien is still there. The eccentric Irish landlord remembers him or rather expertly pretends to, and is still performing tricks with a walking cane and a schooner. He still tells the same jokes and the interior seems even more stuffed with Churchill related paraphernalia than he remembers.

The exterior is now adorned with the most spectacular floral display outside of Chelsea in May, swinging in resplendent baskets bracketed to every square inch of the facade, visible from Notting Hill Gate and presumably by bees a hundred miles away. It is a stunning effort.

The same crowd of city types are mixing with Old Kensington roués and seedy posh, who shuffle in here every night from their multi-million pound white stucco mansions. They cram the cluttered bar, rubbing shoulders with bemused Chinese tourists and gap-year students. The place becomes so full that a sneeze would have brought a ton of Churchill knick-knacks and paraphernalia raining down. In the height of summer it all spreads out into the street.

In a feeble attempt at self-improvement Roberto visits the John Soane museum to try and absorb the poetry of architecture. The house - his home, office, gallery and architectural laboratory is preserved just as it was in 1837. He notices a Hogarth painting in the drawing room and later in the Museum of Cartoon Art around the corner; a Hogarth cartoon reveals some roots of modern political satire. He buys a few original contemporary satirical works to add to his collection - another portable investment which he can enjoy, but which might also one day provide a magic escape door if he paints himself into a corner again.

He then enjoys a quiet evening in the Churchill and settles on a meal in Kensington Place after discovering Gerry's back room Thai restaurant is inconveniently rammed full as usual.

This interlude away in the capital brings further distance from the events in Bradford. He relaxes and stops worrying about a knock on the door from PC Plod when nothing happens on his return to the north. No mention in the papers, no phone calls, not a peep.

Back in Ilkley, his kids don't want to see him. They never do. Their lives are full to bursting with school - after school, pre-school, night school, tuition in music, sporting and social events. They are early adopters of the constant 24/7 digital interaction that is the drug of choice for the late 20th century child, perhaps to escape the confusion and uncertainty of their parents' disastrous marriage.

His ex-wife, Sara appears to be thriving, but his every interaction with her descends into a depressingly predictable shouting match. Life is good for her on Ilkley Moor. The town is ever more opulent, but he has no deep roots and has never spent much time there.

'There is no longer much to keep me here. The interesting folks have been priced out and replaced by upwardly mobile young professionals and more than any small town's quota of slimy mortgage-slave social climbers, wheeler-dealing upstarts and be-suited cringing, genuflecting lickspittles of the kind that I thought were simply an invention of a 1970's sitcom until I moved here, but seem to be your circle of friends these days.'

'What the fuck are you on about? Have you swallowed a fucking dictionary? And what the fuck do you mean, 'no longer much to keep you here?' roars his ex. 'Hello! Planet Earth to Roberto. What about your fucking children?'

Undeterred he continues. 'Your pals are bit parts in a shitcom. They moved in to the town to enjoy "the moors, great schools and easy access by rail to Leeds and London" but they are all uninteresting clones. I may have swallowed a dictionary if being able to populate a sentence without the word fuck is your measure, but I hear you've been swallowing a gardener's dick recently which is possibly the least useful of your many unhelpful adventures!' He spits sarcastically, unbowed by the indefensible hypocrisy of his position.

'Ooooh, here we go! Pissh off. That's only your opinion. It's none of your business what I swallow or what it's attached to anyway. You squandered your right to a say in that many years ago. Murray's an artisht; his gardens are just an extension of his art. And he's twice a mouthful than you if you want to know. He's very busy around town and doing very well'

'I bet he is. I can't wait for the article on him in that glossy lifestyle magazine full of adverts for AGA's and small expensive boutiques you buy. The one with the postcode as its title as if simply living here bestows the reader with some kind of exalted position in the firmament.

'Just the kind of place that a gardener called Murray would thrive. I bet you're not the only spoilt housewife with most of the day free who is polishing his wooden dibber.'

'You're an arsehole do you know that? Ilkley's a perfect town to bring up a family and it takes some considerable ingenuity and effort to find a place in the local schools these days. You're very lucky to live here and have my family stand up to the plate for your kids. When are you going to man up?'

'By which you mean give you more money to spend in Zoe's?'

'Oh jush die and shave me the hasshle will you?' shouts Sara, revealing signs that the wine cellar has been visited recently.

Roberto had succumbed to pressure from his pompous status-driven in-laws to accept their offer to pay for preparatory education for his two children. He saw no fault in the excellent comprehensive in the town despite its ludicrous refusal to accept that it was no longer a Grammar School and hadn't been for several decades yet snobbishly retains that inaccurate but self-aggrandising titular moniker to this day.

Roberto had not missed her dig at him for her parent's well-meaning intervention. It was something which was tiresomely regurgitated during many of their regular but pointless demeaning rows.

She knew that it brought him feelings of emasculation and it narked him to be reminded. That's why she kept it alive. There were not many ways she could get a response.

'Your parents are willing, if not insistent on paying, so who am I to object? They want to do their best and resistance is futile, so all well and good but it's never been an aspiration for me to pay twice for my children's education,' he lied.

'You've never really invested the time and effort in your family to either ensure the success of your marriage or be entitled to intervene in such important decisions.'

Attendance at the small private school on the edge of the moor satisfied his ex-wife's ambition and gave her fuel for the fire she stoked most days. It wounded him for the sake of his ego not his kids' welfare. He was easily capable of fighting his corner. Their infrequent contact these days was all about money and bitter point-scoring. More often than not it ended with a phone being thrown at a wall in one part of the town or another.

Roberto is more on edge than usual at the moment, which strangely made him more verbose and unguarded than comfortable. Each time the phone or his gate intercom rings it shakes him momentarily.

A flash of sunlight picks out Roberto's car as it lifts off momentarily at the brow of a heather swathed hill, where a winding single track road cascades down the precipitous and unprotected valley edge into Hawes from Cam Fell.

Roberto is wearing Oakley sunglasses and listening to Led Zeppelin 4. He has opened the windows to share its explosive power with the hapless wind-blown sheep, who leave it almost too late to saunter out of his way.

After a couple of weeks radio silence from the staff agency who offered him work, he begins to think that he may have blown it by walking out mid-crisis and now wonders if he has shown himself to be unreliable. He is therefore relieved to eventually get a call to attend a remote rural pharmacy way out in a town he doesn't know called West Fell in the Northern Dales.

Never having ventured further north than Grassington and Kettlewell, up the Wharfe Valley on a summer's day, he has to look it up on a map.

Over in Wensleydale and Swaledale there are rivers, valleys and small communities he had no idea existed. Hundreds of square miles of English countryside with almost no sign of human habitation between the tiny settlements.

These fells are the playground of the super-rich. Invisible international billionaires who quietly enjoy their grouse moors from mansions and castles in the vast hills and dales between the Bolton Abbey estate in mid-Wharfedale and the Lake District further north, and between York and Lancaster to the east and west.

Up on the fell tops here, no more than a dozen families own an area three times the size of central London. Land measured in square miles, not acres. Unknown to their immediate neighbours in the valleys, they are only ever seen sweeping through the landscape in Range Rovers or helicopters during the grouse shooting season. Mysterious people who quietly bestride the world, their children marry obscure European royalty and invite each other and the internationally super-rich to shoot and drink with them on the lonely, windswept heather-draped moors. When the season finishes they are gone. To the Côte D'azur, to Zermatt, New York or London.

Unlike many a pheasant shoot where any whiskied up social climber with 300 quid, some tweeds that they imagined the landed gentry wear and an unnecessarily expensive shotgun, can blast away all day merrily at a gaggle of doomed, cage-reared birds who regularly forget that they can fly away to avoid being chased towards obliteration by the rural poor, the grouse shoot is most often a very different, private and exclusive event.

The Upper Dales are little more than half an hour away as a lost crow flies, but in a different galaxy from Bradford.

After a pleasant but challenging drive north through Upper Wharfedale and over the top of the high fells, Roberto eventually arrives in a small market town or is it a large village? He isn't sure. His services are required here for a few days due to a medical emergency.

Just the last minute gig he liked best: in and out quick enough to avoid boredom but for premium fees.

The engine vibrates windows around the narrow streets of stone cottages in the quiet village centre and sets off a burglar alarm across the square. It comes to a halt on the cobbles of West Fell marketplace and ticks as the engine cools. Every other settlement within half an hour's drive is far smaller. There are villages and hamlets of stone farmhouses and barns dotted around the steep narrow valleys by the dozen.

No other settlement however has more than one pub, chapel, shop or restaurant. By comparison to the nearest villages, West Fell is truly cosmopolitan. It has a Chinese restaurant, two curry houses, and many small, independent shops catering for hikers and other tourists. It's most valuable asset, almost its raison d'être, is the enormous public school on the edge of town. It is by far the most significant driver of economic activity within a thirty mile radius and has been for well over four hundred years.

Hill sheep and small dairy farming enterprises come a distant second followed by tourism, second homes and some successful horse racing stables and is often mistaken by intrepid travellers who made the trip up the narrow converging river valleys from the South, East or West for Richmond, Leyburn or Hawes but in fact lies further to the North West. The one single track road over the fells is steep, narrow and impassable for much of the winter.

Roberto takes off his sunglasses as he peruses the tiny stone shops of the market square. There are no national chains represented. These are all independents in ancient, uneven buildings. Until today he was completely unaware of its existence.

Seeing the village pharmacy, he confidently strides in to the sound of a brass bell and after a long wait in an empty shop still offering products he thought had been long ago discontinued, some creaking floorboards above indicate there is life. Eventually an ancient withered man with what appears to be porridge on his lips and a pair of spectacles precariously perched on his head grumpily rejects the outstretched hand, meeting Roberto's introduction with an angry grunt before turning to leave the room.

'Hello - Rob. I'm your locum, yeah? Julie at *Medi-Angels Direct* sent me.'

The man stands staring silently shaking perceptibly with one arm steadying himself on a pillar.

'No, no you aren't,' he eventually replies, before hobbling back upstairs without another word.

Whaaat?? thinks Roberto. *What's eating him?*

He goes back to the car, picks up a mobile and when he can't get a signal, finds some change and astonishingly a functioning call box and rings his locum agency to cancel his engagement.

On the passenger seat lays a copy of the Bradford Telegraph and Argus with the headline *"More drug deaths."*

'I have just driven for an hour north and arrived in the 1950's. I am currently parked in the middle of a film set for All Creatures Great and Small! Can you please tell me why I am here?' he complains, trying only lamely to hide his irritation at being sent on a wild goose chase.

'I found the place, but I have just been insulted by Catweazle who has had a personality bypass and is wearing yesterday's breakfast. He wasn't expecting me. Are you sure I'm in the right town?

'…I know you said it was quite a long drive, but this place is nearly in Scotland!'

Unusually for such a small and remote town there are two small independent pharmacies. He leaves the call box, wanders across the cobbles and pauses by his car.

Should he bin it off and head south or give it a shot? With a sigh he decides to have a look. He could do with the money and he has to be reliable to get the work.

With the lowest of expectations, he finds the other outlet.

4 Speechless Beyond Settle

Everything changes the moment he enters the shop. His eyes are involuntarily dragged out of their sockets upwards and to his right toward a strikingly athletic, tall and blond young woman perched precariously and at full stretch on the top step of a decorative Victorian iron and timber stepladder. Showing far too much flesh, which should be but isn't completely covered by her skin-tight T-shirt.

She says without turning round. 'With you in a minute. If it's a prescription, will it wait until the locum turns up? He should be here by now. Probably lost on the way.'

He doesn't reply.

'Or if it's desperate, could you go across the road to Francombe's.'

He still doesn't reply, not wishing to break the spell of being allowed to examine her freely without censure.

He studies her perfect feet and her perfect legs and allows his gaze to linger far longer than decorum would allow on her perfect backside and her perfect waist, shoulders and hair.

She turns with a raised eyebrow revealing her washboard stomach overshadowed by large impressively self-supporting perfect breasts, larger than he imagined for such a long and athletic frame, not that there is a law covering such things and size being never a measure of quality. He fights internally to quell his base and unsolicited thoughts and prepares himself to introduce.

'Rob, your locum,' he offers timidly, still transfixed, unable to move or breathe, but now controlling the direction of his vision to her eyes, only to her eyes, knowing that the slightest movement elsewhere will expose himself to her mercy. Petrified in the presence of outstanding beauty, afraid of giving away his rapture and half expecting a similar welcome to the one he had just received from the other shop, he stands staring upwards to meet her height. As she moves to descend, his gaze falls to the black iron hinges that connect the two parts of the stepladder in between her legs. Time stands still whilst he admires the ironwork, for that is where his brain tells him safe territory lay.

Mmmm, a cast iron hinge with the words 'Pioneer Ladder' in bold cast metal.

He has time to marvel at the attention to detail of the ordinary Victorian household implement.

There was a pride and confidence displayed in cast metal on many things often proudly patented. He was lost in the moment as a distraction, partly to avoid leering and involuntarily drooling or being caught peeping, and partly it was the automatic freezing of time that he had perfected to gain maximum impact upon a social event.

Her T-shirt only just overlaps her equally taught jeans when she descends the ladder and stands looming over him to offer a handshake.

'Oh, great!' she exclaims. 'At last! Hazel. Sorry, I had better just shimmy that lot further in so it doesn't all fall out.' *The shelves or the contents of your shirt?* he thinks crudely and inappropriately whilst the hundred billion neurons in his brain began racing around in circles, jumping up and down with glee in their nappies crashing into each other creating heat, sparks and joyous pandemonium in his head.

She returns to the top of the ladder to complete her task, cursing as she stretches to reach the top shelf allowing him another chance for his mind to misbehave.

Roberto is so stunned by her he does not at first notice the unbelievable disorder of the shop. It is an absolute bomb site. When he does look around, he wonders, *I thought the first place was a dump, but this! My god, are there no rules up here?*

If she hadn't been here he would have been off out of the door again. There is no way he can work in a shit-tip like this.

Don't complain, he tells himself. *If I get to work with her, I could work upside down in a septic tank!*

'I'm here to dispense healing chemicals for you, with you,' he says with an unnecessary flourish whilst thinking, S*hut up you fucking idiot. Keep hold of your cool and your min*d.

Hazel explains 'The owner is in poor health and should have retired a decade ago. She's been ill for a week and we have a huge backlog to clear. I can't deal with it. I don't know an Anadin from a jar of Smarties. All I've done for the last couple of days is apologise and ask people to come back. It's killing the business and sending trade across the road to the enemy. What else can I do? I'm an architecture student not Robert Winston or Richard flipping Branson. Doing me best here but struggling to find anything. I haven't the faintest clue what I'm doing so you haven't arrived a moment too soon!'

When she speaks he is allowed to look up into her eyes. He drowns in them before she can finish a sentence. His neurons put on lifebelts and swim around holding hands, singing *Hallelujah.* When she smiles he melts.

'I can see you are neither and I am grateful for that. Ah yes, your competitor over the road. He's quite hostile.'

'He certainly can be,' says Hazel as she quickly casts a discerning but far more discreet eye over the newcomer. 'He's been trying to close us down for years so you are last person he wants to see in town.'

'The owner of this mess, Mrs Pickles, and the other *happy* pharmacist over the road, Eric Francombe, are bitter rivals, probably even former partners. They loathe each other so much they *must* have been an item,' she says with an irreverent smirk which makes him tremble slightly.

'Decades ago they somehow ended up in opposition to each other, and now they're locked in a deathly stranglehold at each other's throats', she holds her own throat in her slender fingers to flamboyantly illustrate her point.

'If one of them drops off their perch, the other becomes rich. It's like whatever the opposite of a symbiotic relationship is; I was never any good at metaphors or similes or whatever they're called.' She slows to a halt at the end of her sentence, realising that she is showing off to impress.

Roberto knows something of the complex funding for rural duty chemists.

'I think it may be the fact that there are two that will prevent the NHS from funding them.'

'You don't say! That explains a lot,' says Hazel. 'Tea?'

'Yes please,' he replies before remembering that he never drinks the stuff.

'If there are only two outlets covering a large geographical area like this, where do our customers come from? It's not a big town and very remote.

'…Builder's, fruit or green? …All over the hills really; 20,000 farmers, super rich landowners, retired country folk, various grumpy bastards, the biggest private school north of York and some racehorse stables. All spread out over fifty square miles of bleak moorland. We don't just depend on the village. The school alone provides by far the most business.'

'Builder's, please,' he sings cheerfully, imagining pointlessly that she might like him better if he didn't drink posh tea. 'I guess that's why they are hanging on. Impressive sums are freely available to guarantee out of hours dispensing services.'

'I see, makes sense. That would explain why these two cantankerous fossils determinedly keep going, trying every day to outwit each other. It is not just about money though. Something happened to their relationship which won't allow either to give in, I reckon. No one can remember the ins and outs of it, but the whole village knows they hate each other and has no choice but to listen to them discrediting each other daily. Sugar or are you sweet enough? Sorry, why did I say that?!'

'No thanks and no worries. I know what you mean,' replies Roberto, helping her to move on. 'Seems it's the countryside way. Adults, who once played together happily as children, hate the same people who they then live next door to later in life. They will ignore each other and wish each other dead over some long forgotten slight or deal which went wrong. How old are they?'

'I don't know,' Hazel hands Roberto his tea.

'They appear to be in their late eighties, but they could be prematurely weathered by long term bitterness and hatred. Scowling takes its toll on your skin and ages you.'

'And smiling takes years off you,' interrupts Roberto, catching her eye.

'Yeah, but being children of the Yorkshire Dales, while they can draw breath they will continue to work hard and never ever give up.'

Questioning the viability of the two enterprises he asks, 'Why would you bother to spend your dotage on such a battle to the death here?'

'As I said, there is an enormous public school in a stately home on the outskirts of the village. It's been there for centuries and keeps the village in work. I live there as it happens.'

'You live there? In what capacity?'

'Daughter of Head. My father is Dr Benjamin Anderson MBE.'

'But Dad Ben to you, surely?'

'I wish! No, pretty much Dr Benjamin Anderson MBE to me mostly too. Have a read of that whilst you finish your tea,' Hazel passes him a leaflet. 'I have to put all this shit away.'

Roberto keeps one eye on the leaflet and the other following her around the room sneakily soaking up the sheer perfection of her body and committing it's every detail to a randomly collected memory jigsaw, to be pieced together later. The parochial leaflet explains that West Fell School and the racehorse training businesses on the level foothills of the higher fells for which the village is internationally known, drive its apparent economic success. The tourist trade in this location at the head of the dales and close to the Lake District brings yet more revenue in for five or six months.

'Does it get busier in the summer?' Roberto asks, 'It seems a bit quiet just now. Where's the action?'

'In the summer this place is rammed solid with walkers who spend the days on the hills. Day-trippers from the mill towns of Northern Lancashire and the industrial ports of the northeast flood in like lemmings, if lemmings do flood in. They come looking for the same kind of tea and cake they can get where they live. Special cake deserving a sixty mile round trip. That's what they come up here for, Yorkshire Tea. As if there are fucking tea plantations up here!

'...The narrow lanes are choked on most summer weekends and holidays. Like sugar obsessed zombies they're drawn to the tea shops - "Must have caaaaaake!"' She adds doing a zombie walk as she refills the shelves.

'All the pointless crockery and spoons for everything! That's why I work here instead, really. There's little else. And the tea shop artwork! Oh my God,' she continues, holding her head in the pose of Munch's Scream.

'The lady running them is usually a retired teacher or council clerk whose husband usually fancies himself as Turner or Landseer and proudly shoves his pathetic daubs on the walls expecting to sell them for seventy quid a pop. You can tell those pictures never sell by the dust on them and the different coloured paint behind them on the wall. I'm sure I've seen pre decimal price tags on them!'

Whilst enjoying the shop rant enhanced by her theatrical embellishments his mind drifts to fantasising about the spectacular business opportunity which could emerge should one of the two pharmacies close.

However, business opportunities would have to wait.

Hazel Anderson is rapidly improving his mood.

With nothing but escape from his wife, Bradford and the events there on his mind when he took this job, it's all changing. The scenery, the crazy shop, this amazing animated character and the scent of an opportunity were not what he expected. He has been here less than an hour and he can't see why he shouldn't stick around.

How can I prolong it? What's wrong with the old lady who owns this? He wonders. Roberto sets to work and gamely begins to help to tidy up the shop.

A cardboard box quickly fills up with out of date products as he reviews the offerings with disdain.

'There are products here that have been discontinued for ten years or more. We're going down if we sell any of this.'

'Mrs Pickles told me to bring her prescription as soon as you arrive and let her know if you're up to the job; it's here.'

Roberto takes it into the back room pretending to study the slip and quickly adds some extra white pills.

'Drop her that round when you have moment please,' he eventually asks Hazel.

The new colleagues are immediately busy from the minute they open, getting the shop fit for purpose and dealing with the backlog of unhappy customers. Quickly they adopt a fruity banter and rapport of the kind that is fun for those included, but extremely tiresome for those outside the loop.

A couple of days in, when his assignment should be ending, with no word to the contrary from Mrs Pickles, he carries on. He introduces wine into the shop, for staff only of course, to slow the delivery of tea and allow him more opportunities for control over his new colleague

Hazel's attempts to find out about Roberto's back story and more importantly his love life are carefully rebuffed, lest his baggage puts her off.

They quickly adopt a professional front when customers come in which is equally quickly dropped as soon as they leave.

Roberto sets them both up with a glass of red wine each positioned out of sight, and is careful to have his back to her while he adds a 'sweetener' to hers.

'I'm just a failed husband and an incompetent businessman who is not quite dead yet and still hoping to get it all right one day; but never mind me, what about you?'

'25 next month. Filling time between part two of my architecture degree and then a post graduate course in land economy at St James College in Cambridge after, hopefully.'

'Seeing anyone?' he boldly inquires.

She is sharp enough to keep her options open. 'I *do* have a boyfriend,' she says leaving room for a 'but' at the end.

'Of course you do. You're fabulous. Local lad amusing you for now is it? Or perhaps a University relationship?'

'Local. Intended to finish it when I went to Cambridge and I'll have to get around to it by the autumn when I go back. Unless of course something else crops up!' she deliberately adds.

They are interrupted once more by a public schoolboy sent to buy twenty tubes of toothpaste.

'Thank you Miss Anderson,' says the polite boy as he leaves.

'Aww how sweet, Miss Anderson!'

'Shut it, you! Anyway, Mally belongs here but is never going to persuade me to stay. He won't travel south of Settle if it means an overnight out of the valley. It's like his underpants are stapled to the bench in the town square and he can only venture as far as his knicker-elastic will stretch. Unless it's a rugby match in which case his jockstrap, which *is* necessarily oversized to be fair to him, so will go a bit further,' she adds with deliberate comedy wide eyes which makes Roberto inwardly shrivel before her.

'When he plays away, he can't wait to get back to the village to the home town clubhouse bar where they stay until everyone's fallen over. I've tried and failed to snip it and free him to travel further but he's not interested. Everything he loves is here.'

'Including you,' Roberto chips in.

'Pffffffff,' she expels with a grimace. 'Not for much longer. Much as I love the valley here, it's where I grew up after all, but my roots don't feel strong enough to hold me here. It's too small. My father intends to retire to his farm in Tuscany when he's completed his twentieth year as head. When that happens, I won't be here. But for now he needs me around although he won't ever admit it… We lost Mum recently.'

'Oh I'm so sorry,' murmurs Roberto, not that he is, but he knows when to pretend to show empathy.

'Thanks. In any case, I can't see my future with a man who has *'Young farmers do it in all weathers'* emblazoned across the windscreen of a jacked up Japanese pickup.'

'I notice you said you love the valley but not your man,' Roberto ventures, pushing his luck.

'I see no reason to rely on any man as it happens,' replies Hazel with a theatrical pout.

'What's keeping you from sacking him off then?'

'Well, she says thoughtfully looking heavenwards for inspiration. Let's see. Errr… well winter lasts for 9 months so a boyfriend with a spectacularly huge todger… Um, a car or two in a remote town with no public transport, enough cash to buy me wine…. So he has his uses. Anyway, it's none of your business stranger,' she adds, looking him in the eye and reining him in a little.

Roberto continues preparing prescriptions whilst beginning to regret asking.

'His ability to repair almost anything with an engine has come in handy many, many times. We first met when my Frogeye

Sprite, which is not a goggle-eyed Celtic goblin, by the way but a car – a present, lovingly restored by my grieving father when Mum died, broke a spring when I over did it crossing Cotterdale Bridge.

'...No I'm being cruel; he is a good lad really. Anyway that wine has gone straight to my head. It's a bit early for me. These days I'm out of practice. I'd better shut up now.'

'I know what a Frog Eyed Sprite is, had one when I was a student,' cut in Roberto lying and leaving himself exposed by adding an unnecessary 'd' but, keen to show her his passion for British sports cars.

'Did you? Cool! how old was it?'

'Err...' Roberto digs himself a hole. 'Err, I'm trying to remember.'

'Did it have disc brakes? What colour?'

Wrong footed, he mumbles 'Err, white,' looking at the colour of her T-shirt.

'Err... I'm not sure about the brakes.'

'Anyway,' she continues, after a brief pause 'Mally sourced some parts and fixed it and my reservations and better judgement were too easily defeated. I suppose I repaid him in ways that blew his woolly hat off. It was his handy big hands, huge crevice tool and the lack of any credible opposition that made us an item and for far longer than is sensible for either of us,' she giggles, throwing out her secrets to be judged, revealing her story to him, going to places she hadn't planned with elaborate hand waves and animated facial gymnastics, whilst inadvertently revealing her interest in him at the same time.

'It's doing my brain no good to sit in the pub listening to stories about Land Rover half shafts, banger racing and rugby and it's doing him no good to be so obviously and irredeemably outclassed!' She says with a smile. 'No, seriously. Dealing with *this* "posh bird with a mind of her own", something of a novelty round here it seems and coping with his deep feelings of intellectual inadequacy sometimes can be too much for him.'

'You know I am joking right?' she adds after a pause, 'Well mostly joking anyway!'

'I thought it was none of my business! Sorry I didn't mean to pry,' says Roberto, enjoying the journey.

'Yes you fucking did,' she laughs. 'It's Ok, I haven't really thought it through and it's good to have someone to talk to about it.'

'In bed,' she continues, going much further than it was wise to do, 'I ask him what he thinks of things he never used to worry about and it stresses him out. He'll say *"What the fuck is devolution anyway? What is a Garderobe?"* Or *"Does anyone know or care who the Northern Alliance is? Is it a new building society?...Global warming and the ozone layer?"*... Hello? Anyone in there?! He says the only climate change he experiences is when he watches me take off my clothes!'

Roberto opens his mouth to contribute a predictable response, but she continues before he has a chance. He makes a mental note to find out what the fuck a garderobe is just in case she says it again.

'How about this; One morning I told him I was studying the work of Edgar Allan Poe and would be tied up until lunchtime. His reply was "He must be a shit writer if you have to be tied up to read it, but can't have written much if you're back at lunchtime!"' Roberto laughs out loud, a rare event.

'The thing is I really don't think he was joking! No, I shouldn't take the piss. Who am I, being all superior; but it's definitely time I stopped being a coward and dealt with it.'

Hazel, is no stranger to adventure, and becomes more forward than usual in the presence of someone who interested her. She is used to the suitor putting the work in, but her tongue is loosened dangerously whilst Roberto has avoided revealing a single detail about himself.

'How do you amuse yourself up here amongst these sheep and hills?' he asks.

Keen not to be judged too young or naive, she begins to babble away like a swollen brook, sharing far too much as Roberto refills her wine glass.

'It's not all farmers up here. I know how to have a good time when I feel like it,' she boasts unwisely.

'When I was a teenager I had my pick of the sixth form here. They effortlessly transfer to St James College Cambridge from West Fell. They're mostly privileged, sometimes intelligent, but always ambitious and very randy. Not so much because I am anything special, but for the few who aren't helping out the other boys, I was the only female they had seen for months.'

She doesn't know how to stop herself. She is aware her cheeks are flushed and feels strangely dizzy, but happily blathers on in the moment.

'Shhh just a moment,' interrupts Roberto as a customer comes in.

'Sorry, sounds interesting.... Do go on,' he soothingly purrs after dealing with them.

'Once, in the woodland of the school grounds in the arms of a prop forward who led me away from an after match-party to an oak framed tennis shelter - a memorial to an old boy who lost his life while practicing an aerobatic stunt intended to be enjoyed by the prince of Wales in the 1930's...' As she speaks she continues to illustrate the highpoints of her story with elaborate sweeps of her arms and wipes of her brow with the back of her hand.

'His immature sulking and laziness, I mistook for intellectual depth. Rugby brawn or do I prefer Byronic intrigue... I can't decide. You will learn this about me if you stick around, I'm famous for being unable to make a decision. I juggled both examples once until they found me out. They couldn't appreciate what they had. Both refused to share, which I couldn't understand. I saw no reason why the choice should be in their gift in any case. So when I was cornered and forced to come up with a decision, I surprised them by going further off the rails and adding the new female French teacher to my Harem! Crazy but she was smoking hot and Dad did ask me to look after her!'

'Well done you! Listen. I have another bottle of red in the boot, I don't suppose you would mind if we errrr…' ventures Roberto, seizing the initiative and in his excitement to continue to enjoy being alone with her as she pours out so much detail. He doesn't want to miss anything or be interrupted.

'Wahhay, bring it on - We'll have to stay in the back room though. If I get caught drinking in here it will be an international incident!'

Roberto sprints up the square and retrieves another bottle of Gran Cruz Hermitage he keeps in a specially commissioned velvet lined leather case designed to fit perfectly under the seat in preparation for imagined moments like this.

'Where were we?' asks Roberto, looking to seamlessly continue lest she changes the subject and moreover anxious to press home the advantage he has gained by deftly administering more and more truth serum to her wine glass.

'Well, never keen to be cornered, I told myself not to look back and just enjoyed it all. The poet's threats to harm himself were desperate and the pathetic overdramatised theatrics of a fragile child.

'I was even less impressed by the rugby player's drunken attempts to win back exclusivity. He tried to style himself as a dangerous and tortured romantic hero in the mould of Orlando Bloom playing a cuckolded musketeer, only to hospitalise himself when he fell trying to get into my bedroom via a rusty drainpipe. The resulting kerfuffle led to the French teacher being sacked. She was discovered hiding naked in my bedroom when my father burst in to find out what all the commotion was about!'

'Wow!' Roberto is genuinely impressed. 'Then what?'

'I was hauled to Dr Benjy's study like a disgraced pupil.'

Hazel holds her head in her hands as she contemplates the memory.

'It was awful. His lair has a semi-circular wall-to-ceiling bookshelf with a ladder attached to a rail. All the remaining wall space is adorned with paintings of former masters, royal visitors and scenes of triumph from the rich and honourable history of the school. So it's got a daunting and crusty Dickensian vibe going on in there. Being brought in for a dressing-down like that made me bristle, even though it was only my dad. Before he began to speak I already had my gander up! I cringe now, but at the time I launched into him first.

'"Why can't we have a family chat about this at home, father to daughter instead of parading me here and speaking like someone from the 1840's?"'

'An admirably spirited opener,' encourages Roberto.

'Oh it's still a painful memory. My father is an upright, fit and agile man in mind and body; always well turned out, as expected of a public school head, but who could be an army general or even a vicar! Mum used to call him Geoffrey Palmer after some 70's telly bloke. I remember he was shaking with anger and barely controlled his frustration. Quite unlike his usual buttoned-up self.

'"Your shameful behaviour must change with immediate effect to avoid you being banished from the school grounds. How can you do this to me?"'

Hazel begins to mimic her father raising her shoulders and adopting a comedy pompous voice to imply authority as she sips her wine, jabbing an accusing finger at fresh air to emphasise the drama of her father's admonishment '"*Is this how you honour the memory of your mother? You know how hard it is for me!*"' Now she stands up and adds histrionic hand waving and stamping of her feet as she re-enacts the whole episode.

'"I need you to help me by behaving yourself d'you see? Particularly in the school grounds. I cannot allow you to behave in a manner below the minimum standard that I expect from my staff or pupils and I know that you understand this. It is your lack of respect for my position that I find most hurtful and wholly unacceptable and I have no option but to take action if you insist on disobeying the basic rules of decency and decorum." Blah, blah, blah!' she jumps around stamping her feet, now reliving the episode in real time.

'How did you respond to that?'

'Oh I was on a roll too. I am an idiot looking back on it. I caused him trouble he didn't deserve.'

'"If you mean put some clothes on and stay away from the pupils, why can't you just say it?" Says I, "You warned me off the boys when I was twelve but you didn't say anything about the French mistress," I argued, knowing it would wound him, regretting my words as soon as they left my lips. I knew I was going too far, but I was hurt by his low blow of bringing my dead mother into it.

'I kind of know how to get a reaction from him; he is a bit of a Victorian father. If it was just the sixth form boys it would be bad enough, but my last indiscretion *couldn't* be ignored. He ranted on at me for ages bellowing and slamming his fist on the table. It was terrible but it's all buried and forgotten now. At least we pretend it is; he and I.

'I promised to behave from now on and I have done - for almost a whole week so far... And then you turn up and ply me with wine!' she teases and throws both arms aloft in questioning gesture whilst throwing expensive red wine at the crumbling lime washed wall of the inner sanctum of this quaint but ancient dilapidated shop.

'Ooops - anyway what can I do?'

Hazel's presence on the school premises was indeed causing considerable mayhem. Her mother's death had derailed her trajectory temporarily. She needed her father and missed her mother desperately. They both did, but of course being upper middle class English it was never examined or even expressed.

She enjoyed Roberto's genial irreverent banter unaware that for her benefit, he was making a huge effort to disguise his natural surly detachment. She didn't fail however to notice his interest and begins to deliberately tease him.

'I reckon you're somewhere between the upper side of mid-forties and fifty, Roberto. Does it make you slow down being that old?' she taunts knowing she is deliberately guessing high to provoke a reaction and get an accurate answer.

'Depends what you are referring to,' he replies slightly nervously.

'Anyway, less of the upper side of mid-forties to fifty, I won't see 50 till well into the next decade.'

'Ah that's a complicated way of saying you are pushing 45 but you are touchy about it then. Is that it?'

She mistakenly thinks her openness will encourage him to be more forthcoming in return so she ploughs on.

'The death of my mother three years ago scrambled my brain. I've repeatedly taken the path of the most immediately available escape or distraction.

'It came out of a clear blue sky. I had absolutely no idea that there was anything wrong with her. She was just my mum. A bit miserable sometimes, but mostly exciting and fun when she was in the mood. When she was down she used to be very negative about me and rarely encouraged me, but I thought it was just living with my father that was dragging her down. It was a total shock, a complete thunderbolt when she committed suicide. We just saw absolutely no sign of it coming.'

Hazel suddenly walks out of the shop and up across the square into the park opposite. She doesn't want him to see her cry. She returns half an hour later back on form.

'Are you ok? Where did that come from?' asks Roberto, feigning concern for her, whilst excited and unnerved by the more forward and open discourse. He is smitten by her but it happened so quickly. He is also holding back on her in order to keep his options open.

'Look, you don't have to go there.'

'No. its fine. I'm ok, it's just the first time I have spoken about it. I have no one. It's doing me good'

'Your boyfriend?'

'You have to be kidding! He has the empathy of a wounded rhino. We simply don't engage at any emotional level. Anyway, derailed as I was by my mother's passing, I was more confused and disturbed by the reaction of my father,' Hazel continues.

'He came home and found my mum, his beloved but wild wife, a tortured manic depressive we later learnt, with an alcohol problem far worse than she allowed us to know, swinging from the banister.'

'Shit!' says Roberto this time genuinely almost moved.

'Yes. She had been depressed for years and suffered in silence in the time-honoured way of the English. I've only just learnt this from my aunt. My father can't talk about it and I was away a lot so I just didn't know. Luckily I haven't inherited the ball and chain of the black dog from her, at least not yet anyway. I won't be taking any chances though. Just in case it comes howling, I keep one step ahead by putting fun first. If there's a party I'm the first there and last to go home.' She finishes with a large glug of wine.

'I think we are going to be pals,' says Roberto, trying not to whoop with joy.

Hazel is a beneficiary of the lucky sperm club academically, socially and physically. A keen tennis player, skier and horse rider she is a shade over six feet tall and could pursue a career as a clothes horse on the catwalks of Europe anytime she chose. Not stick thin, but all at once athletic, from some angles gamine and others poised like a thoroughbred, her chiselled features, slightly upturned nose which wrinkled when she laughed as she often did and her mane of blond hair turned heads wherever she went.

Despite all that she can't stop herself from revealing her vulnerability.

Appearances can often be deceptive. Few struck dumb by her poise and presence, her friendly nature and endearing laugh would ever guess that fear of abandonment robbed her of sleep. She missed her mother and cried at night when alone in the , ivy-covered cold stone school mansion.

'Me and my dad keep the upper lip stiff, and present only the stoical grit of the English. Dr Benj thinks that sharing emotional pain is the demeaning behaviour of the weak and the self-obsessed. It's a quintessentially English five centuries old public school, so his responsibility is enormous. Strength for him is proven by continuing with one's duties in the face of all and any personal tragedy. His ilk learns from Royals and aristocrats, who shrug off the loss of a beloved family member as though a favourite apple tree has blown over or a cricket match has been lost.'

So Hazel, who in order not to be emotionally crippled by her family, finds herself opening up to Roberto in a way she has never done with anyone else. It helps that he doesn't know anyone in her small and judgemental world of neighbours who know far too much about each other.

Lost confused and desperately lonely, the subject of her mum never crops up at home, beyond a brief chat about the need to carry on, and this only after the funeral.

Within days her father retreated to his study and buried himself back into his work. They carried on as if nothing had happened. A visitor to their house wouldn't know that pain, anguish and unspoken loneliness stalked the building, especially at night.

Few things are more important in some English households than the refusal to publically acknowledge emotional pain. Her father was a good man, a kind and inspiring leader. He was simply not equipped to deal with such a seismic shock. His only way to survive the grief was to shut it away in a locked room marked 'No Entry' and carry on. Carry on regardless; ignore the pain whilst screaming inside.

The distance that had always been there between father and daughter, common between generations and genders, gradually stretched.

'Somehow I managed to pass the first exams of my architecture course,' she reveals. 'How, I have no idea. The study took my mind off the loss and the partying took hold to fill in the days after I returned home. I took a year out before taking my place at St James's.'

'Sounds very comfortable. Like you mean there is an exclusive travellator delivering the entitled and often untalented from privileged birth though expensive education directly to the levers of power? Who would imagine such a thing.' Roberto offers with unhidden sarcasm, revealing to her the cynical mien and barely suppressed bitterness about his own struggles with academic achievement.

'Ooh, touchy! I don't make the rules!' she says surprised by the mean spirited comment.

She finds his edginess surprising and a little disappointing. It's ok for her to dissect and examine her world, but she bridled at his attempt to comment unfavourably on it.

The next day, feeling distinctly peaky and regretting her loquaciousness, she declines his wine and focuses on her job.

5 Being Naughty and Getting Away with Murder

Summer comes and Hazel's ability to cause trouble at the school continues unchecked. Her father begs her to wear more demure clothes and get a job away from her new friend. The rocket fuelled hormones of the boarders can't be quelled.

Thinking she has found the perfect spot on the school roof behind the castellated parapet accessible from a secret stair in the wardrobe of a master's bedroom she takes to sunbathing to catch the rare moment when this far north the opportunity presented itself. Unfortunately pictures of her stretched out like a porn star begins to circulate through the sixth form and inevitably come to the notice of a housemaster.

One afternoon a boy clinging to the chimney stack on a taller part of the quadrangle, a camera in his trembling hand slips and plummets through a skylight on to tables and chairs below, breaking his ankles in the process. The photos are brought to her father's attention and drugs are found in a dormitory. Defying his earlier warnings, she has now forced his hand. He can't treat her differently. She is banished from the school grounds with the exception of the headmaster's house near the entrance for the rest of the term at a minimum.

The job in the pharmacy is the only thing that prevents expulsion from her family home. She is on probation to behave on the threat of a withdrawal of funding for the next phase of her education. A threat which both she and her father know is empty, but she is aware that to push him to the point where he had to make it means that she is causing him more undeserved anguish. She comes to acknowledge that he needs a break. He had lost his wife and had to carry on with his job whilst managing his grief in the spotlight of the school and the concerned governors.

She is too old for this, but her behaviour, his job and their recent loss traps father and daughter into a dysfunctional emotional cul-de-sac. He doesn't deserve it, so she obeys him and to her surprise, actually enjoys conforming a little.

On a typical day she is first to arrive at work. She opens the shop and welcomes early customers. Roberto then turns up to find a shop full of public schoolboys, injured farmers and pensioners.

'No sign of Mrs Pickles?' he asks after a couple of days.

'Strangely not, it's not like her - she usually pops out of the cupboard or down the chimney whenever you're doing anything wrong.'

'Well lucky for her it's all going great!' he replies whilst emptying a shopping bag full of wine into a desk drawer. A misunderstanding about the nature of the relationship between Hazel and Mally is becoming an issue requiring urgent attention as she neglects him in favour of her new pal.

He turns up looking for her and eyes Roberto suspiciously. Hazel represents everything the mechanic has ever dreamed of. Yes, she had some airy-fairy ideas about architecture, politics and philosophy, but she was the one for him. For her it was fun but just transient. She knows they will never keep each other happy for long. He is batting above his weight like Charles Hawtry being bowled at by Freddie Trueman, like Mr T taking on Julian Clary or a JCB vs a bed of lettuce.

She sees his truck arrive outside the shop and mutters 'Oh shit, no.'

'Haze, where you been?'

'Oh, hi Mally what do you mean where have I been? You know I work here. This is Roberto.'

Mally stands his ground and nods whilst Roberto approaches with an outstretched arm.

'Hi Mally, pleased to meet you, I have heard all about you.'

'Oh aye, you have, have you?' he replies turning back to her dismissively. 'Anyway, Haze, are you coming tonight? It's the team dinner at the club. Pick you up at 7?'

'Sorry I can't,' she lies quickly. 'I've arranged dinner with my dad.'

'Yer wot? You knew it were tonight. '

'So sorry, I can't let him down. He is very low at the moment.'

'But – Oh, please yer fucking self,' he huffs before speeding off.

'Naughty!' teases Roberto, enjoying her discomfort.

'I can't face another one of those Rugby club do's. Sexism, racism, toxic masculinity, really bad wine and a gang of wives and girlfriends lapping it all up whilst bitching about one another - urg!'

'So you might be free for a curry tonight then?' jumps in Roberto, spotting an opportunity.

'I'd love to but not tonight. You don't realise how connected everyone and everything is here. He'd know before we got through the starters.'

'Sounds like you are in a bit of a corner with all that.'

'You're not kidding; I need to deal with it. Anyway, get on with that lot and never mind about my problems,' she scolds playfully.

They rub along very well enjoying each other's company. She has inherited her mother's vinyl collection so she is no stranger to seventies progressive rock and banter about that and their hinterlands make the days fly.

She is unaware how much he is making a huge effort not to show his dark side. More dangerously it soon emerges that they share a wicked sense of humour, hers liberated by whatever it is that Roberto slips into her drinks, her usual empathy and self-regulation forgotten.

They invent weird nicknames for all the regular customers.

'Here comes Mingus and his droopy beard, oh no it's the shoe people and Arthur Pendragon!' they compete to include insults and random chosen words in seemingly innocuous conversations.

Fitting the surnames of the Rolling Stones into discussions with customers about pile creams: 'This is just Watts you need sir' and 'Wyman, you are looking good today'.

The most outrageous word slipped into a conversation with someone over the age of eighty or a vicar: 'Would you like to stay fuckoffy reverend?' or 'Are you from up cuntry madam?'

Completely unprofessional and unbecoming, juvenile and cruel behaviour but they were having a ball. For different reasons they were both there to escape and to forget.

They play to each other their favourite tunes to liven the dance. *'This is what I like, this is who I am, and this is my music'.* So the formerly quiet shop becomes home to the music of Bob Dylan, Leonard Cohen, Led Zeppelin from him and reflecting the near twenty years between them Paul Weller, Radiohead and Suede from her. More than once a customer comes into the shop unnoticed because of the volume of the music and when coming round the back of the counter in a vain attempt to get some service almost catches them drinking wine in the back room.

Bit by bit Hazel takes liberties with her attire and deliberately dresses to entrap him. He can't contain his appreciation of her and doesn't try to. He buys her CDs, gives her books to read, takes her for meals after work, and then by degrees they begin to regularly get drunk at lunchtime and do little or no work in the afternoons.

Coming to work becomes something they both excitedly looked forward to. It is no longer about earning money keeping the shop going for Mrs Pickles nor about escaping from their demons, disasters and deeds. It is by now all about the exquisite excitement of a fruitful new relationship and everything else is forgotten.

Cakes on Wednesday, fish and chips or a curry on a Friday, wine with additional spirit added by Roberto most lunchtimes and rock music every day.

Mally cottons on immediately to a shift in Hazel's attitude towards him and deep down he knows their relationship won't last. He can fix anything mechanical, but doesn't have the toolbox to deal with this. He suffers badly from the small village knowing him too well. He has become used to being seen out with Hazel and enjoys the elevated status it has given him among his peers and fellow rugby folk.

Unable to do anything to reverse what is so obviously developing, he becomes no more than a bystander, pretending not to notice. He makes a fool of himself by being overtly hostile to the newcomer.

Hazel has to get rid of him now and clear the ground for a new relationship, but these things rarely work to order. There is more often than not a distasteful and hurtful overlap and this will be no different. In the pain and complication of parting and moving on there is so often accompanying inevitable hurt to all involved.

Roberto settles into a guest house just off the square run by a Scottish lesbian couple, who pride themselves on their cooking and housekeeping. They are easily capable of out-grumping any English northerner and can be sufficiently parsimonious to make the average Yorkshire tightwad seem like Elton John flexing a platinum card in a florist's.

They are glad to have Roberto to stay as a long-term guest and he will be a life saver when the tourist season gives way to autumn.

To his surprise and relief the spectre of the knock on the door he expected did not materialise and he quickly begins to enjoy his new life.

His hosts are fortunately libertarians too. When the partying goes too far and becomes too much for them they remind each-other of his value: The benefit of having a free spending, long term guest far outweighs the downside.

Roberto experiences no guilt, no sleepless nights and no regrets.

Hazel has unfinished business to tidy up before she can party on with Roberto, but somehow she can't find a kind way to draw a line and move on.

Mally is a powerful human, a near perfect physical specimen, 2m tall and 110kg of solid muscle, topped with a vertical tuft of short blond hair. He has the arms of a man who can mix a tonne of concrete with a shovel without breaking into a sweat.

Sadly the elements that came together to create him were not distributed evenly. An empty vessel makes the most noise and Mally is the biggest and emptiest one in the village. Hazel's obvious flirting with the dodgy old clever bastard that had barged into his long term plans, eventually become something he could no longer ignore.

6 Banged to Rights

Roberto and Hazel could have easily passed each other without getting together and had completely different lives, but circumstances over which they had no control decreed that they would spend too much time together in the shop for nothing to happen. She is healthy, hot and horny; and he is riveted by her youth, beauty and vibrant intellect. They are excited and invigorated by each other, and forced to share the same small space daily. She makes him live life again and begin to consider a brighter future.

Weekday mornings, when the school doesn't send many poorly boys for creams and pills and the weather keeps the elderly and tourists away, the bell above the door falls silent and the dangerous pair, rarely bothered by pesky customers, allows the sexual chemistry to reach boiling point.

They come close to embracing as they lock up one evening, but Hazel pulls back to show him who's boss. The line has been crossed between polite respectful flirting to physical entanglement.

Dressing for work the next morning Hazel catches herself in the mirror and pauses. She discards the bra in her hand and deploys her tightest white T-shirt and skinny jeans.

How can he not? She thinks. *He'd have to wouldn't he?*

'I'm ready for you now, the dance is over. Time for me to pounce,' she says to the tiger in the mirror.

Arriving at the shop she finds him already in place, 'I am feeling alive today and I am hungry.'

'So what can I get you madam?' He says from his position on the floor.

He is toast. The pot boils over. She stands over him as he busies himself with some diversionary shop tweaking. He reaches into a low shelf shuffling some hair products around pointlessly. She throws one long leg either side of his head and looks down on him as he raises his head between her legs. She moves forward and presses her groin into his welcoming face. No need for a preamble of ever closer but tentative contact, she grabs handfuls of his hair and holds his head.

They don't need to speak. He is taken by her at a time and place of her choosing. She pulls him up from the floor and leads him into the store room at the back of the shop. There on the old sofa where Mrs Pickles' cat ruled supreme, they tear into each other throwing away clothes and clawing at skin. She throws off her T-shirt and unbuttons her jeans, before starting on his. He tries to sit up on the sofa to remove his shoes but she pushes him onto his back, straddling him and totally dominating him. He holds her breasts as she grinds into him.

She suddenly jumps off him and lies on the floor with her legs in the air and commands 'Off'. He obediently tugs at her jeans and reveals the black lace of her knickers and endless legs, scattering bottles and packaging everywhere as he tosses her jeans aside.

She leaps up and pushes him onto the sofa, tearing at his shirt. She cares nothing for the consequences and her physicality and vigour make him the weaker participant in the wildest most passionate noisy love-making either have ever experienced.

They come together without removing any more clothes. The electric, sudden and all-consuming animal passion quickly reaches a crescendo for both of them, her frantic thrusting causing him to wince with pain and pleasure.

Before they can part, they are petrified by the familiar sound of the swinging front doorbell. They are trapped and strangled by his partly removed clothing, bound together by his jeans which by then are neither on nor off. One leg is still attached to his foot, the other wrapped around Hazel's leg and he is still inside her.

They momentarily freeze. His torn shirt is turned around Hazel's wrist.

They spring apart without thought or tenderness, still connected but by now only by discarded clothing.

They stumble over the furniture, hopping around like two blindfolded, disabled semi mummified escapologists, halfway through a drunken rehearsal on a bed of nails whose bandages are on fire. They somehow manage to stand up. Hazel cracks her head on an oak beam unhelpfully lower than the already inadequate sloping exposed plank and hand hewn joists of the ancient ceiling and the pain makes her wince.

In heat of the moment, they hadn't thought to lock the door. In fact they were lucky that they weren't in the pub or in the street at the time, as there would be no force that could have stopped that explosion. They were both in desperate need of escape and found each other irresistible from the moment they had met. Pretty much wherever they happened to have been the volcano would have still erupted.

Their rapture is quickly destroyed by a shrill voice like a cheese grater being dragged across the side of a van.

'What in God's name is going on here!! The flames of hell will devour you beasts. Rutting like base animals in a field! Get out! Get out!'

Mrs Pickles is a shrivelled and stooped woman with a strangely young face for someone in their seventh or eighth decade. Her rosy cheeks and shiny skin are incongruous features attached to the body and gait of one of Macbeth's witches. She stands in the doorway and screams a piercing yell at the sight of naked flesh in the shop she has nurtured for fifty years.

For several seconds she can't compute what she sees.

She thrashes at them with a broom shrieking.

'Leave my property immediately!'

Roberto, sweating and breathing heavily after his exertion, cracks his knee on the coffee table and gallantly stands in front of Mrs Pickles taking the full force of her well-aimed broom handle which snaps across his raised arm making him yelp with pain.

'Get out of my shop! I've been in bed for a week and this is what I find!

I was sent here by the Lord who forced me to rise from my bed and come here to bear witness to FORNICATION! Disgusting, revolting fornication!'

*A bit harsh, h*e thinks between yelps of pain as she rains blows on him.

'I thought it was going rather well.'

'I'm sick and old and this is how you repay my trust!'

The experience is far too vivid and rewarding to be spoilt by a thorough battering from a deranged hag, but the next ten minutes feel much longer as Roberto attempts to pacify her. Hazel runs down into the cellar clutching her jeans and quickly tugs from the bottom right up to the top of her bottom until they are mostly in place, before returning up the stairs, unhelpfully but well-meaningly putting the kettle on as she passes it. She'll zip them up later when she finds her T-shirt. Roberto throws it to her from behind his back, continuing to manfully shield her from Mrs Pickles who is still beating him and yelling.

Hazel then succumbs to his frantic semaphore hand signals from behind his back which she understands to implore her to leave him to deal with the crazy woman.

She slips out of the back door and across the yard to the pub, rearranging her clothes as she goes. She orders a double gin and quietly sits in the corner awaiting Roberto, juggling a strange mixture of emotions: shame, breathless sexual excitement, blind panic about what might be relayed to her father and a very strong desire to laugh out loud.

Half an hour later Roberto comes in and as soon as their eyes meet they collapse in hysterics.

'NOOOOOOOOOOOOOOO!!! That was really very VERY bad,' says Hazel with undisguised shame and horror.

'What did she say?' Her head in her hands and her long fair hair covering her face to hide from the world.

'No worries, I've sorted her out. I told her you were having a fit and I was massaging you to relieve your stressed muscles.' soothes Roberto.

'Surely, she didn't buy that?'

'No. Not for a minute, but luckily she was after another prescription, so I put it together and added something to make her sleepy. I told her to go back to bed and rest, and I'll pop around in the morning to see how she is. Hopefully she won't remember any of this.'

'What did you put in her prescription? That is really very wicked of you, she *is* very old.'

'Don't worry, nothing harmful. Just an aid to calm her.'

'Can you do that?' quizzes Hazel.

'Well we'll see won't we? Stop worrying, she'll be fine. Have another one - you have earnt it,' he grins.

7 Taming the Shrew

Mrs Pickles does indeed turn out over the next couple of weeks to lose her sting. A great deal of attention, some flowers and some 'TLC' from Roberto seem to help her forget. She begins to talk for the first time of retirement.

He tells Hazel that he has become quite friendly with her and is genuinely concerned for her welfare. He isn't. She mistrusts him intensely and he sees her as nothing more than a bump in the road to success.

He now has a very specific reason to control her and his medication is starting to work. The excitement of the past couple of weeks and Roberto's attention to her seem to somehow take the venom from her bite. She becomes calmer, almost compliant.

During a visit to her tiny cottage where he refills her pill jar and flower vase, he broaches the future with her while making her a cup of tea.

'I'm happy to stay and help in the shop and if you feel unable to continue, I can leave the agency and invoice the shop directly which would save you 40% in fees and I would happily discuss taking over from you more permanently at some point in the future if you so wish.'

'I'll think about it. Come back next week and shut the door properly on your way out,' she replies.

He spots a door key hanging from a hook and slips it into his pocket.

He eventually convinces her to let him keep the pharmacy going for the time being. He has nowhere else to go and can see some potential in the business despite the restriction on trade which the opposition Eric Francombe represents. He also feels an immediate need to spend more time with Hazel - alone if possible.

He can't believe his good fortune to have met her and his every thought and deed is now focussed upon curating a permanent position in her orbit.

He puts a huge amount of time and effort into Mrs Pickles.

It's very easy to slip her some chemicals which make her drowsy and relatively affable as he seeks to help her forget why she ever wanted to come back to the shop. He has to be extremely careful with the doses as he needs her alive to sign documents. If she dies before he has control, he will be the useful idiot running the shop whilst the beneficiaries of her will if there are were any, sell it on at the market rate.

Her chances of a full recovery whilst her medication is in the gift of Roberto Antonelli and his experimental mixtures are next to none. She is of course, unaware of what he is up to, but he in turn is unprepared for her iron constitution and granite hard determination. She calls her solicitor to her home. He is older than her and like her, until recently saw no reason to hand over his dwindling rural practice.

'My dear Mrs Pickles how wonderful it is to see you. I hear you have been under the weather.'

'Yes, yes. I will make you some tea provided you don't charge me to drink it.'

'What can I help with?'

'Well, privately I have very real concerns about my health. I am feeling weaker as the days pass. I have begun to regret not retiring earlier and wondered if I will ever be fit enough to return. I have headaches like never before, can't sleep and feel sick all the time. I want you to prepare to sell the shop as soon as possible.'

'You do know that the building is in need of extensive repair and the business is still impoverished by the presence of Eric Francombe who is in a better position?'

'I know that you bloody fool, but the business still has a value doesn't it? Or are you working for Francombe? It has seen me right for forty five years.'

The old man leaves with a brief to look for opportunities to offload the business and the building and help her to tidy up her affairs. Before it can go any further her health deteriorates further. She is rushed to Airedale hospital, well over an hour's drive south, where her medication is immediately thrown in the bin and denounced as completely wrong and dangerous for her in any quantity. She takes the doctor's intervention as a gross impertinence and explains the way she sees things in the same scraping voice that Roberto and Hazel had endured.

'I've been a pharmacist for over four decades standing and I'm not going to be told anything by a doctor who wasn't even born in whatever country you came from when I became qualified.'

Roberto gradually settles into the village, each day subtly and slowly making it more to his liking; using alchemy to encourage the populous round to his way of thinking and removing elements he can't control.

His temporary residence at the Fell View Guesthouse becomes a long term arrangement. The owners like having him there, they learn to enjoy the party that follows Roberto wherever he goes and he loves their cooking and the easy going regime. The two women had arrived in West Fell two years earlier and had not received the welcome they imagined.

Back in Glasgow where one was a sports teacher and the other a struggling ceramic artist, they found it hard to make a living and came to the countryside so the artist could create in the garden room and the guest house provide an income. Their first two years were successful financially. The summer months were fully booked but the winters were long and lonely and they were confused and dismayed by being ostracised. In Glasgow their sexual orientation was not judged, but here they sensed the unease of the villagers and were not invited into anyone's home.

So they were pleased to accommodate a non-judgemental guest and his growing entourage who generously include them in his life.

It becomes more decadent by the day. Wine, drugs and cash are liberally distributed to anyone who joins in.

They also take a maternal shine to Hazel, which soon turns into something else particularly for the younger artist of the couple. Quickly, another dimension comes into play in the highly charged atmosphere of free expression and louche experimentation that Roberto enjoys nurturing and curating.

8 Learning to Parallel Park

It isn't the first time that Hazel's clumsy handling of her love life causes painful shockwaves and leaves a trail of destruction.

Mally eventually feels compelled to deal with his perceived humiliation in the village of his birth. The black and chrome Filton car, parked as always in the village square is impossible to miss.

This is the home of the Land Rover defender, the tractor and the pickup truck. The ostentation of Roberto's car speaks directly to Mally's ego. He has been hanging out at the clubhouse more and more since he lost his place in the first team at the end of the last season. He was told his fitness was coming off the boil. During the close season, he had not improved his chances of regaining it in the Autumn by drinking too much. In his last top flight game, West Fell suffered a thrashing from Kendal, a team who they had beaten easily in their last four or five meetings. Mally was judged to have been the weakest player.

Tonight as so many others recently, he drives from the club and sets off in search of Hazel who he knows will have finished work at 5pm. When he can't reach her on the phone, he guesses where he will find her. Time starts to speed up when he sees her unmistakable profile through the curry house window. They are laughing and it's too much.

His blood boils. Eyes blazing, fists clenched, he sees a yellow dumper truck. He has a Lucas key on his key ring, the go-to key which will start most UK tractors or construction machines made between the end of WW2 until the digital age including the four tonne 4WD Benford parked at the top of the square.

Before thinking he climbs up to its driving position, fires it up and points it towards the Filton, stamping on the accelerator and sending the noisy dumper charging across the cobbles, its empty bucket bouncing and clanging in the evening quiet. Picking up speed it bears down on the car, the sprung seat sending his feet in five directions at once whilst he tries to keep the accelerator hard down on the footplate. He holds the steering wheel in his right hand whilst raising the bucket holding the tipping lever backwards. As it tips forward the front edge becomes a blunt battering ram and the back of the bucket blocks his view but still his foot is rammed down to the floor.

This is how it works in Mally's head: his sensible numbskulls in the department of logic and planning are yelling *"What the hell are you doing? No!"* But as too often, they are overruled by the ego and maleness collective, based in his groin. The problem is not helped by the fact that the various departments inside his head and elsewhere in his body are communicating via hand-delivered quill pen messages in ponderously sealed envelopes. He wasn't born blessed with internal neural text messaging, far from it. His controlling numskulls don't even have a fax machine yet, so by the time a plan of action is formulated and agreed with, it's usually too late.

He leaps off when he is sure it will make contact. No more than a second before the steel tipping bucket of the dumper tears along the side of the sports car ripping it open like a sardine can and rocking it up onto two wheels as it absorbs the impact.

The windows smash, one of the gull wing doors flies open, torn aluminium and buckled carbon fibre are thrown in all directions by the impact and the alarm of this and several others in the square go off. The dumper bounces on its wheels and continues driverless in an arc until it collides with the stone boundary wall of the car park and climbs it until it becomes beached and stalls astride of the now partially demolished wall like a giant pit bull mounting a poodle.

The violence of the collision - the 'B' of the bang horrifies all departments inside his brain. They stand peering out horrified at all levels. His anger dissipates in an instant and he tries to run away, he trips over a low wall and is momentarily winded.

In his brain it's every numbskull for themselves. Word goes out from emergency self-preservation *"Damage done; flee now, Mally. Hide until sober, clean up and deny."* Director of logic, at the far end of a lonely and little used corridor is alerted from slumber by a siren and gets into action. Whilst sending down a hastily scribbled note to ego and maleness on floor seven (groin level) with a short message: *"Here we go again you fucking Idiots you know you're not empowered to take action before it's signed off by all departments. You will be the death of all of us."*

But too late, he is spotted by people who know him. It's not his fault. Some people are just wired analogue in a digital age. Unfortunately for Mally he is one of them. Although his plumbing works perfectly he doesn't even have a reliable electricity supply up in his noggin. The terrible noise of the impact shakes the square and brings everyone out into the street. The whole episode takes less than two minutes from thought to completion.

The curry house and the pub next door empty onto the square to join in the fun, Hazel and Roberto amongst them. They love a public scrap up here.

Mally lunges at Hazel but she is too quick for him and grabs his fist, directing him across a pub table as she dodges sideways allowing his bulk to pass without contact like a Spanish Matador outwitting a crazed and doomed *Toro Bravo*. He lands upside down in a flowerbed and when he rises to the cheers and laughter of his neighbours and friends, someone shouts 'Ole!'

He tries again but this time he is restrained by the crowd. His imagined humiliation thus becomes real. By his own actions he makes the whole village aware of his cuckolding. His violence towards his former girlfriend in front of friends, family, workmates and neighbours amid the raucous melée that ensues in the village square will not be soon forgotten.

Now defeated, beaten to his girl by a person who, by his measurement is an aftershave-wearing, elderly woofter and potentially in trouble with the law for criminal damage, he has compounded all this by not only attacking a woman outside the home in front of witnesses (which up in the dales is now at last becoming a tad more frowned upon than hitherto) but, worse still, doing so and being defeated in that enterprise; he knows redemption will be hard won.

He is quickly taken home by concerned friends and Roberto wins the admiration of the throng for not involving the police. He quickly arranges for Mark Deacon to get involved and tidy up the carnage including rescuing the dumper truck from its undignified position straddling the carpark wall. He could have Mally arrested, but he doesn't want cops anywhere near him if he can avoid it. His calm understanding in the face of extreme provocation and violence makes him seem a giant of a man in Hazel's eyes.

As soon as he clocks the scene of mayhem and destruction, he can see 40 grand and six months being spent getting his car sorted. It will have to be returned to the factory in Bristol to sort this. It can't be done in a garage, not even Peckitts in Otley or the Filton Chiswick service centre. It's going to need a partial rebuild in the West Country factory.

He knows this will not end well for Mally, but it won't do him or his relationship with Hazel any harm.

'Oh Rob! Your car! I'm so sorry. It's my fault; I shouldn't have allowed it to come to this. I just buried my head as usual, hoping it would sort itself.'

'It's fine Hazel. It's just a car.'

In truth he is furious and wants the man dead but knows he should keep that in as there is a higher prize for him from this event.

'Are you ok? Nice judo moves.'

'Yes I'm fine. He missed,' she says putting her arms around him.

'How can you be so calm?' She asks whilst stroking his hair.

'Far worse things can happen. I've rung Mark Deacon. He's coming to take it in and keep it until I can have it trucked down to Bristol. It's insured, so what the hell, let's get back to that wine.'

Roberto can't involve either the police or his insurers. Without a crime number he won't be able to claim. He'll have to find the money himself. It will completely clean him out and more but he isn't going to let that appear to be a problem.

'You are amazing,' he praises. 'Truly amazing! Demure femininity is great, but fitness and athletic prowess so much more so. I admire so much a woman who would pick up a rifle and fight back if cornered, rather than cower in a corner squealing!'

'No problem looking after myself,' Hazel smiles.

This incident cements their relationship and compounds the pain for Mally.

As summer shows signs giving way to autumn he retreats into depression, stops drinking at the rugby club, but continues at home and begins to pile on weight. He finds no comfort but escape in food and television and devours far more than he should of both. He can't bring himself to come out in the village for weeks, despite his friends rallying round.

His mother arrives to collect a prescription. The last place she wants to shop is the workplace of her son's ex-girlfriend but Francombe's Pharmacy across the square has unexpectedly closed.

It's very awkward. Roberto tries some small talk on her while he prepares the prescription for her son. It's the moment he has been waiting for.

She ignores Hazel who politely finds something to do in the back of the shop.

'We are all very sorry about what happened Mrs Mallinson, but I've got the car fixed on the insurance,' he lies 'so tell him not to worry about it.'

'Thank you. He's not well. He won't get over this in a hurry but he shouldn't have behaved like that. He knows he's in the wrong.'

'Well, which of us hasn't made a chump of ourselves from time to time?' Roberto smiles benevolently.

'It's only a metal object and it will soon be fixed, so much easier than fixing people, so let's all forget it shall we?' He says comfortingly whilst arranging with relish Mally's prescription.

Hazel, who is listening in the back room, sobs quietly.

I didn't love him and was trying to finish it with him. Perhaps if I had the strength of character to deal with it like an adult, it wouldn't have got out of hand.

'That poor woman, I feel so fucking bad about it. It's my fault.'

Roberto calmly comforts her. Hazel draws succour from his maturity. She doesn't notice him staring into the middle distance apparently devoid of emotion.

'Don't worry. He will be just fine in no time,' he whispers.

9 Busy Digging Foundations

A week later an ambulance is seen winding its way down the valley and it stops for two hours outside the Mallinson family's garage building. When police cars from Northallerton are parked at either end of Miles Beck Lane, word begins to spread that Mally has been found in the office at the back of the workshop.

By that evening the jungle drums report that it was probably a self-administered overdose of prescription drugs, but he couldn't be saved.

Accidental or deliberate, the whole village debates the likelihood either way. His split with Hazel and his decline after the incident in the square are widely assumed to be the cause. She, his family and other witnesses of the dumper truck incident give evidence to the coroner to attest to his bouts of violent mood swings and depression. It began in his early teens and predated the breakdown of his relationship and the unfortunate debacle in the square.

Roberto gives the proceedings a wide berth; he tells Hazel it's to keep a polite distance to save Mally's family from more pain, but in truth, the last thing he needs is for his name to be dragged into it by the village disapproval committee, police or the media.

In the pub he is approached by a rugby mate of Mally's.

'So what's your game plan here pal, what are you doing round here? We don't know what to mek of you.'

'I'm sorry, have we been introduced?' Roberto is in no mind to show any sign of weakness. 'Do I need to fill in a form and submit it to you for approval? If so could you give me your office address? Who do I send my application to exist to? The supreme leader of West Fell are you?'

'Just look out for yourself, that's all I am saying. Mally was a part of this community and if you hadn't come here he would still be alive.'

'Look I am as cut up about him as you are but I don't regard it as my responsibility, so please enjoy your evening and leave me alone.' He resolves to find out who this fellow is, so he can check his records and see if he is a customer.

He is allowed to contribute a written statement to the coroner detailing the exact prescription and likely side effects of the medication luckily originally prescribed by Mr Francombe over the road before he came to the village.

Hazel gives evidence in person about the end of their relationship and downplays any reference to her new relationship and the events in the square.

'We had simply drifted apart and he found it hard to deal with. There were a couple of moments of violence, nothing too worrying; and apparent depression which concerned me, but he never showed any sign on being so low to consider this.'

She hides her shame and desperation about the whole episode to save herself from dwelling on the second suicide in her life within three years.

'I had been trying to end our relationship for some months, his drinking worried me,' she adds, pot-kettle style.

Nearly everyone in the village witnessed Mally's downfall and no one questioned the verdict. They saw him lose control. They saw the anger in his eyes. The court of public opinion made its collective judgement, although the finger of ultimate blame was pointed by some at Roberto. If he had not turned up, then perhaps Hazel would still be happily attached to Mally and they might be on the way to building a life together in West Fell. This judgment was very convenient for him but wide of the mark. He had now perfected his deadly method.

Now he and Hazel can openly enjoy each other as an item, so after a polite interval they do.

Hazel blames herself for Mally's suicide and to temporarily avoid her guilt over another bereavement, she gets high and drunk every day and stays that way for weeks.

Roberto's mature understanding manner and the comfort he gives her over the death of her ex, his calm acceptance of the damage to his beloved car and the careful manner with which he deals with the sensitive issue makes him totally irresistible to her. His surreptitious medication of her has now become routine and she has far less control on her emotions than he does.

Just as in Bradford, a nuisance had been eradicated without consequence.

Dr Anderson is quietly distraught. His daughter is receiving the comfort she needs and though Roberto's presence makes his toes involuntarily curl, he pacifies his dark thoughts with the idea that it will be a passing phase and is unlikely to survive her impending move to Cambridge. Without Hazel's knowledge, her next move to St James College is being quietly eased by her father's discreet benevolent patronage and useful contacts.

West Fell School was linked by its foundation deed to St James, and although the college no longer exercised its right to appoint headmasters to West Fell, the historical links endured.

The school was saved from dissolution by its connection to St James, Cambridge in 1546 when Henry VIII sought to seize its assets. To this day and to respect an ancient covenant which could in theory return the school to the estate of its original founder if it fails to catapult sufficient numbers of pupils to the next level, many pupils who make the grades are encouraged to find their way to Cambridge as her father had done.

Dr Anderson would not have been so keen to smooth her passage back to Cambridge had he known that she had already discussed the move with Roberto and agreed that they would look at the possibility of making it together. Hazel too, would have had a different perspective if she ever learnt that Roberto had made a profit on the repair to his car by fiddling the invoices for handling its move to the factory and back with the connivance of Mark Deacon, his new friend and local garage owner.

Mark, an old school friend of Mally's is also a pragmatist. Roberto keeps him supplied with life-enhancing pharmaceuticals of the kind you can't get on a prescription and, using the astonishingly large sums of cash now coming his way, they have speculatively purchased some restoration projects together. It is a 50/50 arrangement. Roberto siphons profits from drug dealing and launders it through old car purchases, which Mark sources from the classic car trade. He will do all the restoration work whilst Roberto pays for the parts.

Mark's garage has never been busier. In the barn behind his workshop there is now a Riley 2.5, two Jaguar's, the shell of an E-type lightweight roadster and most of an XK120, a burnt out Aston Martin DB5 without a gearbox and a damaged Bristol 404.

They meet to pore over their collection and formulate a plan.

Rob is on his mobile as he walks into the garage.

'Yep, yep Hazel I know, I know. Tell her to come back after lunch. I'll be back in half an hour; I'm just with the bank manager.' He winks at Mark.

'Paradise!' says Mark grinning from ear to ear as he surveys the jumbled mass of rusting and twisted metal.

'Sorting this lot will be three years toil for me in between day to day work servicing and MOT's. I have three Land Rovers and enough farm machinery to fix to keep me busy not to mention bringing in car wrecks for the police and the AA with the tow truck.

'You're the man Mark; I'll help in my spare time. I can do the marketing and handle the money. You just tell me what you need and I will source it. I've got cash coming in which would be very useful to direct into something tangible, so don't be afraid to let me know. Also, if you come across any more interesting projects keep me in the loop, yeah? '

'Don't say that, next time you come we will be stacking them three high and looking for larger premises!'

'Well don't let me hold you back! Buy wisely and as cheap as you can, but only go for quality and the rare ones. If there is a limited edition or a sports version we want that one instead of the bog standard one, do you follow? Top brands, rare models, no matter what the condition. If they are cheap enough you can sort it. If we stick to that you never know where it might go. We're only limited by our own imagination you know, Mark? No one is saying there's a lid on it.'

The village car mechanic had replaced the blacksmith as the go-to man to fix anything metal too, so there is a steady stream of visitors with broken wheelbarrows, snapped pick-shaft handles and drawings of shelf brackets.

Mark is a hardworking man. He has no idea where Roberto's money comes and doesn't ask. He sees Roberto as a kindred spirit passionate about classic cars.

When vital information is withheld within a relationship, it denies one of the participants the ability to make necessary and informed choices.

The urbane and intelligent party animal who is cultured, funny, insightful and capable of enormous acts of generosity is guarded by necessity. There are huge gaps in Hazel's knowledge of what he's been up to.

As soon as he leaves Mark, he goes straight to the park where he meets a sixth form schoolboy under the bandstand. He hands the boy a package and takes a folded bundle of cash. The boy cycles off towards the school. There is another student who visits him regularly and at strange times of the night.

Hazel assumes it to be an occasional exchange of weed and isn't even sure who is supplying who. She has no idea that Roberto has established a significant supply chain into the school and elsewhere which is producing cash quicker than he can spend it.

So she knows he's a bit racy, but doesn't know enough to worry too much. Entranced and intrigued, she likes that element of mystery about him but is just a little troubled by the ease with which he has quelled Mrs Pickle's anger with a small tweak of her prescription.

He has at one point tried as hard as he could to finish off Mrs P completely, but didn't get the mix quite right. A gram more would have done the trick; a gram less and she wouldn't have noticed. The woman is indestructible, but now he wants her ill and defeated, but alive.

A common misconception about murderers is that they behave in a sinister or aggressive manner all the time. It is possible to be the very best person in every way, a family man, a man of God, a Good Samaritan, or perhaps a well-known entertainer and still harbour a devastating dark side.

So no matter how busy Roberto becomes running his side lines, it never gets in the way of his devotion to the concept of being a perfect boyfriend to Hazel. He knows how much she needs him, and throws the kitchen sink at their relationship.

Unsurprisingly then, he also keeps from Hazel the episode involving Brian Calvert, the hill sheep farmer from Deepdale, a miserable old sod, well known for his conflicts, arguments and wars with neighbours.

Roberto had carelessly blocked his Land Rover in at the back of the pub whilst he was absent for half an hour. He returned to find a furious man trying to attach his car to a tractor.

'Hey, hey what are you doing?'

'This yours? Get it fucking moved now you tosser. I've been stuck here all mornin.'

'I am so sorry sir, but I have only been absent for twenty minutes... Give me that - I don't want you scratching my bumper.' The farmer snatched the tow chain back and a punch was thrown in Roberto's direction.

The farmer had the profound misfortune to call in the very next day for some cough medicine while Roberto was alone. He didn't apologise for attempting to knock Roberto out.

'Bloody hell it's you,' he coughed. 'You must be charging too much. Where is Elfrida? 'Ave you got owt fur coughs? I've 'ad it sin' Octowber.'

Roberto was the perfect gentleman. 'I have just what you need in the back. It's new and I'm prepared to personally guarantee that you won't ever have a sore throat again. In fact I will go as far as to say that if you have cause to come back here for anything after taking this, I will refund you twice the cost and give you a hundred pounds for your trouble. I am *that* confident that it will have a dramatic effect on you. That's £12.50 please.'

'Ow much?! Why has it no label? I am not paying £12.50 for something in a bottle unless it says Gin on it.'

'It's a very special new remedy that has only just become available and this is my personal bottle that I am happy to let you have without charge if you are worried about the cost.'

Roberto was ramping up the charm to make sure the farmer took the product, behind his mask, he seethed with hatred for the man and wanted him gone forever.

A dales hill farmer will accept literally anything if it is free. So he took it with a grunt and left without looking back to see Roberto's single raised finger behind his back.

Back at his lonely hillside farmstead the farmer took a big swig neat from the bottle gagged at the taste. Undeterred he mixed it with a large tot of gin and two spoons of sugar and was found a week later in his favourite shabby chair next to his fire.

No prescription, no witnesses, no invoice, no more miserable farmer.

Roberto knows from recent national news that no one is looking for a serial killer until blood spattered bodies, missing persons found wrapped in carpets in laybys or canals turn up, or shallow graves given away by freshly turned earth start appearing in the night. Then, crazed angry loners, weirdos and perverts are the first to come under investigation. Suave, calm, caring health professionals are the last to attract suspicion.

Harold Shipman knew that too, he thinks. Shipman's mission crept from the odd overdose here and there in a weird recreation of his mother's demise to an industrial scale eradication of anyone who he had the opportunity to dispatch, eventually getting caught after changing wills in his favour, which he didn't do until later. If Shipman had left it at a couple of hundred and stayed out of people's bank accounts, the frightening truth is that he probably wouldn't have been caught. It is almost a certainty that there are dozens, perhaps hundreds of more careful if perhaps less busy Shipmans (or is it Shipmen?...or even Shipwomen?) active this very day around the world and some will never be unmasked.

Roberto has no intention of being so busy and decides to restrict his attentions to anyone who displeases him or stands in his path, but selectively and carefully.

You may well enjoy rude health as a result of his care and attention, for the majority of the time he is a very competent dispensing pharmacist. He fancies himself more intelligent than the average murderer and intends to keep the numbers to a minimum, simply to increase his chance of continued success.

He is smart but not smart enough to know that too often our paths are laid out by others.

Mrs Pickles is not expected back at work. The temporary

arrangement by which Roberto takes control of the pharmacy now becomes permanent. She becomes violently ill after reverting to taking prescriptions prepared by him.

She doesn't call a doctor. She knows enough about it all and tells Roberto what she thinks she needs. He prepares it for her to her specification with some additions of his own. She doesn't trust Roberto, but she trusts the local GP even less and has fallen out with him so many times she no longer visits him.

He benevolently calls in on her regularly.

'Worse than useless, those foreign doctors. Not trained properly,' she says.

When her symptoms gradually worsen, she makes the decision to throw in the towel and offers her business to Roberto at a knock down price.

'I would be delighted to buy it but unfortunately, as I told you in the summer, I'm not sure I can raise any money at the present,' he lies.

Maybe not sharp enough to make the link between her medication and her worsening condition, she is no mug when it comes to money.

'I will keep the property. You can have the business for a little more than the value of the stock.'

'Well you know I would love to if I can afford it Mrs Pickles. How much would you think that the value of that might be? I wouldn't know how to calculate it.'

'Well nor would I, without an audit,' she foolishly reveals. 'I must insist again that Eric Francombe never finds out what I am suggesting, and you will undertake to keep the shop open for three years at a minimum and never sell to him.'

'As promised Mrs Pickles, I know how important your legacy is to you and I promise to nurture it and make sure it thrives.'

'Perhaps I can arrange a detailed and independent stock take to save you the cost and any delay. Then if I can raise the finance, I could take over with immediate effect if that suits you?' offers Roberto as kindly as he can pretend to be.

'I will give you a week,' she says. 'I'm too unwell now to get involved myself in protracted negotiations. If we can't agree something very soon I may have to close it.' She rashly agrees to allow him to quantify the stock with the help of an old school friend of Hazel's who is training to be an accountant.

Roberto stays in the shop all night removing stock into the loft and burning delivery notes in a small cast iron fireplace in the back room. Early the next morning he and Hazel meet her friend Natasha outside the shop and Roberto explains the task.

'We need an accurate stock take of everything at retail value and I will calculate a discounted price based on the wholesaler's best prices that we can negotiate, so give it to me when you've finished for me to adjust to wholesale value before we give it to Mrs Pickles, please. If she turns up, don't give it to her. Tell her you've only just started otherwise we'll end up negotiating on every item with her.'

'Aren't you helping, skiver?' Hazel teases.

'No. I will keep out of it then she can't question the impartiality of it. Anyway, I have some business to attend to down in Leeds, so I'll see you back here for a curry when you are done. Good luck. I have left a couple of bottles of red in the back in case you need lubrication.'

In fact he goes further south to check the fencing around his woodland idyll, speak to the farmer who shares the long lane to his land to agree to some new padlocks on the shared gates, and collect some funds and share certificates from his steel box which will help with the purchase of the shop. As always he leaves a five grand cash float for emergencies.

The two old school pals spend the weekend going through the contents of the shop, counting and valuing it against purchase invoices whilst listening to Urban Hymns and Wild Wood, reminiscing about their time as two of only 12 girls at the school. Hazel pours her pal a glass of red.

'So did you ever see that Damien again? The one who played the piano naked?'

'Noooooo don't remind me, he was so horny I had to run away! ...Anyway what's the score with you and Rob then? How long has that been going on?'

'Oh a little while. Don't ask, Nat. It's a bit delicate but we're good. He's kind to me. I don't know where it's going, but we are having a ball.'

'I've heard! You know the whole valley is talking about you two don't you? You hardly know him, be careful.'

'Oh for fuck's sake, why? Are they all jealous? Is no one allowed to have a drink and a laugh?'

'You're probably right, but be careful, won't you? I want to know you are safe and happy that's all.'

'Thanks Nat, I love you.'

'Just let me know if you need help anytime.'

Hazel enjoys the company of her old pal and the weekend flies by in a flurry of work, gossip, talk of future plans and laughter.

Before returning to West Fell Roberto rings around to corral some more cash, check his credit card headroom and find and engage a solicitor who doesn't have a conflict of interest with the vendor. Not an easy task in rural North Yorkshire where many of the local professional classes are often closely related either by practice or marriage and graze at the same very small pond, passing real or metaphorical brown envelopes to gain advantage or often just gaining advantage from helpful tip-offs when properties and businesses are coming up for grabs. He isn't looking for an honest one, but one he can trust to be crooked for him rather than Mrs Pickles.

When Hazel announces that they were done, a quick visit to the photocopier's enables him to present his own version of the auditor's document, resplendent with a fake accountant's logo that he has fabricated on an iMAC G5 he borrowed from a geek at the school. The social misfit gamed away at night and hid in his room for most of the day whilst he honed his hacking skills. He owed Roberto some favours for supplying him. The amended document is considerably more favourable Roberto's way than the original.

Mrs Pickles insists on sky high rent for the shop which by Roberto's calculations equates to the same price per square foot as prime city centre high street retail. He lets her have that one. He admires her for still having an eye for a deal at the same time as fighting off the chemicals he has administered which should have led to her being planted in the ground long since.

I'll deal with her later when the ink's dry, he thinks.

For now he happily agrees to pay her a very good rent. This acquiescence helps the deal go through quickly and keeps her out of his hair while he deals with the opposition.

Such is the antipathy Mrs Pickles has cultivated and nurtured in the village over the years, people are pleased to see the back of her. Her condition worsens to the point where she is hospitalised once more. Few notice and no one cares. Roberto has been *de facto* owner of the pharmacy since the summer and whilst the deal is going through, the cash is coming in so quickly anyway that he can afford it without borrowing.

Mrs P. waves aside her elderly lawyer's reservations about the speed of the arrangement. The transition is made successfully within a month. If she were to have any inkling of how much the shop was now making, she would never agree to terms at this level. Roberto uses every opportunity he can to lay it on thick about how they are struggling bravely to keep her legacy going.

During the take-over, Roberto learns from Mark Deacon of Eric Francombe's dizzy spells. He hears stories in the pub of the doddery chemist stumbling in the street and being rescued from behind his counter when he toppled in the middle of handing over a prescription. Pleased to hear that the mild medication of his nemesis delivered via his milk delivery which was often left on the shop doorstep each morning was working as planned, he was also gratified to note that Francombe's was closed for several days recently.

Roberto benefits from some new customers who drift across. Many of them are people who would rather lose a limb or vital organ than deal with Mrs Pickles due to historical conflict with her.

Some would gingerly peer into the shop window before coming in to ensure she really isn't there. He and Hazel learn to spot them and go out to chat them up and assure them that she isn't coming back anytime soon.

A take-over of all of the lucrative pharmaceutical supply business covering the radius of an hour's drive of the village becomes more than an interesting possibility for Roberto. This tiny outpost lies at the southern end of an area which stretches way beyond the lush green valleys of Swaledale into the vast emptiness of the Northern Yorkshire Dales into Cumbria and the foothills of the Lake District. This is an open goal. Square miles of sparsely inhabited damp valleys, wild moors and stone villages, all of whom rely on the village of West Fell for essential services.

National Health Service funding to support a rural pharmacy is an intrinsic part of the obligation to maintain NHS services to all areas of Britain which are free at the point of delivery for those who qualify, no matter how remote. This support is available only for a sole rural dispensary. Market forces and private enterprise are deemed to be meeting the need if there is more than one viable commercial enterprise involved

Roberto has travelled a long way in the short time he has had in West Fell. He came here almost a fugitive and has found all the cards have fallen in his favour.

He has discovered a thrill from the drama, not of killing, but of getting away with it.

Success is an aphrodisiac, so it does wonders for his performance with Hazel when he is not incapacitated by alcohol. He finds he no longer needs the occasional crutch of the blue pill he has used sporadically to keep up with Hazel's appetite.

Time to strike over the road, while the iron is hot. When it re-opens Roberto enters Francombe's Chemist shop. It is empty except for a steaming cup of tea on the counter. It takes him less than ten seconds to slip some powder into the tea and stir it in with a pen which he then throws onto the top of a high shelf as the old man makes his slow transit from his upstairs lair.

'Hello there; Rob Antonelli,' he cheerfully bellows as a greeting when Mr Francombe eventually makes it into the front of his shop. 'You must be Mr Francombe. I am the new owner of Mrs Pickles' shop. We *have* met briefly. We are now competitors but I hope we can have a friendly relationship and help each other. After all, as sole proprietors, our real enemies are the national chains, eh?' offers Roberto, in a fake spirit of knowing, rueful and conspiratorial joviality.

'Not interested. Please go away, I am busy. Good day.'

Being told to bugger off again makes it easier for Roberto to feel no empathy for his victim and he couldn't have wished for a more convenient opportunity. If the miserable fossil had been found dead in his shop, there might have been awkward questions. Mr Francombe helpfully goes out for some tobacco after drinking his tea and the lethal dose takes him whilst he is crossing the road. He has a fatal heart attack and falls into the road into the path of a white van being driven too quickly through the narrow streets.

Roberto is further emboldened by the simplicity and successful execution of his latest plan and has to stifle a smirk when he hears about it from Mark, who was brought in to remove the damaged delivery van to the police compound in Northallerton.

So easy, he tells himself. *So fucking easy.*

When Mrs Pickles discovers that her nemesis is no more, she is shocked at the news in a way that surprises her. She had fought him toe-to-toe for a lifetime, plotted and planned his downfall and dreamt of the day when he would no longer be able to continue, but now, in a flash he is gone.

Eric is no longer a competitor and no longer an impediment to her domination of the area. But it is too late for her to benefit. She knows immediately that Roberto will take all the advantage from the decades she invested in nursing this ambition, dreaming of this day. The moment she has waited for over four decades to come has arrived, but six months too late.

Initially she is too dazed and confused to work out quite how she has been hoodwinked and short changed. Later, her accountants and lawyers uncover obvious discrepancies and doubts about Roberto's involvement in the stock audit. Her medical condition improves at the hospital, which puts her beyond the influence of Roberto's versions of her self-prescribed medication and enables her to make a dramatic return to confront him in the shop. Fortuitously, it happens when Hazel is not around.

'You despicable cheat. I know what you've done, you fiddled my numbers! I promise you won't get away with this. As God is my witness, I will ensure that you don't prevail.'

It's too late, you foul tempered old prune. You have signed over the business, he thinks, but instead of challenging her he attempts a polite rebuff.

'I'm busy just now but I promise to look into the figures and make any agreed additional payment to you that our respective advisors come up with.'

It is a promise he has no intention of keeping, an easy one to make to someone he thinks will not be around for much longer.

'If you ask your accountant and your lawyer to arrange a meeting, I am quite sure we can get together and agree a resolution,' he soothes.

'They've been trying to do that for weeks they tell me.'

'I will give them a ring first thing in the morning,' promises Roberto.

When he does nothing, she confronts him again, this time in the street.

'He defrauded and poisoned me!' she shouts across the street. She denounces him and accuses him of 'More sinister and dark deeds' He brushes it off with his customary calm detachment and it is seen as the bitter resentment of a greedy old skinflint.

She gives him notice to quit the premises she still owns, but he knows that having just signed a 6 month tenancy for a rate well above what it is worth, all he has to do is make sure the rent is paid on time and he looks after the premises and there is nothing she can do until it expires.

She will have to be gone before then, he thinks.

The last thing he needs now is her tugging at his leg like an angry terrier. The locals' usual reticence and distrust of strangers, something designed through centuries of experience to protect rural folk from outsiders with ill intent, they would have done well to have deployed more rigorously in Roberto's case. Their caution falls away in the face of his well managed 24/7charm offensive.

He knows his time here will depend upon his ability to carefully cover his tracks after Mally's demise. He works hard to fit in as best he can and it is working very well.

He frequently buys drinks, treats people to meals, offers to sponsor hanging baskets and is effusive and attentive with his customers. He gives them as much free advice and help as he can. Anything he can think of to pull the comfort blanket of village life around him.

The ones he doesn't tinker with become the beneficiaries of his need to be an upstanding citizen, so in his eyes everyone benefits. Mrs Pickles' public outburst brings him sympathy, not condemnation. He expects some difficult questions, but receives gratitude for being a breath of fresh air in the village instead. As a result, his growing confidence soars and he becomes ever more dangerously wanton.

Roberto puts it about that she is on medication which suggests the beginnings of dementia.

Mrs Pickles' anger is duplicated tenfold when no one will listen. She calls into the nearest manned station in Kirkby Lonsdale.

'Why do I have to travel all this way to speak to a policeman?' she says to a policewoman on duty. When Geoff Lund was in the police house there was never any crime.'

'Come through Mrs Pickles and tell us again what you are alleging.'

She is patronised and treated as a bit of a local loony as the local PC has primed them about her outbursts and previous complaints, which they chalk up as no more than the ramblings of a crackpot. She mentions it again to the local beat bobby when nothing happens. A log of the allegation is made but not followed up, the local police know her to be vexatious and awkward.

Now settled into the village, enjoying his new position and energised by the thrill of success, rather than adopt a sensibly low profile Roberto feels unbeatable and embarks upon a period of unfettered hedonism that would make the Borgia family blush.

Hazel begins to spend most nights at the Fell View Guest House. After-hours parties, which start with an odd bottle of wine and lively discourse around a log fire gradually become legendary drinking sessions which attract a handful of likeminded youngsters who find a rare opportunity for bohemian expression in a judgemental and inward looking village. The drinking, soft drug misuse and general debauchery begin to get out of hand.

Hazel finds herself the subject of attention from just about everyone. The older boys from the school who gravitate to the house and the women who run Fell View are mesmerised by her and in time, alcohol fuelled physical involvement inevitably become the norm.

She knows this can't go on forever nor does she want it too, but enthusiastically embraces the experience and basks in the attention. It is escapism for her.

Roberto reaches a nirvana beyond his wildest dreams. He now has a new business, and a riveting and interesting partner who is more exciting than he could have imagined. He believes he has found a way of getting away with murder through superior intellect and command of his craft and develops the strutting air of entitlement of a preening potentate. He has lit a fuse and survived the explosion.

Having dealt with Eric Francombe, Mrs Pickles' modest pharmacy is suddenly worth many times what he paid to take control of it. With a NHS grant funding contract in place and no competition for thirty miles in any direction, Roberto is the proud owner of a magic money tree. He needs it to keep everyone happy.

10 Everyone's Trying to Carpe Diem

Peter Manford still has time to occasionally review his blue book and look back for patterns of behaviour and links between crimes and recurring names whilst backing up uniformed PCs on his shift.

Flicking idly through his hand written notes, which are supposed to be a complete as possible daily record of his conversations, observations, meetings and investigations, he is prompted by the notes to remember visiting the Bradford pharmacy following a disturbance.

The female colleague who he is infrequently and casually dating has it on her to-do list. She asks him as a favour to call in and look at it. It is the fifth time they have had cause to visit this particular establishment in the past twelve months.

As it will hasten the end of her work and enable her to accompany him to the pub, he manfully obliges. Yet again there was nothing about the initial disturbance that would normally require his involvement beyond the informal chat he has with the owner. This time it was just a break in with some damage, but his curiosity is tweaked by the coincidence that this is the venue where both of the men who are mentioned in the PC's report had been fighting back in February and are recorded in his blue book, are now confirmed dead.

This place keeps coming up on his radar. He doesn't believe in coincidences and for them both to die after having a fight, albeit apparently from different causes, seems to him to be a very unlikely one. All good detectives have nagging doubts which peck away at them. He decides to track down the strange pharmacist for a chat.

Pete doesn't race his car now but uses it to commute. This common interest will provide the curious DC with an opening gambit in a chat which might enlighten him.

He sees a photo in the file that Peter's DI has passed on to him of Roberto's car taken on the afternoon of the fight whilst he was absent in the pub and knows it to be one of the rarest and most expensive on the road. This pricks his interest further.

How does he afford it? He wonders.

The pharmacist appears to have moved on. The owner says he hasn't been back there since and his mobile number appears to have expired; he doesn't know why.

The truth about the car is more unlikely than the policeman could imagine. Roberto had found himself meeting a representative of the ruling family of Ligeria in Manchester which had changed his fortune.

The sons of Moataz Manoosma were known to be preparing to cling to power beyond the life of their revolutionary father who had taken the oil rich country and run it for over 40 years.

A customer at a pharmacy where he briefly worked in a greater Manchester suburb told him that he was printing tickets and documents for sporting events. He had been approached by a man who worked for one of Manoosma's sons on a major charm offensive launched by younger members of the mad dog's family which came about as a part of George Bush's 'War on Terror'.

Tony Blair had been to Ramalia and shaken hands with the pizza-faced crazy man to try and build Bush's coalition against terror beyond the UK, America and one or two smaller nations. The recent thaw in relations delivered fruit. Compensation for international terrorism in the form of huge payments had been cynically put on the table. The Ligerian government had never admitted culpability but were now up for paying a billion dollar bribe to enable their pariah status to be downgraded from 'Don't touch with a barge pole', to 'Friendly but potentially dodgy'.

It only lasted for a short time but this window enabled some opportunist trade with the oil-rich desert nation and its dysfunctional ruling family to flourish. This extended tentacles of lucrative business opportunities which reached as far as Manchester, UK.

Rather implausibly, in the wake of this, Manoosma's soccer-mad son Kamel and the relatively more urbane and western educated Musa were looking for opportunities to cement their regime's legitimacy and make it seem more benign and western-facing. They had put together the beginnings of a bid to hold the 2010 football World Cup in Ligeria. Fifa, the world governing body of football had indicated that the 2010 World Cup would be held in Africa and encouraged nations to bid for it; some would say to live off the process whilst countries outbid each other with bribes and presents.

Their hubris-driven and inevitably unsuccessful venture brought their fixers to Manchester as part of a 'bid to benefit' scheme which encouraged countries and sporting bodies to pitch for major sporting events, not with the expectation of success, but the process itself was lavish and long winded enough to create a multi-million pound industry around it.

Roberto's customer had obtained a contract to design and print the bid documents. He was searching for a craftsman to provide hand carved wooden boxes in which to present the documents to Fifa. The presentation format could accommodate the inclusion of 'incentives' hidden within the sealed boxes if one were inclined to enhance one's bid. These boxes could only be opened by the delegates themselves who would then decide where the World Cup would be held.

Roberto realised that this was a ruse to introduce the bid in a box that could then subsequently be used as a cigar or jewellery box. To add to the fun for the pampered delegates, who were reputed to be enriching themselves by supervising the process, the box could only be opened by using a two-part key which would be presented on separate occasions.

It left Roberto with the headache of finding someone who could make forty luxury hand carved boxes to a very high standard at extremely short notice.

As a proposal, it was way beyond the craft skills of a pharmacist, but not necessarily beyond his creative and entrepreneurial abilities. Roberto had no idea why he was being asked to help with this but he did know someone who could help.

A man he had spoken to in the Bar T'at pub in Ilkley was struggling to find work for his joinery business and employed just the kind of people who could jump on this. They arranged to meet.

'Working on television set construction we're well used to turning out creative work at very short notice,' explained the struggling contractor. Only the week before, Roberto had been discussing the guy's lack of current work and he had promised to keep his ears open for opportunities. He had expected to be able to pass on his number to someone who wanted a kitchen fitting out or perhaps some new windows .They took their pints to a quiet table overlooking the car park.

'This is a different kind of opportunity altogether. I will manage this and make a turn on the deal for myself. A presentation box for bid documents would have to be sumptuously luxurious and I feel sure it will attract a healthy budget,' explained Roberto.

'Let me have as much info as you can and I'll work out a price. How many will they need?'

'Forty odd. I will get all the info to you.'

'I saw a news item which showed one of the Manoosma boys boasting of having unlimited funds to bring the football World Cup to Ligeria. He spoke in terms of billions rather than millions.' said Roberto's new friend.

'I could perhaps have a small slice of that cake,' replied Roberto 'You would get a good job out of it.'

'We can do it for sure. Some of the lads in the workshop are superb and love a challenge. The Ligerians are very unlikely to be successful in bidding for it, especially in view of the opposition. They're up against South Africa who are surely a shoe-in for the first world football tournament to ever be held in Africa don't you think? The irresistible PR advantage of sports-mad Mandela hosting the football World Cup will trump any other bid?'

'If they pay the bill, who cares?' said Roberto.

'Besides all that, isn't it a bit dodgy distributing sealed boxes as presents from Manoosma? I wouldn't fucking open one and I wouldn't be happy getting on a plane with 40 of them either!'

'Again who cares about that? I just have to deliver them to the printers in Manchester, I couldn't care less what happens after that as long as they pay.'

The likelihood of failure of any bid from such a dubious regime didn't prevent a great deal of ill-judged and self-generated delusion building up to fuel a bid process which enabled a gaggle of Manoosma family ingrates and bid process facilitators to greatly benefit. The boxes would have to be very special. Compared with other things he had delivered to people recently, he saw this as by far the most risk free.

Roberto knew nothing about cabinet making but correctly deduced that he didn't need to. He took on the job and arranged cherry wood samples left over from a restaurant renovation in Ilkley to be shown to the Ligerians.

He met a very understated, smartly dressed man in the Jewel of India restaurant on the Curry Mile and swapped the samples for a printout of the lid carving they required. During the conversation, he told the man that he was a pharmacist. As soon as he said this, there was a perceptible mood change and the Ligerian leaned forward and whispered 'We know this.'

'Who are "we"? How did you know that?' asked Roberto puzzled and more than slightly worried.

'You would be very surprised by what we know, my friend. Would you like to work in Ligeria? Our leader has many tasks for you. We would pay very well and you would live in very safe and beautiful house. Do you wish to experience a new country and live a life of great luxury?'

Roberto was taken aback.

'I'm not planning any new career moves right now, but thanks for the offer.'

The man said 'Take this card and phone me if you change your mind. I can promise you a very comfortable life at the heart of the Ligerian government with the Manoosma family.'

'What? Are you serious? Why me?'

'As I say, you must contact me if you change your mind.'

The joiners delivered the goods on time and Roberto pocketed a significant arrangement fee, some of which he hid in a stainless steel box buried at his woodland hideout.

A month later the same man arrived in Yorkshire out of the blue and asked for an urgent meeting.

Roberto was made an offer he couldn't refuse, to deliver some pharmaceutical products to a Manchester hotel.

A week later he found himself back in the city. He took a room and waited in the foyer with a leather man-bag stuffed with the products requested as instructed.

He recognised the same well-dressed man he had dealt with previously, who came in shaking the rain from his expensive suit. He quickly gave Roberto a briefcase and said

'This is from our leader. He wants you to know that he is grateful to you. Our leader, the father of our nation has demanded that I give you the number of our office in London. He implores you to contact us and help us again very soon. You must spend it wisely. Remember you have now a friend in North Africa. You are a part of our family.

'No, do not open it here!' said the man suddenly alarmed. 'Take to a safe place now and come back.'

Surprised that the briefcase was given without handing over the drugs Roberto took it to his room and opened it carefully. The size of the payment took his breath away. He had never seen so much cash. He looked at the cash and the man-bag and considered for a moment, absconding via the fire escape with both but dismissed this thought and correctly assumed that the trust offered by the Ligerian must mean they were 100 percent confident that there was no risk in leaving him alone with both.

Unused to dealing with international crime and sovereign espionage he missed the armed assassin in the corridor outside his room pretending to look for his room key and returned downstairs politely handing over the bag.

Unsure as to what would happen next, Roberto offered 'Drink, sir?'

'Tonic water, please.'

Roberto went to the bar and returned with a bottle of Montepulciano and Malvern water. The Ligerian vanished.

The key fumbling man, now wearing sunglasses on a dark Manchester evening exited the lift and left the hotel unnoticed.

Roberto was able to jump the queue for the sports car he had long coveted and closed his mind to what might have happened to the chemicals. He didn't need or want to know what they were for. He could imagine no circumstance where he would ever need to contact them again, but he did however, keep hold of the business card.

11 A Grand Trip Out

Peter Manford's DI finally responds to a note Pete had left for him regarding the pharmacy deaths and asks him to tidy up a few questions relating to the rising number of other unexplained deaths in the city.

It had been a busy year for murders, suicides and bodies turning up randomly. He now agrees with Peter that it is worth a quick chat to see if there is any other known link between the two men. A pint and a chat about cars could be interesting anyway.

The older man who died that day had a history of heart problems but there is no evidence to suggest that his death was in any way connected to the scuffle in the shop. The heroin addict he tussled with was discovered dead in an alleyway soon after. If he was guilty of bringing about the older man's death it would probably only have added up to manslaughter at best and they wouldn't be able to produce a direct causal link that would have made it past the CPS.

With the potential victim and possible culprit both dead and the circumstances of the altercation in doubt, plus no direct cause of death linked to the scuffle identified, there was probably nothing in it.

He is about to file it away as a 'no crime', when, at the last moment, some background digging throws up a few links to Ilkley and a name change by deed poll from the parochial Robert Andrew Peckitt, to the Italian sounding Roberto Antonelli.

No crime to change your name. Just very unusual that's all. Well, unheard of around here to be fair.

He digs out the registration documents for his car, finds the address he is after and leaves his card through the door of the art deco flat on the edge of Middleton Wood. He had visited before when he dropped off the pharmacist and collected the spare parts on the day he took possession of the Ginetta.

When it fails to smoke out a response, Manford calls around again.

He spots a neighbour washing his car

'Hi, just looking for Roberto. Seen him today?'

'No, not for some time.'

Cobwebs over the key hole on the front door, a pile of unopened post and the calling card he had left a week earlier, all visible through the letterbox seem to support the view that the flat has been unoccupied for a while.

'Try his ex-wife, she's still in town. I saw her in the gym just this morning. I don't know her, but I think she rents the old reservoir cottage on the corner of the Keighley Gate track. Oh and if you do see him, ask him to arrange something for his bins would you, we don't mind putting them out the odd time, but it's been every week for a long time now and my wife has sciatica.'

DC Manford soon finds himself outside the door of an attractive stone dwelling on the south side of the valley on the edge of Ilkley Moor. It's a typically inviting cottage with a tidy garden and beautiful view across the steep, verdant valley. The setting sun completes a vision of perfection and is not diminished by a rag top Porsche and a healthy looking blond woman who meets him at the gate. The striking, smiling vision of expensive and carefully manicured sophistication looks puzzled and amused. Momentary initial impressions shouldn't dominate our thoughts but often they do. Pete immediately creates a biography from what he sees.

Ilkley is ram-packed with women like this, he thinks. He imagines her owning a high-end fashion shop in the town that clothes her and her friends and gives her a reason to get up in the morning but has never made a penny profit.

He imagines her driving a Range Rover wearing skin tight jeans whilst dropping off a ten year old future estate agent and

Rotarian called Jolyon wearing a cherry red cap, pristine uniform and leather briefcase to Brookdale preparatory, before rushing to meet a friend called Tilly at Harvey Nichols in Leeds.

True or not, his potted somewhat cynical biography is forgotten when she shrieks 'Manly Manford! What are you doing here? Is that Roberto's car you have there?'

She is an old school mate he hasn't seen for well over twenty years. She left Ilkley at sixteen to attend London school of contemporary dance.

'Sara, my God it's you! Are you still dancing?' They walk towards the house.

'I wish, no-one needs a thirty-something heifer galumphing across the stage. You have to be a twelve year old anorexic to get work and its decades since I was one of those. Great while it lasted but what can you do? …What are you up to?'

'I'm a detective now, but don't be so hard on yourself, you look great. It's a bloody small world and no mistake. Are you with this Roberto guy then?'

'Was, God help me. Met him at the zenith of my pomp, but before I knew it, I was shackled to the bastard with two kids. Me stuck back here with a crippling rent, while he carried on like a teenager on heat. What a mistake…Glass of wine?'

'No. Thanks, but working. Why so harsh on yourself? Who doesn't make decisions when we are young, naive and arrogant which place us on a track we didn't intend for the rest of our manky lives? I know that more than most. No one is immune from the sands of time and you seem to be faring very well if I may be so bold.'

'Don't be fooled by what you see, it was great for three or four years. After which we spent a decade leading each other a merry dance. He dragged me through marriage, infidelity, childrearing, civil war, deceit, humiliation, divorce, then eventually a fragile negotiated peace for the sake of the children. I'm exhausted with it all and wonder why I bothered to pursue this life.'

'How did you and he end?'

'Oh I don't know. I blame magazines, the bright lights, wine and everyone except myself... Ah, here it is,' she says with a smile and hands him an address high in the dales.

'I have no idea what the hell he's up to up there. It's so not him to be in the hills among the sheep. He hasn't seen the kids for weeks - no, months.

'Tell him to sort his life out when you see the sad fucker. Tell him he isn't Beckham's twin brother, more like the third chuckle brother!' she says, not really expecting the message to either get through or make the slightest difference if it does.

'What the hell are you doing in Rob's old car? I remember having some fun in there. God, it looks so much smaller now. Can't imagine getting jiggy in there again, there's hardly room to swing a cat. I hope you didn't pay too much for it. He told me it was knackered.'

'*Now* you tell me,' says Pete with a pained expression.

'How does he afford his lifestyle?'

'Do you know, he won't say. '*Bit of luck on the GGs'* one day, profit from the sale of a flat the next; some bullshit about Ligeria, blah, blah. I've given up asking where he gets it from. It's not funny. He claims to be skint when the kids need important things, but then by magic he shows up in something from a Jeremy Clarkson wet dream! Anyway, let's catch up in the Crescent sometime soon,' she says with a smile.

'Yes, sure, I had better crash on, I need to have a chat with Roberto and I want to get up the dale in time for a pint and get back before dark.'

'Tell me seriously, is he in trouble?' she asks, chucking the levity.

'No, no not at all. I just think he might be able to help me throw some light on something'.

'Getting Mr Mysterious to give some important information up? Well best of luck with that.' She bids him goodbye with a hug and a wave.

'Oh and by the way, she adds as he walks towards the car, if you catch him ignoring you and staring into space like he has been hypnotised, click your fingers and tell him he's back in the room, he absolutely hates it. See you soon.'

'Thanks I'll bear that in mind and yes I hope so, I really do.'

Why did the idiot let her go? he wonders as he watches her return up the path.

As he leaves Ilkley, rather than take the A65 up through Skipton, he decides that it is a perfect evening to follow the River Wharfe to its source. He turns right in Addingham and hits the road up the dales.

He sweeps through Bolton Abbey, past the beautiful stone entrance to the recently extended Devonshire Arms Country House Hotel, past Bolton Hall, the ruined abbey and the elaborate stone waterfall, a memorial to an aristocratic politician murdered in Dublin. Then Strid Woods, up and down over a ribbon of tarmac laid over the landscape like a slate grey silk scarf floating on the naked torso of a shapely goddess.

It all flashes by in a blur of unspoilt natural beauty of rolling hills enhanced by centuries-old stone walls and ruins. He powers past Barden Tower, the Clifford's derelict hunting lodge, through a string of beautiful stone riverside villages. The tight corners between the cottages of Burnsall slow him. Then he follows the Wharfe to the West of Grassington where the lush green valleys and gritstone buildings meet the Craven Fault. The landscape becomes less verdant and opens out to moors and crag and the distances between settlements stretches out from one or two miles to five or eight, revealing limestone pavements and escarpments near Kilnsey Crag then Kettlewell, where drinkers sitting on the Wharfe Bridge scatter as he slides on the gravel when the car lifts off over the peak of the bridge.

Better tone it down, he thinks, *nearly lost it there.*

Next Buckden, after which he slows as the lanes narrow, turning left through Hubberholme and Beckermonds, where Greenfield and Oughtershaw Becks join to form the often raging River Wharfe, *the second fastest rising river in England.* Now just a trickle, starved by the dry summer from being fed by the tiny hillside streams, it quickly becomes a raging foaming torrent after heavy rain. The narrow winding road takes him past Oughtershaw Hall and over Cam Fell.

The distances between settlements stretches further still and the roads narrow to bumpy tracks devoid of tarmac in places with occasional strips of grass growing between the tyre tracks. The sense of remote wild country where a breakdown could quickly result in frostbite in the winter, a misjudgement on a bend could leave you rotting to a skeleton to be discovered next spring by a walker or farmer.

At the summit Pete pulls over and gets out to walk up the side of the wild and windy moor for a couple of hundred yards. He finds a spot where the view down each side of the fell and beyond to The Three Peaks and The Lake District to the north and back down over Wharfedale to the south can be drunk in from one position. There is no place more remote, nowhere more perfect for silent contemplation on a warm evening.

God's Own Country lay out before him. It can't be fully appreciated until seen at the end of a clear summer's day. Pete drinks it in, feeling more awake and alive than his work had allowed for months. What a contrast to his daily grind, what an honour and a pleasure to be alone up here.

He returns to the car and goes over the top, down through Gayle where in the middle of the river ford a man had parked a van and was washing it.

Yorkshire Dales car wash, haha!

He roars past Gayle Mill which still saws timber, inches from the cottage walls through the narrow zigzag and then down past

Kit Calvert's Wallace and Gromit Cheese Factory before winding through the traffic in the centre of Hawes.

The most remote and charming roads in England, perfect for a summer evening drive in his aging sports car.

He is now in the Northern Dales, a land he knows less well. The remote and narrow valleys with no road wider than a millionaire's driveway and the inconvenience of an hour's drive to even the smallest market towns means it is largely ignored by the industrial revolution and is still a unique landscape of small stone farms, dairy herds grazing in the lowlands, sheep on the hills and the occasional mill by the river. It's well away from the rush of industrial construction in the late 19th century that created the urban landscape further south. Now still largely dependent on farming and summer tourism, it is the most remote and unvisited; so consequently, also the most unspoilt part of England. Neither a destination nor a stopping point on the way to anywhere, the distances stretch out forever.

What employs the people in these cottages? He contemplates as he drives along. *How do they survive the winters up here?*

His London friends may visit York but never the Dales, they will holiday in Marrakesh, take train journeys across Siberia, jet to the West Coast of the US, to India, China, anywhere in the world, take the train, a plane or even drive up the M6 to Scotland or fly up there from Heathrow on a Friday evening; Some of the more adventurous will have even visited Windermere in the Lakes on a summer day, but few if any venture sideways and find this wild paradise so it survives mostly undiscovered.

As he concentrates hard to stick to the road on the tight bends and powers up the passes that split the dales, Peter smiles when recalling the chat about old times with his high-maintenance looking school mate. Taking this trip in his own sweet time temporarily erases the burden of another day shovelling shit against the tide. He resolves to take her up on the offer of an Ilkley night out.

It takes him a good forty minutes longer to get up there than he thought. The distances are so much greater and the roads so narrow, twisting and random that ten miles seem like twenty five but he doesn't care. He loves the journey.

DC Manford arrives in the West Fell Square to meet a happy band of hedonists, the like of which he had no idea could be found so far from the metropolis.

Roberto and Hazel's debauched behaviour after drunken sessions in the local pub and elsewhere was always going to make them some enemies. Their new friends also attract unfavourable comment. The contours of the valleys create an isolated world where everyone knows each too well - or think they do. Judgements are harsh and small-minded at the best of times. If someone appears to be enjoying more than their allotted quota of fun, they are bound to be condemned here.

The annual village show, fell race and Christmas pantomime in the Village Hall are the universally acceptable outlets of exuberance and frivolity. Anything outside of that framework, if alcohol is taken, has to be a wedding, birthday or royal event to avoid outright condemnation.

For anyone but the retired or disabled, even simply being seen leaving a café during a weekday is enough to attract judgemental opprobrium. You will be equally judged if you live in any small community the world over, except here in the fells people are mandated to explain your shortcomings directly to your face. Phrases like 'Who ate all the pies?',' Who do you think you are?' and 'Not a day's work in you!' are shouted across the high street daily; opinions are rarely kept hidden.

For the daughter of the headmaster and local chemist to be having a boozy weekday lunch is to be brazenly challenging the order of things as prescribed up here by John Wesley and so they are roundly and universally condemned in this po-faced land.

After working hard to win over the collective judgement of the village, Roberto is now quickly draining the reservoir of goodwill and understanding that he has carefully built up and nurtured. Folk are measured daily and spend their spare time measuring others. Often judging very harshly on the subject of how hard each-other are perceived to work, how brutal and relentless their toil.

A farmer here who, during recuperation from illness, surprised everyone by learning to paint extremely well and quickly earned a peerless national reputation with beautiful depictions of the Dales at work, became accomplished enough for his work to attract the interest of the Royal Academy and high end art dealer's on the Kings Road.

Rather than enjoy local admiration for pulling a creative rabbit out of his hat in difficult times to enable a new and exciting artistic career, he attracted relentless unfavourable comment whenever he was seen painting in the woods or on the side of the road in the hills during the day. Eventually he took to travelling fifteen miles away from home to avoid the guilt of the 'openly idle'. Painting quietly at an easel on a work day was not on the invisible list of approved activities.

The owner of a new car that might for instance sport a racy set of wheels or a jaunty stripe is considered to have ideas above their station.

'What does he need that for? ...Just who does he think he is, eh?'

The court of public opinion up here does not have a jury to mull over all possibilities, just hundreds of self-employed volunteer judges.

Periods of grief after the illness of a relative are carefully measured, monitored and reported upon. Anyone appearing to find happiness outside of an undefined but collectively and silently agreed period following a death will be roundly denounced. But grieve too long and you attract similar disapproval. '*When is she going to get over it and get on with her life? She won't find anyone else, moping around like that.*' It's a tightrope keeping on the right side of the Weslyan committee of appropriate behaviour which still thrives.

The flip side of this is that in any real crisis all this is forgotten and there is no more mutually supportive community on Earth. It takes a monumental crisis to expose it, but beneath the seemingly unmovable wall of stone, warm-hearted and caring characters hide. They work harder to put food on the table here and have no time to dance around emotions.

Roberto and Hazel represent a more challenging prospect to the order of things altogether. Roberto overheard a conversation as he passed a bus stop.

Stepping off the narrow pavement to pass them, 'Good morning ladies,' he chirped. No response.

Then as he walked away he heard, 'That's the bloke I was telling you about. He's no better than he ought to be.'

'Is he from London?'

'Probably, by the look of his shoes.'

It's water off duck's back. He now has a significant income but the village cannot contain him much longer. He is uninspired by many of the people and begins to wish some of the innocent folks of the village to be dead simply for boring him. The easy success so far has led him too quickly to become complacent and arrogant.

His mission had begun to creep on the back of the ease of success.

Mrs Pickles just refuses to die. She is back under his care and bedridden. She refuses to receive prescriptions from him and pays her carer to travel to Skipton to pick them up. The carer, who drinks in the same pub as Roberto simply gets them from him anyway and keeps the petrol money.

If he tweaks her medication any further, the bottle will emit poisonous vapours and probably boil. Fortunately for him, no-one is listening to her complaints about him and her ill health is dismissed as payback for being a sour old cow. But he fails to finish her off. He suspects that she is not taking her medication in the doses he has recommended on the bottle - she couldn't be or she would have expired weeks ago. For the time being however, she is too ill to be a problem to him. And so there are absolutely no consequences. He doesn't even lose any sleep.

Here, enveloped by the hills and lonely valleys, it is easy to forget the world beyond the fell tops to the north or south. Lives are smaller and contained, people from villages over the hill may be only ten minutes flight by alpine chough but their paths will never cross.

Roberto didn't know this when he moved to West Fell. But he discovers the distance between here and the austere Victorian metropolis of Bradford, although barely fifty miles away, might as well be a million. Even though well into the new millennium, almost no one from Bradford, bar a few intrepid hill walkers ever visits the area. Not since the exodus of farm workers to the mills of Victorian Britain, has anyone made the journey south. Even now, one has to drive to the hilltops to make a mobile phone call and then the connection is slow and unreliable via the over-burdened phone lines which often fail in the winter.

The four hundred pampered boys of the huge and prestigious school, most of whom are 7-day boarders and the staff of the racehorse training businesses provide a very healthy income from the sale of legal and illicit drugs. Pick-me-ups and weight loss pills for jockeys, harder stuff for partying, starter drugs for posh schoolboys at sky high prices. The cash is now rolling in through the shop till, from the NHS and under the counter sales and into his bulging back pocket.

Roberto fixes the prices at double what they would have to pay for their happy pills and powders in Leeds and Bradford. He has no empathy for anyone but certainly not the boys. He holds the view that now that they no longer have fags and butlers and the internet is beginning to create the laziest generation of youngsters in the history of the human race, they are there to be exploited.

To Roberto, the rich spoilt know-alls are more than happy to spend enormous amounts of their parents' cash so why let them give it to someone else? His premium service saves them the inconvenience of travelling to Leeds to engage with the great unwashed in order to score.

The supply of illegal substances to the school and the jockeys has become by far his most lucrative side-line, and the NHS money which flows in after the closure of Eric Francombe's business is easily manipulated.

A period of debauched excess accelerates towards disaster. There is no longer any police presence in the village. Locally based policemen in tied houses are a thing of the past and team policing have promised to ensure fast response from mobile units controlled from headquarters far away. Mostly they fail to deliver.

In this case HQ is 44 miles away. Resources dwindle, priorities have shifted and now there are often no policemen within an hour's drive of some of these remote places. Visits from the police can be a year apart in some of the most remote villages.

Until the 1980's there was one in every village. The Local PC knew everyone, and everyone knew where he was to be found, even if he could usually be found fishing or enjoying an after-hours pint. He was a constant reassuring presence, a man who you would run to when you were in trouble and away from when you had caused it. This meant that crime was quickly nipped in the bud by a visit from a figure of authority. A man who could steer the young and foolish away from a life of crime while they were still apprentice crooks. At a time when a testosterone fuelled teenager with a troubled home life could go either way, there was a rudder to steer them to a better path, a social structure which included consequences for transgression. It was the flipside of judgemental and nosey village life. Often the judgement was correct, if unwelcome.

Then the cost of this service became analysed in only annual financial terms. The long term benefit to the community of embedded local police was not measurable on a spread sheet, and so the concept was removed from the minds of those in charge. Criminals became more mobile and so it was easy to justify a reduced car-based system, the crime figures showed relatively little or no rural criminality, so the police presence was reduced. The service removed as a result of its success.

Huge cuts in budgets brought the police out of the countryside to deal with the visible urban crimes of alcohol-based civil disorder, drug-related crime, thefts from motor vehicles and traffic offences. There is now no police presence in the countryside at all unless there is an emergency.

The population looks after itself and knows that it's pointless asking for help unless faced with a very serious problem. Drink-driving has made a comeback (if it had ever gone away) and recreational drug use, drugged driving and petty crime are perfectly normal, often unreported. Without the likelihood of being apprehended, speeding, using a mobile phone while driving, throwing litter from car windows, failing to stop after an accident, road rage, threatening abusive behaviour towards other road users and fly tipping are barely considered crimes up here.

You can only guess at what takes place within the thick stone walls of the farms and cottages dotted over the hillsides, particularly in winter. It reminds Pete of a trip to the west coast of Scotland as a teenager, where car tax discs were ten years out of date and behind the roadside walls there were piles of whisky bottles thrown from cars.

Fortunately for civic harmony, most people are minding their own business and living and working within the law. They watch television if they can get a signal and keep warm, but they could all be printing false banknotes or be devil worshipers and they would easily get away with it. It's a good place to start over and rinse the stains of shame, regret and disappointment from a life gone badly wrong, whilst evading the long arm of the law. It is this environment which has helped Roberto to enjoy a new and unfettered, carefree and hedonistic life

The Fell View Guest House has become something of a fun palace. The owners were saved from imminent financial disaster by a loan from Roberto. He will never seek repayment. He can easily afford to bail them out from their rash and un-researched leap into the bed and breakfast business in a world where they are rejected by their neighbours and largely ignored by all but the few potential guests who come here out of season to brave the sodden fells.

This allows him to treat the place as his own country seat. He behaved like he owned the place from the outset. Now he almost does.

A folk musician who rocks up in the village looking for shelter before he heads to the south west for the summer festival season takes up residence in the converted garage. He becomes the court minstrel. Youngsters from the village tasting their first teenage freedom yearning for expression and a place in the adult world gravitate towards the house and there is an impromptu party most nights.

It looks like sex, drugs and rock and roll to the neighbours, but for the participants it is physical, intellectual and spiritual stimulation and experimentation. It represents expansion of the mind through discourse and challenging debate, through the exchange of ideas and passionate intercourse of all types late into the night. It's somewhere to go where, no matter what time of day or night there is a happy young face, an open fire, a hot drink and some mind stretching. Somewhere beyond parental scrutiny, where people smile and the rain stops for a while.

This nirvana of hedonism could never go unnoticed in West Fell for long. Late night impromptu jam sessions around a fire pit in the garden had to be curtailed after complaints. Hazel is eventually again hauled over the coals by her ever more angry father whose reputation for strict discipline is at odds with the very public behaviour of his daughter in the village and worse still, now even within the school grounds where his ability to control and keep order depend upon his reputation. There are rumours of drug fuelled orgies involving the older boys and for the first time in the history of the village, drugs are being traded and used.

Haze spends most days living in one. Swept along on a tide of excess, she loves it. She ignores the worried warnings from friends and family dismissing it as jealousy. Upper Dale's folk didn't set out in life to become miserable, negative sour-faced trouts. It is perhaps the cold, the incessant rain, the isolation and the near impossibility of earning a decent living on a sodden lonely hillside which for some sets the face, tightened against a freezing torrential gale into a petrified grimace.

The unified condemnation and loudly broadcast condemnation reaches Dr Anderson and he is determined to remove his daughter from this shameful episode as soon as he can. He calls her in for another lecture.

'Some voluntary service overseas is in order for you young lady,' he tells her.

'Oh come on Pappy, I am not twelve for ffflip's sake.'

'I realise I no longer have the influence over you I would like, and your strong will and hunger for adventure reminds me so painfully of your mother and only amplifies the pain of our loss. It's not your fault, I admire your spirit and I am comforted by the knowledge that you are easily able to look after yourself but, in addition to my concern, I also have my own position, my life's work and career to consider. It is apparent to me that unless your decadent hedonism can be reined in immediately my career will be compromised.'

'Ok, ok I hear you.'

'Yes but now I am telling you that your promises are no longer sufficient, I want immediate action to improve your behaviour before it's too late. Parents are now becoming aware of the changing atmosphere in the village and they're beginning to write to the Governors and you, my own daughter are at the heart of this unacceptable behaviour. It simply has to stop now. I have no choice but to act decisively to distance the school from this outrageous distraction and threat to good order and discipline.'

In fact, her most recent indiscretion was no more than a drunken embrace with one of the girls from the guest house in the pub. High spirited horseplay which sounded far worse with the retelling. A repressed and single middle-aged man who still lived with his mother and considered East Enders to be too raw a depiction of the disintegration of the moral compass of England was hardly the best judge of a frivolous peck between tipsy youngsters.

In truth, as well as some illegal and irresponsible experimentation with class A drugs at the house, more often they would only get a bit merry while watching an interesting film or discussing art or politics around the kitchen table until the early hours.

Inevitably the stories of what might be going on take on a life of their own and tales of drug taking and sexual excess are blown into the open when an outraged family withdraw their son from the school after he becomes ill at the guest house.

Dr Anderson's public proclamation (which he privately extends to include his daughter) forbids anyone connected to the school from visiting the guest house and consorting with its residents, and is delivered with the threat of immediate expulsion. This ignores the fact that Hazel is by now living there permanently and so comes to nothing, which brings an inevitable collision between them much closer. Rather than confront her father she avoids him and so the lecture and proclamation are politely ignored by all, illuminating his impotence.

She is no longer a child but not quite yet blessed with the insight that would later guide her to more fully respect and understand her father's impossible and publicly delicate position.

She would live to bitterly regret not stopping to think about what he was trying to communicate to her. Such was the excitement in her life, fuelled in part by drugs she had no idea she was ingesting. Roberto is becoming more skilled at tinkering with her. She dismisses Dr Anderson's protestations as the blinkered rantings of a bitter and repressed old man.

Perhaps also she is stretching the boundaries to punish him for not protecting her mother and depriving her of the love of a complete family. Possibly to test his love for her and challenge him to save her, like he failed to save her mother from the demons that tore her away. Who really knows why we behave the way we do towards our family?

Whatever the seeds of her rebellion, the more he tries to restrain her, the wilder she becomes. There becomes no limit to her exploration - nothing she won't try. For a while she stops caring who knows.

DC Peter Manford arrives amid the unrestrained bacchanalia of the Fell View gang. After an exhilarating drive over the fells he appears mid-evening and it doesn't take long to find them outside the pub in the cobbled square.

The evening sun is still warming the stone walls and people are sporting sun glasses not wanting a rare dry and warm day to end well aware that winter will be along too soon.

'Excuse me folks, mind if I join you? Hey, you're Roberto, the Ginetta bloke from Ilkley aren't you?'

Roberto recognises Pete immediately but decides not to let on. 'Guilty as charged.'

Pete is on a rogue mission out of hours but as copper, he automatically remains vigilant. If Roberto's heart missed a beat as he instantly remembered what Peter did for a living, he doesn't show it but Pete isn't convinced that he passes the unexpected moment without giving away his shock and alarm.

He is not here to interview Roberto as a suspect - not yet, but he is trained to be alert to reactions and be aware of body language and speech. *Is he nervous? Are his hands shaking? Is he touching his nose when he speaks? Does he make eye contact?*

He eventually has to concede that there is little evidence of any negative reaction. Friendly banter about the Ginetta, cars in general, ex-wives and the tragic state of the city they both know takes hold. Pete is driven by curiosity at this point. He has no evidence of any wrong doing and has nothing more than a vague niggle at the back of his mind that drives him to find out more about Roberto.

In Roberto's company this warm evening there is a radiant and animated young woman. She clearly is either slightly drunk or under the influence of something stronger. She is smiling too much, for no apparent reason, a sure-fire giveaway that skilled functioning alcoholics and addicts imagine they can pull off but singularly fail to do. She is astride a pub bench and has to retract her long slender limbs to make room for Pete at the table. Her leather boots become entangled in the bench legs and Pete leans forward to politely help her free.

'Cheers,' she says looking at him for the first time. 'Who are you?'

'Peter. My pleasure. Drink anyone?'

The sun is now on its way down over the top of West Fell throwing long shadows across the square, but the warmth of the day is still radiating from the buildings. It is still T-shirt warm.

Roberto introduces his girlfriend. 'Peter this is Hazel, I sold him that car,' he says pointing to the Ginetta. 'I'm pleased to see it is still running.'

'Only because I've sorted it out,' Pete says darkly.

'Oh shit, what happened? It was fine when I passed it on. Do I owe you anything?' lies Roberto charmingly but rather too quickly.

'No, forget it, water under the bridge.' Pete waves a dismissive hand. He seeks to make friendly enquiries, not start an argument.

When the drinks are lined up, and her probing reveals Pete's job, Hazel proceeds to engage with him about crime and punishment. Ordinarily in social situations, a copper won't reveal his trade unless there is a sound reason to do so. It's hard for them to be off duty if they ever want to be, once it is known who they are. Pete finds this extremely tedious but is happy to make an exception in her case. It's a conversation he has had a thousand times with drunks who have an issue they want off their chest. How best to get off a drink-driving charge, policing of demonstrations or some gripe about an unsatisfactory encounter with a rude traffic plod or to raise a complaint about an unsolved burglary. They are too often pestered to describe the most gruesome case they have encountered. 'How many dead bodies have you seen?... What are you working on now?... Are all your bosses still freemasons?'

On top of that, if the policeman is out and about on a sniff to gather information, as Pete is doing now, it puts everyone on the defensive and won't bear fruit.

Pete is able to chat uninterrupted with Hazel for half an hour. Roberto keeps out of it. Very happy to chat freely with her, she is looking very spaced out. His training enables him to analyse the possible cause of her intoxication. Roberto is concentrating hard, listening to them whilst engaging in jovial banter with someone else and doing his best to appear cool and calm.

Pete immediately gets on well with Hazel. She is intelligent and naturally inquisitive despite the obvious inebriation. Time passes quickly in her company.

The group have a couple more drinks outside the pub and by the time another is offered the sun has disappeared. Pete says his goodbyes and is only mildly disappointed when his Ginetta won't fire up. It's not the first time. He knows he shouldn't be driving now anyway, but up here it is well known that there is still a tacit acceptance of a certain level of cautious drink-driving, even with the police. No-one ever talks about it, but the unspoken rule is: If you can walk in a vaguely straight line, you can drive carefully. Otherwise, no one would have a social life of any sort. Wrong technically, but true. This time such judgements are unnecessary as the dam thing won't start.

'Oops, that's embarrassing,' says Roberto, 'The fucking thing had to do that now! Let me get Mark Deacon to have a look at it for you sometime.'

Pete has enjoyed the company, and is knocked sideways by Hazel. The journey back, even if the car started, will be in the dark and he is well over the legal limit. It's best not attempted. He wasn't sure of the roads, even in the daylight while sober.

'You can't drive now. That would be crazy. You'll end up through a wall or through the parapet on a pack horse bridge. Stick around for the rest of the evening,' Roberto offers.

'Stay over,' whispers Hazel as she put her hand on his leg under the table.

He readily takes up her offer. They continue drinking and chatting. He is pleased that she offered and she is pleased that he accepted.

Hazel, though very drunk and feeling strangely light headed is just hanging on to some control. She doesn't want Pete to leave, not yet. She excuses herself and in the toilet, regarding herself in the mirror for a moment, tells herself to behave. Her head is spinning and she is experiencing a dizziness which is new to her. *'Be careful Haze,'* she tells herself.

Several drinks later, her brain now soaked in red wine and turned upside down, common sense leaves, animal instincts take over. She is having fun, still unaware that her behaviour is being tweaked artificially towards relaxed hedonism through drugs administered by the man she trusts. She loses the ability to restrain herself.

Roberto has been spiking her drinks since they met, nothing life threatening, just enough to alter her mood temporarily. Chemically liberated from social restraint and her natural English reserve, she is free to like what she sees.

He cares not. He enjoys it very much. He knows he can turn her mood in whatever way he chooses, like a dimmer switch. He feels he can let her free and rein her in when he pleases. This feeling of power allows her as much rope as she chooses to take within their relationship. The only thing that really concerns him is to preserve his own freedom.

Roberto's manipulation has opened Hazel's eyes to a kaleidoscope of possibility. Experiencing many things she knew nothing about five years ago, life and energy is now bursting from her whilst she soaks it up with new confidence and hunger.

Hazel throws her arms around Pete's neck and she pulls his ear to her mouth.

'Do you ever throw yourself into a fire?' she purrs.

Glancing at Roberto and seeing him engrossed in conversation or choosing to ignore his girlfriend's behaviour, Pete can't resist encouraging her.

'If I throw myself in will you make sure I don't burn too badly?'

'I can't save you, I'm already in the flames beckoning you!' she whispers, sending warm breath into his ear. 'You have to be man enough to look after yourself; I might need you to rescue me. Are you a *real* man? Will you follow me into the fire?'

Pete is shocked by her direct invitation, and unnerved by the potentially risky direction the evening is quickly beginning to take.

'I don't think I could deny you anything.'

'Come with me, I want to talk to you,' she says leaning over him and pressing the full length of her young long and lithe body into his as she tries and fails to lift him from his seat.

'Whoa careful', he says standing her up and darting another look towards Roberto who is now taking interest in what is going on across the table. Shooting him an apologetic glance, Pete raises his eyebrows in a 'Help me out here!' kind of way

Roberto waves them away with some dangerous advice.

'Take her away, do whatever she tells you or you'll regret it.'

Pete is astonished but obliges, lifting her upright and following her to a bench across the dimly lit cobbled square. From here they can talk without being noticed or overheard and keep an eye on the rest of the drinkers.

'I don't know who you are,' she slurs, 'but I need to talk to shomeone from the big wide world beyond thish valley. I'm normally a shaintly good headmaster's daughter. I do have moralsh.... I just I left them at home and gave them evening off.' She rambles on poking him in the chest whilst screwing up her face and staring him in the eye.

'Is every evening like this up here?' asks Pete not knowing what to make of it all.

'What's your story? How did you hook up with him?'

'Well it all began a very long time ago, a loooong, long way away....' Hazel explains in a strange semi-Pam-Ayres-on-Absinthe voice. 'Mother's unexpected death knocked me sideways.' She was garrulous at the best of times but now it all flowed even more easily to this stranger.

'They want St Jame'sh College, Architectural practice, job with English Heritage overseeing church reshtoration. Parents saw things panning out that way not this! Oh yes. First classh education and career, classhical piano at the weekend, marriage to cricket playing, church going hedge funder. BUT NO!! Fucking NO!' she shrieks, now using a loud male voice.

'This is not my beautiful life, it's someone else's. This is not my fucking destiny... Are you listening stranger?' She bellows when she notices him looking across the square keeping an eye on Roberto.

'Sure I am, carry on.'

'Took too long to finish with old boyfriend properly didn't I. Messy, messy, messy...'

Pete was enjoying the theatre of it all, intrigued to be given a potted history of her life that would have taken weeks to learn otherwise.

Hazel isn't finished yet.

'Shexshy Scottish landladies given the Purple Haze – me!' she sniggers.

'Fresh ecstashy, freshtasty... in fact,' she continues, employing a spindly finger in an arc through the air towards herself as she plays out the pantomime dancing around in her head.

'Not enjoyed shince the Frenchie teacher taught me how to jig with a girl. Pleasure drawn to repeat whenever skinny elderly lover keels over, the two headed monster falls ashleep long before I am ready to retire!'

Pete decides it best to help her back to the throng before she goes any further.

'Come with me, curry. Forget them elves,' she says dragging his sleeve in the opposite direction.

'No, come on Hazel, let's see if we can get you some water.' Pete had been around people the worse for wear through drink and drugs to know that it was probably the latter that was behind her loquacious ramblings, and she shouldn't be left alone.

The evening gives way to night and wine continues to flow in the curry house after the sun has gone. They all have a great time. Despite the curry by general agreement not matching the sublime offerings from the Aagrah, it's as good as it gets this far north.

'Drink more water,' Pete implores Hazel when she reaches for the wine, sending plates and glasses crashing to the floor.

Pete awakes on the sofa in the guest house by the embers of an open fire. There are wine bottles and discarded clothes everywhere. He groans and stumbles around looking for his shoes and trying to find milk, coffee and a kettle vaguely recalling helping Hazel up the stairs long after the rest of the household had retired.

She still lay across the landing at the top of the stairs where she had dismissed him insisting that she was perfectly capable of getting herself to bed.

'Who the fuck are you?' asks a Scottish voice as he peers into the fridge

'Ah, sorry. Pal of Roberto and Hazel's,' he explains.

He turns to see a fierce gypsy woman with jet black hair and a kind of ethnic drape hiding the shape of her body, who would he would have sworn was Italian had he not first heard her voice.

'Everybody's a fucking pal of theirs, was that you last night fighting on the stairs?'

'Ah, yes sorry. We weren't fighting. I was just trying to get Hazel up to bed.'

'Ay I bet you fucking were. There hasn't been a single person in this hoose for the past six months who hasn't been trying to do that and no mistake. Every last man, jack and woman of them!'

'I wonder if you could help me, I have to get back to work urgently but my car wouldn't start last night. Rob mentioned a friend of his who might be able to help.'

The woman passes him a card from her notice board.

'Try him. Probably who he meant.'

'Where is Roberto by the way?' asks Pete

'Left an hour ago before you woke up.'

'What about Hazel, is she ok?'

'Dinne wurry you about her, we'll make sure she gets everything she needs,' says the woman firmly focusing a suspicious and steely eye on him.

Mark Deacon gets the Ginetta started with a pair of gargantuan tractor jump leads zapping life across from the engine of his 4WD truck.

Mark wants to talk cars, but Pete has to crack on 'What do I owe you?'

'Not a penny, Roberto is my best customer. He'll sort me out, I owe him anyway so forget it.'

Pete returns down the valley stopping at the top of Cam Fell to use the only mobile signal for miles to check in with his partner at work. The wind howls through the phone making discourse almost impossible.

'Have I still got a job?' He asks his colleague, Adrian Collingbridge.

'Only just. I told the chief you were working beyond your mobile signal and checking an address on the way in. He's bought it for now, but you'd better check in sharpish and come up with something good.'

A sheep runs to the nearby fence and bleats, giving away his rural location.

'Where the fuck are you? Emmerdale Farm?'

'No, way more north.'

'Where's more north than that? Orkney?'

'Tell you later. On my way.'

Pete sits on the grass and runs over the events of the previous evening whilst the raging wind rocks his car and blows hard against this face. He stays there for ten or fifteen minutes gazing across the wild and empty moors willing the wind to blow away his hangover, wondering where all this is leading until the biting cold drives him back to the calm of his vehicle. Even then when inside, the buffeting of the gale and the matchless view keeps him temporarily mesmerised anew.

Despite the urgent need for him to return to work, this isolation and connection to nature in its most raw and unspoilt form is hard won and very rare in his busy life. It's not easy for him give it up and return to Bradford having stumbled across this alternative world.

He should know better, but he is he is confused, intrigued and more than a little excited by Hazel. Her physicality and her smile are imprinted on his brain and despite her fuzzy condition he thought he detected a connection between them. It's been a long time since he has felt such a strong stirring of attraction towards a woman. He finds it both invigorating and disturbing.

He uncovered nothing that he can identify as a genuine policing reason to spend any more work time on this, but already he wishes for it if only to be able to revisit her... But for now it's back to the mean streets.

12 Bad Penny Returns

Before it drifts into memory Pete decides to return to West Fell. He didn't find anything relevant to the Bradford incident on his first visit and if he had, he may have forgotten it due to the quantity of alcohol consumed and the intoxicating distraction of Hazel's presence.

He tries to convince himself that his reason for returning so soon is strictly work-related. He is vaguely seeking background information to follow a hunch rather than a specific line of enquiry... Or is he? Does he envy the life up here or is it simply an escape, an antidote to his life of grim duty to an uncaring employer and a failing city?

He and Roberto share the frustration and anger at the state of Bradford and the difficulty of delivering anything which would help to make it a better place. Although he is so far unaware that Roberto is only paying lip service.

On his return he finds that everyone except Dr Benj are turbo charging the party. Pete cuts the journey down to an hour and ten minutes by taking a slightly different route and knowing where the passing places and the stretches where he can fly are if he keeps an eye on the horizon. On the days when there are no farmers driving sheep or cattle in the road, he shaves a few more minutes off the trip.

The Ginetta now knows the way and can almost make the journey on its own. It was made for this. 'Always be first in the phone book' an album by the Aardvarks entertains him.

'Calling out to the fallen of the broken world', his favourite on repeat; the thumping bass line shaking the car from speakers behind the seat, he arrives refreshed and energised.

Maybe it's just the way Hazel looks at me, the way her eyes are speaking to me. I'm probably imagining it, but I think she really likes me.

Something else is tormenting him. Pete finds himself fighting feelings of extreme jealousy over Roberto's apparent life and relationship, he concedes that much, but that's not all that makes him uneasy. Casually he tackles Roberto about that day in the pharmacy.

'Do you think it strange that both of the men who fought in your shop are now dead?...and they both died within 24 hours of each other?'

Roberto's answer is friendly, confident and politely dismissive: 'For a start it wasn't my shop, and people visit pharmacies when they are ill. Even my good work can't keep them *all* alive. They die all the time and the pharmacist isn't a doctor, he just hands over what the paperwork instructs.'

He protests a little too much and is talking down his role, 'I shudder to think how many people who I have served are no longer with us. If I knew that number, I would probably not be able to sleep.

'...Do I think it strange?' he asks himself out loud, 'That a drug addict who lives rough and a stressed out overweight middle-aged man with a long-diagnosed heart condition both die younger than you or I? Not really... No, I don't. The only thing they had in common apart from their death on the same day, being that they were customers of the same pharmacy in the street near to where they both lived. Nothing odd about that is there?

'Anyway, you're the copper. Perhaps I am missing something. All I can say is that if you went back through the files of any pharmacy in the world for say six months and asked for an audit of who had died, you would be fucking amazed at the size of your workload!'

Without anything tangible, Pete lets it drop, until one evening some days later when he detects the first glimmer of a very dark side to Roberto's character.

Whilst very drunk and showing off, perhaps feeling some competition for Hazel's attention in the face of her apparent growing interest in Pete, Roberto begins to loudly discuss the various ailments and treatments being delivered by him to customers he recognises in the pub.

'That bloke has had piles for fifteen years and spends thirty quid a week in the shop. It's not doing him any good, but he is too good for business for me to point out to him other treatments and solutions, like not wearing his punders too tight!'

The obvious discomfort of the elderly man sitting no more than 4 meters away shows that whatever is going wrong inside his trousers, there is nothing wrong with his hearing.

It is embarrassing, but Roberto's voice is too loud and he can't be silenced. This is cruel though funny to begin with, but takes on a more sinister tone as it continues and becomes ever more uncomfortable for those present. He is behaving not only unprofessionally, but unnecessarily cruelly as he continues to reveal private and personal information with a hint of disdain and almost hateful contempt for his hapless customers.

Out of nowhere Roberto has become far more indiscreet than is sensible for a man trying to keep a low public profile.

'See him in the front bar,' he continues warming to his theme; 'He's had three heart attacks in the past six months. He shouldn't be in here drinking! Oi you, put that drink down you should be on the wagon!'

'Ssshhhhhhh, Rob for fuck's sake what's got into you? Leave them alone. Stop being a dickhead,' says Hazel desperately trying to shut him up. It's not the first time she has detected aspects of his character that unnerve her. For now she will bury them, but they are piling up and may one day deserve more careful examination.

'Ohhh fuck the lot of them the miserable moaning bastards!'
This is interesting, thinks Pete.

One appalled elderly customer leaves in disgust and is followed into the street by Hazel. 'I am so sorry, he's not himself today; I'll have word with him.'

'Too late for that miss, my personal ailments are now in the public domain in the village of my birth. What's done is done.'
'I'm so sorry, when he's better I'll make sure he comes to apologise.'

'Please don't, I can visit Skipton for my needs in future.'

As Hazel leaves the room Pete, rather than helping to silence him allows Roberto to continue, making no attempt to stop him as it gets worse.

Maybe the frustrating missing nugget is now emerging. Roberto continues to dig the hole he has started. The landlord wisely brings it to a close by throwing them all out before he gets around to revealing the publican's own medical condition to his unforgiving customers.

Pub regulars can often be thoughtless bullies and regard their landlord as naughty schoolboys do a teacher who has shown weakness. It would have been impossible for him to maintain order if they discovered that he is allergic to synthetic fibre and has to apply cream to his privates to control his ceaseless itches!

The pharmacist and his friends are removed unceremoniously and told that they were not welcome until they learn some manners, no matter how much good trade they have brought.

'So, patient confidentiality isn't a prerequisite up here then? Pete ventures as they wander back to the Fell View with some bottles from the Co-Op in the village square.

'Oh bollocks to them,' Roberto grumbles, 'You have to make your own sport up here. Baiting the punters keeps me going.'

Their behaviour is now becoming uncontrollable. Pete is a serving police officer, albeit in another force area and he technically has no official business here. This is a good thing. A professionally embarrassing situation could threaten his career. But somehow he can't give it up.

Hazel has begun putting her hand on Pete absentmindedly, smiling across the table at him and always placing herself near. Roberto has noticed, but is focussed upon keeping his cool whenever Pete is present, apart from today where he has let himself down spectacularly.

Pete is becoming drawn ever closer to Hazel and becomes sure that there is something about Roberto that is only now revealing itself. This 'quiet, sophisticated man' has a hard and unfeeling edge to him which an excess of alcohol has revealed.

13 Going Native

Pete's Bradford workload over the next few weeks becomes ever more impossible to manage. Something has to give and he can no longer justify using up all his spare time playing out in the dales, but he isn't done yet.

A force budget cut of twenty per cent on a service weakened by endless cost savings whilst fighting horrendous drug wars, dealing with prostitution, the grim and depressing consequences of alcohol abuse, sporadic street violence, more and more domestic burglaries and now more unexplained deaths makes it all too much. The threat of more cuts to come and the *'you think this is bad, you wait and see what's coming'* kind of mood coming from the higher ranks does nothing to help force morale nor his own waning enthusiasm for confronting what he increasingly sees as an impossible and endless task.

His colleagues are dropping like flies, either leaving mid-career, transferring to more rural forces further north where there is relatively less heat, taking long term sickness, stress related absence or turning up and freewheeling while crimes are not investigated.

Recently his visits up the dales have become more frequent and longer as he has ever more need for diversionary escape.

By now Pete no longer sees his long term future in the force. The cuts, justified by manipulated crime figures designed to show reductions in all categories, have made the job impossible and he has begun to look out more keenly for alternative employment in the live music industry.

His attitude to his employers and his respect for them finally disappears when he is reprimanded after refusing to obey an instruction to omit a whole list of crimes from his reports. In the office, he is approached by a DS and handed a pile of files.

'Here, Manford. The boss needs you to lose this lot and forget you want to pursue them. We don't have the resources.'

It's the final straw.

He has been pressured before to bully career criminals into making false 'Taken into Consideration' admissions which erroneously clear up unsolved crime statistics and add nothing to sentences, but appear to improve detection rates. He has been pressurised into dropping jobs 'without legs' and cutting off lines of enquiry 'at the knees' and to stop making his enquiries 'all encompassing' by which he understands to mean that if his enquiries reveal other potentially interesting information, he is to ignore it. He refuses to be complicit in what adds up to the wholesale falsification of crime data, and failing to do the job he signed up for. His career is now stagnating as a result of being considered 'not one of us'.

As a night duty DC, he is covering a division the size of Cumbria pretty much on his own. But actually dumping files without completing investigations is crossing a line for him and it's a pivotal moment which changes his trajectory.

A small number of very active drug dealing, thieving and feral criminal families have had the whip hand in Bradford for far too long. A good proportion of them are the leftovers from the mill working families who must be looking down in horror at the behaviour of some of their descendants. Some, but by no means all, have their roots in the Irish travelling community which itself sprang from the industrial past. In the 1800's ten percent of Bradford's population hailed from Ireland. The criminal mind-set is multi-racial and reflects the diverse community, so there are also Asian and Eastern Europeans, now the 2nd and 3rd generation of the influx of workers who arrived in Bradford to work in the woollen industry and build the city.

Criminals, wherever they come from, are now allowed to continue unbothered by the police due to the lack of a force with the funding, the motivation and work ethic to tackle the problem.

Large-scale fraud cannot be investigated with the manpower available. It is too time consuming and complex, and so is mostly ignored. The foot soldiers on the ground are left the impossible task of having to make judgment calls on what priorities should be, deciding in real time what to chase and what to ignore.

Furthermore Peter believes that far too much of their time is wasted dealing with paperwork to record actions necessitated by the petty squabbles of total fucking idiots. Trivial arguments between family members, neighbours, other motorists and workmates swallow most of every average coppers day and it gets him down far too frequently. There are no-go areas and crooks who are now untouchable; Men with £100,000 cars who live in £40,000 houses with no obvious source of income; some with large new houses in the hills around the city with electric gates, CCTV and roaming dogs guarding the grounds.

Pete was prevented by his Inspector from raiding one such house where a man on his radar is known to have just received a huge shipment of cocaine. His boss said he doesn't have the manpower and the man in question has evaded prosecution seven times in the last four years. This was increasingly due to the ongoing success of the local mafia solicitor, an Iranian with a dubious history, who drives a Bentley and has a beaky face and large nose with a pencil thin moustache. He only needs whiskers and he could play a water vole in Watership Down without need for make-up. Despite, or perhaps because of his comic appearance, he manages far too often to keep his reprehensible clients out of prison.

The crime division of the force is far too under-resourced to find the time to investigate obvious signs of dubious activity. Firearms are becoming commonplace and the police becoming reactive never proactive. They don't have the manpower to respond to the incoming calls most nights let alone build intelligence and take on long term investigations.

Over the summer, Peter becomes a frequent resident of the Fell View on his days off. The food is good and the entertainment is a welcome distraction from his day job. The apex of their hedonistic summer is another day when Roberto abuses his professional responsibilities and runs his mouth off again in the pub.

It had begun quite sensibly. They had got ahead of the dispensing side of the business and as often, persuaded themselves that this deserved a celebration. They left a student in charge in the pharmacy telling him to defer any further prescriptions until the morning wherever possible and tell everyone else to fuck off if they are not happy.

After a liquid lunch and a swim in the river, they stagger back to the bed and breakfast cottage and throw Roberto on his bed; he has some sleeping to do before the morning when he will have to use his most charming lines to rescue his business and credibility.

It's particularly hard to sleep in the ancient building. The first floor walls are no more than thin planks. The noises from either side of Pete fire his imagination to unbearable levels of frustration.

He keeps this to himself but it doesn't go away. He has never met a girl who has such a dramatic effect on him as Hazel.

Furious with Roberto and having no intention of sharing a room with him, Hazel is outraged by his behaviour in the pub and feels embarrassed for the customers he has abused.

Sexual tension in the house is strong enough to provide more sparks than an offshore wind farm in a gale. Pete doesn't need to be a detective to know that the footsteps in the corridor between the bedrooms tell a story.

He can hear giggling followed by passionate groans in the owner's bedroom long after there is snoring coming from Roberto's room. On a trip to the toilet he tiptoes into Hazel in the half-light. She is naked and heading back to the room she is sharing with Roberto.

She is not fazed, smiles and holds a finger to her lips.

This is a vision he will never forget. It is tattooed on the inside of his eyelids and he sees it in perfect technicolour just by closing his eyes for years after. She tiptoes towards him, he is literally petrified.

They exchange a delicate silent kiss in the cold corridor. They hold the moment, lips locked together. He breathes in and can smell and taste her. He cannot move. She parts and floats silently back to the correct bedroom smiling as she goes. Roberto continues to snore.

Over breakfast on the patio there is a warm and genuine vibe of togetherness. Roberto is up and out and working his magic on the locals while the owners make breakfast for the late sleepers enjoying the beautiful garden and exchanging knowing smiles.

Pete resolves to get serious. Last night's display from Roberto has reminded him of his original reason for coming up here given some clarity to his foggy and non-specific suspicion.

Roberto clearly has anger issues which are not far below the surface and despite appearing to be easy going, when his guard is down, true feelings of hatred appear. Pete can defend his interest professionally now. He feels he can justify putting some time into it. If it doesn't bear fruit, he will have serious questions to answer, but for now he has justification.

There is little or no sharing of information between police force areas and although all serving officers are empowered throughout England and Wales, they have separate data protection policies that make collaboration occasionally far too clunky. However he has no business working in North Yorkshire without notifying them and his own superiors too.

A chance to push on presents itself over a glass of wine in the Fell View garden: 'Business seems to be going well for you here,

Rob. Is it always so lucrative or have you just fallen on your feet?'

Roberto isn't sure where Pete is going with his persistent questions, but keeps a cool head. He doesn't know how much, if anything, the copper has learnt, but he does know he must keep calm and answer the questions as accurately as he can without leaving any clues that lead to his door. This is difficult and he is beginning to find Pete to be incredibly annoying a potential threat to his new life, but Roberto can handle it - he has to.

'You could say that. It's swings and roundabouts really. What you gain in having a captive customer base and no competitors, you lose in the footfall.

'If everyone who lives in the village came in at once, it would still be fewer than you would get wandering in if you were next to the rail station in Leeds for instance.

'However in that instance you would be working four days out of five to cover the rent and rates, as indeed I once was. The base costs here are miniscule compared to a city outlet. Living out here is obviously a lifestyle choice, but you can't escape your customers up here, which can be a pain.'

'You don't just rely on the village though do you? The school must benefit trade.'

'Mmm not so much really, it varies. They're not here all the time you know,' replies Roberto.

It's a stressful conversation, but he is getting away with murder. He begins to think he can walk on water. If this inquisition passes without going further, then maybe he can.

He could well do without this line of questioning, and in an attempt to deflect it, says 'To be honest the best thing about living here is not the business, but meeting Hazel. Were it not for her, it's unlikely I would have put down any roots. She's changed my life.'

'For the better clearly! You worked all over the place before here didn't you?'

'Yea, but no more than anyone else, that's typical for a locum; the clue is in the job description.' He replies a little too defensively and after a pause.

'You can't help it, you fuckers can you?' Roberto smiles as he says this, hoping to make the point whilst having a joke about it.

'Why are you always here by the way? Is it me you're after or Haze?'

Pete knows from the answers and subtle changes in Roberto's body language that he is now getting somewhere. Exactly where, he has no idea.

'Well no worries, just wondered,' Pete takes the heat out of the conversation.

Roberto's experimental creep happens so slowly, he doesn't see that it is consuming him and there is no way back to the time before he became a killer.

Pete has no evidence yet but begins to believe that the casual and urbane chemist has some secrets. He can't believe Roberto's car and lifestyle can be funded by his work and cash is everywhere around him all the time. His behaviour is reminiscent of some of the chancers he encounters in Bradford. Men who become shifty and guarded when pressed and give away too much when they are observed close up. Pete's background searches show a clean record with the exception of some drunken misbehaviour when he was the teenager Robert Peckitt, but no sign of evidence of any earnings which would explain his largesse.

He ponders what will happen if he arrests Roberto now to see what an interview under caution might throw up. *Without any clear evidence it's a crazy notion. It would lead to North Yorkshire police getting involved and his input being side-lined*, but he decides to quietly persevere with the social interaction and see if Roberto incriminates himself, perhaps to a point where a formal investigation can be justified. *It could be drug dealing or importation perhaps; too early to say.* Pete cannot be more aware of his potential conflict of interest.

His suspicion is ramped up to red alert when he bumps into Mrs Pickles while he is sipping a restorative coffee after yet another wild night at Fell View. She is in a wheelchair in the sunshine outside the café. Mrs Pickles' anger at what has happened is just about all that is keeping her alive. Her indignation and determination to see justice done is her reason to live now. She still has the strength to push herself around the village, haranguing anyone who can't avoid her. Her lawyer is asking awkward questions of Roberto and getting nowhere. She wants answers.

After some banter between them she probes Pete to reveal what his job is and for what reason he is regularly seen in the village.

'I know a spy when I see one. You're not from the village and you have no work here. You're a policeman aren't you? He tried to poison me. He stole my business and I think he killed Eric Francombe.'

'I've reported him to Detective Sergeant Clowes but she's absolutely useless. A woman shouldn't be doing that work.'

Bingo! Thinks Pete, not believing everything he is hearing, but thinking it would explain a lot even if half were true.

He replies quietly 'I'm sure she would be delighted to hear your sisterly support for her efforts.'

'What did you say?'

'I said: Let me look into this Mrs Pickles. Would you mind if I come to see you next week? By the way, who is Eric Francombe?'

'Why do you want to wait until next week? Why not arrest him now?'

'I have to make some inquiries first and I would appreciate it if in the mean time you don't tell anyone we've had this conversation.'

'I will wait until Wednesday and if he isn't arrested by then, I'll want to know why.'

'You'll have to trust me. I need to do some research and check out the background first before his suspicion is raised. Don't worry I'll have my eye closely on him.'

'Wednesday. That's all.'

'Eric Francombe?' Pete enquires again. 'He is?'

'Ask him!' she shrieks, pointing across the road. 'He knows who Eric was.'

Roberto had spotted Pete speaking to Mrs Pickles.

'Murderer! Thief!'

'Hey, steady! You can't shout at people in the street like that, for fuck's sake, go home and have a cup of tea.'

Roberto crosses the road towards them casting a conspiratorial glance to Pete and behind her back rotating his finger in a circular motion about six inches from his ear, using the internationally acknowledged semaphore for 'bonkers.'

'Can I be of assistance Mrs Pickles?'

'Keep away from me if you know what is good for you.'

Roberto tries to push her wheelchair up the road in the general direction of her house, partly to get her on the way home to shut her up and partly to demonstrate a caring side to Pete.

It doesn't work on either front.

'Get off will you!' she shrieks whilst thrashing at him ineffectively with her walking stick.

'Police! Police! Arrest him he is kidnapping me now!'

He gives up and turns to face Pete.

Pete is trying to hide it but Roberto can see in his eyes and sense in his manner, the way his eyes are darting from left to right and avoiding contact, his stuttering words and pained expression a world away from his usual detached nonchalance that something important has changed.

'She's err, regretting shelling up, selling up. It's hard for the elderly when they have outlived their usefulness; it takes some getting their head around... I see it all the time. I guess it will happen to all of us before we know it,' he laughs, lamely trying to lighten the mood.

'What can she mean?' asks Pete as he shoots Roberto a glance before walking away.

It has not gone unnoticed recently that Pete is gently asking more probing questions about everything related to Roberto's work. Roberto knows that to remain ahead of events, it is time to bring the debauchery here to an end. If he does nothing and sticks around his life could quickly crash again.

14 So Slippery We Need Wellingtons

Back in the shop Roberto takes a business card out of his wallet.

Harry Pippin, an odious commercial estate agent usually drenched in aftershave and carrying a leather-bound diary, represents a nationwide chain of pharmacies. He had recently paid Roberto a visit and told him that they were desperate to expand and get their hands on the NHS money and the North Yorkshire monopoly.

Roberto knows Pippin from Ilkley, his natural environment. The man had been involved when Roberto had lost his original pharmacy.

Pippin was so oily that he could enter a room under a closed door. He was so slimy he could slither underneath and reform before you with an outstretched hand, the touch of which resembled fondling a wet kipper through a silicone glove. His personality is so revolting that just being in the same room made you want to shower.

'Their wholesale arm supplies you Rob. They know how much stock you're shipping and they want a piece of it my good friend,' said Pippin sniggering conspiratorially and using the standard terms of engagement of a lying cheat, who seeks to use familiarity to deceive. Pippin considers himself a master salesman.

Roberto suspends his involuntary revulsion at being in his company and arranges to allow him to set up a meeting with Wellingtons. He can't believe his luck. A battle between the two largest chemist chains was in full swing and domination of the market was the prize.

Business sales agents have been dispatched to target small operators all over the country in a rush for market share through takeover.

Pippin is getting rich touring the country chatting up small independent chemists and successfully doing deals. Merging and arranging takeovers for both Wellingtons and their competition, the Lion chain.

In common with the salesman species, he will tell any lie to nail a deal, pour any amount of fake praise and attention on a target until it is signed, then forget them forever.

When Pete calls round to Mrs Pickle's cottage, it is empty. Her neighbour peers out of her window watching him.

She throws it open and leans out calling out to Pete.

'She's been taken in to Airedale again. It's looking bad for her apparently. She fell ill over the weekend and went downhill very quickly, the poor love.'

This gives Pete a problem. There are now some clear indications that he is onto something and if it was on his area he would deal with it immediately. But he is moonlighting on someone else's patch and he wants to deal with it himself. For no other reason, than to remain connected to Hazel, he makes the error of deciding to wait before calling it in.

Unnerved by Pete's presence but aware he can't react to it and sensing that he is running out of time, Roberto begins to plot his next steps. He arranges to have accounts prepared quickly by Hazel's friend and again uses his tame schoolboy forger to amend them favourably. He then invites interest and an offer from another competitor to create the impression he is not in a hurry and has other options.

This simple act of manipulation costs him no more than two hundred pounds and a morning in the photocopier's, but nets him an extra £75,000 on the sale price, a sum larger than he had earned the previous year. There is no point in approaching Mrs Pickles to suggest they take over her premises, and in any case her ramshackle building, although possessing the quaint charm of the Dale's stone vernacular, is completely unsuitable for a modern retail chemist.

So Wellingtons buys the business from him and take the lease on the empty former co-operative store opposite, arranged by Pippin the eager, parasitical dealmaker. It gives Roberto a huge profit in little more than six months, and delivers a healthy wedge for the lucky agent to spend on Hugo Boss suits and Mark Warner ski trips.

They meet in the Red Lion, on the outskirts of the village - a pub Rob didn't frequent so as not to attract attention, to tidy up a few minor details and toast the rapidly concluded deal.

'So, what's next for you Roberto my main man? Retirement?'

'Harry, I'm looking to make a move south, could you have a look at Cambridge for me? Hazel is due there to complete her studies and it would suit us to move there perhaps. Only the thing is, I don't want anyone up here to know that. Her father hates me and she needs to get away from him, so I'd appreciate it if you would keep it totally confidential. In fact, I will double any commission it might bring you if we conclude a deal, if you can promise me right here and now , that you will not discuss this in West Fell with anyone before, during or after the deal.'

'You have my word my good friend. If I'm known for one thing Robbie boy it's my integrity and discretion and my ability to see the wood from the trees. I'll get on it immediately. I'm sure we can do more business. I am the dealmaker's deal maker and I have got your back, pal!'

That's three things, none of which you are actually known for, but it won't help me if I point out what you are actually known for you reptilian arsehole, thinks Roberto.

The deal is completed quickly. Roberto and Hazel leave town just as an investigation at the school reveals the source of the recreational drugs that have flooded the village of late.

Rumours coming out of the school suggest that a sixth-former who had inherited his well-known father's legendary entrepreneurial zeal in creating a worldwide media brand, has gone into business with Roberto to supply the voracious appetite of the school for the consumption of recreational stimulants.

This business was intended to be no more than a sideshow, but the enthusiasm and arrogance of the budding business tycoon schoolboy had created an enterprise with a turnover too impressive to be ignored by the authorities. The upstart's bank manager in the village had no choice but to report the unexplained sums of money entering the lad's account and there were an alarming number of transactions taking place between his account and the pharmacist's.

This was very reckless and bound to be discovered, as the only bank in the village held both their accounts, but Roberto's success in evading investigation over the deaths in Bradford and now three in the village, leads him to believe that the police up here neither have the resources nor the nouse to keep up with him.

As an empire expands and the core mission creeps, one's eye can come off the ball, and that's how it is. Roberto has become complacent. He is drunk too often, under the influence of narcotics and too puffed up by success with Hazel and his other adventures. Too busy and too arrogant to be concerned that he is leaving an obvious trail behind him.

When Pete hasn't been around for a while Hazel, careful not to seem too interested, asks Roberto, 'What happened to Pete then? Has he had enough of us?'

'Yeah, I don't think you'll see so much of him from now on. He told me he was in love with you and asked me if I saw us together forever!'

'What? Really? Well do you?'

'Do I what?'

'See us together forever of course.'

'Of course I do Hazel, you know I love you.'

'Do I? I love you Rob but we will have to rein it in. I can't keep this up forever. It's been a blast, but I will have to get real and get my education finished. My dad is at the end of what he can take.'

'I know,' Roberto agrees, 'We're on the same page. Let's keep our heads down for a while and see what comes next.'

She is secretly not unhappy to know she is desired by Pete. She knows that the investigation into recreational drug use at the school will lead to Roberto, but agrees with him that if they leave town before its revealed, the police are unlikely to be informed.

Hazel's father knows that the success of the 500 year old school, which has been at the top of its game for all of his tenure, depends entirely upon the highest possible probity. It is a vast, private educational enterprise, which is one of the largest, oldest and most revered, iconic rural boarding schools.

Hazel's father is two years from retirement. She guesses correctly that despite his anguish over the path she has taken and the danger to his professional legacy that this outrage could potentially bring, both he and the school will sweep the whole episode under the vast carpet of shame that insulates the ruling elite. They will ensure it can't happen again, but will move on and forget it. That's how it works, how they have survived for centuries in a changing world. No fuss, no drama. Stay aloof. Keep quiet and carry on.

Parents must have total trust in a boarding school for it to work.

Having to ignore his moral compass for the sake of what he believes to be the greater good fires Dr Anderson with a rage that he can't quell. He secretly vows to bring down this scoundrel when the time is right.

If he can keep control for now and perhaps retire a year earlier to Tuscany, he can then find time to put in the hard yards to expose this man and have him put in jail away from his daughter.

A new headmaster could keep above the scandal which would protect the school.

For Roberto, a new direction is vital if he is to evade disaster and escape Pete's increasingly obvious infatuation with Hazel. Roberto's career won't stand up to close inspection. He fully expects Pete to investigate him more thoroughly or report him at any moment and paranoia stalks his thoughts when it doesn't happen.

He feels that a candle he has lit is now awaiting a hurricane. All undiscovered murderers and master criminals must live with this thought daily.

Roberto recognises recent events to be a huge potential threat to his liberty. His misdeeds cannot be undone, but the reputation that he now has in the village for being at the centre of drink and drug-fuelled mayhem and Pete's intervention in their relationship gives him a good story to sell to Hazel - a move south as the only option to avoid more trouble and the attentions of a potential suitor.

Peter and Hazel have indeed become close of late. He is very near showing his hand to her when she and Roberto leave for Cambridge.

Pete has a lot to think about.

He now knows Roberto is not what he seems. Pete is a very experienced detective with a peerless track record, but he is not a narcotics expert. He feels vindicated that his gut feeling is bearing fruit but needs more time to build sufficient evidence to make a move.

In the weeks leading up to their flight from West Fell, Pete stops visiting altogether. He ignores most of Hazel's phone calls and texts and they meet only once in Bolton Abbey on a confused and unsuccessful tryst when Roberto is absent on a mysterious trip south.

He works hard in secret to assemble the facts but key pieces of information are still to be discovered. He knows that it is unlikely that Roberto will step out of line now given the scrutiny he is under and Pete enjoys taunting him knowing he is close to trapping him now.

He has one message for Roberto and he calls into the shop to deliver it.

'Hazel tells me you're moving for the sake of her education. You can escape from West Fell for now, but you can't escape from yourself.'

Roberto avoids eye contact, stays silent and studies his newspaper intently until Pete leaves.

15 By the Skin of their Teeth to Cambridge

Roberto cruises slowly through the historic streets of Cambridge near the market square and comes to rest opposite the Fitzwilliam Museum. This is to be their new home.

The previous month has been a whirlwind of activity and he is looking forward to relaxing and turning the dial down.

Profit from the sale of his business has bought a pharmacy enterprise in a prime location amongst the university boarding houses, museums and restaurants. The premises have been a chemist's for over a hundred and fifty years, but under many owners. Roberto is very lucky to get his hands on this one after Pippin pulls it out of a bag for him. Small pharmacies are still being swallowed up and many of them were proving profitable.

'This is a peach of an opportunity, Roberto, pal. Cambridge has sailed through political and economic tumult over the centuries, unconquered. The worldwide reputation of its academic institutions underpins a vibrant local economy that is immune from most recessions.' He reads from the brochure. 'The current middle-classes of the emerging economies of China, India, Brazil and the Middle East can deliver enough students to fill the colleges a hundred times over even without the UK and European elite. The roadside position of this corner shop, on a major arterial route into the historic town centre with an attractive flat above is too good to be true!'

Roberto doesn't need any of Pippin's cobblers to sell the business to him and recognises its potential instantly. Pippin has identified it as a perfect takeover target for Wellingtons that he will then recommend they move into the market square and he can again get two bites of the commission cherry.

Pippin, true to form is up for shafting his best customer, Wellingtons if he can extract a larger cash commission from

Roberto. The possibility that a sale to Roberto is a backstop if Wellingtons aren't interested, or the other way around drives Pippin's narrative - He can't lose! A Brussels sprout can make a living doing this. After his success in West Fell, Pippin can't keep his excitement to himself.

The jewellery-wearing, Bri-wax skinned bullshit-monger is, like many salesmen, too verbose for his own good and no match for Roberto's cautious, studied skills of manipulation.

'Just like your last gaff, Lions and Wellingtons are fighting to take this one after the owner retires. He's run it for twenty years.' He foolishly shows his hand, before he realises Roberto is more than capable of working it all out for himself.

'I'm playing one against the other to ramp up the price,' he chortles.

'Wellington's intend to close it down if they're successful, to focus their trade in their larger market square branch. The vendor will sell to the other interested party if no sole trader can be found. A lower offer from an independent will swing it if the vendor discovers their plans. I'm not going to tell them of course, It would scupper my percentage, but for you Roberto, I might be able to do something in view of your promise to cash me up.'

'I would be up for bunging you four high figures in a brown envelope if you could send it my way,' said the spider to the fly.

Knowing that a cash bung will be untraceable and there are ways of getting what he wants out of this without parting with any money in Pippin's direction, Roberto sees a clear path to success.

'The vendor strongly believes that the building should remain as a chemist's forever. He feels some kind of romantic loyalty to the sign above the door and is no fan of the dominant players in the market. He's already lost a business when he was undercut by one of them. They bought his ailing enterprise elsewhere in a fire sale. Despite their assurances, they closed it down before the ink was dry on the contract. He isn't going to let that happen again.'

During Pippin's pitch Roberto gives little away. He says nothing.

Rather than wasting time and negotiating money with the greedy agent, Roberto plays his next chess move. He stalks the vendor and makes a direct approach.

It takes him just one visit and a meeting over a drink in the Falcon pub near the market square to persuade the guy that he is just the man to take it on and retain it as an independent store, as it had been since the 1850's.

Without key information gleaned from Pippin, Roberto would have had no chance against the big chains. Even with the bonus windfall from the sale of Mrs Pickle's shop, he only had 80% of what was needed to secure the business. He still had money in one last property in West Yorkshire but it was partially funded and tied up with a commercial mortgage and 6 month tenancy agreement, so not easily redeemable.

In the Cambridge pub, an ancient building divided into small rooms and timber divided nooks all full of relaxed university town drinkers, they shake hands. Roberto lines up the drinks and launches immediately into his well-practiced offer.

'The thing is this. I can't afford the business but I desperately want it,' he says using the same charm and enthusiasm which seduced Mrs Pickles.

'How about I keep you on as a silent partner until I can earn out the remainder of the purchase price? I'll pay you in instalments for the remainder either monthly, annually, in cash, with interest based on the length of time it takes to settle it at ten percent over base? Or whatever best suits your tax situation.'

'This could work. All I want to do is to retire and prevent the shop falling into the hands of Wellingtons. It's been independent since 1851 and I won't be the one to let it go. I don't need the money urgently. To get paid this way would be more tax efficient and fits with my wish for a succession to a like-minded person and also keeps Wellies out. I don't need you to pay me in cash. If we stagger the payments over, say three years it will keep me below the higher tax bracket. As I try my hand at writing it would be good to have a trickle of income. I think we can do business Mr Antonelli.'

'Fantastic!' Roberto is barely able to believe how easily it falls into his lap.

The deal takes an hour to formulate and as Roberto doesn't feel inclined to risk losing the deal, the vendor leaves the Falcon with a spontaneous non-refundable deposit in the form of a large cheque.

After the happy chemist leaves, Roberto takes Pippin's business card out of his wallet and throws it on the fire muttering 'Fuck you, Tosser,' sipping his Jack Daniels as he watches it burn. He then changes Pippin's name on his phone's contacts from 'Harry' to 'Wanker'.

If Pippin stays alive long enough to chase his promised commission, Roberto would simply threaten to reveal to his biggest corporate customers the fact that he had offered him a cash deal which would have lost them important business and was lining his pockets by representing Wellies whilst at the same time rushing around like a sewer rat using their data to do whatever deals he could on the side.

He is also confident that the potion he had slipped into Pippin's drink will begin to take effect over the next three weeks or so. It is a new slow burning formulation he is tinkering with.

He doesn't care much if it works or not, as if Pippin becomes a problem, he can simply arrange to meet him over a drink with a promise of cash, something he knows Pippin won't be able to resist, and sort him quickly with a chemical cosh. He needn't worry. He receives a text from 'Wanker' a week later, sent by Pippin's unfortunate wife with the details of his funeral. He sends flowers.

When the purchase contract comes it includes a first refusal buy-back clause which hadn't been discussed, but Roberto signs and returns it immediately without due diligence. He doesn't even read most of it. The details didn't matter; his eyes are on the jewel.

Hazel, back in West Fell punches the air when he rings to tell her the news and begins to plan her move south. Whilst packing she comes across a cherry-wood box amongst some of Rob's stuff in a crate at the back of the Fell View garage. She sits on the floor and tries some keys she finds in Rob's bedside table. The box is about 400mm square and 100mm deep. The lid is hand-carved with what looks like a Viking longboat with an oblique pattern of squares randomly carved beneath.

After ten minutes of fiddling with keys the lid springs open. Inside, lying on the vivid green silk lining is a business card with a Ramalia address and an elaborate crest. Underneath, there lays some paperwork referring to preparations for the 2010 football World Cup. There are also a large compressed bundle of fifty pound notes, a Swiss army knife and three glass bottles, two containing liquid and one some white powder.

Bit James Bond, she thinks.

Finding this prompts her to consider how little she knows about Rob before they got together. She makes a mental note to pull him up about it.

She too is feeling a lot more in control and inspired by the prospect of a new start and is unaware that her new less rampantly reckless perspective has more to do with Rob's absence from the village and therefore his inability to surreptitiously medicate her.

He spends time in his wood down in Hertfordshire while he negotiates the move. It is only 30 mins south of Cambridge, less when the roads are clear and as long as he remembers the lone speed camera in Foxton which has caught him out from time to time. He still hasn't told her about his modest property, still hanging on to his escape door.

Hazel looks back on her recent behaviour as that of another person. She has been present and a willing participant, but barely recognises herself these days. She also has good reason to put distance between herself and her father. For the first time in his life Dr Anderson has failed to contain a problem and it has spiralled out of control. This disappointment manifests itself in rages that hasten the disintegration of his relationship with his daughter. He worries deeply about her and agonises about what will happen to her when she is even further away from his support and guidance, but he hears his late wife's voice telling him he must trust her to deal with her own problems. He won't be around forever and in any case, he will be best placed to rebuild their relationship from a respectful distance and position of professional and emotional strength once he is able to regain respect and clean up the reputational damage done to the school and his own standing by his all too apparent inability to nip the drugs scandal in the bud.

He promises his wife's ghost that he will show leadership and take control once more. Then he will focus on his relationship with his daughter. The move can't come too soon for either of them.

Hazel and her father need some time apart. Enduring the finger-pointing and open disdain of the village has become tiresome for both of them. Not to mention the baleful stare of Mally's mother and the deranged ranting of Mrs Pickles, who isn't going to take the theft of her business lying down. Even though at her age and in her medical condition, lying down was now her default disposition. She does recover once more, now her prescription is again beyond Roberto's control.

He is puzzled by her resistance and thinks, *I will one day study that woman for a research paper.*

He has absolutely no idea how she has survived his carefully prepared and increasing doses of poison. In desperation he breaks into her house in the dead of night using the key he had stolen to administer a deadly dose, but still she lives!

Hazel needs a new start and manages only just to hang on to her place at St James to begin the next phase of her education. She ignores the mail reminding her that the term was about to begin; she had not arranged accommodation, paid any fees or filled in any forms. The course began a week ago and her place has been taken.

Despite his anger, shame and disappointment over the drug scandal and blind fury at her wanton disregard for his efforts to help her cling on to a way forward for her, Dr Anderson has enough love left for her to pull some strings at St James. She benefits from a personal tragedy that prevents another student from taking his place. She just gets in.

He calls her to his office for one of his official summits. Hazel arrives on time at his office door and he deliberately makes her wait for ten minutes while he scribbles a picture of his Tuscany farm.

'Come in, sit down and listen to me.' There is no hug, no welcome and he treats her as any other miscreant.

'You look like a streetwalker. You are at a crossroads now. You have ignored my advice and I don't expect you to listen now, but I am bound by my duty as your father to give you the best advice, guidance and assistance that I can, despite my fear that it is likely to be a complete waste of time.'

Hazel sits silently, hungover from the previous night when the thought of this meeting had made her drink more than usual. She had dreaded it and her fear made her more reckless than she had been of late.

What he sees before him is representative of a blip in her new more sober life, but he takes it to mean that she continues to career towards a cataclysm.

'I am ordering you to take the advantage I have provided for you and to appreciate that it is a privilege. Go from this room and start anew. This is the last time I can rescue your education from the disaster that it is about to become. Go to Cambridge; leave that disgusting man behind you, stop drinking and taking whatever drugs you are taking for your own sake. Are you listening to me?'

Hazel doesn't answer. She is feeling sick and trying to concentrate on not letting go. Frustrated that he isn't getting his message across, he gets up from his desk and grabs her, lifting her from the chair he shakes her and yells.

'Grow up you fool, don't disgrace me, don't disgrace the memory of your mother!'

The last few months have all but destroyed him. He has endured whilst grieving for his wife for the sake of his daughter and the school, but he is no longer sure that he will now retire to his Tuscany hillside. Who with? Would he be able to cling to the last remaining part of his family?

His clenched English reserve makes it impossible to tell her that he still loves her and the conventions and rules he lives by are all that he knows. They prevent him from showing her his feelings.

As expected of a man of Dr Anderson's standing, none of this terrible torment has ever been apparent to anyone. He simply never refers to any of it; confides in no one, seeks guidance from no one and suffers alone.

Hazel slurs 'Have you finished? Can I go now?'

Her father lunges at her, drags her to her feet and for the first and only time, slaps her as hard as he can.

It is so hard her head rocks sideways and she collapses across his desk.

He will never get over the shame of that moment; the force of his own actions shocks him to the core.

Hazel throws up lavishly all over his desk drowning his very important papers in the contents of her stomach. It is the last straw.

'Get out of here! You disgust me. I am utterly ashamed of you. I never want to see you in this building again.'

He calls the caretaker and asks him to remove her from the school grounds via the porter's entrance.

Roberto returns to West Fell to pick Hazel up in a van he has hired in Stevenage from Mick's Minis. Graham there obligingly agreed to store his car in his garage in exchange for the keys and permission to take it out until he returned the van.

Roberto chooses a larger motor than he needs, but it was the only one not sign-written with a Stevenage phone number. Graham has looked after Roberto's vehicles before as it is a convenient place to store the low slung Filton which he can't risk running up the long gravel lane to his wood.

Graham has no idea where he lives or where he comes from, but is happy to oblige. He enjoys taking the car home to his wife to give her a heart attack by pretending he has spent their retirement fund on it.

Back in West Fell, Roberto has to hide in Mark Deacon's garage whilst Mark heads up to the school to pick up Hazel's stuff. He has a similar relationship going with Mark and Graham who were 220 miles apart. They would get along famously if they ever met.

Mark is very concerned for his business having invested months into the vehicle restorations.

'Don't worry I'm still committed to it, I just won't be around to help out in person anymore,' he says ignoring the fact that he has never helped physically anyway.

'Just crack on with it and text me when you need funds. Get the Riley done first. That's the nearest to completion, then text me when you want me to put it in Bonham's next sale brochure. Send me photos that I can use when it looks right.

Wheel it out across the road and make sure you get the Fells in the background. Do it in colour in the early morning for the best light.'

He can't risk showing his face in the village again. He tells Hazel that it's due to his shame after the partying and the drugs scandal. Her father, Mrs Pickles, the family of Eric Francombe, Mally's family and worst of all, Peter Manford are surely only moments away from joining the dots.

He also knows his return will do nothing to help Hazel.

'Give me some wet and dry and I will do a bit of sanding on the Jag wings until you get back.'

Instead he walks up the Fell behind the garage to get a phone signal and spends the time arranging more of the details of their move south until Mark returns.

By moving to Cambridge Roberto has pulled off yet another escape and, if only temporarily, has swerved the consequences of his actions.

The distance between him and his kids grows larger, but he doesn't often think of them. When he does he easily persuades himself they are better off without him.

He has done this before and will do it again. Life in Cambridge is a world away from the Yorkshire Dales, as similarly his move north from Bradford was a total contrast.

Yet again he is pleasantly surprised how easy it is to change scenery in such a small country and leave a troubled past behind. He wonders how many times it will be possible to pull it off.

What is life like in rural Wales, in the West Country or even in Scotland? He wonders.

He laughs out loud when he sees a news article about a Dutch dentist who had committed murder and disappeared. Her plan for a new life fell apart when her new surgery in Scarborough, North East Yorkshire hit the news simply because she had decided on a policy of re-admitting national health patients, bucking the trend towards exclusively private work. A queue had formed around the block which became a national talking point after a local news item percolated to the attention of the London media. The woman must have been squirming whilst her identity was publicly displayed and discussed. 'Who was this Dutch woman who had so kindly opened her surgery to the poor?' asked the press.

The metropolitan hacks scrambled to secure an interview. Her cover blown, she was unmasked and arrested. The residents of Scarborough had to dig deep again to pay for their treatment.

I must make sure I keep out of the national news, Rob tells himself. *No random acts of kindness, no interviews, no profile. Perhaps the car should go?*

The centre of Cambridge is not a place to own a supercar anyway. The market square is closed to traffic most days and the one way system is a tedious imposition on the freedom of movement for vehicles. Cambridge is a bicycle town and he only ever goes to the pub, the bookies or the bank anyway.

He finds a yard at the other end of the terrace from his corner shop. Accessible through a courtyard entrance next to a newsagent's and secured by a lockable gate, it includes an unused lockup garage. He persuades the shop owner to clear it out to house his car permanently by offering a generous rent. Gradually the car stays in there more often than not, only emerging occasionally on a sunny day. There is nowhere to park when it comes out and he can walk into town quicker than it takes to get the car out and navigate the one way system. As he plans to keep his head down while putting distance between where he now lives and his crimes, this arrangement helps to lower his profile.

He is pleased to have put distance between himself and Pete and remove Hazel from the detective's orbit too.

He knows that Pete at the very least, now has grave suspicions about him but will find it hard to establish any facts. At worst,

Pete can perhaps nail him for drug supply if he perused the links between his financial dealings with the pupil at the school. The upstart has by now left and quickly started a magazine funded by his father and so is presumably keen to put the misdeeds of his schooldays well behind him.

This is a test if there ever was one of covering his tracks and his research into disguising the effects of medication on the human body are paying off. He imagines like the perfumier from Grasse in the Patrick Süskind novel, he moves around quietly leaving scant trace, but an ice cold gentle breeze.

Roberto resolves to end his experiments before getting caught and considers himself far too clever for prison. If Pete gets closer he knows he will have time to eliminate his nemesis, or at the very worst, ingest something to put himself to sleep and beyond the reach of his accusers.

I will never willingly succumb to a judicial process for any of this. Prison is for losers, he tells himself. He knows how to painlessly put himself into a permanent sleep. He finds that plan far more agreeable than the idea of a life behind bars.

For the time being, he has no need to consider such inconveniences and will carry on enjoying himself.

17 Cam and Have a go if You Drink Hard Enough

Cambridge suits him very well. The more cerebral, positive and youthful residents of the university town enjoy a drier, slightly warmer climate with an earlier spring and a marginally shorter winter. It is no Canary Islands, but it is perceptibly sunnier and the people seem to possess a disposition to go with it. They believe with good reason that they have a bright future and behave accordingly.

It gives Roberto a buzz to be free from the dales and his lighter mood is in part buoyed by a belief that he can evade arrest and do pretty much whatever he wants. His ideas about slowing down are overtaken by the new opportunities that the move presents.

He will have to remain sharp. He will keep his skills to himself and do everything he can to wipe the slate clean and maintain his relationship with Hazel.

She is due at her course immediately and quickly buckles down after a slightly delayed start, genuinely chastened by her last meeting with her father.

She loves living back in Cambridge and has a few friends still here from the first part of her architecture course. She knows the river, the streets, the restaurants and bars, and London is less than an hour away for research, fun and vibrant breaks from study.

She was born in the town but moved away when she was five as her father climbed the elite school ladder. Despite that, it feels more like home than West Fell ever had. She had only returned north to be with her father after her mother's death curtailed her studies.

She finds she misses Pete, but buries that thought as best she can, deciding to redefine herself and try to forgive and forget the recent past. She blames herself for everything getting out of hand.

Still oblivious to Roberto's experimental intoxications, it is easier for her to love him without that knowledge. Asking an honest person to understand the mind of a killer is like asking a goldfish to describe how a diesel engine works. There are no reference points to start to understand or explain. So, intelligent and perceptive as she is, she has not even the slightest understanding of what he is capable of, no portal through which to illuminate the darkness within his soul.

They settle into the flat above the chemist shop and enjoy being able to walk to the Falcon pub, the market square, the museums and the riverside.

Her bicycle is retrieved from the back of a store used by stall holder pals and is revived by the market's mobile bike-fixer. Roberto buys himself one too. Living in Cambridge without a bicycle is like trying to live in Los Angeles without a car.

Roberto starts to frequent the Falcon more regularly than is good for him or his business, regular intoxication keeps self-doubt at bay and he loves the conversation in there.

He is enthralled by the pub's history and its wartime ceiling decorated by lipstick, coal-dust, and whatever the American and British air crews could find to leave their messages to loved ones during blackouts before flying missions against Hitler. This extraordinary ceiling has been preserved superbly and covered with a lacquer which enables those who know to look up and imagine the lives of the courageous young souls who drank here in between missions abroad in lethal aeroplanes. Their chances of survival slim, their missions deadly. This room must have hosted the best wartime parties, with blackouts giving cover for all manner of misbehaviour, to escape the thought that each day might have been their last.

For centuries, the Falcon has housed the dons and elite students from the whole world and remained very much unchanged since the 18th century. A place where bright young minds with new ideas who know answers to big questions can meet and debate, educate and learn.   A vibrant, welcoming magnet with great food and the best wine, Roberto and Hazel both enjoy this pub and feel they have found a place where they can relax, nurture a new social scene and stretch their minds together.

17 Mission Creep

Roberto relaxes, enjoying his new life and feeling he has easily escaped. But his confidence is shaken when out of a clear blue sky six months after they had moved, Pete turns up without warning.

Conflicted to the point of derangement by the growing realisation that he is infatuated with Hazel and at the same time aware now that it is more than likely that her partner is a murderer, Pete has become demented with frustration.

Hazel lets slip the details of their move to Cambridge during a drunken exchange of text messages with Pete. Whether she was trying to hang on to him and keep him in reserve at arm's length, she isn't sure, but in the sober light of day she doesn't regret it.

Pete has followed up several leads since Mrs Pickle's outburst in the street. He now has to make a move to arrange to have Roberto in for questions under caution or at least pass on his very real concerns to his bosses. In any other circumstances, he would not pause for a moment before blowing the whistle. To do nothing now with the information he has would be a dereliction of duty which might end his career.

This will more than likely lead to Hazel and Roberto's separation and might present an opportunity for him to reveal his feelings to her with his nemesis out of the way. Or equally, if she is involved or even just aware, if implicated it could also put her behind bars.

This is the cause of his torment and has deprived him of sleep for weeks. Either way, he can only be with her if she chooses him over Roberto. He has had relationships in the past where he has been second best and he has learned the hard way that it is better to be alone than to learn that you are merely the next best thing.

He has to act, and has an idea that might deliver a 'third way' out of this.

After a search of the town centre he arrives at their pharmacy. It's a corner shop at the end of a brick terrace opposite the Fitzwilliam Museum. An elaborate Victorian copper sign says 'G. Peck and son dispensing chemist est. 1851'.

Under normal circumstances Pete would have had the pair checked out by colleagues in Cambridge. He would have asked for some covert observation on them, but despite the fact that he now feels sure that Roberto is a very dangerous, devious and clever man, he has not shared this with anyone.

He has checked out where they are living quietly by using police cover to trawl information on Cambridge pharmacies and colleges. He has travelled unofficially. It's becoming a bad habit, pursuing this man for professional reasons, but doing it unprofessionally. Pete knows he has the advantage of surprise. Roberto does not know how much Pete has worked out nor what he intends to do about it.

As a backup, Pete visits his most trusted colleague and drinking partner Adrian Collingbridge and leaves him with an envelope before leaving Yorkshire.

"Don't ever open unless I tell you to or if I disappear." He instructed in bold felt pen.

'What the fuck are you up to now?' demanded Adrian over the phone.

'Can't tell you yet, but you will find out soon enough.'

As soon as he is alone with the envelope, Adrian immediately tears it open. He has to. If he is going to back up his mate, he has to understand what Pete is getting involved with. The content shocks him. He hides the envelope in his shed at home.

There is an apartment above the shop on the corner of Fitzwilliam Street. Pete assumes correctly that this is the one they are occupying. Hazel has kept in touch with Pete by text sporadically and has mentioned living over the shop.

Whilst asking him not to follow them, she leaves enough of a chink of light to allow him to believe that there was the slimmest possibility that one day they could perhaps be together. Or at least that's how he read it. If she wanted a complete break she didn't have to keep in touch occasionally. He knows that Roberto is unaware of their contact, which gives him hope.

They are not in the flat and the shop was closed.

The sign in the window says 'Sorry, called away for emergency. Back tomorrow 9am sharp. Keep your legs crossed, head back and don't take any sweets from strangers.'

Business as usual, thinks Pete, as he trawls the pubs and bars in the market square and around the centre.

Eventually he spots the Filton on the footpath next to the bread stall in the market. He has never seen such an impressive array of artisan bread. He had no idea there could be so much choice. In his home town it's brown or white, big or small, sliced or not sliced and that's your lot. Here, the whole world is represented in bread form. The jovial Glaswegian in charge says that Roberto has taken to dumping the car there when he is around the shops. 'I don't mind, it brings a touch of je ne sais whitsitt to the ambulance of the locale or whatever you call it,' he jests. 'I sometimes keep the keys for him and pretend it's mine while he gets wrecked round the corner but I don't have them this time.'

'Do you know the owner?' asks Pete.

'Quite well. He's a good customer and a fun fella. A few years back he was around a lot, but then went back north. He's recently moved down from Yorkshire again to the chemist's on Fitzwilliam Street.

'Yeah it's closed. So he's been around for a few years then?'

'On and off. Sometimes don't see him for years. I think he's always had somewhere to stay south of here, but I don't know where.'

'A mate of his, are you?'

'Aye, as much as you could say. We go back. Why d'you want to know?'

'Tell me, was he in the company of a stunning woman when he dumped that there?'

'Aye. You've met Hazel then, have you? '

'Yep.'

'She helps me a couple of days a week. She's not supposed to; her college forbids it, but she's got away with it so far, thank God. Takings shoot up when she's here. I'm sure men buy bread, shove it in a bin round the corner or throw it in the river, give it to the ducks and the swans they do, and come back for more an hour later, just to speak to her. She's a bonnie lass is Hazel.'

'Where can I find them?'

'Who, the men who buy bread?'

'No no, Hazel and Roberto I meant.'

'Och I know that, ye puddin, I was having a laugh. Well never mind. As it's been there for three hours I would say he is probably in the Falcon. It's just the other side of that big building there.' He points a baguette in a southerly direction.

'Try the snug at the back; he'll no doubt be sampling the single malts. Have one for me! ...You could also tell him to shift that thing before six or it'll get clamped again; I can only keep the powers that be off it whilst I'm here and I have an early start in the wee hours. No in fact, tell him Hugh saw it lifted on to a parking truck, that'll put a bat up his nightdress!'

'Can't guarantee I'll find them, but if I do I will pass that on. Meanwhile if I'm trekking around I'll need a couple of those massive samosas please.'

'Here take 'em, if you're a pal of Roberto's, you can have them on me.'

'Thank you.'

Roberto and Hazel are not in the Falcon this time, but the landlady says they were earlier. He goes back to Hugh's stall for more suggestions.

'Try The Devonshire down in Petersfield or the White Swan. He watches the football on a Saturday in there, big Man United fan he is, like most armchair fans. He meets the gambling guys in the Bedouin later in the evening some days.'

'How do I find that? Is it a taxi ride or what?'

'No just go left out of the square, then second right and go down there until you see Parker's Piece on your right. Cross that diagonally then cross the road. Petersfield is the area beyond there. Ten mins tops. By the time you find a cab and get round the one way you will be there and back.'

'Tell me; since Roberto came here how you would say he is compared to before? '

'Well we were never really that close so it's hard to say, but I do have to remind him sometimes how lucky he is. He can be very quiet and I would say almost depressed like he carries a burden, but no more than anyone else. I suppose it annoys me that he can't be happier as I would if I had his life. Not that I'd swap him mind you. Not permanently ... but you have just given me an idea!' His thumb and forefinger rise to his chin thoughtfully.

'Parker's Piece?... Give me a clue.'

'It's a large area of grass not the appendage of Lady Penelope's chauffeur.'

'Glad to hear it!'

'First place proper football was ever played under what became known as the Cambridge rules. Meant you weren't allowed to pick the ball up and run with it which distinguished it from rugby. Hollowed ground for football that is.'

'Hallowed surely?'

'You haven't played on it yet have you?' chuckles Hugh.

How does he do it? Wonders Pete, as he wanders across the grass, dodging the students on their bicycles and the tourists and shoppers. *Roberto has everyone eating out of his hand. Everyone loves the bastard. He causes mayhem and is in the pub while his customers suffer God knows what ailments. If they cross him, they fall over somehow.'*

A keen footballer in his youth, having learnt of the significance of the expanse of grass before him in the history of the game, Pete can't resist returning a football that comes his way. He runs towards it, dribbles around a player who has left the pitch to retrieve it and thumps it towards the goal.

When it misses the net by a yard, he shouts, 'Sorry lads, Hollowed ground!' to the boys he leaves to retrieve the ball.

After a good ten minutes or more, wandering the streets, he asks for directions to the White Swan from a gargle of winos on a memorial garden bench.

Pete gets a better steer on it from one of the more coherent drinkers and gives him a spare samosa. He's been eating one of them for the whole journey and is full already. There is no way he can eat the other.

They are not in the White Swan or the Devonshire, but eventually he finds them in the Bedouin.

Roberto is very much the worse for wear and slumped over his meal. Hazel is in the middle of telling a story to a couple they are sharing a table with. Her arms are flying everywhere as she strives to dramatise her point and she freezes mid-anecdote when she spots him.

Her delight to see him is obvious. When Roberto hears her shriek with delight he sits bolt upright and stares unemotionally as Pete looks into his eyes over Hazel's shoulder. She hugs him for long enough for both men to feel uncomfortable.

Roberto is rigid as if fossilised. Pete joins them.

'How did you find us down here?' asks Hazel.

'Your car is causing a nuisance in the market square. Hugh is it?'

One of their mates offers to move the car from the market square to avoid a drink-driving charge.

'No, I'll take care of those keys if you don't mind,' says Pete, grabbing them from the table,

'I'll move it for him. You lot must be miles over the limit.'

An opportunity arises when Hazel leaves the table to say goodbye to their guests. Pete whispers to Roberto. 'I have more than enough to take you down and I have every intention of doing so.'

'If you have what you think you have, you would have arrived here mob-handed and done the deed,' says Roberto calmly but with menace. 'You wouldn't give me the chance to escape by telling me that.'

Good point you bastard, thinks Pete, wrong-footed by Roberto's response but still confident he can tackle him and take him in.

'I can't deal with you in this state. I have another suggestion. Meet me in the Falcon at 11 tomorrow morning.' says Pete calmly.

'Where are you staying?'

'None of your fucking business!' he smiles. 'You think I would tell you that and let you to pop round and put something in my breakfast or coffee? Who the fuck do you take me for?'

'Calm yourself. Be careful, making accusations without any evidence. And it *is* my business if you are thinking of pestering Hazel again.'

'Don't push your luck. You have one chance and if you're not there at 11, the roof will come off your flat and a hundred coppers will land on your bed. I'm keeping the keys to your car and it will be bobbing around in the Cam by 11.15 if you're not there. Every road out of Cambridge will be blocked, and I'll find you wherever you are.' Pete lies. 'I will spend the rest of my life bringing you down. This *IS* your one and only chance. Don't fuck it up.'

'Leave us alone,' replies Roberto sternly, but revealing for the first time a tremulous twitch.

Roberto's ice cold demeanour slips momentarily and he reveals the tiniest weakness. It's fleeting, but enough to embolden Pete. Like it or not, our bodies reveal tiny signs of our real feelings and Pete is trained to spot them a mile away.

'11 am, the Falcon, the rear bar,' Pete insists.

Roberto knows very little about Pete. A worthwhile career in the force is now a romantic memory. Promotion, if it came would mean fronting an office and being a part of a huge lie.

He joined the force for the challenge and the pleasure of taking out criminals, to remove from circulation those who make the world a darker place and to help the vulnerable. Now, it depresses him beyond measure to be a small and ineffectual part of an underfunded and demoralised bunch of low grade losers and backsliders. Little more than the rump end of a once proud and successful organisation. The few who are still trying to uphold the law and do the right thing are carrying a dead weight consisting of unnecessary paperwork, lazy colleagues and lying bosses.

He is in no position to make a difference and knows by now he never will be.

The serious organised criminals who are responsible for the marketing and distribution of drugs, prostitution and child exploitation, illegal immigration, protection racketeering, large scale internet fraud, burglary and gang warfare are now mostly left free to carry on their work with impunity.

The enthusiasm and dedication of this once proud and passionate detective has been squandered by spineless bosses who are too afraid for their own pensions to fight for the resources that the task demands.

Pete still wants passionately to strike a blow for the good of his community and get some serious results to make a positive difference. After racking his brain and torturing himself for weeks about his own future, Pete thinks he may have stumbled upon a creative solution.

Despite being horrified and repulsed by what he believes Roberto to be responsible for, Pete has to concede that if he is right, the man is very, very good at what he does.

He seems to have developed the knowledge and ability to strike out anyone who crosses him, without leaving a trace. He has no idea how the science of it works but it's clear that Roberto has left no finger print for forensics or autopsies to implicate him.

Pete wonders what would happen if he arrests Roberto?

Would the CPS see a clear path to a conviction and back a prosecution? Probably not. Most of the people Roberto had targeted would not have had many champions seeking justice on their behalf. He would be able to come up with top drawer legal advice and there would be huge scientific challenges in proving what he had done. It would take months, if not years to convict him. Then how long would he be taken out of action for?

He sees Roberto as the kind of clever-dick chancer who will have the system eating out his hands and get a quick route back out on to the street. *He'll probably end up with a government drugs advisory post, bestselling autobiography and a column in the Guardian.*

Pete has been trying to nail a big-time drug dealer who has been prosecuted twice for being engaged in organised class A drug supply and importation but still remains at large. He supplies drugs which find their way on to the streets of Lancashire, Yorkshire and the North East and has dodged conviction for years whilst building a criminal enterprise as large in turnover and staff as a small regional supermarket chain. The man has become so untouchable as to become an informer for the sole purpose of elimination of his competitors and built a multimillion pound property empire to launder his fortune.

He is close to having enough evidence to nail Roberto, but better after he has served a purpose. For the time being he may well be more useful as a free man.

At eleven o'clock on the dot Roberto enters the Falcon. Already it's busy. Breakfasts are being served; hardened drinkers are already on the way, Sunday broadsheets everywhere and lively conversation drifting through the warren of rooms.

Roberto gets a whisky and finds Pete in a quiet corner.

Happy that there is no-one within earshot, there is no need to waste time.

Pete goes for the jugular, leaning forward into Roberto's face, ignoring the conventions of social discourse.

'You murdering cunt. I'm only giving you ten minutes. If I don't get the answer I want, I go straight to the nick and call an urgent meeting about you, right?'

Roberto freezes in shock but knows not to show fear.

'Ok, there's a problem in Yorkshire and if you do exactly what I say, I will leave you alone. If you waver in any way from my instruction, you'll be in a cell before the day is out and you will stay there until your trial.

'I know exactly what you've been doing and exactly how you're doing it,' he lies.

Roberto attempts to speak.....'Bu-'

'Shut the fuck up, I haven't finished.' Pete interrupts, red-faced and shaking.

'I will send you the medical records of a man who has caused mayhem on my patch. We've tried to put him away and end the misery he causes but my team and my bosses are too depleted, too tired and demoralised to deal with him and he is laughing at us. He gets stronger by the day. I can't let it continue.

'Here's where you come in and that's why I spent so much time up in West Fell. I was about to give in; take a career break

~ 187 ~

and let someone other mug deal with this, but now I realise no-one ever will. It will just continue to get worse. There is no cavalry coming along behind to help me.'

'Why should I help you?' interjects Roberto, taken aback by the ferocity of Pete's onslaught. He can tell from last night that Pete was angry and on a mission, but he didn't expect this.

'You will help me because you have absolutely **no** fucking choice. None whatsoever. Don't mistake this conversation for any kind of validation of what you've done. I have nothing but contempt for you and there's only one reason why you don't have handcuffs on you right now.'

'Pray tell. I thought we had started to get on well.'

'Cut the sarcastic shite. I've just explained it to you. Which part did you not understand? I haven't arranged your arrest yet because there is a small possibility that you might be able to do some good.

'Look, you don't need to know the detail. The police are at full stretch. You are in the shit and have no options. I will give you a once-only deal. I have a huge problem with the way that organised crime is dealt with. We are told that we have no resources to tackle it and that certain lines of enquiry are not pursued because social cohesion, integration, budgets, community initiatives and other levels of bollocks.

'Only last week I was with a senior colleague and we were tasked to visit a cross-dresser with a secret life in Manchester who had been regularly observed changing in a layby near Leeds. We were ordered to interview him away from his wife and workplace and told to discuss ways we could help him to continue with his life choice, his perfect legal right to pursue apparently.

In short, two senior detectives wasted a whole morning - no, probably a whole day including paperwork, to enable and assist a pervert to continue with his secret life and deceive his colleagues and spouse.'

'Is a cross-dresser a pervert?'

'Shut up and listen. This is important. We were then told to attend some bloody diversity panel in Leeds to explain why we made a joke out of it. We said we couldn't see why we shouldn't just turn up at his home or work with a suitcase full of his lady clothes and ask him in front of his wife or boss why he couldn't in future get changed at home or work before he trawled the streets of Manchester dressed as Madam JuJu.'

'Why are you telling me this?' Interjects Roberto now smirking, 'People should be free to live how they live, surely?'

'Because this is not a joke. It's not why I joined this job. I didn't join to be told to help him to deceive his wife, whilst the serious criminals steal, deal drugs and commit crimes every day with impunity.' Pete regrets using this example to illustrate his position, but it was simply the first one of many to come to mind, he is now involved in a debate about sexuality and gender issues. He needs to get back to the point.

'I don't see where he was breaking the law,' says Roberto, trying to lead the conversation on to safer territory, but further winding Pete up to a state of red faced fury.

'THAT IS NOT THE FUCKING POINT and you know it,' he seethes, trying but failing to rein his anger in. 'I've had enough of fighting crime without back-shovelling shit while the powers-that-be have taken the shovel away from me and tied my left bollock to a lamp post.'

Roberto jumps in 'Oh come on for fuck's sake, this is very interesting, but it all seems very much like your problem and not mine. If it's as broken as you say, then what gives you the confidence to assume that I wouldn't just walk from the court a free man, even if I were guilty of anything - which I am not.'

Pete has to concede he had a point but couldn't give him an inch.

'Because I've been on to you for months and I have been recording you audibly and on camera. I have stills, videos, mobile phone recordings and detailed statements, details of your financial transactions, you name it, I have the lot.

'Why do you think I've spent so much time in your company?'

Pete is making it all up as he goes along now; he knows full well that if he had it would be inadmissible.

Roberto downs his drink to give himself a moment to think then says 'Because you're in love with Hazel, you loser, that's why.

'In any event, if you have all that, it would have to be sanctioned by your bosses and court orders would be required, so how do I know doing a deal with you would prevent your bosses taking action in any event? In fact they would be obliged to do so. Your attempt to do a deal with me compromises your position so I have nothing to gain by dealing with you. You are attempting to blackmail me, so I will take my chances, thank you.'

Roberto buys time with robust defence and he hopes he appears unruffled but his mind is racing: *Have I grossly underestimated PC Plod?!*

Pete has to think on his feet. He is taken aback by Roberto's instant and accurate assessment but has to press on now and not reveal his bluff. It's a crossroads. He knows what he says next has to be good or his plan will go nowhere.

'Ok ok, you did kill Jimmy Murphy, Ahmet Altouyan, Eric Francombe, Brian Calvert, Steven Mallinson and quite probably poisoned Elfrida Pickles and no doubt many more, but those are the ones I know for sure you killed. I know you did and I have all the proof I need.

'It doesn't matter how I got it, what does is the fact that I have you in my sights and I've left the whole of my evidence in the care of someone I trust. I've told them that if I don't return by Tuesday, to take it to Cambridge CID without telling anyone In Yorkshire.'

Pete's gamble works.

Roberto is now inwardly panicking. The only one he had missed was Pippin and no-one would mourn the passing of an estate agent, surely? He wasn't even sure that one was a crime. How did he know about the farmer? No one knew about that.

I need time, he thinks.

In fact Pete, acting on a hunch and researching Roberto's recent movements as carefully as he could, had collected information on all the unexpected deaths in Wensleydale, Swaledale, upper Wharfedale and the Southern Lakes since Roberto arrived there and adding them to the ones he knew about in Bradford, by a sheer fluke had made a complete and accurate list. All present and correct. No one else had died in the valley since he arrived either unexpectedly or inexplicably. There was only Mally and Mr Calvert and Eric Francombe. Three or four others had died during the relevant period, but mostly of extreme old age, cancer or in one case a vehicle accident whilst a West Fell resident was on holiday in Florida. Pippin had died at his Ben Rhydding toad hall after Roberto had left Yorkshire. Normal everyday deaths, sad for the families involved but none included suspicious circumstances or revealed evidence of foul play.

Pete had spent several weeks investigating every possibility. He treated it as he would any other job, only he didn't share what he was up to with anyone. His partner in the force knew that he was on a mission, and knew that it had something to do with Hazel, who he had met once, but he knew Pete well enough to know that he should leave him to it. He trusted Pete to involve him when, in his judgement the time was right, but retained the right to intervene at any moment if he sniffed danger for his pal.

Pete tested every coincidence, examined every fact he turned up to build a picture. He hadn't documented it as carefully as he led Roberto to believe, because he didn't want questions to be asked in the office about what he was up to.

As he was relatively new to the business of murder, Roberto's victim list was relatively modest. So it wasn't too hard to identify all the people he had killed. Convincing him now that he was stuck and had no option was not easy but Pete senses that he has the upper hand.

'You couldn't stop interrupting me a few minutes ago and now you are silent,' he goads with a smile.

Roberto stares impassively at the wall without comment for longer than he intends. His usual studied coldness not the reason. This time ignoring it isn't going to make the panic go away.

'Are you recording this conversation?' he asks after a huge and profoundly uncomfortable space in their discourse.

'Me to know and you to wonder,' Pete spits.

'Ok,' replies Roberto. 'Let's assume that I was in some way involved in what you think I am. Which I am not! Then what am I supposed to do for you? What do I have to do to ensure my freedom? From you I mean?' he continues. 'And what comfort do I get that you won't just send that file to your superiors when I've done what you ask?'

Roberto gets up from his chair before being pushed back down by Pete who makes it clear he will physically prevent him from leaving irrespective of the concerned glances from other drinkers.

He pauses with his hand still on Roberto's shoulder.

'You just have to eliminate one person for me,' says Pete quietly.

'What? How so and why?' asks Roberto, guarded and puzzled, pushing his hand away.

'He's unwell. He eats too much, takes all manner of drugs and attends a clinic regularly, we think for diabetes; I'll get you his medical record from the NHS by pulling in a favour with a DP9 request to his dodgy doctor, who is on my radar for unrelated issues.

'His doc is in a similar if not quite as precipitous a position as you are. He's my bitch as well as you are; difference being, he can see his best chance is to help me out.'

'I didn't have you down as a one-man bribery merchant. I just thought you were another dozy copper.' Roberto fights back. 'You sure you're up to managing this venture?'

'Fuck you. I'll tell you where my target goes to collect his prescription. You'll arrange for a swap of his medication like you do, and you'll make sure that he leaves this world in a way that has some link to his lifestyle or his medical history. You don't need me to tell you how to do it.'

'What is a DP9?'

'Permission to release records to the police... Surprised you don't know that. I'll send you a copy of his records which you will return to me when you've read them.'

'I'm a pharmacist not a copper. No one denies me access to medical records.'

'So you could get them for me then?'

'What and leave a trail back to me? Not a chance. If you want to do this you are on your own.'

Roberto is now convinced that he will have to go along with this, or at least appear to for now, but he wonders where it will lead to later.

Maybe I could take Pete out somehow. He likes a social drink, so administering a kick would be easy, but what about the file he says he has deposited somewhere. Who with? Who does he trust? Roberto needs time to work it out.

Pete's poker face is holding up well.

'You've missed a crucial point. I'm not his pharmacist. His medical records would educate me in how to knock him over, but I can't get his medication down his throat without dispensing it to him. And I'm guessing he isn't fortunate enough to live within my catchment,' says Roberto, exasperated and looking for a way out.

'I'll arrange for you to have shifts in his pharmacy in Bradford. I'll tell them it's part of a covert observation operation, leave that to me.'

'Oh no, I am not going back to work in Bradford again. Shifts? What the fuck do you mean shifts? I cannot and will not start working in that dump again. Not for you or anyone else, I would rather do a twenty year stretch. Take me down now! I've promised myself I will never go back there - I couldn't bear it; you will have to arrest me now.' Roberto pleads, only half joking. 'Even if I wanted to help you, which you must know I most certainly do not, I have a business to run here.'

Pete leans over the table and grabs him by the throat, 'You have no fucking choice if you value your freedom. Hire a fucking locum. If you can find one you can trust! Oh just one other thing. If anything happens to Hazel, I'll kill you myself. I'll be watching you.'

'I will think about it,' says Roberto smoothing down his shirt collar as he gets up to leave.

Pete stops him in his tracks by pushing him against the wall of the pub, 'You have an hour to think about it. Then I might give you back your car keys.'

Pete lets Roberto go and leaves by the rear entrance. He stops in the back yard for a few minutes, his heart pumping. He has just put his own career and freedom on the line. Anything is better than continuing to deal with an impossible deluge of despair, putting himself in harm's way for an ungrateful world.

An hour to the dot after their meeting Roberto rings. 'I'll do it.'

Pete replies 'This is the last time we communicate directly. Ever. Delete my number and don't ever ring me. I will contact you when I need to.'

18 The Will to Love Tears us Apart

Roberto has no choice but to cooperate.

Pete's entire life is now upside down. He knows he has crossed a line, now on the wrong side of the law, he has become an accessory to murder.

Abuse of his oath to the Queen and the corruption of his duty will send him away for a longer stretch than his accomplice and on top of that, any time inside will leave him at the mercy of those he had worked so hard for so long to defeat.

He knows that if it goes wrong, he mustn't be caught. It will be far too ugly.

He secures a time-old offer to join an ocean-going sports-fishing vessel captained by an old friend. If he can keep ahead of the game, Pete has an escape strategy but he will have to live with the guilt. He knows it will be hard but provided the right people are targeted, it will be possible and worthwhile.

Before Pete leaves Cambridge he texts Hazel and arranges to meet her on the Bridge of Sighs behind St James College, accessing the elaborate formal gardens from the rear gate on the west side of the Cam.

The moment he sees her walking straight and proud, her hair caught by a gentle breeze, through the college grounds framed by the ancient stone arch, he is bowled over anew. Her presence is so striking it hurts him.

They meet on the crown of the bridge and embrace for at least ten years. He begins to cry, he doesn't know why; he is overwhelmed to see her.

'What are you doing here?' she asks, her face resting in his neck.

Her scent melts his heart.

'I had to see you. I think about you day and night.'

He yearns to tell her that her partner is a murderer.

'My future is here for the next three years, If I don't finish my education and put some time between us and the mess in West Fell, it will break my father's heart. I owe that to my mum too. She wanted the choices that slipped through her fingers to be available to me. I wouldn't be able to look myself in the mirror if I ran away from this opportunity.

'..And I love Roberto as well you know. He came along at the right time and I can't turn my back on him.'

'Do you trust him?' asks Pete, his heart sinking.

'What do you mean, trust him? With other women you mean? Of course I do. Look at me! Is it likely he could cope with more than this?' She says in jest, sweeping her hands from head to toe and raising a comedic eyebrow.

'Well, when you put it like that! No, I mean do you feel you *know* him?'

'Of course I know him, what are you getting at?'

'Forget it,' says Pete, frustrated. He's bursting to tell her what he knows, but he can't. Once she knows the whole story, it will take Roberto out of contention and he will never know if she would have chosen to be with him.

He yearns to tell her *"Hazel. You are by far the most incredible woman I have ever met. How can I not love you but I would rather live without you than spend the rest of this life wondering if I was your first choice or just someone available."* But instead he stays silent and looks at her.

The numbskulls in his comms room stubbornly refuse to sign off those thoughts and allow them to be distributed, despite those in the heart-pumping department being in intensive care with the last rites being read.

The words won't come.

Hazel breaks the silence. 'Pete. As much as I love Rob I know there is a dark side to him that I can no longer ignore. This madness mustn't continue, for both our sakes. I want to go straight and buckle down and I've decided that my future with Rob depends on him doing the same. I don't know if he can do it.'

'Going straight can mean a number of things. What are you driving at exactly?' asks Pete carefully steeling himself for the bombshell that she is aware of what Roberto has done.

'Oh, you must know.'

'Know what?'

'Oh where do you want me to start?' she pleads, her forehead wrinkled in puzzlement. Pete was there for much of it, how could he not know?

'How about: misuse of recreational drugs? Drinking, partying, dangerous, shambolic unprofessionalism? Or cruel disregard for some of his customer's welfare and dignity? Will that do? Don't tell me you hadn't worked him out by now?'

Pete breathes for the first time in a couple of minutes.

'Are you ok?'

She is only scratching the surface, he thinks.

Seeing Hazel again puts his passion for her back into overdrive and though it's mutual, she is at a crucial point in her life. Hazel now begins to acknowledge the existence of dark thoughts that have slowly taken root in her brain. She has pushed to the back of her mind suspicions and doubts about Roberto for some months but they are now breeding and spawning unanswered questions and itches that will have to be scratched. *And what about that box I found?* she remembers. *It's past time I challenged him about that.*

Pete doesn't need to spell out his love for her. He has shown his hand through his actions. She will have to decide soon whether to tell him there will never be a chance for them, or ask him to wait.

Why is her love life always so complicated? It has never occurred to her to leave Roberto. She hasn't given it a moment's thought since they met and not even now. Despite her misgivings she is loyal still. If she embarks on an affair with Pete everything will be destroyed.

Why can't I have them both? That's what we would do if I was the male or if we were French.

During the meeting in the Falcon, due to Roberto's acceptance of a mission to kill, Pete was satisfied that his hunch was correct: the man who had the woman he loved in the palm of his hand is really a murderer... An innocent man would have no reason on earth to contemplate such an action.

Conflicting moral challenges race through his mind as they walk the college gardens on the bank of the Cam. Doubling back, pausing at the river's edge and retracing their steps to extend their time together.

They are approached by an elderly smiling porter.

'I'm sorry but these gates are closing now as dusk falls. If you have business within the estate you can sign at the porters lodge at the other side of the building, I'm so awfully sorry to disturb you.'

Hazel flashes him a smile. 'We're on our way now, thank you.'

'It's so English down here isn't it. Up north you would be given 2 minutes to piss off before the dogs are let out,' contributes Pete unhelpfully.

They part with a passionate kiss in the narrow passage that leads back to market square. The romantic location matches the warmth of feeling between them.

'Where have you been all afternoon?' inquires Roberto when Hazel returns.

'Oh, nowhere in particular. Just got a lot on my mind.'

'Where have you been all afternoon?' he repeats, 'I didn't ask what you had on your mind. I tried to get you on your mobile.'

'Can't I go for a walk without applying for a permit?'

'Whoa, I just wondered. Why didn't you pick up?'

'Oh, I left my phone in the basket of my bike, didn't I.'

'Where was your bike? '

'When?'

'This afternoon.'

He stands in her way blocking her path to the kitchen demanding an answer.

'Oh I don't know, I can't remember.'

'You don't know where your bike was this afternoon whilst your phone was in the basket?'

'Are you checking up on me?'

'No, I'm not'

'So why the nosey questions?'

'Why the defensive replies?'

'Which defensive replies?'

'Shove out of the way, I need the loo,' she says hoping to move it on.

'The ones you're shooting back at me.'

'Why do you want to know?'

'Know what?'

'Where my bike was.'

He remains in the doorway still blocking her. This is a small action but a telling and worrying one. Never before had he used physicality in such a menacing way with her.

She stops short to avoid a collision and having tested him, retreats.

'Oh for fuck's sake, I just wondered why you left your phone in your basket all afternoon when you normally can't go ten minutes without picking it up to see if there are any messages.'

Now he *is* getting suspicious.

He wasn't before, but the defensive and incoherent answers are now making him wonder if she has met Pete.

'Look this is crazy. We're better than this. I met Pete, we spent the afternoon together. He told me he loves me. We're not having an affair and I told him I was happy with you. Ok?'

'Yeah, fine,' Rob is satisfied.

How come he is so cool about this? She wonders. *Completely, disarmed. Why the fuck didn't I just tell him and save all the pressure?*

Roberto is now calm and can live with the competition from Pete as long as she doesn't learn what he knows.

Roberto is in love with her too as much as he ever has been with anyone. He wishes that he could leave the recent past behind and just spend the rest of his life in her company. His grip on the future is now loosening and he knows.

Hazel takes a bath, not because she needs one, but because she needs to be alone to think. She is grateful that Roberto is not kicking off, but puzzled and confused about why Pete is here.

Later, on the sofa when the tension has evaporated, she hopefully suggests

'Shall we go to the Falcon tonight? I feel like a drink.'

'I can't do a late one; I'm up at 2.30am.'

'What the fuck for? You don't open until 9.'

'You wouldn't believe me.'

'Go on.'

'I have to go to Hitchin for Hugh.'

'Whaaaat? What for? '

'To collect his bread.'

'Rob? What are you on about? You are joking right?'

'Nope. Lost a bet. He is having a morning in bed. I am going to do his job for him.'

'No! Are you working on the stall all day as well?'

'Fuck that, I lost a bet on the FA cup final with Hugh and the loser had to do the other one's job. He says it does you good to find out what others have to do. He thinks I don't appreciate you and my life. It's a part of his 'walk-a-mile-in-my-shoes campaign' to make me appreciate my good fortune.'

'Hugh can't dispense chemicals to people!'

'Yeah and I can't sell bread so I am going to do the collections of the new bread.'

Hazel has done a few days here and there on Hugh's stall. She loves the crack with the punters and knows how hard the day is.

She had however, never thought about how the bread gets there fresh every day and is astounded to learn that it involves early travel every morning to Hugh's craft bakery thirty miles to the South.

'What would you have done if you had won the bet?'

'I suppose Hugh would have been in the pharmacy. People with migraines and heart problems would be given a stollen cake or a German rye with olives or one of those massive samosas or something. Probably do them just as much good as the addictive shit I hand out. Anyway, it's not an issue because I didn't win the bet did I?'

'You're totally mental,' says Hazel as she leaves the room.

'You don't know the half of it my sweet,' he replies quietly, to the back of the closed door.

19 Happiness Defined

The next morning Roberto is up and off in Hugh's van.

2.30am! I had no idea that it was possible to begin a day this early. It's still fucking yesterday!

He had been out at this time many times but only as a part of the previous day. He zips down to Hitchin following a map and Hugh's notes to his craft bakery and then to a specialist who supplies samosas the size of pillows and doughnuts the size of lorry tyre inner tubes.

He collects all manner of weird and wonderful delightful smelling fresh breads and cake. During the trip Roberto encounters several revellers, still enjoying the day before.

After shaking off the shock of functioning at such an unfamiliar hour he begins to enjoy it. The bakery is staffed by cheerful East Europeans who are surprised not to see Hugh. The job done, he is back in Cambridge with a yawning hunger and unloaded before Hugh arrives to set up and man the stall.

'You can't possibly do that, then sell the bread all day, then pack up and do your paperwork. No-one can! I had no idea there are so many hours in the night; I never knew what happened between 2am and 5am. I've gone to bed early and I've got up early, but I never knew what happens in-between. It's brutal man! Those hours are brutal!'

'Aye, seven days a week mostly. I get the odd day off and have some help on the stall some days, but that's pretty much a normal day,'

'You're fucking kidding me?'

'No, that's what I do. I love it!'

'You are made of something else.'

'Ahh it's not so bad. It's not work if you're enjoying yourself is it? Work is when you have to go every day and you would rather be anywhere else but there. It's the same with happiness.'

'Happiness? Remind me?'

'You know, happiness is when you are exactly where you want to be. When you know for sure you don't want to be anywhere else, doing anything else, with anyone else. There is no better description of happiness than that. Surely you have that with Hazel? Christ, if you don't, there is no hope for any of us. How can you not be happy when you have the love of her? I tell you what, if it's not working out for you, drop her round mine anytime.'

'No of course I am happy with Hazel. I know how lucky I am. Just sometimes it's easy to forget the day before she came.'

'I should fucking hope so. Stop looking so fucking haunted all the time. It dinna get any better. What's happening today. That's all there is. This is your life now you know. There is no yesterday and may be no tomorrow. Learn this,' he continues, now dispensing with the levity. 'The only rich people in the world are those who know how lucky they are to be alive and enjoy themselves. To be here now, in this place, at this moment in history, on this planet makes us by far and away the luckiest living creatures of any kind that ever had life within them, so wind yer neck in and put a smile on ye face, you've already won the lottery by being here. Or if ye canna manage that, shove this in it,' he completes his lecture by poking a foot-long sausage roll into Roberto's startled face.

Their banter is stopped dead as a white transit van reverses along the side of the market square. There is nothing unusual about this. The stallholders are setting up and vans are everywhere on the pavement and the roadside. But when it accelerates backwards into Hugh's stall, bending the roof supports and sending boxes of bread flying, they momentarily stand open-mouthed.

Hugh springs out of his shock and quick as a flash, shouting abuse at the driver, runs around the side of the van, opens the door and drags the occupant out into the road where he proceeds to kick and punch him to the floor.

'You work for Quinn don't you, you bastard? If you think you can frighten me, you are mistaken sonny.'

Hugh's accent becomes twice as Glaswegian as it was a minute ago.

In a moment of Herculean power and dexterity, Hugh picks up the driver who is, to be fair, not much more than a scrawny ferret, holds him aloft and throws him over some iron railings. Hugh then runs around to the other side of the railings and down some stone steps.

Roberto rushes up to the railings and peers over just in time to see Hugh bundle the injured groaning youth through a door into some subterranean room. Hugh slams the door and locks the combination latch. He bounces back up the stairs shouting 'I will deal with you later you skinny shite.'

Hugh, still travelling at speed runs back around the railings throwing his apron towards Roberto and shouting 'Keep an eye on the stall for me. I'll be back in ten minutes.' He leaps into the van which is still running, and shoots off around the corner, wheels spinning.

Roberto is open-mouthed surprised at what has just happened.

Before he has time to put his apron on, a queue is beginning to form from the small crowd that has gathered.

Roberto fumbles loaves into bags, tearing them as he tries but fails to match the hanging paper bags to the correct sized loaves. He drops doughnuts on the floor and trips over boxes as he tries valiantly to sell bread for Hugh. He has no idea what anything is supposed to cost, so he just guesses. It's a shambles and after a few minutes, he gives up and stands next to the stall asking people to take whatever they want and put money in an honesty box, which they all happily do. Fortunately the customers don't hear the muffled shouting from the subterranean dungeon beside the stall.

Half an hour later, Hugh returns on foot. He is sporting a huge gash across his forehead, a cut lip and torn jumper.

'Jesus Hugh, what the fuck is happening?'

'Och, it's a long story. It's nothing. There is a guy who runs a car business near here who sold me a dog of a motor. When it broke down, I went around and asked him to fix it but he refused, so I reported him to the council, which gave him a year of grief and lost him his tenancy. Since then, he's been trying to see me off by reporting me with false claims about food and all sorts o' shite. He'll have paid that twat down there to come and do that. I collared him outside his new premises just now and gave him a proper woodening, and then he had a couple of his men take me on with spanners.'

'Jeez I thought Cambridge was a refined sort of town. I had no idea this kind of thing could go on. It must remind you of home?'

'Aye, it's like any place. There's scum floating on every pond,' replies Hugh with a resigned sigh. 'I'm too fuckin old to be scrapping in the street.' he says leaning on the iron railings and holding his chest.

'You look badly injured, you should go and get that looked at.'

'Not as bad as the other bastard. You should see him,' he laughs.

With that Hugh goes down the stairs and releases the youth, sending him packing with a slap to his neck and kick up the arse.

Just as the youth flees to the sound of a torrent of abuse from Hugh, a well-known white bearded figure with bushy eyebrows cascading over his spectacles like a white owl peering through an unkempt hedge, wearing a black cloak and a concerned expression arrives at the stall.

Hugh's smile immediately returns.

'Oh, good morning, your royal Archbish!' cries Hugh forgetting his injuries and falling into his usual banter. 'What can

I get you, your usual? Five barley loaves and two small fish is it?'

'Now you know I've retired, it's just two croissants and a sourdough on a Wednesday as you know,' replies the clergyman with a weary resigned sigh.

'I hope everything is alright, Hugh. Only I could hear some fruity language from my lodge.'

'It was nothing Rowan, just a happy customer returning to say how much he enjoyed his doughnut.'

'I believe you Hugh,' replies the retired clergyman with a benevolent smile as he saunters off with his breakfast. 'Don't forget your fishes Rowan,' shouts Hugh as he disappears with a wave.

'Was that?--'

'Aye, we have some interesting customers here. Clive James is here twice a week mostly on Derek's bookstall. Paperbacks on Tuesday, hardbacks Thursday, but I've been feeding the poor sod for years too. A top man but not at all well, sadly. 'He spends a lot of money between me and Derek and we sometimes have to drop it off for him. Clive lives what I was talking about. He is far more iller than he will admit but he's had a great life and been a right tinker. He still wakes up every mornin' with a twinkle and makes the best of his day.'

'I'm beginning to get the message, although I can't imagine I could be so cheerful after dealing with that just now. Anyway, I must be off. It's been an interesting morning. I was wondering what keeps you at this job year in, year out; but if every day is half as much fun as this one I get it completely.

'Get those wounds seen to as soon as possible. If you need any bandages, Dettol or anything, drop in.'

Roberto, dropping the levity for a moment takes Hugh to one side and says quietly, 'Listen, if you need help dealing with those people, let me know Hugh.'

'Oh, I can manage, thanks for the offer though,' shouts Hugh getting back to his stall.

The same afternoon, an ugly, angry, tattooed man with black oily hands comes into the pharmacy with similar wounds to those he had seen on Hugh in the morning.

He asks the assistant for something for a headache and some bandages when Roberto has a thought.

'Are you Mr Quinn by any chance?'

'What's it to you?' snarls the man.

'Oh, I have a car and my friend told me you might be able to help me to service it. It's a Filton. It's quite rare.'

'I know what that is,' snaps the man. 'No, I can't see to it. You have to take them back to the manufacturer. You should fucking know that anyway. Can I just get something for my fucking headache? It's pounding.'

'Oh never mind. Headache was it Mr Quinn? Let me deal with this Steph, just give me a moment, I'll see what I have in the back for you.'

Roberto rushes down into the cellar in a repeat of his action in Bradford and lifts a stone flag in the floor. In a flash he is back at the counter handing Mr Quinn a bottle. 'Take a good gulp of that and your headache will be gone by supper time I can promise you.'

'Fucking better do,' grumbles the unpleasant man, 'Or I'll be back for my money.'

'Oh you won't be back for your money. I can assure you of that Mr Quinn. Enjoy your day. It could be your last, I always say.'

Roberto later scolds himself for his relapse.

Must be more careful, he tells himself.

Hugh has no more trouble from Mr Quinn.

He does send a tray of cakes and doughnuts and a couple of boxes of pillow sized samosas to the wake though. Hugh is like that; a very generous man who holds no grudges.

20

Thank You for Visiting Bradford, Please Drive Carefully and Take Our Rubbish Away With You

We've been busy whilst I was out says Roberto approvingly as he flicks through the incoming prescriptions.

'Not half boss,' says Steph, 'Oh by the way there's a letter for you here.'

'FAO Roberto Antonelli. Urgent - Strictly confidential'

No one noticed it arriving. There is no postmark or full address. It has been handed in by a ghost.

It is the medical records of someone called Declan Arthur Lewis. Roberto was sceptical that Pete could obtain access to these, but he clearly wasn't bluffing. There are some notes with the package detailing his home address along with a printed Google map showing the location of a chain store pharmacy next to a health centre.

The package instructs Roberto to be there at 10am the following Wednesday morning.

He is now a part of someone else's mission, no longer in control. He doesn't want to do this. In truth, if he was asked to hand over a dodgy prescription for the same aim, but without knowing its destination he would not have been so concerned.

He is more put out by the thought of returning to Bradford against his will, than the thought of committing murder; but that's Bradford for you.

Roberto now has the need of a locum that day and he can't ignore the irony of that.

The contents of the envelope show that Declan has a doctor's appointment that day at the health centre next to the pharmacy at 11am. The files give plenty of clues as to what the man is likely to need. There are several options. Roberto has to concoct a bespoke powder and a liquid which will do the job.

He wonders how they know the target will go for his prescription immediately after his appointment. He might just as easily leave it for a minion or his wife to pick up elsewhere, or he could perhaps come and get it himself, but at a later date.

Roberto decides to do this once and if the man doesn't turn up he will tell Pete to forget it.

He tells Hazel that he is going North to see his kids. He has missed a birthday and is in trouble. This is true but without this unavoidable mission, he wouldn't have bothered to see his two youngsters. He is now completely estranged from them. He likes to believe that they are happy with their new stepdad. The gardener (or landscape designer as his ex describes him) has now moved in and they all seem content. Avoiding asking any probing questions about their welfare makes it easier for him to think everything is ok.

Hazel has been trying to get him to do the right thing for his kids for months, so for her this is a welcome development.

He has forgotten about a standing order that is still in place for them which is most probably spent in wine bars and shoe shops by their mother. According to his wife his kids still hate him for his abandonment. To what extent that is fuelled by propaganda from their mother and how much of it is real he can only guess, but he feels sure that as soon as they are old enough, they will come looking for him. He is unmoved as he believes they are better off with their mother without being in the crossfire of their parents' dysfunctional marriage.

Inspired by Hugh's example, he gets a very early start. After taking care past the speed cameras in Bedfordshire, he plays with the car on the wide four-lane lit section of the A1 between Peterborough and Alconbury. He knows it has no fixed cameras so he fleetingly hits 190mph.

There are few places where irresponsibility is possible to this extreme and Rob knows he will have to sell the car very soon, so *what the hell* he thinks.

As he roars northwards, what appears to be a wide straight road to an ordinary traveller is now twisting right and left whilst occasional lorries come into view and disappear behind him in fractions of seconds, his speed turning the terrain in his peripheral vision into a blurred video game.

The times when he can use it are so rare and exciting to him he can't resist the thrill. He covers the 13 mile four-lane wide stretch of tarmac in a little over 6 minutes for no sensible reason, just because he can.

He is in the Bradford area within two and a half hours. Without a refuelling stop he could have made the journey even faster. It's recklessly irresponsible, but next to his other exploits, it's probably the least dangerous and antisocial thing he is involved in at the moment. He can't think of a good excuse to keep the car now. He will need the money before long to build a nest for Hazel and he has got it out of his system almost, but he resolves to enjoy it as much as possible before the day it has to go.

Roberto realises that he will be early if he carries on at this rate and so decides to make a small detour into Otley for breakfast in Dunnie's café by the river - if it hasn't been bulldozed for housing yet.

Roberto used to go there regularly for a full breakfast when out cycling or as a hair of the dog after a wild night out.

He is astounded to discover that it is in fact still there and impossibly still turning out a full breakfast with two eggs, three sausages, beans, a side of bacon a pint of tea and as much bread and butter that you can eat for an unbelievable £3.50.

After passing some time along the riverbank Roberto calls in on his 'uncle' Colin Peckitt on the old Leeds road to see what he is up to. Now almost eighty, Colin's garage is still buzzing with activity, fixing everyday cars to keep the cash coming in, whilst restoring everything from vintage wagons to Bentleys and modern supercars, putting far more time into those jobs than is economically sensible.

Not remotely interested in accompanying his wife Moira on her trips abroad, Colin is only happy when covered in oil and sharing his passion with anyone who will listen.

Despite never being anywhere near close, Colin is the nearest Roberto has to a male role model and was the inspiration and catalyst for his interest in sports cars. Colin knew that he only called in when he needed parts, expertise or help, but preferred it that way. He thought little of and knew next to nothing about his sister Irene's life and preferred lifting the bonnet of an exotic car to trying to understand people. Colin had given up trying to fathom his sister long before she passed away. She was way too naively socialist and bohemian for his taste and they spent no time together as adults.

He could rebuild the engine of a Rolls from memory, but couldn't begin to understand how his sister's mind worked and had no intention of trying. For him a mutual interest in exotic cars was as useful as any blood ties could ever be.

'Have a look at this. It's a 1928 Chevrolet. I'm having to go all over the world for bits, but that internet is marvellous for it. My grandson does it all from his bedroom. I just need a distributer cap and it's done. Last one came from Florida by post but it were the wrong size.'

Any car nut could chat to Colin all day long. For decades, with a spanner in his hands, he has worked on everything. He and his staff soon have the bonnet of the Filton open and a small crowd come out to listen to the engine.

'It's a supercharged Chrysler v10 which produces 628 bhp and is capable of 210 miles per hour,' Colin explains to the small but enthusiastic crowd.

He is a wiry-framed thin-faced man who would not look out of place herding sheep in the fells. His eyes are bright and wide when holding forth about engines. Work has never been a chore; he loves every minute of it still, 65 years into his career, 55 of them with his name above the door and an encyclopaedia of stories he'd share with anyone who had the time.

'They've not even made ten of these yet, they are the rarest and fastest production cars built in the UK...'

Just boys who don't want to grow up, playing out instead of getting proper jobs. Good luck to them, thinks Roberto, as he tears himself away from an impromptu lecture from Colin on the improvements made to the radiator of a Maudsley wagon in the 1920's.

As he reaches the roundabout up the Chevin Road Roberto can see them in his rear view mirror on the pavement admiring the sight and sound of his car shaking windows and vibrating the pavement.

As the sound fades, Colin returns to his class.

Roberto smiles at the thought of grown men being as excited by cars as they had been all their lives and wondered what working there might be like.

How different, my life could have been, he ponders.

Half an hour later he arrives at the pharmacy in Bradford and takes his place behind the dispensary. His predicament depresses him. He doesn't appreciate taking orders from others.

OOH, What the fuck am I doing here again? Nothing changes. It's the same ungrateful crowd of chancers, addicts and fossils...

'Thank fuck this is no longer the way I have to make a living,' he mutters.

Half an hour ago he felt jealous of the guys working in Colin's garage. Now he feels lucky that this is no longer his life.

It's another chaotic muddle. Illegal recreational drugs are believed to be the cancer that destroys the young and foolish but the misuse of prescribed medication across a wider section of the community is an equal scourge; if not yet an acknowledged problem.

At 11.20 a gleaming red Rolls Royce Phantom turns up outside. Roberto clocks it to be the latest centenary model, it can only be months old and would cost nine or ten Bradford terraced houses. Three men get out and he can see from a hundred yards that this has to be his target. Only someone immune from arrest would drive such an obvious car in such a deprived area. In that colour, in this town, it could only be a drug dealer or Michael Winner on his way to review a curry house.

Roberto has parked his car half a mile away in the Rawson market multi-story car park to give it half a chance of still being intact when he finished. He is heartened to realise that following the orders of a serving police officer, he is pretty well immune from arrest.

He knows that won't save him, but the trial would be interesting. It would be easy enough to claim that he did it under duress. Or that he believed that he was doing his civic duty.

Before long he looks up from his desk and standing before him is a Caribbean man in a black suit wearing a gold watch who must be seven feet tall and twenty five stone. In his hand is a prescription. 'Give,' is all he says. It is for Declan Lewis. This man mountain is not Mr Lewis but staff, Roberto assumes.

The man stands silently and doesn't move but his eyes follow Roberto wherever he goes in the room.

In any other situation like this he would ask a series of questions to establish the man's identity and confirm his relationship to the person on the prescription. On this occasion he can't serve the man quickly enough. He doesn't care if this is the wrong man. He has done his job. He just wants to go now.

He takes the prescription to the back of the shop and quickly prepares it adding the phial of white powder he prepared earlier.

"Four times a day and not before eating. Avoid alcohol" he prints on the label.

The vast mountain of muscle in front of him grabs it with a hand and arm so big it could pick him up by the head and throw him across the room whilst he rest of his King Kong size body was busy doing something else entirely. He leaves without a word and shimmies sideways to get through the normal sized door allowing daylight back into the room. It's all done in a flash. It's still 35 mins till noon.

Roberto desperately wants to leave as soon as the monster disappears in the Roller. He doesn't want anyone to remember his face or his name but if he leaves early it may be remembered, so he grudgingly endures most of the remainder of the day.

This is madness, he thinks. *I am paying a locum in Cambridge and I am here.*

He sneaks away ten minutes early telling his workmate he has completed all the prescriptions, which is almost true and drives out of Bradford towards Ilkley. He stops at the lights at the bottom of Great Horton road. The Jacob's Well pub to the right is still open, but has a 'For Sale' sign above the door.

He had taken the precaution of paying his own locum in cash and leaving his name on the register and the prescriptions he prepared for dispensing today so that if there is an investigation, in time, he can claim to have been there all day.

To that end, he parks on the edge of Ilkley Moor in the Cow and Calf car park and waits till dusk. In fading light he walks across the moor below White Wells to the corner of the Keighley Gate track and drops off some presents for his children in the dark and slips away. He could then, if asked, claim to have had them delivered by a friend. He is only doing this to gain brownie points with Hazel but he doesn't want to be seen in Ilkley.

The journey back to the car is more hazardous than he would have liked and despite the moon offering some illumination, he trips regularly in the shaded stream valleys. Stumbling around in the dark on Ilkley Moor reminds him that he is no longer the master of his own destiny and he genuinely does not know how much longer he can stay free in England. He might have to do a Lord Lucan if Pete won't leave him alone.

Back in Cambridge he has a quiet week and puts in some genuine effort to heed Hugh's wise words and become a better, happier person. He reflects on Hugh's mini lecture and realises how right he is. However that's easier said when he was completely unaware of what Roberto was responsible for. He convinces himself that Hazel is having a calming effect on him and making him a kinder human. He sees a future with her but he will now have to cover all the traces of his misdeeds and leave it all behind.

Hazel persuades him to arrange a trip to London to meet his kids who are coming down with their mother to shop and see a concert. He cooks and cares for her as she digs into her study. He drinks in the White Swan and the Devonshire but keeps life tidy and cuts down as much as he can. He avoids the Falcon as the banter and intellectual competition in there is invigorating but often leads to trouble.

Down there away from the gentile historic centre around the colleges, the Cambridge student head count is lower and the folks more grounded. Although Roberto is doing very well, he can easily remember when things were far more difficult and he is all too aware of how easily the money supply can diminish, or disappear completely at any moment.

It is in the White Swan on a Saturday afternoon at the end of the Sky premiership football coverage, that a news item catches his attention. Across the room on the big screen is the same photo of Declan Lewis that came in the envelope.

But it is the headline running across the bottom of the screen that stuns him.

"Three dead and seven injured in Bradford drug war gunfight at gangland funeral"

'Jesus!' whispers Roberto, 'eleven for the price of one.'

That should keep Pete off my back, he thinks.

And so it does.

Newspapers and the television are taken over by this unprecedented event.

The power vacuum in the underworld in Bradford leads to an all-out war between the three families who either seek revenge or to make capital from the resulting tumult.

The Lewis family blame the Asians and the East Europeans blame the West Indians. The crime families on the periphery of the travelling community all display the usual paranoia and over-reaction of the guilty.

The police appear to be taking little or no action, but why should they bother? The criminals are sorting each other out. There are a handful of arrests and another murder linked to the death of Declan Lewis, but Roberto draws great relief and comfort from the fact that no one mentions the victim's heart condition, medication or his visit to the doctors.

Lewis very helpfully chose the moment of a secret meeting with a rival criminal family to succumb to the chemicals that were eating his body and die of suspected heart failure. The timing of his death convinced his family and all who knew him to believe that he had been set up, perhaps poisoned by his rivals.

This was becoming very interesting. It is one thing taking out the odd random nuisance, but quite another level to be taking on criminal families with tentacles everywhere. Not least to see multiple positive outcomes from one untraceable action. Pondering the potential and revelling in the ease of it all excites him.

Up in Bradford, DC Manford is experiencing the same rollercoaster that Roberto had gone through in the days following the Bradford pharmacy fight and the death of Jimmy Murphy and Ahmet Altouyan.

His thoughts travel from deep concern in the first forty-eight hours or so, to relief and incredulity when the dreaded knock on the door doesn't come. The unexpected and immediate success of this initiative in the fight against organised crime leads to the arrest or death of fifteen of the most active and dangerous criminals in the area. The collateral damage spreads. When the opposing criminal families react to the situation, it brings them right out into the open and exposes them to scrutiny that would not have been possible a year earlier. The media attention brings the politicians and the home office into the equation and Pete's colleagues upstairs are able to successfully make the case for increased manpower and resources. It brings world-wide media attention to the problem of inner city organised crime and other forces start to benefit too.

DC Manford now finds himself put forward for local interviews relating to the war on drugs and organised crime by his bosses, keen to take credit for the clear-up rate since the death of Declan Lewis. This brings with it in an increasing public profile for the reluctant copper, which is noticed by national media organisations in London.

The very last thing he or his bosses want is national public exposure, but to decline could jeopardise the local message that is bearing fruit. He does his best in television interviews to press home the case for more resources and to explain where the inquiry is and to appeal for more information. He is tutored by the press office on how to deliver to the camera and implored to keep to the script.

His lowly position is a part of the attraction for the media who become more interested when he goes off message and becomes passionate and angry in the face of hostile questions. Without his permission they begin to market him as the man at the sharp end fighting the good fight without sufficient support from his superiors. It suits their usual *modus operandi* to present a complex and difficult problem in simple terms to fit in with their insatiable hunger for controversial content and simplistic solutions. With an election less than a year away, no Home Secretary wants to be seen to be starving the police of resources.

This is now way out of hand and reaches a tipping point when he is hauled in by the chief constable for a dressing down.

'You're taking every opportunity to criticise the police service. You're a serving officer and bringing the service into disrepute.'

'I am not. I'm helping you to leverage vital money for improved resources; I believe you've been promised an extra four million pounds a year. Is that not what you want? The press office put me up there and you were aware of it.'

'It is not your place to criticise the structure of the force and to involve yourself in matters so way beyond your brief that you have no idea what the hell you are talking about. You're a detective constable for Christ's sake! You're being asked to contribute to the media more often than the boss. It has to stop! Anyway, no one believes that promises of extra funds from politicians leading up to a vote will ever materialise. If you think you've secured extra funds, you are stupid as well as an attention seeking tosser!'

'Every single one of my interviews has been cleared up front by the media strategists in the press office. I've spoken to no one without an email clearing it, I will send you copies.'

'Well it's over now. No more.'

This hypocrisy is too much for Pete. They wanted him to present the force positively and encouraged him to speak to the media, and now they don't like it. He forgets his rank and goes for it.

'What I do know is that I've worked here for 18 years and in that time I've watched the service collapse. You know it, I know it and every serving copper here knows it. Most of the good men and women have left. The ones who remain are so thin on the ground and so demoralised and ill equipped that it's impossible for them to carry out their duties.'

'THAT IS ENOUGH!' shouts his superior 'YOU ARE SUSPENDED PENDING A DISCIPLINARY HEARING AND YOU ARE FORBIDDEN TO SPEAK TO THE MEDIA , IF YOU DISOBEY THIS ORDER YOU WILL BE ON A DISCIPLINARY, DO YOU UNDERSTAND?' Thrusting a piece of paper at Pete, and yelling as loudly as he can he continues, purple faced with rage.

'THE PSD WANT YOU IN ON MONDAY AND THE CHIEF WANTS A REPORT FROM ME WITHIN A WEEK. DO YOU UNDERSTAND WHAT THIS MEANS FOR YOUR CAREER AND YOUR PENSION? YOU ARE IN DANGER OF BREAKING THE OFFICIAL SECRET'S ACT AND THAT WILL BE THE END FOR YOU.'

'I UNDERSTAND THAT YOU HAVE LOST THE PLOT AND ARE UNFIT FOR OFFICE. THAT'S WHAT I FUCKING UNDERSTAND,' Pete shouts back, turning as he approaches the exit.

'COME BACK HERE NOW! COME BACK! I ORDER YOU TO RETURN TO THIS OFFICE!'

Pete hears the tirade continuing as he walks out of the building.

He crosses the road, walks into town across the busy roads to the Jacob's Well and orders a pint.

He realises he has forgotten to leave his radio at the nick but he ignores it and his mobile which are both going off and holds the outstretched palm of his hand in the face of the landlord to ensure he doesn't even try to engage him. Both devices continue to go off one after the other. He only picks up when he notices an incoming call from his pal Adrian.

'What the fuck did you say to Wiggy?'

'Meet me in the Well as soon as you can get away.'

As Adrian walks in, twenty minutes later, he hears Pete say to the landlord.

'Yes yes I know that but what the fuck can I do about it? No, seriously. What the fuck do you want me to do? Buy the city? Become Prime Minister and move the houses of fucking parliament here?'

As they move as far away from the bar as they can and beyond earshot of the landlord Adrian asks 'What were you on about? Leave him alone! If you get barred from here we have nowhere else to drink.'

'Yeah, I know, but for fuck's sake have you heard him banging on. I swear I'll do time if he speaks to me again.'

'Forget that.' says Adrian looming over his pal trying to get him to focus on more pressing matters by trying a serious face.

'You have a big, big problem. His Royal Wiggyness has gone completely crackers. He even said you should be arrested if you won't come in to speak to him!'

They both laugh at this. It's no secret that the divisional commander was out of his depth in the role, promoted way above his ability when his two predecessors ended their careers early in various levels of disgrace.

The depletion of the force and early exodus of the talented left few quality coppers with over five years in the job.

'I'm not concerned and I won't be intimidated. He can't arrest me or even fire me without having a disciplinary hearing. We've just facilitated the biggest blow against organised crime that has been struck in the area for decades, and on top of that helped to secure funding to expand the fight back not only in Bradford but all over the country. I'm going to resign so it doesn't matter.' Peter downs his pint.

'No you don't understand, you twat. It's worse than that! He *really does* want you arrested on sight. I shouldn't be in here talking to you.'

'What for?' asks Pete momentarily concerned.

'Insubordination, bringing the force into disrepute, organising a strike..'

'Hang the fuck on a minute. Organising a strike? What are you on about? There aren't enough of us to go on strike and it's against the fucking law anyway. I haven't spoken to anyone about striking, nor would I.'

Adrian continues, 'The whole nick are backing you and say if you are not re-instated, they will work to rule. It's spreading too. I've just had a call from GMP and they're having the same kind of problems. If they hear about this they will too,' says Adrian excitedly.

'What? What are we going to do now?'

'What do you mean "we"?' jokes Adrian. 'You dug this massive hole, not me!'

'Who took that bullet through me trouser leg for you? Equipped with no more than a Parker pen, a notebook and a plastic torch.'

'Yeah, but if I hadn't thrown a chair at him and booted him in the nuts, you wouldn't be able to play the piano now.'

'I can't play the fucking piano.'

'Well exactly. Get the beers in. Let's have a think.'

Pete was sorry he couldn't tell his oldest pal on the force the full story.

It was just one more thing that was dragging him down.

They had joined the job together and worked closely on and off sharing the same dark humour. Over the years they had honed their double act to perfection and bounced off each other as sharply as Morecombe and Wise and without a script.

What he didn't know was that Adrian had already read the contents of the envelope. This was different now. This mission had been completed and Pete was trying to protect Adrian by not informing him of the link to Roberto but he was wasting his time worrying.

Pete's fear of being poisoned by his nemesis is now nothing to the possibility of him being either sacked and possibly jailed on the one hand or killed by the mob on the other.

'Listen pal there's something I have to tell you,' says Adrian firmly but quietly.

'I opened the envelope and read the whole thing.'

'You twat! I thought I could trust you to obey a simple instruction!'

'I did, I looked after your envelope and didn't grass you up when I read the contents. I worked out why you were so interested in obtaining Lewis's medical records. It's that pharmacist with the hot girlfriend and the fancy motor isn't it? You somehow arranged for him to put a Mickey Fin in his tablet didn't you? You forget, I know you too well.' He stands in front of Pete and addresses him directly.

'I figured this was serous when you went up to sheep shagging country when you should've been here working. I don't just mean on to someone else's girl, which you obviously were, understandably.'

Knowing that denying it would be fruitless, he replies 'Are you supposed to bring me in then; like in a cowboy film, is that the idea?'

'Don't be fucking stupid' says Adrian, genuinely offended.

'You know I won't do that. You don't realise I am 100 percent with you. We all are.'

'WE ALL ARE??? WHAT THE HELL DOES THAT MEAN? WHO DID YOU TELL??' yells Pete, now panicking.

'Calm down you tit, I didn't tell anyone.'

'Calm down? How can I calm down? No, you calm down. You don't tell me to calm down, I tell you to calm down and if you tell me to calm down it's because I have told you to tell me to calm down and not before!'

'Alright alright. Wiggy will calm down anyway, he has to. Otherwise he is going to lose control of the dressing room.'

'What would happen then?' wonders Pete.

'I don't know, probably bring the army in like they did when the fire brigade went on strike and we had to drive round at thirty miles an hour in front of those Green Goddesses.'

'So you worked it out then?' asks Pete ruefully.

'Aye'

'You are a detective as well then, after all.'

'As well as what? '

'An extremely thirsty man and frequent downer of beverages.'

'Steady on old chap!' complains Adrian, well used to the abuse.

'Anyway, I am starving. Shall we go to the Kashmir? Hey I've just had a fucking brilliant idea. Why don't we invite Wiggy for a curry and a chat?' asks Pete with a smirk.

They both burst out laughing at the ridiculous suggestion that the Divisional Commander would socialise with them outside the office, let alone agree to an off-the-record meeting with a feral officer who could easily bring down the force and end his career. Despite the unlikeness of success, they pause, staring at each other and shout, 'Do it!' in unison.

Pete rings the commander and after a long conversation he confounds them by agreeing to meet over a curry.

The conversation begins in a very heated and confrontational manner.

'Manford your career is over.'

'You are correct, Sir, I've had enough and your threat is two years too late for me to give a shit, frankly.'

Eventually after exchanging blows they remember that they are on the same side, both struggling with their respective briefs and over a couple of hours and several bottles of wine, they gradually begin to see eye to eye.

'Look, Manford you know that there is a reorganisation on the way. Large investigations will soon be handled by a new Homicide and Major Enquiry Team and if you want to go forward in this job you should be looking to keep your nose clean so you can fit into that. I'm telling you that this will all be reorganised for the better very soon.'

There has to be a compromise and so Pete agrees to take a desk job researching cold cases, collating 'Taken into consideration' admissions, working with the scenes-of-crimes teams and working with the application of new pathology and DNA technology to old and unsolved cases. It does enough for peace to break out for the time being.

'This deal has to include you being banned from working outside the station and speaking to the media on any police issue or having any media profile whatsoever. And you must undertake to refer any enquiries to me and keep your head down,' his boss says, who is now almost paternally avuncular as the wine soaks in.

In exchange, Pete avoids any censure or blight on his record. It is a gentleman's agreement that won't stand up to scrutiny if it comes to an inquiry, but as Pete knows he's skating on very thin ice regarding the Declan Lewis case, he takes it on the chin and stays out of the way of trouble.

He revives his music connections as a distraction, profiting from the more regular hours of desk-based work to have a life outside the job.

Eventually the media move on and forget him and the force quietens down enough for them all to get on with the job.

21 Mundus Transit Et Concupiscentia Eius

Roberto comes home early to get a shower. He has been out delivering prescriptions and Hazel has Suede's "Coming Up" turned up to 11. He is in the room before she is aware that he is home and she has a bundle of his files spread out over the floor.

She found them in an old holdall by accident.

She hadn't had the time to study them to see what it was all about, but Roberto's actions tell her that it is something significant that he doesn't want her to read.

He immediately flies into a rage and pushes her to the ground before quickly gathering up the papers and shoving them back into the cardboard files.

'What the fuck are you doing? This is nothing to do with you.'

She is shocked senseless by his outburst and for the first time is in his company when he loses control of himself.

'Rob what the fuck?' she says as she gets up.

He lunges at her and she dives behind the sofa.

Hazel grabs her coat and races out of the flat.

She takes refuge at a friend's flat and turns off her phone.

Later in the evening she switches it back on and eventually takes one of his many calls. She allows him to explain and although on the face of it lets him believe his charm offensive has brought her round and it's all ok, it isn't.

It was a turning point. For the first time she begins to question who he actually is. She doesn't believe what he tells her about his reaction but lets it go to give herself time to work out where she is with him.

Back in the north Pete is still side-lined. His requests to resume work as a front line detective are rebuffed again and again. He eventually realises they are keeping him in limbo until he voluntarily leaves or retires. If they sack him he will attract more attention from the media and he will be free to speak his mind. While still in the force, he can be controlled.

He seeks one last meeting with the boss, but it comes to nothing. For the tenth time in six months he is told that something is happening soon and to be patient. He has now lost belief.

Later the same week his partner asks for an urgent meeting in the Jacob's Well.

'I am leaving the job,' says Adrian quietly, staring at the floor. 'I've had it now.'

'What's eating you? Don't leave me here fighting on my own for fuck's sake.'

'Well you know I was shot in the leg and vilified for not supporting the force's defence against Katie's compensation claim. I claimed nothing for myself. It was her prerogative to go for compo and good luck to her; but I wanted to keep out of it, put it behind me, support neither side and move on.

'...News is they're saying that declining to help the force and not giving evidence against her to prevent her claiming compensation is reflecting very badly on the "future prospects for the advancement of my career." They're threatening me, the bastards. The final straw today is that I have just received a gift from the police federation for my trouble.'

'Why are you bringing all this up now?'

Adrian throws an envelope on the bar.

'Take a look,' he challenges.

Pete takes out a voucher.

'I kid you not: twenty-five quid to spend in M&S for taking a bullet!'

'I've got more bad news for you, Drain. It's twenty, not twenty-five'

'What? I would have stayed on for twenty-five, but twenty quid, that's an insult that is. I am leaving!' says Adrian smiling for the first time.

'I've just been told that I won't be able to put in for promotion because I'm not committed to the job. They're right, I'm not. I was, but no longer. I'm off to run my parent's hotel and to do a bit of freelance detective work here and there. But before I go, I have something your mate might be able to sort out.'

'Which mate?'

'You know, old pill fiddler.'

'He is NOT my mate.'

'Yeah, whatever. Anyway, it's the Flaxtons!'

'Who?'

'You know, the Flaxtons, the pikey twats who prey on rich old ladies and lonely farmers. I've been looking into them since they fixed a tile on old Ma Quarton's roof and took her down the building society to clean her out?'

'At least 6 years since they painted her roof with brown emulsion paint and told her they had re-roofed it, took her bank book, forged her signature and so on.'

'Oh yeah, twenty grand for painting the roof tiles the bastards. That background info any good? Been updating you on them for the last year since I was confined to the barracks.'

'Of course you have.'

'And now I am this close to nailing them,' says Adrian holding his thumb and forefinger in a calliper pose about three millimetres apart and pausing to drive his point home.

'So? Get on with it.'

'Anyway, they seem to have a sixth sense for the kind of vulnerable people who live alone, usually in the countryside, particularly those with piles of cash stashed at home, or in building societies or whatever.

'They turn up, lay tarmac over mud and weeds and spread it out until it's thinner than a bat's wing, fix a roof that doesn't need fixing and ram in a massive invoice.

'If it gets paid, they return a few weeks later and either straightforward rob the poor buggers or stitch them up to hand over a pile of dough from their accounts on some pretext about urgent extra work or an unpaid invoice, bounced cheque or whatever. I have to put up with them laughing at me in the street. I was standing in the fish shop the other day being openly mocked by one of them about our inability to stop them, the arrogant bastard. He left his feral son in the truck and the evil little shit spent the whole time sticking two fingers up at me and waving an axe. He can't be more than 12 for fucks sake!'

'So what's this leading to?'

'Why don't we bring in your mate, do a Declan Lewis on them? Look at the result there! We reckon thirty criminals are out of circulation and God knows how many crimes won't happen now because of that. It has to be the most successful strike against organised crime ever to happen in this area by miles.'

'No. I don't know if it's wise to try that again,' cautions Pete. 'Aren't we best just leaving it at that? Is this big enough to justify risking everything after we got away with it last time? And by the way I've told you before. He's *not* my mate. Just talking about it here is enough to have us cuffed. You aren't wired are you?'

'Don't be a knob. Of course not,' wails Adrian offended again by the suggestion.

'No, I concur. Up until today, I would've agreed with you but three very very significant things have happened...'

'Four if you count you buying a round at last,' chips in Pete.

'Be serious for a moment will you? As if there is a snowball's chance in hell of that! ...One: I have just found out my career is going nowhere from here so I am leaving.

'Two: This gang who have got away with millions in the past five years have just taken 400k's worth of antiques and cash from an old dear in Bolton Abbey and tied her up and left her for dead. She's ninety by the way, in hospital and they say she's done for. Drove an ambulance in the war, took in foster kids, ran the village hall and played the piano at the pantomime every year. Terrorised her and beat her until she handed over the key to her safe, didn't they? We know it's them. Their vehicles were seen; its same M.O. and we got prints.

'Three: I've found out that they get their fish and chips from Peel Plaice in Burley at 6.30 every Friday. They send in one of their family; he drives a red pickup and takes away 22 portions of fish and chips, sometimes more. I stumbled across this a couple of weeks ago. I was starving and dropped in to the chippy. It's amazing what you hear just standing in a queue. It took Jack and Edna a lifetime to deal with the Flaxtons' order and by the time I got out of there I was related to half of the people waiting. In fact, I'm sure one of them grew a beard before he got his supper.

'…Anyway, Jack told the whole shop about their regular Friday order and an idiot in front of me said out loud what the whole village knows already, namely that it's during their Friday fish supper that they have a share out and arrange the following week's activities. He even claimed to have been there, to know them and to be able to get anything you want from drugs to stolen tellies and cars; you name it.'

'Slow down Gonzales, take a breath and have a pint.'

'So I felt like cuffing the maggot on the spot, but I knew who he was and I told the gypsy patronisation unit and the gaffer what I heard, but he won't let us take them on. We don't have the resources to do it without help. Upstairs have looked at it and done feasibility and a health and safety audit on the idea and said "We need a hundred strong force to get through the fencing and ensure everyone's safety. Never mind deal with the dogs, film it, round them up and take them in before they leg it across the fields.'"

'They *will* fight. It's a job for the army really,' chips in Pete.

'If we catch them together we'll save the force thousands of man hours and millions of quid. They're like locusts turning up all over the North. We can't stop 'em.

'It should never have been allowed to get to this point. They should have been tackled years ago. It goes right back to when Billie Flaxton was in property and joined the Freemasons. There lies the seed of this. They became immune and allowed to expand to the point where their organisation is too big to be brought down.

'Rumour is, our gaffer stayed at their Spanish holiday gaff every year when he was in the ranks as all the top brass did back then. If we don't round them up on the spot - and all of them mind, they will be gone and we won't be able to establish who is who and they will blame whoever isn't there. If we don't hold them until charged they will vanish.'

'So why now?' asks Pete hoping that Adrian will get to the point before the bar closes.

'The gaffer banned me from tackling them. We just don't have the manpower. All that shite about fighting for the resources we need was forgotten as soon as the election was over, surprise, surprise; and they got you out of the way. You were the only hope of getting some attention for this problem. It looked good for a few months after Declan Lewis, but it all disappeared when the press forgot us.

'I have to walk away from this job and let them get on with it; there is nothing I can do. That being said I wondered if your mate could get something in the fish and chips and sort the fucking lot of them out in one go.'

'How many times? He is *not* my fucking mate for a start. Anyway, how the fuck does he spike their fish and chips?' asks

Pete, not enjoying the thought of taking on another, larger mission.

'The batter. That's how you do it.'

'What you mean? Put a plant in the chippy?'

'No, old Wanky Jack wouldn't play ball; it's just him and his wife in there, we should intercept the fish and chips on the way and swap them.'

'Whaaaaaaat ? Hide in a layby with some fish and chips and swap them at a fucking road block or something? Have you completely lost it?' retorts a now very exasperated Pete.

'I don't know, but we can find a way. I can't just leave and wave goodbye to five years of work on these bastards. I have all the dirt I need on them but I'm told to leave it because of budget cuts. Can you believe it? Help me do something useful before I go.' Adrian pleads. 'In any case, mate, I don't need to tell you that I know how you persuaded that chemist twat to do your dirty work for you.'

'What exactly are you saying?' replies Pete, unnerved by his friend's darker tone.

'I'm saying I want you to do for me what he did for you. You know I could make it hard for you.'

'You bastard, I thought I could trust you.'

'You can, but I need you to help me strike the same blow that you did. I'll go speak to him myself if you won't.'

'No, for fuck's sake don't do that, you might put Hazel in danger. Let it lie will you.'

'Think about it. We could check out with another big success. Something which would strike a blow to these bastards who we have to just watch taking the piss while we're pushed around and sent on gender awareness courses for trying to have a laugh and given twenty-five quid M&S vouchers for being shot.'

'Twenty quid I keep telling you. Anyway, I *will* think about it. I'm on my way out too, I've taken a place on a round-the-world boat trip; I'm off in a month.'

'What? Leaving or career break?'

'I dunno yet. Depends. Can't see myself coming back to this shit, but you never know. By then the whole thing could easily have collapsed and a new start may be underway.'

'That's all the more reason to do this. It could be our goodbye job.'

'Leave it with me. I'll have a ponder.'

Pete fancies an excuse to get near to Hazel again. It's been over a year since they met on the Cam Bridge. He has thought of little else. She haunts his waking thoughts and is the subject of his dreams. He had resolved to get away and forget, but it wasn't working.

Pete goes for a hike over Beamsley Beacon and up the Wharfe to Burnsall on his next day off to have a think. He decides that Adrian is probably right, it was worth a shot. If they could pull it off, it could save many years of police time for dozens of coppers. As he walks up the river through the Bolton Abbey Estate admiring the superbly restored barns and farmhouses, he begins to see some sense in taking the opportunity to mastermind one last strike against dangerous criminals rather than just walk away and leave Bradford and perhaps all of West Yorkshire to suffer.

He speaks to Adrian again. 'I'll see if I can arrange something. I'll be back on Thursday. Be ready for Friday; but I can't promise anything.'

Roberto has his back to the door when Pete walks in to the shop. Pete clicks his fingers and shouts 'SO! We are back in the room.'

Roberto swings round when he hears his ex-wife's favourite taunt.

He stands in silence staring at Pete trying to compute how this can be happening.

Pete relishes Roberto's discomfort and is urgently keen to press home the advantage of surprise.

'No, no, not you! Not you! No way. I'm not going up there again. My life has turned around.'

'It doesn't work like that. You behave yourself for fifty years, murder someone, then behave yourself for another fifty years and you are a hundred year old murderer. There is no statute of limitations.'

'Look you can't do this. I paid my dues and helped you out. You can't keep turning up whenever you have a problem. What do you want now?'

'How is Hazel?'

'She's fine. Stay away from her.'

'Where is she?'

'Fuck off will you and leave us alone.'

Roberto looks older than Pete remembers. He is still a stylish bloke, dressed like a younger man from a distance he looks in good shape but close up it is easy to see he is a worried man.

'What's up with you Roberto? Pressure getting to you is it? Don't know when the knock on the door is coming?'

'You don't worry me anymore. I've followed your story in the press. Your management had to shut you up didn't they?!'

'Don't believe what you read. I've been busier than ever on covert work and I have a job for you.'

'Yeah, right! Who the fuck do you think you are? The Six fucking Million Dollar Man? The Equaliser? Do me a favour.'

'Ok ok, I'll see you in the Falcon usual time in the morning.'

'Where did you say Hazel was today?' He taunts.

'Fucking stay away from her. I will not be in the Falcon, I have a pharmacy to run.'

'Just put a note on the door like you usually do when you're off your face.'

'I don't drink.'

'Whaat?'

'Not for six months.'

'Well, it's doing you no fucking good at all, that's all I can say. You've aged badly.' Pete knows how to stab the urbane and preening narcissist.

'What happened six months ago then? To stop you drinking?'

Roberto's silence is all Pete needs.

'She's left you, hasn't she?'

'Leave her alone and fuck off will you. We're just dealing with some issues and the last thing we need is you sticking your fucking oar in again.'

'The last thing *you* need, you mean.'

'Just fuck off.'

'11am tomorrow. The Falcon.'

Pete leaves the shop and goes up to Hugh's stall to find out what's been going on.

If Hugh won't tell him, he'll make St James College his next stop.

It's his lucky day. Hazel is running the stall. She has decided to disobey her college's ban on her working there and their insistence that she devotes all her time to her studies. She decides that she likes working there and will continue until they catch her.

Unlike Roberto, time and their split has done her no harm at all. Her beauty he expects and it doesn't disappoint, but her overpowering persona and presence is stronger and more irresistible than he remembers. She looks like an advertiser's dream woman from a 1970's chocolate commercial. Blue striped apron tied in a bow over a white vest, her hair tied up and her long slender legs shrink-wrapped in tight jeans.

He takes up residence on a wall opposite the stall and waits while she works her way through the polite queue of foreign students, London media-types and tweedy retired dons. He doesn't have to wait long. She looks up and sees him, drops the bread she's holding and runs across the road tossing her apron in the vague direction of the stall behind her.

Hazel flings her arms around him and holds him tightly.

A flock of pigeons play peck football with the discarded loaf.

'Take what you want and leave some money,' she shouts over her shoulder at the customers. Such is the good will that Hugh has cultivated by decades of his generosity, again they do as instructed.

Their clinch again lasts forever. Einstein once explained his theory of relativity as "five minutes sitting on a hot stove seems like a lifetime and five minutes in the company of a beautiful, woman passes in a second." For Pete, five minutes in the arms of Hazel Anderson passes in a second but he had waited a lifetime for it and he would remember this moment for the rest of his days.

'Where have you been and why didn't you come for me?' She demands.

'But you are with Roberto down here. You could have rung me anytime. Have you left him?'

'No he left me. Well kicked me out in fact.'

'You're kidding. Why?'

'Oh, I'll tell you later, where are you staying?'

'Later? When? I've no idea yet, I'll text you when I book in somewhere?'

'I finish at five and I have a lecture at six. So come to the north gate of St James at 8.30. And stay away from Roberto if you know what's good for you. He's unwell at the moment. Really not well at all.'

Pete leaves her to it but feels better than he has for as long as he can remember.

For the first time since he had met Hazel, he can believe that they might one day be together. But why hadn't she contacted him?

He wonders what could be wrong with Roberto, he looked like shit.

But so would I, he thinks. *...wait a minute did she say he threw her out?*

Pete meanders around the Cambridge streets. On the corner of Bene't Street he comes across a large crowd surrounding a small man in a wheelchair. It is the unveiling of the Corpus Clock. Pete watches as the strange locust-like beast that Professor Hawking introduces as 'The Chronophage the *eater of time'* for the first occasion in public view, it leaps forward above the huge gold clock face to gobble up some seconds.

'Mundus transit et concupiscentia eius,' he continues one word at a time *'The world passeth away and the lust thereof.'* It takes half an hour for the stunningly bright but physically challenged genius to say via his voice machine.

'Designed to be accurate for two hundred years and containing six newly patented mechanisms. It's a polyandrous marriage of 17thand 21st century engineering, and the artistic genius and entrepreneurial philanthropy of a talented and grateful Corpus alumnus.' That Pete should pass that way just then whilst trying to eat some time, is somewhat ironic.

'The world passeth away and the lust thereof,' he mutters. He has more than enough lust for life. He now wants it to be spent with Hazel and away from the North.

He browses the second hand bookshops and has coffee in the subterranean haven of Carrington's Café under the street.

He avoids the Falcon and the White Swan in case he bumps into Roberto and then falls asleep in a park by the river and dreams the afternoon away waking only at dusk when the early evening chill and some light drizzle reaches his skin and makes him shiver.

He books into the Varsity Hotel on Flaxtons Lane off Bridge St, for no other reason than it was the Flaxton family whose demise he was here to engineer and the fact that there should be a hotel on a street bearing that name, makes it seems like a day when the stars are aligned correctly for the first time in years.

The Hotel is five-star and way out of his league but seems to confirm that it is his lucky day. He gets a small discount on a double room for being on his own, which he needs.

He showers, changes and catches up with the news, and texts Hazel saying 'Wish you were here,' but he is still really killing time. The day of the Chronophage. Counting down the moments till he can see the woman he loves who has just for the first time shown real sober affection for him and perhaps the hint of a future.

The beast swallows time; far too slowly for him.

After a lifetime, 8.30 finally arrives and she is there. They walk the streets hand in hand rehearsing what it might be like to be a normal couple and pick an Italian restaurant at the furthest end of Magdalene Street, as far as possible without leaving the town centre, from Roberto's flat. They take a quiet table and Pete, in Yorkshire form gets straight to the point.

'So what the hell is going on with you? I've torn myself in two trying to stop myself from coming to see you because that's what you wanted, but you still text me.'

'Look, it's very complicated. Roberto and I haven't been getting along too well recently. For some time I've been aware that there is something big haunting him. He's been distant, quite absent, and it's getting worse. I once took it for mysterious edginess and I like being with a man with hidden levels. Melancholy and brooding contemplation *is* interestingly sexy. But in time you get curious, you want to dig down. Even though I'm aware that by finding out what's there can kill the magic and can be disappointing. But with him, the more I dig, the more he tightens up. The more I probe, the less he will tell me, which drives me mad and us apart. I wanted to help him. He said no-one can help.'

Despite the subject matter, he is entranced anew by her animated delivery, her earnest furrowed brow and propeller hand gestures emphasising her message.

'I wondered if he missed his kids, then I wondered why he didn't. I just know something happened before he came to West Fell - but I don't know what. I know now that I was trying to escape from my grief over my mother. It nearly broke my father. And my ex! What did I do to him? Did I kill him? I treated him so badly. I can't sleep sometimes. I should have dealt with it long before I got involved with Rob. I was just using him. I don't recognise myself from that time. I was too spaced out to care what I was doing.

'I thought it was just me. Now I know Roberto was escaping too, but I didn't then and I just can't get to the bottom of what it was.'

'I was searching for something there and I found it,' says Pete, 'But I also found you and I haven't been able to think straight since. Don't blame yourself for all that. I suspect that you were taking bad stuff you probably shouldn't have been without being aware, but Roberto certainly would have known what it was.'

Hazel looks at the floor. 'I'm so sorry; I just don't know what to do.'

Pete doesn't want to hear any more about her feelings about her relationship with Roberto. He doesn't want to hear that she wants to fix it.'

'Anyway, why did he throw you out?'

'He came home and found me reading through his paperwork and he went berserk. It was so out of character. He hit me. I know it was in the spur of the moment and in shock at finding me looking through his stuff, but I won't stay with a man capable of such violence, I just won't.'

'What did you find?'

'Nothing at all, but I now know there is something he doesn't want me to find, something he will risk losing me to keep from me.'

'So you left?'

'No, I didn't get round to it, I meant to but I was weak.'

'But you said you couldn't stay with a .....'

'Oh shit, don't judge me!' she snaps 'I was trying to leave him, I really was, I just didn't get round to it.'

'So he threw you out?'

'No he didn't, not then.'

'So you left?'

'No, I didn't'

'So come on. What happened?'

'Just give me a chance will you? What is this? A fucking interview under caution?' she hisses and kicks him hard on the shin showing a strain he hadn't seen her display before.

'Ow! Hazel. I'm sorry. In your own time,' he looks at his watch. 'Interview suspended at 8.45pm. Suspect becoming violent.....Really I'm sorry, do go on in your own time,' he says gently putting his hand reassuringly on her wrist and smiling.

She kicks him again.

'Ow that fucking hurts. That's my dancing career over.'

'You're a northerner. It's unlikely you have ever been happy enough to dance.'

Pete rubs his leg and was now genuinely hurt by the truth and the pointy toe of a handmade CHL leather boot.

'Where was I? Oh yeah anyway, I have been kind of shagging a younger guy at my college.' I couldn't resist, she is sheepishly embarrassed but keen to be honest. 'He was so sweet and called me darling. It was only twice and I didn't want it to continue. His arms were strong and he was so bright, but do you know what clinched it for him?'

'Not yet.'

'Shut up and learn! For the first time I was the older, wiser one looked up to. He adored me.'

'Hazel, everyone looks up to you,' Pete has a go at inappropriate heightist humour.

'Oh shut up, I said,' retorts Hazel displaying more of a harder edge than he knew.

'I know it was wrong, but as Rob and I drifted apart, I justified it to myself that for all I know his hidden life, his secret could be another family, another woman, or maybe he's a freemason... Who knows? But the point is, once you reach a hurdle you can't get over, a brick wall of silence, you feel distant. You feel the bond between you is weakened.'

She leans forward and looks him hard in the eyes. Her chiselled face earnest, electrified and vibrant, making Pete feel like holding it in his hands and kissing her there and then. Her words dampen his spirit though. 'I love Rob but I never want to be with a man who can't be completely honest; so for the first time I began to see an end to us. I want a family one day, but I can't have one with a man who holds big important secrets, I just can't. I don't care what the secrets are, do you understand?'

You would care; it really would make a difference if you knew what his secret was. Pete has no idea what to say. He sadly stares at the floor.

To fill the silence, Hazel presses on. 'So you see, we were just passing time from then on. As I say, I love him and we have fun together. More than I could ever imagine with anyone else. He helped me grow into who I am. But until he can tell me that there is nothing hidden and I can believe him, we don't have the basis of a stable and committed relationship. So that's why I allowed myself to play out. That's the way it is, I will have my own secrets in a relationship that is not whole.

'So yes, he threw me out when he caught me in bed with my little beau. He wasn't worth the trauma, but I hope you understand. We needed to part. It's just unfortunate that it happened that way. I might add that Rob has had a few months to redeem himself and come clean and I would have been up for it. But now, I'm not so sure. If he comes to me when he's ready to open up and gives me full disclosure then perhaps we can do something to patch it up. Sadly, I think it might be too late now. It's on a knife edge.'

'You don't need to justify yourself to me. I won't judge you. Maybe he just can't tell you things, maybe he can't tell anyone what has happened to him,' says Pete not too helpfully.

Pete is heartbroken now because he knows he can't ever be her partner. Not now she has defined her rules of engagement. Pete now has the same kind of secrets that he would have to keep from her too and he understands that if either he or Roberto are truthful to her, which is what she deserves, then they are going to jail. It's as simple as that.

Is she prepared to wait fifteen, twenty years? Why should she wait? She has the whole world at her feet. Why would she wait for a murderer; him or Roberto?

'What's up Pete? No, don't cry, what's the matter with you?... You know something, don't you?'

'No, I have to go, I'm sorry, I shouldn't have come, I must go...'

Pete rushes out of the restaurant throwing some cash towards the waiter and runs away giving her no chance to follow. He can never tell her the truth.

Back at the Varsity he downs a double whisky in the bar, then empties the mini bar in his room. He sobs and yells into his mattress and wishes himself dead. So near to winning this woman but he knows he never can. He loves her too much to lie to her and he can't ever tell her the truth. He is broken.

He falls asleep and awakes before dawn. His head is pounding and he decides to walk the streets until breakfast. It is raining heavily and still very dark. He slips out of the hotel into the narrow lane and quietly clicks the front door shut.

A cold wet hand grabs his wrist tightly. He swings around in shock. It is Hazel. Soaked to the skin, freezing cold and red eyed from tears, her face has changed shape. It is taught with a rage he has never seen in her nor imagined possible.

'Tell me what the fuck is going on. Tell me. NOW!' She screams. She holds a knife to his throat and presses it hard into his skin. 'Tell me before I fucking kill you!'

She pushes it forward and draws a shocking amount of blood. It's only a nick, but the immediate claret flow shocks them both. She drops the knife. She is no killer, just demented by frustration and fortunately the power went out of her lunge before it made contact. They look at each other and she throws her arms around him sobbing.

They stumble towards the hotel, he tells the startled night porter, with a beaming smile 'It looks like the wife is joining me after all. Don't worry, cut myself shaving.'

Reaching his room, his blood soaking them both. They fall onto the bed and cling together. Hazel is shivering and crying.

'Help me; help me understand what is happening. I don't know what to do,' she pleads. She beats his chest and tears at his hair pleading with him to come clean whilst he fights to wrap a towel around his neck to stem the flow.

'For fuck's sake! Calm down and let me sort out this wound or you'll have to explain why you're in bed with a corpse without even checking in properly.'

The concerned porter knocks on the door.

'I'm so sorry for the disturbance, I would be grateful if you could let me sort this out and I will explain in the morning.'

'Do you want me call an ambulance?'

'No honestly, it's fine. Just a nick. Here take this,' says Pete emptying his wallet into the man's hand.

'I'll come and see you later this morning. Now if you wouldn't mind, my wife needs some sleep, thank you so much for your concern, good night.'

He eventually calms her and pulls the covers over her and they fall asleep in each other's arms.

They awake to Pete's alarm. Hazel pulls him to her and pleads again 'Tell me.' as if their sleep had not intervened. 'You have to tell me, you bastard.'

'Ow fuck. Stop hanging on to my fucking head, its coming off already since you cut me,' cries Pete holding her away from him, exaggerating his injury to deflect attention from her persistent line of attack.

'I will. Look, I'm meeting Roberto at 11 o'clock this morning and I'll talk to him about this. After that I will meet you anywhere you want me to, anytime; and I will tell you everything, I promise.'

'Why not now? Why not here, now?'

'I can't; I just can't'.

'What has he done that's so terrible?' She looks into his eyes scared, confused and angry.

'Please trust me until this afternoon. I will take this room for another night and give you a key.'

'No way! Stop treating me like some frail sap in a Victorian frock. I'm coming with you to that meeting, then neither of you can bullshit me any longer.'

'Okay, okay, come.'

'Good. Now I want some breakfast. How is your neck by the way?'

'It's fine. Looks worse than it is, with the blood and the rain. Thanks for asking,' he grins. 'I'll have to get it dressed. Can you recommend a chemist's?' He jokes.

She takes a shower while he organises room service.

It gives him no pleasure to be in her company in such intimate circumstances. He is torn in two, fighting to contain his infatuation and the strong desire to tell her everything. There is only one thing he can now do and that is to change the time or location of the meeting.

He is heading up the lane into the market square by the time she comes out of the shower. His note just says. *"Sorry, see you later. Apologise to room service for the blood for me will you?"*

She texts him, 'I'm going to sleep now you fucking coward. If you don't come back I won't come looking for you.' There is no 'x'

He barges into the pharmacy startling Steph, the assistant.

'Emergency. Please just leave for half an hour.'

When she hesitates, he flashes his warrant card. This is a mistake. He had so far kept his occupation secret in Cambridge. Now he can be identified.

He turns the door sign to 'closed' and drags Roberto up the stairs into the flat above the shop. Pete is slightly shorter, but perhaps two stone heavier and has no trouble manhandling Roberto. His strength comes from his rage and pain. He is out of control now.

'I saw Hazel last night.'

'I told you to stay away from her. What did you tell her?'

'Nothing. I want you to do one more thing for me and then I will leave you and her alone forever. That's the deal. You do one more job for me then that's it, you have my word that I will leave you to tell her whatever you want to. It will no longer be my problem.'

Roberto is sprawled across the floor with Pete's foot on his head.

'She knows nothing of any of this. I've protected her from that. I can't tell her for her own sake.'

For the first time Pete sees something human almost even noble in Roberto.

The rage subsides. *He is right.* By not weakening and telling her the truth, he protects her from any future prosecution. She didn't have any part in the hideous path that Roberto had taken; if she had known of it and did nothing, she would be condemned and wouldn't be able to avoid jail assisting an offender.

Pete had endured her anger for only a few hours and Roberto had to live with this permanently. He now understands why the man is losing his charm and good looks and ageing before his eyes but you can't expect peace if you cause mayhem.

'Karma, isn't that what they call it?' Pete keeps his foot in place.

'What do you want me to do?'

'I want something I can put on my fish and chips.'

'What?'

'I want to poison 22 portions of fish and chips.'

'How?'

'You're the expert. I don't know.' He says lifting his foot from Roberto's head and allowing him to get up. The salt? Vinegar? Batter? Fish? Potatoes? It's not like there are a hundred ingredients. It's simple northern fodder.'

'Don't tell me the location. Salt and vinegar. That's how to do it.'

'Ok, so you give me something to put in the salt. It's for...'

'SShhhh don't tell me. I don't want to know who, where or why. Anyway the shop would be instantly closed down once the first person goes down. That person could be anyone. How are you going to prevent it being administered to the wrong people before your targets get to eat it? You can't.'

'I'll worry about that.'

'I need to put you right on something,' Roberto continues. 'You seem to be labouring under a false premise, namely that I am capable, even if I were willing, of producing from nowhere, a magic potion, which can pass as table salt, lethal enough to kill twenty odd people at once.

'Perhaps it's the sign above the door which says this has been a dispensing Chemists since 1851 which may have lead you to the wrong conclusion. I don't have sacks of base material and shelves heaving with bottles of potions which I have collected myself to invent my own fucking potions.

'The prescriptions here are dispensed under specific guidelines from products supplied by factories which are using traceable and verifiable ingredients. Most often, all I do is pass on packets of pills unopened. Do you think the witches of Cawdor are out the back inventing all this stuff? In many ways I'm no different to Hugh in the market square, a middle man between manufacturer and customer. What you're asking is technically impossible.'

'Bullshit!' spits Pete. 'You're forgetting that I know your history. Now you are here with your own empire, it must be much easier. I don't need to remind you it's already been market tested. That's the only reason I'm here.'

'No it's a totally different proposition,' pleads Roberto. 'Poisoning someone's food is a million times harder than tweaking a prescription. How am I supposed to make all these people eat what is put in front of them? What about damage to the chef or the waitress who steals some of what's left of the meal?'

'I don't know which chip shop *you* use' replies Pete 'but where I'm from, a fish supper on a Friday is still a treat and it is not prepared by a fucking chef, you ponce. It's wrapped in yesterday's free newspaper by a man who's ability to avoid first degree burns whilst standing on a slippery tiled floor next to a vat of boiling fat is his fortune. That and knowing when to reach in to remove the fish. Usually while treating his customers to an array of bigoted opinions. He is no more a chef than I am... Anyway, let *me* worry about how it is delivered and who has access to it.

'The salt and vinegar. We'll swap the dispensers. It needs to be odourless, invisible and release a terminal dose after a delay. And I need it in Yorkshire before Friday.'

'You don't want much.'

'You can do it.'

'I don't actually think I can. Not overnight. I'm not sure it is possible to come up with anything that meets your requirements and I'm not sure I intend to help you,' says Roberto attempting to bring the conversation to a close.

'Look we both know that you can come up with something. Cambridge is bursting at the seams with the knowledge and expertise you need. You can work it out in the library of Corpus or ask one of the boffins in the Falcon to look into it.'

'You know I can't ask anyone what you need. Hi guys, mine's a pint. Anyone know how to put a controlled-release poison in table salt, I'm having a dinner party for the mother-in-law,' Roberto rolls his eyes and shakes his head at Pete's stupidity.

'Here. I picked this up in the market for you,' says Pete throwing an old book at him. 'Hugh's mate Derek with the second hand bookstall... This town is overflowing with everything you need.'

"Forensic pharmacy by H. Glyn Jones 1929 London Pharmaceutical press 17 Bloomsbury square. Price three shillings and sixpence."

Stick to police work. That's no fucking use to me.' Roberto becomes angrier and more defensive as the conversation continues but there was no stopping Pete, who is becoming more agitated.

'I didn't suggest you ask anyone what you need, you just have to ask someone where to look for relevant information don't you? There's no reason for there to be any link between me in Bradford and you here in Cambridge. Think about it. Deaths in Bradford wouldn't make waves here. No-one knows I'm here so you'll never be implicated - unless any more harm comes to Hazel that is. You don't have to go up to Yorkshire and you don't need to know why, or see me again. Once you've delivered

I am gone forever. I'll take it North, or we could even send it by courier.'

'Look,' says Roberto. 'You can't blackmail me. You're in the same boat as me. If I could do something, it can't be posted. That brings in too many random possibilities. You have to stay in control. I would only hand it to you. In any case you made all these promises last time. I believe *nothing* that you say. How do I know you won't keep returning until we all get caught?'

'You don't,' says Pete. 'I'll come back in the morning to pick it up. 11am of course.'

As he leaves the shop, Pete's parting shot is to take a dictaphone out of his pocket and say 'Thanks, I think I got all that.' He sprints up the road and melts into the weaving throng of tourists, shoppers and cycling intelligentsia, just to make sure that Roberto isn't following him with a weapon.

Pete picked up the Dictaphone for a fiver on a second hand market stall. There was no battery in it but Roberto didn't need to know that.

Pete rings Adrian as he weaves in and out of the Cambridge crowds and tells him to go to the fish shop to check out the salt and vinegar dispensers and get duplicates.

'Someone will have to be in there just before the runner comes for the food. Swap the salt dispensers and swap them back as soon as he leaves to avoid collateral damage.'

'What if they put the salt and vinegar on when they get home? Or don't have any?' asks Adrian.

'Get in there and have someone inside who's ready before the scumbag arrives. You might need two plants. One to swap the dispensers, then another to put them back again, got it?'

'I don't like the sound of that, says Adrian sounding concerned. 'Who the fuck is going to do that for us? I can't do it, they know me.'

'Oh for fuck's sake,' says Pete. 'They don't know me; I don't live on takeaways like you. I'll have to do it then. I'll have to make sure I'm out of there by the time the shit hits the fan.'

I'll bring the stuff back up tomorrow morning and sort it, if the knob-head can turn out the chemicals in time. Just be sure you have the replacement dispensers.

They will find how it was done in time. Does Wanky Jack have CCTV?'

'You are kidding aren't you?' says Adrian 'He's only just got fucking electricity in there and he didn't take decimal money until five years ago.'

'What about CCTV in the village?'

'I'll check, but I don't think so. Do you remember when those two fire engines collided at the bottom of Station Road or when someone smashed the window of the Conservative Club on election night?'

'Yeah, so?' asks Pete as he dodges into a doorway to avoid a delivery truck that came flying down the narrow, cobbled lane between ancient brick walls.

Adrian continues 'We spent two days trying to find anyone sober in the village who either saw, or heard anything, but found nothing. Up here they think CCTV is a new sailing channel on SKY. Anyway what if he recognises you from the telly?'

'I'll wear a disguise then.'

'Come to think of it you have disguised yourself with two stone of blubber since you've been working behind a desk.'

'Fuck you, George Clooney!' bites back Pete, genuinely hurt.

Pete returns to the hotel and finds Hazel still in bed.

She wakes when he enters, so enticing and perfect, it makes him whimper.

She is half covered by a twisted and crumpled duvet, wearing his shirt and jogging bottoms rifled from his bag. Her clothes are drying on the radiator. On the bedside table there are the remnants of a room service breakfast. Pete helps himself to some left-over orange juice.

She is in no mood for games and when he tells her that the meeting is off, he can resist her questions no longer. All he can do is lie to her. It breaks his heart.

He's saving her from being dragged into what they are up to. She must not get the slightest inkling of what is really happening.

'Right, that's it now. You are going to tell me everything,' she demands.

Pete tells her a story: 'Roberto foolishly got involved in fraud when his first pharmacy went bust and he was prosecuted. At the trial he gave evidence that convicted a very dangerous criminal. That is why I knew Roberto when I came to West Fell. It wasn't just over the car. He's been helping the police to crack another scam perpetrated by the same crime family and he's been sworn to secrecy.'

Pete hates portraying Roberto as a hero, but he has to give her a tale she will accept. It does explain why such a flash bastard showed up in West Fell. It's an ideal isolated place to make a fresh start. We helped him relocate and I was his liaison. His real name is Robert Peckitt.'

'I know that,' Hazel processes the story as it explains so much and has elements of truth in it.

'Yes, but that's how he had the criminal connections to be able to supply recreational drugs to the school,' says Pete adding colour as he spoke.

Hazel reaches out to him from the bed. He avoids her outstretched hand and stands away from the bed. Avoiding physical contact with her is the most difficult and counter intuitive challenge he has ever endured.

There is nothing he would rather do at this moment than to climb in with her and he is sure he will regret this moment for the rest of his life because it is unlikely to be presented to him ever again.

'I can't get involved,' he says moving back.

I have found it. This is real love, he tells himself. *The torture! Our self-imposed denial of what we **know** we need.*

It's a sacrifice he has read about but never before encountered. It is so fucking hard to be an adult sometimes.

'You know I am completely in love with you. I will wait for you, but we can't be together now. Not until you are free from Roberto,' he tells her quietly.

'Why couldn't Rob tell me all this himself? Tell me why!' She pleads, still confused.

'He doesn't yet know whether he will be further implicated in future legal action and while he helps the police, he's in danger from the criminal gang he used to be tangled up with. It's best no one knows because they're either likely to reveal his whereabouts under caution or duress or be implicated themselves in any future legal action. He is stuck in the middle and trapped. It must be hell for him. Torment. He was trying to protect you.'

'He should have trusted me. Thanks for telling me all this.'

Pete hates himself for lying to her but he has to stay focused. More so, he hates having to doubtless drive her back into Roberto's arms. He had just described a flawed but trapped hero in a difficult situation who was trying to protect her. He had just made it possible for her to love Roberto again. It was the very last thing he wanted to do, but it was all he could come up with in the moment to hold it together. In any case Hazel seemed still minded to try and patch it up with Roberto. She hadn't at any point said she had left Roberto for him.

'I have to leave,' he says abruptly.

She doesn't object. He can see that his words have changed her mood.

He gathers his luggage and quickly leaves the room. 'You can keep the T-shirt,' he tells her.

As he starts to close the door, she says 'I love you Pete, I don't know what will happen but I do love you.'

He can no more embrace her or kiss her goodbye than he can hold his hand in a fire. He doesn't possess the self-control to touch her and then pull away. If he grabs her now, he will never let go.

'You don't love me. You don't yet know what I've done. You don't know me yet.' He mutters as she listens to his footsteps fading down the corridor.

Pete spends the next night in a Travel Lodge, coming back to his life with a thud. Hazel must have caned the bar in the Varsity when he was out. The bill makes his eyes water.

The following day in the pharmacy, Roberto gives Pete a plastic container about the size of a jam jar. He can see that it contains a white granular powder that in any other situation could be mistaken for table salt.

'That looks very good for fake salt,' says Pete, impressed.

'That is because it isn't fake salt. It *is* salt.'

'Are you taking the piss?'

'Not at all' replies Roberto 'You want the people who eat it to taste the salt, otherwise they might reject the food. So it is 99.9 percent standard table salt. Don't open it until you need to. Don't touch it. Don't sniff it or drop it. It will dissolve in vinegar but will effervesce, so decant it before you need to use it. It is largely odourless, but not completely. When it is dissipated on the food portions, the smell of the fish will disguise it....If it was bright orange and smelt of pig shit, no one would put it on their food would they?'

'Is it going to work? '

'Well I don't know what you want it for do I? All I will say is that if you were to put it on your food and eat it, you would be dead before the day is out.'

'What sort of quantity do I need?'

'Well you need about the amount you could fit on a pin head to kill someone, but a good table spoon full to make your chips salty so I think it will quite easily do the job,' says Roberto, getting seriously cheesed off with Pete's continuing questions.

'Look you bastard, I've come up with this only because I spent the whole night on it. I was in the library at Corpus Christi all afternoon, had a meeting at lunch time and another in the evening to collect some books. Dusty tomes like this.' He waves *Forensic Pharmacy by H GLyn Jones.*

'So it did come in useful then.'

'Only for background, to point me in the right direction. I had to arrange for Hugh to collect a package from a bloke in a Stevenage doorway at three o'clock this morning, which puts me and him at great risk if this goes tits up. I told him it was a gambling debt I was collecting on. I had the powder I needed encased in a plastic bag and sandwiched between a wedge of cash. Arranging this with an addict who owes me a favour puts me in danger.'

'I don't much care how you managed it. You're a killer and I am a policeman. You are lucky to be on the street,' says Pete with unnecessary venom.

'As a serving policeman, you are as bad as me, if not worse, so get off your fucking pedestal. Oh, and by the way, it has not been tested, of course, and I produced it overnight without all the ingredients I needed. I had to improvise, so don't come back to me if nothing happens or if it blows up in your face on the way home.

'By handing you this I draw a line. I will take any consequences that come my way as a result of that final decision. So, if you don't mind, fuck off out of my life forever.'

22 Peel Plaice will Peel your Face

Pete takes the train back to Leeds via Stevenage and then the connection to Ilkley.

Getting off at Burley in Wharfedale, an agreeable rural commuter village two stops short of the Ilkley terminus, he meets Adrian and carefully decants the contents of the jar into the dispensers.

The salt is easy but dropping only a tiny amount of powder in the vinegar dispenser causes a minor Vesuvian eruption which sends noxious gas into the car. They both flee and only return when the windows clear. A passer-by tells them 'Your radiator must have overheated and burst. You need to get that fixed.'

'That's very kind of you to take the time to tell us, we hadn't noticed, thank you and welcome to Yorkshire,' says Pete under his breath.

The liquid settles in the plastic dispenser and resumes the appearance and smell of vinegar, but they are stunned to see that where it had overflowed onto the free paper Pete had brought from the train, it had curdled the newspaper into to a paste.

'That doesn't look good,' says a shocked Adrian. 'No-one's going to eat a fish supper that looks like that.'

'It depends how hungry you are I suppose. It could perhaps just make the batter spongy. It may not react the same way on warm food. We don't have time to try it out. In any case, we aren't launching a new product for the shelves of Tesco's you tit, we just need to get this done and away. We have no fucking choice now do we? This was your idea. We have to at least give it a bash now.'

'If it gives one of those bastards the shits it will all be worth it,' says Adrian. 'No time to waste. We have ten minutes. Get on it'.

Adrian drops Pete off at the top of Peel Place and leaves the village. He stops in a layby next to the river at Leatherbanks about a mile away and waits for a call.

Pete enters the small chip shop wearing a baseball cap pulled down over his brow and some clothes he has bought from his mum's charity shop on the grove in Ilkley. He told her it was for gardening. The chippy is the end of a stone terrace no different to the Bradford Pharmacy except spotlessly clean and arranged in every detail by a pedant.

The fish fryer dominates the room and the space for customers is so minimal that people have to repeatedly leave to let people squeeze out past them before re-joining the queue. Pete orders fish and chips to take away.

The elderly lady serving at the counter has prepared a vast array of chip wrappers which are being filled with chips pedantically by her husband.

'No, not like that, Edna,' he chides her. 'Put them on the counter or you won't have enough room....We'll be with you in a moment young man, we have a big order on at the moment.'

'Can I help while I am waiting?' Offers Pete as he grabs the salt and vinegar dispensers and drops them onto the floor where his open bag lays waiting.

As he bends down he stands them upright behind his holdall and lifts the new ones out of his open bag onto the counter in one seamless move.

'Oh I am sorry,' says Pete 'Sack the juggler, eh?'

He is pleased with how well this move worked out. He had managed to make the switch undetected and she takes charge of the situation before the idiot in front of her does any more harm.

'I will see to it thank you,' she says curtly ignoring his levity.

She grabs the dispensers from him and vigorously shakes them over the open packets of food. She wraps the first batch and lays out some more.

Meanwhile her husband is too busy nattering about how 'No-one eats curries in Burley' and how unconcerned he is about the opening of the new Asian restaurant across the way. Whilst speaking, carefully placing, removing and tweaking the battered fish in and out of the boiling vat of oil with a pretentious flourish in the time honoured tradition of a Northern fish and chip shop proprietor. Jack fusses over his deep-fried battered fish with the furrowed brow of a top scientist or master craftsman. This charade is most likely an affectation developed in order to publicly take all the glory and avoid any of the more tedious tasks in the enterprise like peeling potatoes, dealing with the money, or cleaning.

'You've missed one there,' says Pete helpfully. 'That last one you wrapped had no vinegar. You put salt on but no vinegar. 'Are you sure?' she says as she reopens the last one to check.

This gives Pete the chance to swap the containers back again and zip his bag.

At that moment a red pickup pulls up outside knocking over a bin. A fat dirty teenager with a cigarette and an obnoxious attitude saunters in, ignoring the queue and hands over two crispy new fifty pound notes.

'Oh I'm sorry we can't take them. There are too many fakes around.'

'All I got,' says the youth, in a manner that invites no further discussion.

'Oh well, I suppose we know you; it should be ok.'

'We can go to the fucking Fish Dish in Ilkley if you don't want the business,' the teenager sneers aggressively. 'Keep the change, you sad old cow,' he adds just to add some glamour to the discourse as he snatches three bulging carrier bags from the counter.

'Err excuse me, it comes to a bit more than that!' calls Edna to the back of the yob.

'Oh never mind, we'll get the rest of the money off them next Friday,' says Jack from his exalted position.

You may well not, thinks Pete. As he politely waits for his fish supper he keeps his head low and avoids eye contact with the arrogant toe rag as he leaves.

Job done. He rings Adrian and waits at the top of Peel Place.

'Piece of fucking cake,' says Pete as he climbs into the car, high on the success and relief at its completion. 'Go, go, go!'

They carefully empty the contents of the bottles into the river from the Old Bridge in llkley three miles up the valley. The fluid disappears as it hits the clear water cascading over the stone paving beneath the ancient pack-horse bridge.

'Is this going to kill the fish?' asks Adrian innocently.

They burst out laughing as much as a release of nervous tension than at his concern for the river fish.

They gingerly wrap the containers in plastic bags and put them and the rubber gloves they used in the boot for discreet disposal later at the landfill site at Snaygill, then wash their hands in the river.

They then celebrate by sharing the fish and chips ignoring the possibility of contamination and down several Hoegaardens.

'You *could* have got fish and chips twice,' chides Adrian.

'Expenses wouldn't cover it!' replies Pete. 'If this works out, we've just probably saved a million quid a year in insurance claims, prison places, police and court time. Not to mention the removal of the fear and trauma caused to the community by us allowing that gang of bastards to roam free… And we can't afford a fucking fish supper each.'

'Says it all, Pete.'

A stray dog begins to attack a fish and chip wrapper next to the bin where they are perched.

Neither of them speak for several minutes.

'We're like Simon and Garfunkel,' says Adrian out of nowhere.

'You what?' replies Pete staring at his colleague with a baffled expression. 'Sitting on a bridge over troubled water listening to the sound of silence whilst in a clearing stands a boxer, you mean?'

After the laughter dies down Adrian stares into the water and says quietly, 'No. The day 'Bridge Over Troubled Water' made No.1, they were sitting in an old car eating their chips, listening to the radio. One said to the other, "Gee those guys must be having fun."'

'What the fuck are you on about? Anyway, that is a labrador not a boxer and I bet it wasn't chips they were eating in New York.'

'Well, here we are quietly contemplating something we've done which could change our worlds. It's out there now. We can't take it back. It's done and we have no more part in the outcome. Just like Simon and Garfunkel listening to their hit on the radio,' says Adrian sadly.

'Yeah! Just the fucking same! They did songs about peace and love and we poison criminals in Yorkshire, I can see where you are coming from there! I wonder about you Adrian, I really do. I don't have the faintest idea what you are rambling on about sometimes, do you know that?'

'Simon and Garfunkel eating a bag of chips?'

'Well it might not have been chips, it could have been a chilli dog with pastrami on rye, but that's not important to the story.'

'No part of that story is important.'

'I think I should perhaps remind you at this point that we're both serving police officers and this is on our patch,' Adrian points out, trying hard to maintain some levity to keep their minds off what might be happening at the Flaxton's compound.

'By this time tomorrow we could be on our own trail. How do we manage that tricky conundrum? If I arrest you first then you can't arrest me!'

'I'm going to arrive early to work tomorrow and lie in wait for you. You are going down mate.'

'That's a joke,' replies Pete. 'You're the only person I have ever met who could fuck up the investigation of your own crimes. If you arrest me first, then it turns out you were involved, my lawyer will make mincemeat of you.'

'I'll take my chances. I got shot remember! I could claim it was PTSD that turned me into a killer.'

'I could claim the same thing after working with you!'

'Seriously Pete, what do you think is going to happen?'

'I'm not sure to be honest, but that's it for me anyway; never again. I'm out of the job on Friday whatever happens. I join the boat in Southampton on Saturday and I'm gone. I don't know if I will ever come back.'

'Are you not going via Cambridge to pick up Hazel on the way?'

'No, I can't see her again, it's impossible. There's no sign she'll leave that bastard and if she did, I'm no better than him now. I can't tell her about this,' he sighs bitterly.

'No it's over now. It has to be. In truth it never got off the ground. One day she'll be able to move on and leave all this shit behind. If she becomes an accessory, she *will* go down with the rest of us.'

'We're not going down, Pete. We'll make this work just once, forget it and move on; that's the plan isn't it?'

'Yes, we will but after what we've done, whether we get away with it or not, we've crossed a big line. The biggest! We've embarked on something that's taken on a life of its own.'

'Hopefully we tidied up the two biggest organisers of crime in the North without the help of our employers, that's what we did. Don't beat yourself up about it,' says Adrian.

They don't know how to behave in this void while they wait to see the outcome.

'Are you telling me you are not concerned about the moral implications of all this? We're supposed to bring people to justice and uphold the law. Not go around killing anyone we don't like.' replies Pete, already having severe reservations about what they have done.

'Not anyone we don't like so much as anyone the system has decided to allow to continue ruining other people's lives,' says Adrian. 'We're supposed to protect the weak and vulnerable as well. If this works, how many old ladies will we have saved from losing their savings and sense of contentment? How many crimes will we have prevented? I bet we'd be heroes if the general public knew what we were doing.'

'The public don't know that I received no help after being shot. Just got a twenty-five pound Marks and Spencer's voucher from the police federation, a bollocking from the boss and the threat of arrest if I didn't help them resist my colleague's compensation claim. That's what happened to me mate, when I was out there doing my job. That's all I got.'

'Yeah, of course the fucking crime figures are falling, there's no fucker there to record them!' an angry Pete joins in.

'Anyway, how many fucking times, it was only twenty fucking quid not twenty-five!'

'We'd be supported if we got caught and the truth comes out,' says Adrian hopefully.

'Don't you believe it,' says Pete. 'Privately perhaps, but not publicly. Look how we turn on nurses who make honest mistakes when people get killed. Coppers and soldiers who shoot the wrong person when they're in a no-win situation. Even when they shoot the right person they are savaged by the media. Social workers who cock up and let nutters and paedo's off the hook and are just doing their best with the kind of shit we have to deal with on a shoestring with no backup. They are treated the same. Dumped, blamed and savaged by the press.

'Suffice to say that if this blows up in our faces we're going to the big house, make no mistake and you know what they do to coppers inside,' Pete shudders.

'I'd better crack on; I'm on duty tomorrow,' says Adrian rising from the bench and collecting the empty cans and chip papers strewn around where they had been sitting on like a couple of winos.

'That'll be interesting,' says Pete.

'I feel like doing a long-term sickie like the rest of them,' replies Adrian.

'Don't do anything to attract attention, just carry on as normal. And that includes not changing the habit of a lifetime and getting good at your job. Solving this one would be out of character and not at all helpful! Keep it in your trousers for a couple of months if you can as well. The last thing we need is one of your secret affairs going Pete Tong again with you letting the cat out of the bag when you are throwing the kitchen sink at a potential conquest.'

'Calm down, calm down. What's eating you Pete?'

'What do you mean what is fucking eating me? What do you think? It's what's eating the Flaxtons that worries me! Just ironic really, the one time you get a job where you know all the answers and you can't chalk it up!"

They finish another bottle each and shake hands knowing that by daybreak nothing will be the same again. They go their separate ways.

23 The Hurricane Arrives

Six o'clock the next morning, Adrian inevitably gets called in early.

Three of the Flaxton family have arrived at A&E at Airedale hospital at around midnight in a taxi. Calls came in from many sources, firstly hysterical mobile calls, neighbouring property owners and some anonymous.

The first two PC's on site are assaulted by friends and family of the owners who have gathered outside. No-one will enter the yard until someone says it's safe.

Everyone available is hauled in from all over the division to control the mob outside the compound.

It is declared a major incident. The first bobbies who turn up know who lives there and the screaming about dead bodies freaks everyone out. The coppers don't get paid enough to put themselves on the line for these scumbags, who have been giving them headaches all over the North for years.

It is not until armed response from Leeds arrives to take out the loose dogs that a forward party go in. There are fears of poisonous gas.

It's 6.30am. The full horror is revealed before sunrise and the crowd is restrained. A woman in her fifties died in the hospital foyer and two children, one aged 7 and one aged 12 are under observation and very sick. Something has burnt through their intestines. It is less than 50/50 that they will pull through.

Dawn has broken when Adrian arrives to the full horror.

The balloon went up and the division dropped everything in order to respond. The night shift are told to stay on as the first day shift arrives.

The Flaxton family occupy a former quarry site not far from Ilkley Moor between Burley and Hawksworth. It is a five acre hole in the hillside, hidden from the road by a small forest of pine. Hundreds of thousands of tonnes of stone, used to help build the Victorian boom town of Bradford and the mills all around West Yorkshire, extracted from here. The quarry was worked for over 150 years, but its output declined through the 20th century and ceased altogether in the 1960's. Much of the stone then came back in the form of reclaimed materials from demolished mills which was then recycled and re-dressed to suit modern cavity walling methods by Billie Flaxton and his family.

The 70's and 80's housing boom brought enough cash in to enable a brief foray into property development. Stone flags from the mill floors were trucked down to London to enhance the streets and gardens. When later the few remaining mills were saved from extinction, the supply dried up. 'Reconstituted stone' (posh name for concrete), newly quarried stone and cheap imported Indian flags, hand-dressed by cheap labour, became the norm.

The Flaxtons, who had for years mixed honest, hard work and enterprise with the occasional dodgy dealings, handling stolen goods, car and heavy goods vehicle thefts, got out of the stone and demolition business completely. The next generation became full-time criminals, primarily drug dealers, housebreakers and exponents of the cheap tarmac driveway or roof repair scam which has caught out many a hapless landowner or lonely OAP, a scam which begins with an apparently very cheap quote using square feet instead of square meters and ends with a terrified customer being frogmarched to the bank or building society to hand over tens of thousands of pounds. When they spot a rich, lonely and vulnerable person, they come back time after time until there is nothing left.

Despite having no planning permission to live on the site, the whole quarry floor gleamed with expensive chrome caravans and bungalows on wheels. Brand new four wheel drive pickups and flatbed beavertail trucks fitted with hi-ab cranes, the go to vehicles for the nocturnal plant and machinery thief were parked everywhere.

The overstretched council had its hands full dealing with the travelling community, especially those who never got around to travelling. The local authority had never followed through any of the eviction notices that they timidly delivered to the quarry, anxious not to cause offence to people known to use the cover of victimised minorities to pursue lives of lavish and barely concealed criminality.

The family had owned the site for 40/45 years. It was hidden from view, out of sight and out of mind on the edge of the moor.

It could not be under a brighter spotlight now.

By the time Adrian arrives, the media have been alerted and are turning up in hordes. Local, national and international television and all the papers are there.

The narrow lane leading up to the quarry is completely blocked with cars and trucks.

A common path in and out of the quarry is established to protect the scene and PC's are posted in a wide arc across the fields surrounding the quarry to prevent the rapidly growing crowd from interfering with the site.

Mutual aid from surrounding force areas is called for to bolster the overwhelmed local team. This is clearly an unusual situation which requires an exceptional response. The divisional commander has taken full control of the whole area. He instructs his own team and takes full charge of the incoming assistance, keeping the chief constable informed from his car during the morning.

It's too early for an effective investigation into who was responsible. They are still at a loss to describe what they have found. Even the longest serving officers present have not the experience to enable them to deal with what they see before them this cold dark morning. The younger ones are completely numbed by it.

Adrian is ushered in as he has been at the front of the many attempts to rein in the known criminals who reside here. He is shown the scene of the carnage he has caused. There are possibly seven large new caravans clothed in gleaming chrome, some with small garden areas around them and amongst them a patio area with several wooden tables where they had gathered for their last meal. This is where most of the bodies still lie: A grotesque scene of dead humans, vomit, blood and horror.

'It's hell in there,' says a uniformed officer.

'Can we get the road cleared?' asks Adrian.

'We can't even get ambulances out,' replies his colleague.

'Get rid of this lot. Tell them to park down in Menston in the pub car park and walk up... And keep them behind some tape. We have too much to do deal with.'

There are twisted faces frozen in grotesque yawns. Partially dissolving corpses, their mouths dripping yellow foam, streaked with blood like vomited custard trifle. Overweight men in T-shirts slumped over the remains of their meal. There are signs of incontinence and nausea; fear and anger frozen on their faces as the last roar of terror and defiance against an attack they had no way of expecting or understanding, brought the end of their lives.

There are men he recognised, men he had dealt with time and again who evaded and belittled his attempts to cow them. These men had caused havoc and fear. They took whatever they wanted whenever they felt the desire. They now lay silent like a mound of rejected abattoir fodder waiting to be shovelled into a covered skip. It reminded Adrian of the cattle culls of the foot and mouth epidemic when mountains of animals were piled up, burnt and buried. It is a colour photograph from the scene of a massacre in hell. One that no one present will ever forget.

He is numbed and shaken to the point of delirium and stumbles over a fence. He begins to cry. Fortunately for him this is not an unexpected response for anyone encountering such a scene and the few moments that it takes for him to gather himself back from a retching, horrified and blubbering wreck is taken as the emotional reaction of any normal human being. *'Shit shit shit,'* he says to himself. The reality is a million times more horrific than the theoretical exercise they had planned in the pub.

He is confronted by dead people, human beings no matter how unutterably disgusting these people were, *did they deserve this?*

Of course, he realises - *They are a fucking family not just a crime syndicate.*

*H*e gazes upon the horror scene he had instigated and sees the implications and the consequences of their naivety lay before him in all its horror.

The kids! The Women! The inexperience of mass murder dawns on him for the first time.

They had investigated dozens of murders but had never perpetrated one. *Why didn't we consider collateral damage?* He curses himself.

During the discussions leading up to it, he and Pete had stupidly spoken only of the male members who would hopefully be present, nearly all known to the police: A grandfather, three sons, several grandsons in their teens and older cousins, uncles and hangers-on. There may even have been some slaves.

The silent and scared Romanians he had found in a container during a raid on the site last year were clearly not in there rubbing down the metal before painting it, as the Flaxtons had claimed. They were obviously living in there. By the time the border agency arrived with social services for a half-hearted raid, they had vanished.

There are dead bodies everywhere, mostly males and possibly four women and six children. Twenty-four casualties in total, including those who made it to the hospital: two children at death's door and three survivors. One was a vegetarian and had cooked her own meal, one arrived late and one had decided on a burger so passed on the fish and chips. He was in the nick with the family's dodgy lawyer creating hell with some family who had arrived from elsewhere.

Some interesting characters were turning up from the criminal community, some from far away. Some of those who instinctively showed up to help their family out or were there out of morbid curiosity, would later wish they had stayed away. The force begins to secretly film the crowd of onlookers. A move which will bear much fruit later in the investigation.

Once the police regain control and some order out of this horror there will be a lot of explaining to do about bundles of cash, stolen goods, vehicles and the contents of the warehouse, but that will be weeks away and is far from the priority at this moment.

If the force had been in control of things, this place would have been raided years ago and regularly, until they were contained. It is too late now. No-one wants this scene from hell. Now the West Yorkshire force has the biggest case for years on its hands and the world's media, the home office and the politicians are going to hold them to account.

Despite his involvement and culpability, this disaster is even more devastating to Adrian. It was inevitable that he would be brought in to be central to this investigation as he had been here so many times before and had tried so hard to alert his bosses about the place, pleading many times with them to shut it down. He was overruled and slapped down on several occasions. He wishes now that he had ignored it like the rest of his colleagues, the council and the revenue and customs people.

A HAZCHEM team in white SOCO suits with breathing apparatus scour the quarry with gas monitoring devices before anyone can enter. The team quickly ascertain that the presence of apparently healthy dogs amongst the scene of carnage combined with evidence of a communal meal being eaten, point quickly to the cause of death being the human's food.

The dogs have to be destroyed to protect the investigating team.

'Fish and chips everywhere,' the senior scientist barks at the lead investigating officer.

'No idea how or what we're dealing with here yet, but the meal is certainly the starting point. Must be poison. Get on it.' the SIO says to Adrian. 'Cover every fish shop within five miles. Start with the nearest. No-one is to eat fish and chips anywhere in Yorkshire until I say so.'

Even in the most serious of situations the boss is capable of making a complete tit of himself. That statement would be hilarious if not here and now. *Everyone stop breathing until I say so,'* would be on a par.

Adrian knows exactly where to go first of course. He locks down the chip shop as a crime scene and leaves two uniformed officers there taping off one side of Peel Plaice and interviewing neighbours. He has no option but to go through the motions. He knows which questions to ask Jack and his wife and he already knows the answers. After half an hour at the fish shop he phones his boss.

'Ok. It looks like we have a source. Peel Plaice fish shop. Jack and Edna Winkler. He tells me that the Flaxtons come to Peel Plaice every Friday around 6.30pm.'

'Is that usual Collingbridge?'

'The owners say for the past three years or so, almost without fail. The only time they were absent was when they were doing the Horse Fair at Appleby.'

'Never heard of it. Who would know about this regular tradition?'

'Everyone knows about the horse fair. Except you, Sir.'

'No! You idiot, I mean the Flaxton's fish and chip habit. I know this is overwhelming for all of us, but do your best to concentrate will you?'

'Many people would know about the Friday fish and chip run, Sir.'

'We must look at this as a horrific attack on a family and forget our view of them. We can deal with the peripheral issues later.'

Once Adrian has got his boss off the line, he continues to interview the Winklers.

'They've been coming in fer years and everyone knows who they are.' Jack tells him. 'Although we don't like having them around,' he continues, 'They *are* our best customers by miles. They must not know how to cook up there, they don't just come in on Fridays, they're in here nearly every day in ones and twos, but on Fridays it's the only day they come in and get it all at once for their family gathering. Old Billy Flaxton pays for it apparently, his father used to do it for the farm labourers and travellers back in Ireland they say.'

'Anything unusual yesterday?'

'Nothing. It was a normal day as far as I can remember,' replies the stunned old man.

An edict from above comes in when Adrian reports back.

'Seal it off. Nothing leaves the premises. Take the owners in. Tell them to bring the clothes they were wearing. Interview anyone who went in there last night I want every single name number and pack drill of every customer who has been in there this week. Make a full list. Names, numbers, any previous, any relationships to the victims. Do a door-to-door and seal off the street. No-one goes in the building until forensics have a chance to look at it.

'They will have to look at ingredients in stock on the premises plus packaging, sources of all ingredients, any CCTV. Turn over all we know about the shop owners and anyone who works there. The lot.'

'Sorry boss, I can only do one of those things until I get the cavalry.'

'Just do it!' The boss barks down the phone.

'I am telling you. There *is* only me today. Uniform are mostly at Elland Road for the 2nd division playoff semi, and if, as we expect, Leeds blow it again, those animals will tear the city apart. We just don't have the manpower to deal with this. Weekend overtime cover is now restricted to the Saturday evening shift. I'm in my own fucking car since the vehicle pool was 'rationalised'. To be fair sir, we *have* been trying to tell you for years that we don't have anywhere near enough cover to deal with anything big. And here it is.'

'Alright, alright. You've made your point. You ought to try and walk in my shoes for a mile or two. See where that gets you.'

'To Ilkley wearing your shoes?' Adrian mutters.

'What?'

'Nothing, Sir, carry on.'

No matter what the challenge is, front line workers use humour to get through. The darker the event, the darker the humour. It's not an indication that they are devoid of empathy; it's just a survival mechanism.

'You have no idea what I have to do to keep the show on the road. We've borrowed twenty men from North Yorkshire and they'll be here in half an hour.'

'Perhaps if the lack of funding had been challenged publically earlier, then the politicians would have had to find some more money?'

'This is *NOT* the time!' bellows the chief down the phone.

'Well we don't even have the manpower or the vehicles to seal off the site never mind investigate it,' continues Adrian. 'We're snowed under as it is!'

'You're beginning to sound just like Manford and it's not helpful to this situation or your own career. By the way, where is Manford?'

'He's working his notice back at base remember? You took him out of service last year and I'm well past caring about my career.'

'Get him back now.'

'He's leaving on Friday.'

'Is he hell! Tell him to ring me. Get on it **now** for fuck's sake!'

Here we go again, thinks Adrian.

When eventually the ambulances and fire brigade are allowed onto the site, there is no one alive to rescue. Firearms have to shoot the loose dogs to avoid the possibility of infection or attack on the emergency services.

A brief foray into the quarry establishes that there are no apparent signs of life, but that has to be confirmed as the initial sweep had been a rush in and out by a foolhardy detective in a white paper suit with only a dust mask for protection. He is now under surveillance in Airedale Hospital but so far showing no signs of illness.

The scene of horror is more than anyone who attended that morning could take in. Some of the bodies had been feasted upon by the dogs and the bodies appeared to be decaying around the throat as if they had swallowed acid.

Strewn around the site and blowing in the wind, were thousands of twenty and fifty pound notes. No-one touched them. No-one went near the cash. They eventually noticed a warehouse behind some trees. It was stuffed with antiques, motorcycles, televisions, computers and luxury cars.

This was the first time the compound had been open to view, the Flaxtons had created a no go area and it was a revelation. Just inside the compound were parked an array of pickup trucks , sports cars and brand new pimped up transit vans with black windows.

Deep into the quarry hidden from the entrance there was a huge industrial building which formerly contained the stone cutting and lifting machinery. At the back of the biggest shed.

Under a tarpaulin covered in dust there was a red Bentley Mulsanne. On a shelf there lay a number plate: JBT 600. Adrian held it next to the Bentley.

'Well look at this, they even have Jeff Bartlett's motor in here. That was nicked from outside the Green Frog last summer.'

Speaking off the record to a journalist, Adrian pulls no punches.

'I've been flagging this place up for three years and earlier raids had revealed nothing to bite on. They always knew when we were coming somehow. It's clear that this kind of hardware can't be purchased from the occasional driveway tarmac job.

'There were rumours of drug supply being coordinated here, but all we managed to find was some stolen lawnmowers, nothing big. Whenever we got near any particular individual linked back to here, they would disappear for six months. No-one on site would know where to, of course. By the time they came back into circulation, the trail had gone cold, the file put away and that was the end of it.'

Adrian has to fight his way through the throng of media hounds to get in and out of the quarry. The next day, whilst returning to his car which he had left at the rear of the Menston Arms, he finds himself plied with alcohol in the bar by a persistent investigative journalist.

Having decided to leave the force, and now as a desperate man seeking at the same time to justify his involvement and distance himself from culpability for a horrific mass murder, he sees no reason now to keep quiet. He always liked a drink and could never resist a free one but lately his drinking has become a daily event. His tongue becomes far too loose.

'The force only has the resources now to investigate each day's incoming jobs. There's no time to look at anything from the recent past or connect the dots with patterns of behaviour. *"These essential spending cuts will not affect the public and will create a more streamlined more efficient service"* is a mantra from government that we've heard too often and we knew it to be a worthless statement. Look at us now!

'It's only in this environment that a crime gang like the Flaxtons can live openly, knowing that the forces of law and order are so depleted that we're a joke.'

The journalist goes away with some killer quotes to add to his article which depict an incompetent force out of control at the top and demoralised throughout the rank and file.

'Whatever had killed them must have been slow to take hold,' deduces Pete, when he arrives at the quarry, equally shocked. He has to be seen doing his job. He had thought about ignoring the calls and setting off a couple of days early, but that would obviously arouse suspicion. Now he has to go through the motions and not forget to say *I told you so, Sir,'* as he would be expected to do.

He must make sure that he avoids Peel Plaice. He had worn a hat which hid his hair colour and a charity shop tracksuit that he had never worn before when he picked up the fish and chips. Those clothes are now three feet under the surface of the landfill site at the Snaygill quarry landfill site in Skipton with the rest of the kit. He is confident that no-one will suspect the police to be involved.

He knows that the impeccable cleanliness of the chip shop will make it very hard for forensics to place him there, and even if prints or DNA put him there, he can always admit to being an occasional customer and hope that Edna wouldn't recall him being there on any specific occasion.

The Winklers had thoroughly cleaned the shop floor and counter as they always did before turning the lights off. They had even wiped the salt and vinegar dispensers. His fingerprints and DNA were recorded at work and so if they came up during the investigation, they would be discounted as being those of a known and authorised person. He was right.

As with the Declan Lewis case, criminal rivals were universally assumed to be the culprits.

The boss begins a briefing for the few local coppers available plus the twenty brought in reluctantly from North Yorkshire.

He is a tall and very serious man near to retirement who wears his years in the force heavily and he knows that this case will be the largest and most remembered of his tenure in a force area that has seen a great many major incidents.

'Right, we have a very serious and difficult situation here, one which we have to deal with without the resources we would wish for, but I know you will rise to the occasion. So, imagine you are in the middle of a family meal and some of your relatives begin to melt in front of you, you would have to be very hungry to continue eating,' he begins.

'We have reason to believe that this is the scene of a regular weekly meal for a family who are also probably, I should say potentially, the most prolific criminal organisation in this area. Almost all the adult males amongst the dead are known to us, some have been for decades, but we must not let that colour our judgement nor dictate our pace in investigating this crime. The nation is watching. We have to not only deal with this as we would any other, but we have to produce answers very quickly.

'We know that suspected stolen goods, drugs and the proceeds of extortion and fraud are here within the crime scene. Everything here must be photographed where it is found, collected, recorded and kept securely in the barn until we have time to go through it.

'For now however, the focus of our efforts must be on revealing the cause of the poisoning and to identify the perpetrators of this horrendous crime. I need not add that women and children are involved and we have a couple of survivors. We have appointed family liaison officers, uniform to control crowds, a media spokesperson, and we are carrying out a community impact assessment. I am assured by the home office that we will be given all the resources we need.

'Firstly we must secure the outer cordon and a common path in and out and make absolutely sure it is 100 percent secure, 24/7 until I say. We must prevent anything walking off site, any contamination of evidence and allow forensics and SOCO to carefully examine the quarry here and the Peel Plaice chip shop in Burley-In-Whaferdale without any interference. We need to secure and assess potential witness statements from the survivors, the fish shop and neighbouring properties and put out a call through the media for anyone who may have been in the area to come and speak to us.

'I'm particularly interested in regular customers of the chippy on Friday and indeed on any other Friday, motorists taking short cuts down the lane to and from Hawksworth, over the top to Baildon and Bradford. Get round the boozers in Menston too and see what you can find. We have no suspects yet, but our witnesses are so far: five survivors from the extended family who live here and the husband and wife who run the fish and chip shop. Until we know differently, the owners must be our number one and two persons of interest.

'DI Frankland is leading the allocation of tasks, but I stress that we must remain open-minded and be prepared to change tack as information comes in. We need to find out when the poison was introduced to the meal. We suspect before delivery, but we can't yet be sure.

'Finally, no one must speak to the press unless sanctioned to do so by me personally. Do you all understand that? There will be a press strategy. Don't be tempted to speak to anyone outside the investigation.'

Adrian looks at the floor and says nothing.

'Any questions?'

Pete raises his hand.

'Not you Manford, I will speak to you in my car in ten minutes. Do your best boys and girls. We need very quick answers.'

In the car the boss jumps in first.

'Before you start, I don't have time for any bullshit. None of you are to speak to the press. Particularly you.'

Thank fuck for that, thinks Pete. The last thing he needs is the chippy bloke or his wife to clock him on the news and make the connection. He didn't see any CCTV there or in the village but he has to be very careful.

'You have no need to worry, Sir. I've learnt my lesson on that score,' he lies.

'This is my last week, Sir.'

'Are you still leaving us then?'

'Yes I am. You promised me some action on resources. I was patient, loyal and did my job, and you shat on me. Now because I was right, you want me to stay on. Sorry, but no chance. I will work my notice, but I'm joining a boat in Southampton on Saturday.'

'Don't make me beg you. Despite your lack of support for me and your cavalier attitude, you're one of the most promising detectives we have.'

'Had, Sir. You had my full support until you dumped me in the backroom and expected me to leave. Now I arrange to leave you want me to stay. It's too late.'

'Look, I don't need to spell it out. I am asking you to delay your departure until this is sorted. We can't deal with this and everything else. You can't walk away and leave your colleagues in this position.'

Pete is furious. 'That is the lowest form of guilt trip possible. You created this situation and shoved me into the broom cupboard. Now you dare to suggest that it is me who is letting down our colleagues!' He frowns and pauses, looking out of the window for a moment to consider his options.

'If I want to look myself in the mirror, you're right,' he sighs.

'I can't walk away. If I do, I am as bad as you. I'm officially on holiday this week to catch up on some time you owe me. So if I stay, I want a written guarantee of double bubble for every hour I work on this.

'I know that this job is so big that you'll be able to invoice the home office for it. I want a car and fuel and I want you to tell me to my face that you will not censure any officer who raises the subject of lack of resources.'

'I have no choice. Despite your blackmail, I have nowhere near enough officers to deal with this. But the deal is off if you speak to the press. You are now a lightning rod for trouble and insubordination. You must promise to ensure that all complaints and comments are internal and come directly to me, not even the police federation. You understand? I can't deal with this without that assurance.'

Pete knows that most of these promises will not be honoured, but he has to stay to avoid any suspicion his abandonment of the force might attract.

'Ok, ok. Two weeks, that's it. Then I go, even if it's not sorted. And I can't speak for what all the others might do. I don't control the rank and file despite what you think.'

Pete slams the car door so a hard when he leaves that it triggers its alarm leaving the chief fuming in the back while his driver tries and fails to disable it.

He didn't fall for the bullshit from the boss but he needs to show that he is prepared to stick around. He would be investigating himself, so it would be helpful to spread some false leads and perhaps he could frame someone on the long list of other local career criminals who were avoiding prosecution.

They had this conversation not knowing that the horse had already bolted and Adrian's impromptu interview in the pub was already on its way out to the newsagents, proving the boss's point graphically.

He and Adrian purposefully ignore each other unless they have operational reasons to speak. Their last conversation is on board a double-decker layby café near Wetherby.

Pete gets there first from Bradford and Adrian arrives ten minutes later from the Harrogate side of town. He had been up at his family hotel in Grassington.

Pete speaks first. 'We can't afford to be seen to be plotting. If we do come under suspicion, we will be observed and recorded without our knowledge.'

'Hang on, we're mates, won't we be expected to hang out as before?'

'No. Everything has completely changed now. If we meet we might slip up, if we don't we can't.'

'I know I can trust you not to break down and confess or discuss it with anyone else. But our mission has spectacularly and tragically over-shot. Innocent children have died. It is the reality we have to face. We must avoid detection at all costs. It is the end of the road, we are on our own now. Don't ring me.'

Adrian follows his leads. The chip shop couple can't remember anyone unusual that night. They have a vague image of someone offering to help with the salt and vinegar, but they are not encouraged to elaborate by Adrian. He persuades them that they have to be sure to avoid a defence solicitor tearing their evidence to shreds if they hesitate or appear unsure in court. The thought of publicly confronting the remains of the Flaxton family in court makes the Winklers visibly shudder, so they agree it wasn't relevant and it doesn't make it into their statement.

Jack reminds whoever will listen that he served over a hundred and fifty portions that night so it was hard to remember.

The truth was, it was over two hundred, but he had been conducting a dark trade of 25% of his business by purchasing potatoes and fish for cash direct from a farmer and fishmonger.

He had been doing this for twenty five years. *Just like all the rest of them,* he thought. He had used the money to set up his retirement bungalow in Whitstable next to the fish port. Jack and Edna went down there once a month on a Sunday morning and spent Monday and Tuesday in the port, arriving back in time to open on Wednesday lunchtime. They couldn't wait to retire and could well do without this fuss.

'How can we sell the business now? Best fish and chips in Wharfedale for over 20 years only to have this disaster?' Jack asks Adrian.

He isn't the only person to have little or no regard for the people who had died. The consensus in the village is one of relief and incredulity that it has taken the police so long to wake up to the scale of the problems that the Flaxtons have created.

Fretting about all this, considering their age and the fact that they are operating a cash element to their trade, the details of which they don't want to reveal to the police make Jack and Edna potentially unreliable witnesses.

The boffin's report on the likely chemicals involved takes a fortnight.

During that time hundreds of interviews are carried out. The contents of the quarry are recorded and photographed. There are several attempts to break into the warehouse by associates of the Flaxton's, some of whom claim that they were the owners of vehicles and equipment. A 24 hour guard of three officers has to be posted at the quarry. It was particularly vulnerable out of hours and as a crime scene, it is vital to secure its perimeter until it can be handed over to the proceeds-of-crime investigation team. They wish to assess the financial status of the quarry, its contents and ownership of goods where possible. They are also under constant scrutiny from media reporters, which although dwindling, is still a nuisance. In view of that and as a result in part of Pete and Adrian's delaying tactics, little real investigative progress is made before Pete leaves to catch up with his boat.

The criminal fraternity is in tumult again. It is a repeat of the Lewis murders.

Collateral damage begins to emerge, much of which is extremely helpful to the police. With most of the Flaxton family gone and the police all over every aspect of their lives, dozens of associates are apprehended, stolen property returned, proceeds of crime seized. It is looking like they will be able to round up an incredible £7million worth of goods, assets and crime clear-up. Many trials follow from this and an enquiry into the handling of the case leads to the formation and implementation of Homicide and Major Enquiry Teams to handle murders and large enquiries in tandem with the more day-to-day workload. A move which changes the way crime is investigated for the better and benefits the legal system enormously to this day.

Adrian's shame and guilt over the death of innocent children breaks him and his drinking engulfs him. As soon as he can, he bows out of the force and his already gargantuan appetite for alcohol marches on unabated. It is no surprise that Adrian's nickname in the force was 'A drain'. The torment he feels over the poisoning of the Flaxtons tips him over the edge.

Running a hotel for his parents, which has a large well stocked bar, does nothing to help to dissuade him from the bottle. By the time he leaves the force, it is known how the poison had been administered, but still there is no idea who was responsible for it.

It will be another month before laboratory testing can prove the chemical breakdown of the poison beyond the first preliminary finding to enable a more detailed investigation into its source.

Fortunately for Adrian and Pete, the Flaxton family's many enemies within the criminal fraternity still look like the most obvious culprits.

24 All at Sea

The Conquistador is a 600 tonne 165 ft converted oil rig supply vessel owned by an Italian billionaire. It was refitted in Florida and converted to be the luxury mothership of the 'French Hook' a blue marlin sports-fishing boat which piggybacks on the bow and is lowered into the water when elusive marlin fishing grounds are found.

Super rich, self-made men spend their later years engaged in expensive leisure pursuits. Some buy Formula One motor racing teams, others go down in flames whilst trying to fly their own helicopters.

Men never grow up. They just have to pretend they do in order to get paid work and persuade women to marry them.

Stephano Lagna, the owner of The Conquistador and its French Hook hanging at the stern was no exception. Rich beyond imagination, he could easily afford the luxury of a vast permanently crewed ship to circumnavigate the globe in pursuit of blue marlin in order to harpoon it and drag it aboard for a photo.

The crew enjoyed the best of the good life as long as they towed the line when the boss was in view. The ship had no helicopter pad, so the boss couldn't turn up at short notice. His visits had to be arranged weeks in advance, giving the crew considerable freedom and ample prior warning of a royal visit to conceal their mischief and tidy up.

It took £4 million and two years to transform the vessel in 2002 and the honour of piloting around the world fell to Stephano's trustworthy Captain Bertram Sedgwick - Berty to everyone except his mother. He was a large and cheerful man who never took life too seriously. The four state rooms of the ship wine cellars, a cinema, dining and snooker rooms, staff accommodation and bridge were meticulously fitted out in burr walnut, ebony, leather and oak with polished stainless steel. It was a big expensive toy for a big, fat rich bloke.

The plan was to follow the blue marlin fish year in, year out in the Atlantic and black marlin in the Pacific and the Indian Ocean, stopping off wherever the action was, when the fishing was good or when the F1 circus was in town. Whatever took Stephano's fancy. He would fly out and join them for a week or two, never stay long and frequently change his plans. He was a busy man and easily bored, so he was constantly on the move.

The joke amongst the crew was that Stephano was the unfortunate irritation in an otherwise perfect existence. Dealing with him was the price they paid to live the life of luxury, sailing the oceans of the whole of planet Earth. Sometimes a whole year would pass without seeing him. When he was on board, he was the king who had to be served, but as soon as he left it was party time.

Berty had swapped his life as a chef in his wife's restaurant in Otley for the open sea, firstly as crew and eventually captain. He passed his ocean yacht master's certificate in Florida and gradually upgraded his qualifications until he was ocean ready for almost any craft.

Berty knows Pete from his days in the Green Frog burger and pizza joint on Ilkley railway station. Berty and his indefatigable wife Liz made their mark in the eighties, blazing a trail for consumer choice by introducing a whole new and exciting dining experience to the ill-served northern epicurean. The irresistible, if somewhat geographically questionable mixture of pizza, burgers and Mexican food quickly became huge hit in the hungry town. Up to that point the only choices for supper had been fish and chips, a trip to Bradford for a curry or staying indoors for a Fray Bentos steak and kidney pie served up directly from the tin with a choice of two anaemic over-boiled vegetables.

The Green Frog had enriched but exhausted Berty's family. It had strained their marriage to a state where a prolonged absence was a good way of avoiding permanent separation. He was reborn on the open seas. A summer break turned into a ten year adventure across the oceans of the world.

Berty helped Pete to secure a temporary position as security man and first mate for a six month meander from Portugal to Thailand. Pete was required to join the boat in Portsmouth but couldn't get away in time. Fortunately Berty's timetable is flexible and within his gift, so he takes his time calling into one or two Basque ports and eventually down the Atlantic coast of Spain.

Pete is grateful for the helpful delay. He sells his car through the Ginetta racing club and rents his house through a letting agent, clears his savings out and leaves his current account to deal with his mortgage. The rent will cover it with a surplus which he will never touch.

His grief over Hazel's decision is with him every day and the scene of carnage he perpetrated in the Flaxton's compound gives him nightmares. He hopes that a change of scenery and a new adventure will give him time to reflect and consider what to do next, a chance to escape and recover. The alternative is too much to contemplate.

Berty dawdles as he navigates down to the Bay of Biscay then around the Atlantic coast of Spain, dropping anchor off Viana do Castelo at the mouth of the Lima, off the Portuguese coast to give Pete the chance to catch up.

A cheap flight to Santander and a hitchhiked ride in trucks across the Basque country brings him to their rendezvous. *Yorkshire with sunshine,* he thinks as the lush countryside speeds by.

The Zodiac inflatable picks Pete up from the very end of the extended seaward mole which enlarged the harbour area. Using this small craft to come aboard the mother ship saves Berty the hassle of port-office paperwork, the details of which might have found its way back to Stephano's office in New York.

They slip anchor and get the mission back on track without the owner's office knowing exactly where they are. Not that they were likely to care, provided the ship was able to show up in the right place when required.

When they can no longer see land, Pete is reborn. He doesn't contact Hazel or Roberto again and doesn't return to Cambridge before he leaves England. He ignores a couple of texts from her. She asked how he was and where he was. He doesn't want the pain of distant connection. He was passing through hell and hoping to escape to the other side if he could. All he wanted to hear was that she had left Roberto forever and couldn't live without him. Even if she did, it would be impossible. He loves her, but can't lie again and so eventually her texts peter out. He jots a few phone numbers down from its memory and throws his phone over the side of the boat.

Back in Cambridge Roberto has been following the case in the media. He is well ahead of the game. He draws great comfort from the knowledge that he is so far nowhere near being connected.

Hazel doesn't move back in with him and takes a room at the college.

'You need to show me who I am going to be with before I come back. If you can't then maybe it's the end for us. Until I know you and I know that there is nothing hidden, then I am happy as it is,' she explains in the pub.

They are getting along much better since Pete had gone, primarily because Roberto is making a genuine effort. But Roberto still hasn't owned up to any of the false details that Pete has told her, and she takes that to mean that he is still holding out on her. Their sex life dies as they drift into a routine of diligent husbandry of his new and lucrative pharmaceutical enterprise and her architectural studies. Pete isn't the only one at sea. Roberto no longer leaves notes on the shop door when he escapes to the pub. His only respite from work is Saturday afternoons watching sport, some light gambling, good food and wine. He tries to clear the majority of his prescription work before noon on Saturdays and leave his staff to handle the shop. The rest of the week he now works very hard and stays out of the Falcon.

All but a few customers co-operate with this and pick up prescriptions later, the rest he can pacify by delivering locally in a blizzard of activity between the end of the Premiership coverage in the pub and a meal out in the evening.

To deal with this, he hires a retired van driver who knows Hugh to chauffeur him from the White Swan or the Devonshire and drop him back at the Bedouin or the Falcon after covering the deliveries all over town in less than two hours.

He is trying to be sensible and is working hard to win back Hazel's trust, make some honest money and build a sustainable future.

Roberto is still clinging to his looks and charm but he feels tired for the first time. He feels the creeping unstoppable erosion of youth and passage to middle age. He knows he may well be still not half way through, but he feels his youth slipping away. He frames the old passage from Dylan Thomas – *"Do not go gentle into that good night. Old age should burn and rave at close of day; Rage against the dying of the light"* and hangs it above the counter to amuse his customers and remind himself.

Hazel rebuilds her relationship with her father over time. Although he refuses to engage on any level with Roberto, he begins to accept that he can't influence her choices.

In West Yorkshire, the extensive scrutiny upon the police force while they battle to solve the Flaxton murders begins to have dramatic consequences. The spotlight is on them with an intensity not seen since the Ripper enquiry.

Top brass are moved sideways. The Home Office and the police authority agree a new budget which enables some recruitment at the bottom end to resume work on the aftermath and to try and restructure. Three new senior officers are brought in.

Adrian has been able to bow out without a stir, blaming the pressure of the catastrophic Flaxton Murders. As he isn't the only one desperate to get out of the job and he has made known his intentions ahead of the compound poisonings, Adrian successfully ensures that his expressed intention to leave will not implicate him. His time on the Flaxton case effectively investigating himself whilst keeping it from his door takes its toll on his mental wellbeing.

It is easy for him to cover their tracks regarding events at the fish shop. A passing lorry had parked at the top of Peel Plaice and blocked the road around the relevant time. He knows what kind of truck it is as it appeared ten minutes later on CCTV at the Ilkley traffic lights. He suspects that it was most probably the driver who had been the missing witness, but as it had licence plates from the Newcastle area he counts on the fact that if he doesn't follow it up, the driver won't remember any details from the evening if by any chance, he is found and interviewed later on. In other circumstances he would have traced the vehicle and obtained a statement.

The forensic evidence eventually leads to the salt and/or vinegar, but as the lad who collected the supper was one of the casualties, no-one can be sure that he wasn't apprehended on his journey back to the compound or had his attention diverted in some way. Perhaps he was guilty of the crime and by badly handling the poison, unwittingly finished himself off as well.

There is evidence of internecine warfare in the Flaxton family as there is in most criminal enterprises. Many suspects are identified, framed, or implicated by rivals. When added to the volume of crime that is uncovered during the investigation, it becomes bogged down and there are enough potential suspects, most from the criminal fraternity, to make progress impossible.

A review of the case at the six month mark brings more questions than answers. 32 arrests, 20 charges for unrelated crime, near on a hundred suspects and thousands of interviews later, they are no nearer to identifying the murderers.

A murmur in the community begins to question the sense of pursuing this with the extra resources that the police now have at their disposal. The service has been starved of the funds it needed to do the job properly for years and this disquiet is shared by the team investigating it.

Proceeds-of-crime bods have identified millions of pounds worth of assets. Apart from identifiable stolen items, the Flaxton's legitimately owned assets, which included land and property which can't be touched without a conviction. Most are dead and for those left, it is felt they should be given a wide berth for a while. A line has to be drawn. Minor prosecutions of grieving family members before they had caught the murderers would have gone down like a lead zeppelin.

The universal judgement is that the world is a better place without the Flaxtons and the culprits had done the community a big favour. The suspects are probably competing criminals and already known to the police so why waste time and effort on it? Why not celebrate their absence and use the extra funding generated by the major incident to create a more effective service generally?

Higher up, the issue is one of law and order and the need for justice to be seen as well as done. Investigating the deaths of criminals has to have the same priority as any other. Inevitably though, without any solid leads and a lack of motivation, the investigation is eventually scaled down and slips out of the news.

Jack and Edna are in the clear, but publicity over the case and Jack's misjudgement over the appetite of his customers to embrace more exotic takeaway options results in the sale of his business falling through. After they retire, the shop soon becomes a residential property.

Meanwhile, life on the Conquistador is idyllic. The sun shines every day, dolphins travel with them, the wine cellar is plundered daily, the chef is a French genius, the crew of nine plus four 'guests' become expert party animals. They are very good company and the captain is a man so busy enjoying the attentions of the female 'crew' he had collected at African and South American ports, that he is happy for the boat to run itself.

'In-between the boss's rare visits to the boat, I am he.' announces Berty during one of many relaxed evenings around the upper deck dining table where the crew congregate most evenings to watch the sun go down.

'I run the ship with just five rules:

Rule one - Don't crash the boat.

Rule two - The week before the boss visits the boat is when rule four comes into play and the tidying up begins.

Rule three – No-one talks to the boss on the radio or the sat phone except me. Ever, unless I am dead.

Rule four - When the boss is on the boat he is the king and the crew are the slaves to do whatever he wants, no matter how ridiculous, illegal, debasing, irrational, dangerous, boring, embarrassing, pointless, humiliating, unwise, repetitive, or just plain wrong - What the boss wants, he gets!'

In the six years they had been at sea, rule four had never been in force for more than fourteen days in a row and that included four days ashore at the Rio carnival. On the basis that anything can be endured for a week or so if the prize is worth it, they deliver his extravagant requests in exchange for the life of privilege they enjoy in between Stephano's infrequent visits.

In many ways, they got more out of it than the owner, who was the one who had to pay the bills and do all the paperwork. The 'grown ups' in the New York office dealt with the port authorities, port agents, with customs permission at ports of entry, berths, immigration, licences, taxation and paid the wages.

The crew were all paid tax-free into Jersey accounts arranged via Stephano's bank and despite this incredible lifestyle they had no need of cash. The boat's credit cards allowed re-supply of anything they needed.

Berty had worn no shoes, paid no bills nor filled in a form for seven years. Nor had he touched a penny of his wages.

'..Oh yes and *Rule 5* - A full understanding and obedience of rules one to four is the only way you can stay on the boat.'

'Finally *rule six* - What happens on the boat stays on the boat.'

'But that's six rules' complains Pete.

'SO?'

'You said there were five rules?'

'Ok well I forgot rule seven.'

'Which is?'

Rule 7 - You don't ever talk about the rules or question the captain's memory or mathematical prowess!'

Pete had attended navigation classes and had seamanship certificates gained three or four years back, but his police career had prevented any serous nautical miles being chalked up. He is more than happy to obey these rules in exchange for the freedom of the sea. He takes to it like a whale to seawater, but has no interest in the pursuit of blue marlin.

His conscience instinctively tells him that such rare and beautiful sea creatures should be left alone. Not chased around the globe by rich brutes. He finds the sport to be cruel and indefensible but fortunately they only fish when the owner is on board and that is almost never. They only ever catch smaller fish to eat by line. In any case, after the recent events in his life he is no longer entitled to nor minded to question the actions and motivations of others.

Life aboard the Conquisador is the perfect distraction for someone needing escape. Being in the middle of an ocean at dawn or dusk, sleeping in a luxurious cabin after a bacchanalian banquet and waking to find yourself surrounded by the sea, several miles from where you were the night before, still unable to see land.

Sunbathing on the deck, reading and photographing the dolphins ahead of the boat, makes it very easy to imagine the recent past is just a bad dream.

After a few weeks Pete wonders why he ever spent so many years engaged in the hopeless task of fighting the forces of evil. He now has time to read, think and he becomes fit and healthy after years of junk food snatched on the hoof and curries late at night washed down with gallons of alcohol. Making himself unwell fighting to protect the vulnerable from the relentless misdeeds of evil doers for a pittance and no mention of thanks. It wasn't a life worth living.

The boat carries 160,000 gallons of fuel and drinks 40 gallons every hour off the anchor. It holds enough fuel to keep the two main engines and one generator going at sea for 24 days or more. It can cover thousands of miles depending on the conditions, between refuelling and victualing.

On a visit to Mohammedia in Morocco where they take on fuel and supplies and enjoy a day exploring the markets around the port, they pass between the Canary Islands, then swing way out into the Atlantic and follow the West African coast south, a hundred miles out beyond the reach of pirates who hunt in fast day boats.

As a mobile pleasure-palace, The Conquistador is a spoilt westerner's luxury toy, which presents a provocative enticement to impoverished and desperate people.

Piracy is a thriving and noble tradition off the West African coast and the Conquistador doesn't enjoy the protection of the navy or a multinational company as do the larger commercial vessels. The crew has to think defensively to avoid being picked off and so they give the coast a very wide berth.

After two blissful months in the open sea dawdling without any specific dates in their diaries and visiting the beautiful Cape Verde Islands they eventually turn in to Walvis Bay, Namibia.

Following a week in the deep water harbour amongst the fishing boats they press on to Cape Town, then Durban, where it takes a month to repair some damage to the ship's hydraulics. A worn cutlass bearing had resulted in one of the propeller shafts rotating slightly elliptically and wearing a seal loose. The hull became breached and it began to leak; not seriously, but it had to be fixed before they venture around The Cape of Good Hope and across to the Indian Ocean. This gives time to travel inland and even take the Blue Train to Pretoria, followed by a relatively short hop back down to Port Elizabeth to prepare for the Indian Ocean leg where they don't see land for seventeen days.

They later decide to check out Port d'Ehola on the South coast of Madagascar, including a visit to Taolagnaro for no other reason than they can get away with a sneaky bit of tourism on their employer's credit card. They anchor offshore and take the Zodiac into port for day trips.

By now Pete is a fully integrated crew member and is unofficially in charge of the vessel on a few occasions when Berty is sleeping or otherwise occupied.

'Show me how to steer it will you?' he asks one afternoon in the high-tech nerve centre that is the wheelhouse.

'It's all computers these days. I can plot a course then have nap. This thing here will start hooting at me if anything comes into our orbit. It's a bit like a plane really. They can take off and land themselves now pretty much. The captain is just there to stop the punters crapping themselves... Someone has to keep a look out though. I don't trust this kit entirely to keep us from smacking into an oil-tanker or a rock. The depth gauges are the most important things in here when we're anywhere near port. Just like a plane, once you're out at sea or half way up in the sky, there's plenty of time to go for a shit or go down the wine cellar.'

'Do they still have wine cellars on aeroplanes?' Pete jokes.

'You know what I mean, you tosser. Here have a go. Just hold this joystick and keep the front of the arrow pointing at that horizon on the monitor. Keep having a look out of the fucking window as well of course! I'll go have kip. Wake me up if you're about to crash.'

With that Berty is gone and Pete is alone and in control of hundreds of tonnes of steel in a vast ocean with no sight of land. A grand position for a novice, but out at sea it involves no more than keeping an eye out and rousing him from his state room if there is anything to be concerned about. ..which there never is.

Pete is now fully immersed in boat life and uses the time to focus on learning the ropes.

On the upper deck over breakfast at dawn, Berty ventures to find out what is driving Pete away from his career and family.

'The radio tells me that there's certainly some heavy shit going down back in Yorkshire. *Many murders amongst the criminal fraternity.*" What's going on? It's getting like New York in the 1970's!'

'Yeah we've tried hard for years to warn the grown-ups. It's not just me who's throwing in the towel. Most of my colleagues have had enough of it. We've seen this coming for ten years. We're just not given the tools to do the job.'

'Well the criminals appear to be doing a better job of sorting themselves out than the police could ever manage.'

'Yes it's not all bad news. This will make them wake up and throw some resources at the problem but it's too late for me. I've made my choices. I'm not going back now.'

'Looks like you are better off out of it,' advises Berty.

'Why don't you apply for permanent crew?' He continues. 'I can wangle it for you if you want to stay.'

'Tempting, but I don't know at this moment. Maybe I will take you up on that, but not before I've explored on land a bit first.

'And forget that fancy bird as well eh?' chips in the captain.

'Yep. Her too,' says Pete wandering off in order to take in the view and prevent further discussion.

Their ultimate destination is Phuket in Thailand where the boss is due to join them for a week's fishing with his family. That certainty allows a further window of opportunity for indolence and so they have a leisurely time in the new Madagascan port. Their patronage is appreciated by the local traders and poor families who gather on the shore, some even tried to sell their children to the boat.

These western visitors are godlike kings of the sea to the locals representing temptation and opportunity. The crew have to drag themselves away before any news of misbehaviour gets back to Stephano.

A few weeks later they arrive in Phuket. By now, Pete has no concept of time or place. He just awakes at daylight and lives the life of a decadent stateless seafarer.

When they come alongside and are visited by customs, their passports are checked and stamped on board quickly with no record taken. The customs officers are more interested in touring the luxurious ship and checking for illegal immigrants and drugs than focusing on the Caucasian crew members, who they assume are traceable through their employment records if necessary.

Pete isn't sure where he is heading, but Australia begins to crop up in his mind. He thinks it best not to form definite plans. If he doesn't know what he's going to do next, no one else will either.

Wanting to leave the ship before the owner arrives, he persuades Berty to drop him at the airport in the boat's hire car.

Berty shakes his hand outside International Departures.

'Sorry to lose you. Remember to keep in touch'

Pete reminds him 'You ain't seen me right? I need to lose myself for a bit and I would appreciate it if you don't tell anyone where I left the boat, or even if I'd been on it at all if possible.'

'No worries pal. I'm off the grid myself anyway. Haven't spoken to the wife for a month, haven't seen my kids for over a year and haven't paid tax for seven years... No one ever asks me for an opinion anyway.'

'They would if they knew you'd found the secret of a perfect life, swanning around the globe on your ship and getting paid tax free for the pleasure!'

'Ok, here is a deal then,' suggests Berty helpfully. 'I won't tell anyone I've seen you if you don't tell anyone about my job. I couldn't handle any competition for this position and I don't think I could return to normal life now.' he smiles and winks.

'You have a deal. Look after yourself, Berty. Maybe I'll be back sometime soon'

'Welcome, anytime.'

Pete doesn't get on a plane..

He takes the packed bus west to Surat-Thani, already immediately feeling like a student on a gap year. From there he travels by train south to Hat Yai.

His eyes are glued to the window, a permanent travel channel showing the poverty in shanties on the cheapest land at the side of the railway. People are going about their personal business no more than two metres from the track. The teeming mass of traffic and busy human mayhem is an extraordinary education for him.

Once into the countryside, the pace slows. The palm tree jungle flashes by, but the people, busy in their fields make him think he can lose himself there forever. He imagines what their lives might be like. The rural poor when viewed from the speeding cocoon of a train can often seem like the lucky residents of an enticing organic idyll.

He sees what looks like a hardworking but relaxed and healthy life away from the pressures of western suburban industrial economies.

Hat Yai is bonkers, a packed and chaotic shambles. He can only stand amongst tourists and gaze open mouthed in bewildered amazement. To escape the mayhem he drifts into the Wat Hat Yai Nai temple on Phetkasem Rd.

He is as far from being a religious man as it is possible to be. He knows nothing whatsoever about Christianity and has never visited any church for the whole of his adult life, unless someone close to him was being hatched, matched or dispatched. But now, in search of escape, peace and understanding, surrounded by the mayhem of the Thai city which matches the turmoil in his mind, he finds in the Buddhist temple the tranquillity he craves.

The 35metre reclining terracotta Buddha astonishes him, and the respectful silence within the compound brings a surprising but comforting new peace to his mind.

Without understanding or in any way agreeing with the reality, motivations, rituals and scriptures of organised religion, it is possible to seek and find solace in their calm places of worship and contemplation; and so he does, taking deep breaths of the calming incense and closing his eyes to the world.

Six months on the Conquistador has put distance and some perspective on the recent past for Pete. Despite the visual and spiritual distractions, the torment of his guilt and loss continue to stalk his every quiet moment day and night. He has instigated terrible acts of violence towards others and allowed himself to be dragged into the worst thing a police officer can ever be involved in but he can't re-write any of it.

All he can do is to search for some spiritual comfort. It is available in spades here if he can tune in to it. Meditation, contemplation and peace surround him.

It seems here that there is a life not yet overtaken by the hunger for material possessions and not yet a deranged obsession around the constant valueless digital conversation of the internet. He learns nothing about how Buddhism works but relishes and feeds upon its tranquillity. He resolves to return to this place of peace to learn more, once he has made sure that he has put enough distance between himself and his past... if ever possible.

For now however, in order to outrun his demons, he must keep moving.

After a week in Hat Yai doing nothing at all, he decides to move on and explore Malaysia. He takes the night train from Hat Yai to KL Sentral. He thought the cities in Thailand were busy but blimey, Kuala Lumpur! This is chaos at another level!

Wanting to avoid the crowds, he doesn't stay long and flies from KLIA to Perth only to draw some unwelcome attention from customs officers. He is using a false passport acquired in Bradford from a man who he had arrested several times for fraudulent cash transactions between the UK and Pakistan. He had never managed to make anything stick to the likeable rogue. The man's travel agency was a front for a wide range of illegal practices. Despite their obvious professional differences, they had developed a strange friendship based on mutual trust and respect. Pete told the man he needed it for an undercover job and if he asked no questions, it might help in the future to keep the force off his back.

That was a lie, no such deal could ever be offered, but it did no harm to let criminals believe that they had some level of immunity in order to obtain favours or useful information. The man had given Pete some good leads to clear up several drug and violent crimes and Pete knew that a dodgy passport was something the man could quietly arrange.

The Australian customs staff treat him to a proper strip-down and he has to suffer the indignity of his privates being enthusiastically sniffed by an overexcited spaniel. His time at sea has given him a tan, a beard and the hair and air of a hippy. He actually enjoys the fact that he no longer looks like a copper, and is relieved in the extreme that his passport has not attracted attention, but could have done without the attentions of a wet canine nose snuffling around his nudger. He blesses the lord that he had avoided the recreational drugs enjoyed by some of the boat crew.

His job had taught him to ignore all the 'cool' bullshit about drugs. He had seen far too much of the darker side to ever risk it and besides, he had enough problems restricting his intake of food and alcohol.

Once cleared to go, he bends down and strokes the sniffer dog in a risky display of innocent posturing. The last thing he needs is another vice to control. He is grateful that he doesn't have to worry about being apprehended or turned away from the country. Deportation would deliver him right back into the spotlight and could result in questions he can't answer. Mercifully for him, he clears customs with no more than a couple of minor heart stopping moments. Playing a straight bat, whilst interviewing criminals had honed his poker face to perfection.

After a couple of days in Perth he flies to Cairns and works his way down the coast to Sydney following the backpacker's route. He has some raucous nights and makes some friends who in another time he would have hung on to, but right now he wants to be invisible. He moves on without a word whenever he gets close to anyone. He has to disappear whenever anyone becomes close to discussing his identity or his past.

In the Waterfront Grill at Sydney Harbourside where he hangs about looking for work he picks up a five-day old copy of the Sunday Times. It carries a detailed *insight team* article about the Lewis and Flaxton murders.

The journalists are getting nearer than the cops he flashes back. For the first time someone has made a link between those two incidents. It is only in terms of the geographical proximity and the inability of the local force to deal with the aftermath so far, but the article includes speculation about the causes of the death of the principle characters, and the paper has consulted forensic and pharmaceutical specialists who have been persuaded to provide quotes, extensively sprinkled with possible chemical ingredients and speculation about poison agents that could have been responsible.

There is a clear description of the possible method, which accurate or not, Pete thinks is the height of irresponsibility on the part of the journalists to print openly.

Although now himself a criminal, his years of police training and experience leave him with an automatic default reaction towards the preservation of law and order. Journalists who survive by presenting 'scoops' will not consider the fallout from publishing details which can harm people and investigations.

Pete's newly found relaxed demeanour comes to an end on reading this. He is thousands of miles from home and his brain had allowed all this horror and pain to belong to someone else. This article brings it all back in a second. There is nowhere on the planet he can go to hide. No amount of time will change what happened. It is only a matter of time before someone works it out.

What about Adrian? He wonders. *What if he talks about it?*

He and Roberto are the only two who know the truth. He has no fear that Roberto would speak to anyone about it, not even Hazel.

Hate him as much as he did, Pete had no choice but to acknowledge the strength of his enemy.

25 When Love Breaks Down, the Things You Do

Adrian's hotel is going down the pan. He is unable to avoid the bar and bookings are beginning to fall. By his own admission he is turning into Basil Fawlty. The stress is too much.

Just like Pete, he is trying to distance himself from what they did, but by climbing inside a whisky bottle. This makes him a dangerous hotelier. He becomes intolerant of his guests and a rude and very difficult employer.

Asleep on the floor behind the bar he mistook a late returning guest for a burglar. Still in a drunken stupor he attacked the hapless guest with an empty bottle.

'Aaaaaagh!!' screamed the guest 'Get orf me. Take whatever you want!'

'Oh shit, Mr Soppet , I am so sorry, forgive me, I thought you had broken in.'

'I told you I would be back after midnight you lunatic.'

Adrian helped him to his feet and led him to a sofa.

'You reek of whisky young man. I am going to leave in the morning so have my bill ready and take my advice: in future when you attack the guests, make sure they are not retired barristers!'

Resulting legal threats and ex-gratia cash payments kept his former colleagues in the force from finding out, but mostly cleaned him out of reserve cash for his retirement fund. The debts are mounting and room occupation is falling. One night when completely out of ideas and common sense and completely wrecked by liquor he has a thought.

In front of him are a pile of unopened bills and a list of outstanding invoices to be paid. He is on the stop-list of most of his suppliers and the dam is about to burst. Recklessly leaving a trail back to himself, he emails Roberto's pharmacy.

"Hello Mr Antonelli. I am a colleague of Peter Manford's and I have a file here which you might wish to discuss with me over a pint. I will be in Cambridge at the weekend and I will pop in."

Roberto is enraged by this email. He agreed to help one last mission on the understanding that he would then be left alone. He will not tolerate this. He considers himself a rehabilitated man and no-one, nothing will intervene in his life now. He is working towards reconciliation with Hazel to the point where they are talking about looking for a new home together. Hazel will be starting a new job in a month's time and things are relatively stable.

Hazel has not forgotten Pete. But she has chosen to try again with Roberto. She doesn't know that Pete has not received any post for over six months. Her letter asking for his patience and for understanding of her indecision lays unopened in a basket of junk mail in the cellar of his home. The students renting his house have no idea who the owner is and do not care enough to pass the post on to his letting agent. The rental income and the surplus slowly accumulate in Pete's account, which he doesn't touch, for fear of leaving a trail. Hazel's confidence is shaken by the apparent rejection. Despite appearing to have the world at her feet not so long ago, she hits a spell of self-doubt.

Roberto ramps up his efforts to portray himself reborn and surprises her with a weekend in 'the pigsty' near Whitby. It's a Landmark Trust elaborate folly long since cleaned out and converted for weekend occupation. She is turned by the gesture and taken anew by Roberto's charm.

Walking the harbour late one evening after a romantic meal, he proposes to her.

'Not yet Roberto,' she replies, 'but we are heading in the right direction. Why don't we look for a place to do up and move into together and if it all goes well, we can start to plan long term. Ask me again in a couple of years.'

'Ok, I will begin to search for that rectory with a south-facing garden you dream of where we can have our wedding reception. I won't ask you to marry me again though.'

'Why not?'

'I will know you are ready when you ask me!' he replies.

If she learns the truth about him, they are over forever. But the sad irony is that her feelings for Roberto are renewed by Pete's revelations about his past. By lying to her, Pete had secured Roberto's hold over Hazel as she feels that perhaps she has been harsh on him. Roberto decides it's time for the car to go and reluctantly sells it to a railway entrepreneur who is building a business based on the resurrection of old class 56 diesel locomotives to pull freight around the crowded rail network late at night. The purchaser is an engineer and car nut, so the Filton now has a good home.

As a child, when on the knee of the man he then thought was his father, Roberto would go to the Harewood Hill Climb in an Austin Healy and watch while his mother's lover threw it gamely up the hill to the farm. The glamour and excitement stayed with him and when he realised that a passing sports car made some girls turn and look, he never again saw a car primarily as a means to get around.

True, it did bring freedom to roam and a way of getting to work, but he learnt early on that the main purpose of a sports car is to make little boys feel like confident men... men who are not scared to ask women out. This would be his first attempt at facing life without such a prop.

As he is now on the way to regaining the love of the most exciting woman he has ever met, he can risk it. Its sale to fund a sizeable house deposit shows his commitment to building a long term future with Hazel, and the symbolic nature of this development makes her happy so the loss is bearable. To accompany her architecture degree, Hazel immediately embarks upon a part-time post graduate Land Economy course and begins work in the estates' department of St James College. She sees it as a vital stepping stone towards her dream job with English Heritage. The college of St James owns and operates from fourteen Grade II* properties, as well as 7 Grade II and 4 Grade I listed buildings and acres of listed parklands. Learning to manage, restore and preserve these superb buildings will contribute greatly to her CV.

That it was the parent college of her father's school and indeed his own university, makes him proud and contributes to their healing relationship. She is able to show him things he didn't know about the university he attended and he is able to explain how the university works and lives within the ancient walls. St James is no different to the other Cambridge colleges in its care and investment in its traditional buildings while also spending significant amounts of its vast wealth wisely on the finest new buildings. This will give her an unmissable opportunity to learn from the country's best designers and architects in matching the grandeur and historic assets with modern well designed and built halls, laboratories, accommodation blocks and lecture theatres.

Now having funds and opportunity to begin to look for a village rectory in the Fens or the Mendips, for Hazel it represents a clear sign of intent from Roberto.

The pharmacy is now providing a healthy and sustainable income. Roberto begins to wonder about building a small chain of perhaps eight or nine outlets, selling it to a multiple before retiring. In five years or so he could start a new family and walk a retriever with a shiny coat to a village pub.

They find the house they are looking for in a village five miles south of Cambridge which is close enough to town to enable a short commute by train. They stay in the flat above the shop while they engage a designer and builders to sort out the house. They are well aware that moving in and living on a building site will only remain bearable for a month or two and sensibly plan to keep out of the way until at least the upper floors are ready.

Roberto secretly thinks that Hazel will provide too much of a distraction to the builders and knows she will be keen to get her hands dirty as soon as possible. He would have loved to restore it with her over a long period of time as she wanted, but he knows it to be impractical and thinks it best that they focus on earning money to pay professionals instead. He knows that sharing this view with her will most probably prove to be counterproductive, so keeps his counsel. He is convinced that paying the mortgage and the restoration bills whilst building a business when Hazel is so engrossed in mastering her new job will leave no spare time for building works in-between.

They eventually agree that it is best that they concentrate on making a success of their work and leave a project manager to deal with the house.

Zipping around Cambridge on his bicycle also inspires Roberto towards an idea for business expansion. So far there are no prosecutions for drunk cycling. He employs students to expand the cycle delivery service in between lectures. It proves to be popular as the large chemists in the town are less adaptable to such ideas and he begins to steal market share. He outgrows the Fitzwilliam Street pharmacy and decides that the market can easily sustain another branch less than a mile away.

He struggles now to be in two places at once, especially when the new shop so quickly becomes another cash cow. The profits are very encouraging and the timing is perfect to give his favourite employee Steph Baskaya a leg up. She has the qualifications and more importantly the incredible work ethic of the self-motivated self-starter from Eastern Europe. Her parents brought her and her siblings across Europe begging for petrol and food, fleeing from desperate circumstances. After living for two years in a car with her family, she had worked endlessly since she arrived to gain a degree and find a good job.

Roberto marvelled at her success, knowing that her ambition wouldn't stop there as she would soon seek to start her own business. She is happy to learn the ropes in the meantime and help him go the extra mile that makes all the difference. They were introduced by Hugh when she ran his bread stall in his absence while she was a teenage student.

Working on the bread stall was a handy way of networking. It was also there that Hazel met the perfect person to oversee the restoration of their new home: A cockney lass with a Hong Kong Chinese father and Malaysian mother, Kim also had the work ethic and strength of a shire horse. She represented the perfect mix of technical 3D CAD skills and practical knowledge of construction, a flair for design and reason to provide a good service. This project could help to set Kim up. She is a building designer with a new studio: a loft over a mews garage in the centre of town. She had five years' experience at project management and design in rural property restoration and had decamped from a London commercial design house. After ten years the glass ceiling of the testosterone fuelled practice she toiled for had failed to open as it had done effortlessly for her less capable male colleagues.

Now starting out on her own, Kim is hungry for work and new clients so she grabs the opportunity that the restoration of their rectory presents.

Hazel learns much from her and they work well together.

Within two months she has agreed a plan which involves removing walls and creating long, high splayed windows running from floor to ceiling, cleverly disguised by having the outer brickwork re-modelled around each window in matching brick to create sharp angled reveals leading to much wider openings inside the room but barely visible slits on the outer skin. She introduces oak, ash and Scots pine, interior ironwork fittings and shutters and buys rope from Hawes in the Dales and light fittings from Hebden Bridge. The centrepiece of the opened up ground floor is a vast sweeping oak stair. She includes an oak-panelled office with long views across the fields and her piece-de-resistance is a freestanding copper bath in the bay window to the south.

There, Hazel will be able to relax while watching the swaying oak trees in the garden and the endless views beyond. Hazel loves the plans and agrees a programme of works which Kim submits for planning permission.

They get cracking immediately with essential repairs whilst they await consent. They order bespoke joinery items and engage the services of yet another of Hugh's customers to do the works. Hugh's stall and the contacts he makes through it prove to be useful beyond measure. It seems he knows almost everyone in Cambridgeshire.

Roberto is happy to see Hazel grasp the nettle on the restoration works, pleased that it is in better hands than his own. He is best left to drive the business forward and earn the cash to pay for it.

But just as he thinks there is nothing else to stop their happiness, another unwelcome visitor from Yorkshire arrives.

Adrian looms in the doorway and tries friendly bonhomie to greet Roberto.

'Afternoon squire. A good day for a visit to the south!'

Roberto's blood runs cold as he recognises the northern accent. Although they had never met he instinctively knows who this is.

Adrian's out-stretched hand is ignored.

'Fuck off.' Roberto doesn't pretend to be anything other than disgusted to have to deal with this.

Adrian's smile disappears. 'Adrian Collingbridge,' he announces unnecessarily.

'I know who you are. Leave me alone!' shouts Roberto.

Hazel, in the stairwell leading from the shop to the flat hears raised voices as she wheels her bicycle towards the side door that leads to the street. She is on her way to discuss plans for a car port with Kim, but she stops short and quietly listens.

'You have to hear me out.' counters Adrian, failing to gain the momentum he had rehearsed.

'Why exactly?'

'Because I can put you away.'

Roberto's eyes narrow.

'The newspapers say you are no longer on the force. If you are, show me your fucking card.'

'In this case, I don't need to be in the force to put you away.'

'How are you going to do that without going down with me then? Where's your partner?' Roberto stares at him with unconcealed hatred.

'No-one knows exactly. Away at sea somewhere.'

'Drowned, with any luck.' Roberto blurts with as much venom as he could muster.

Just as Adrian lunges towards him, Hazel bursts into the shop.

'What the fuck is going on here!?' she exclaims.

Adrian recognises her and she him, but neither of them acknowledged each other. He and Roberto immediately stand down from their fighting positions.

'What time do you finish, old Pal?' asks Adrian quickly trying, unconvincingly, to change the mood.

'We close at 5, but you needn't come back!' seethes Roberto.

'See you at 5 then.'

'Who the fuck was that?' asks Hazel.

'He's an addict who I am trying to help. He won't have it, but if I give him methadone, it won't do him any good at all.'

Roberto silently curses and bangs his head against the wall once Hazel briefly leaves the shop to stand her bicycle in the street.

The fucking thing won't go away! I can't sit here waiting to be picked off! he thinks. *I told them to leave me alone. If they had, I could just get on with my life, but here they are again, wanting another piece of me. I'm done with this!*

…He was here for five minutes and already I am lying to Hazel again. I will not be defeated by this.

He prepares some chemicals from some jars in the cellar that he had hidden beneath a stone floor, draws them into a syringe and hides them in an inside pocket of his jacket.

When he returns to the shop Hazel has come back in holding the plans.

'What will you do when he comes back?' she asks.

'When who comes back?' he asks, distracted.

'That addict of course.'

'Oh, him. He won't. He comes round regularly trying to ponce some methadone.'

Hazel says nothing more about it. They have a conversation about the plans for the new outbuilding and agree to get a quote for it. He kisses her and waves her off as she rides away with the plans in her basket. He fails to notice that she is sweating, her heart is pounding and she is shaking.

She calls in to the Falcon still trembling with fear and rage and downs a double gin. Her trust in Roberto, challenged of late and put to the back of her mind, now drains away quicker than the gin in her glass.

What did the copper mean, "I can put you away!" Why were they coming to blows and how can I be contemplating a future and having children with someone I neither know nor understand? She recognised Adrian. They had met once when he interrupted a stolen night with Pete in the dales.

Roberto had been away down in his southern hideaway so Hazel had booked into the Herbert Royal suite of the Devonshire Arms in Bolton Abbey. She'd invited Pete there to talk.

They couldn't speak candidly about their emerging feelings when in West Fell as they were never alone. If they weren't with Roberto, any one of the Fell View collective present would prevent an honest and open conversation. They were in the grip of fever for each other and heading towards an affair. Pete had some urgent police business to deal with which involved a quiet conversation in the bar with Adrian who had rung to find out where Pete was and driven up from Bradford.

Adrian called their room from reception and they met in the long lounge bar. Pete left his phone in the bedroom and when it rang Hazel brought it through to the lounge where she had a brief introduction to Adrian before leaving them to it.

Pete and Hazel didn't make love that night. They both wanted to but instead they talked until dawn with room service delivering food and wine.

The fever didn't subside. Being together alone in the room and the self-imposed distance made them both fizz and boil with passion. It was an exquisite and almost masochistic pain and pleasure. Neither of them understood why, but without words they both held back, not wishing to dispel that magic. The wine and intense conversation lead to intimate contact but could go no further. Eventually, they fell asleep in a tight embrace.

Yearnings for lost relationships that nearly get started but remain unconsummated are engraved in memories for longer than ones that go through the whole dance to the end. The longing for what might have been clings in the mind with a tighter grip than the certainty of a failed relationship.

Adrian's gaunt physiognomy was something you would not easily forget and his accent confirmed beyond doubt who he was.

This was the man that Roberto had just described as a local Cambridge addict. She couldn't be mistaken.

She had previously had her doubts but submerged them with exciting events. Now she instinctively knows she has made the wrong call by staying with Roberto. Huge doubts about his hinterland and the unknown had surfaced and troubled her for some time. She can no longer ignore them.

The story that Pete had told her about why they were interested in Rob no longer gave her solace. If it was true, there was clearly more to it than she had been told. Otherwise why would Rob be arguing and lying about Pete's colleague? It probably meant everyone was lying to her. It was too frustrating and confusing. She needed to get away from the men in her life.

Her decision to return to live with Roberto had been based on a promise of one hundred percent honesty. He vowed there would be no more lies, no more hidden truths. Yet here he is, lying again.

The protective layer she had created to anesthetise herself from the pain of grief which had allowed her to ignore many important and obvious signs is suddenly washing away. Now she has a hundred questions about her partner that she should have asked long ago.

Where was Pete anyway? she thought. She must find him if only to get to the bottom of what is going on. She had believed Pete's explanation of Rob's behaviour and promised him that she wouldn't reveal what she knew.

But what is it all about? All she knows is that Roberto had a choice to introduce Adrian as who he really was, but didn't. He chose to lie.

She remembers that he said he was coming back at 5pm. It was 4.40pm.

After necking her gin she dumps the plans for the house in the bin outside the Falcon. There is no way she is going to continue to plan a life with a man who can't level with her. She no longer knows who he is.

She rings Kim. They had developed a good working relationship which was developing into a friendship. They had enjoyed a few nights out in town and at the theatre together. She knows how important the job is to Kim and she genuinely imagined that they could work well together on overlapping work in the future.

'Hi Kim, how are you?'

'Good thanks, did you get the garage plan? What do you think?'

'It's great, lovely... but, listen,' she has to get it over with, 'Look, I'm *really* sorry. Rob and I are splitting up and we have to sell the Rectory. I know this will be a huge blow to you. Please believe me I am gutted about it and it's not your fault. I love your plans and you have looked after us so well, I'm really sorry.'

If Kim was angry she didn't let it show.

'Hey, no hard feelings, I won't lie, it's a huge shock. So quick! I needed the work, so maybe you could put a good word in if you find a buyer for it. Are you ok? Do keep in touch.'

'Send me your bank details and email me any outstanding amounts when you know the numbers. Don't send any more bills to Rob, we've agreed that I will settle everything.' she lies.

Up to this point Roberto has been dealing with the bills for the house, but Hazel wants to make sure that her decision doesn't leave Kim out of pocket.

'Please ask the builders to tidy up and send the bill to Rob, if he doesn't settle it within a fortnight, let me know and I'll sort it. I have to leave town, but I'll soon be back and we'll have a meal and catch up so I can explain.'

'I'm so sorry. See you very soon.'

Hazel ends the call with a heavy heart and then jogs down Tennis Court Road to the rear of the old Addenbrooks site. She crosses the road, entering the Fitzwilliam Museum from the courtyard entrance, so as to not be visible from the pharmacy and watches from an upper window on the staircase for Adrian's return. She has to move around a bit to avoid the attentive staff who are well trained to discreetly keep an eye on things without appearing to be managing the flow of visitors. She pretends to peruse the Lucien Freud etchings, which are on temporary display when the attendants wander by. In between which, she stretches to her full height on tiptoes from where she can see the front door of the shop and observe Roberto still in there working.

The museum starts to close and Adrian still hasn't returned. Hazel needs a new hiding place. As she leaves the museum she sees the pharmacy door open and dodges behind Henry Moore's 'Large Reclining Figure' which she figures is largely reclining on the main entrance Lawn for the sole purpose of providing her with something to hide behind. Moore helpfully provided climbing aids in his sculpture which she uses to clamber up and with a foot on its elbow and peer over the top, just in time to witness Roberto leaving the shop and fixing a note to door, locking it and heading into town on his bike. When he has gone, she jumps down and runs across the road to look.

"Apologies, had to shoot out. Falcon 5.30pm." She reads. She unlocks the door and removes the note before changing her mind and replacing it.

Sprinting down Fitzwilliam Street and back up Tennis Court Road avoiding the obvious route back to the Falcon, assuming correctly that Adrian would be coming out of town that way towards his 5pm assignation; she takes a sly peek into the Falcon. Roberto is there in the rear bar with a drink and a paper.

Right you bastard. This is your last chance to level with me.

The last moments of a relationship are often ones you dredge through looking for blame or justification later, like a council worker sifting through effluent in a sewer searching for a lost wedding ring. Roberto and Hazel's ended like this.

She walks round to the market square and rings his mobile. Speaking as calmly as she can, she says 'I'm up at the rectory with a contractor interested in quoting for the outbuilding,' She embellishes with details about the man she was meeting, adding 'not impressed.'

'I think he's talking too much, and if he says "no problem, darlin" once more, I think I will kick him in the nuts. He seems more interested in my tits than the plans.'

I'm now a liar too, she thinks to herself.

'When are you done this evening?' she inquires.

I know you're already in the pub.

'Oh about eight I think, I'm still in the shop.'

I am lying to her again but I must get rid of Adrian before she asks any more questions, he wishes he didn't have to lie.

'Shall we get a curry later?' she asks, thinking *Please discuss something else.*

'No, not tonight, I have some research to do.' *I have, but nothing could be further from my mind just now!*

'You're still in the shop, are you?' she challenges him to lie to her again just to make sure. *I can see you through the window of the Falcon you lying bastard!*

'Yes. Why?' *Why does she want to know that*? Has he been rumbled?

'Don't bother with a quote from that bloke if you don't trust him.'

Please talk about something else, he begs silently.

'Oh, I was just worried about that bloke who came in,' she feigns concern.

I was worried because you are lying about who he is and it's not the fucking builder I don't trust, it's you. The fucking builder doesn't exist! Neither does the slightest chance that I will spend a moment more with you than I have to, you lying bastard!

'Why are you worried about him?' Roberto enquires.

Why are you asking me that question? 'Who?' she asks.

You know exactly who I mean! they both think.

'Oh, he said he was coming back, only I think I know him from somewhere... where would that be?' she tries again. *There you are right there, your last chance not to lie!*

'Ok, Hazel what the fuck is this about? Unless you have been hanging out with Cambridge addicts I have no idea where you know him from so for fuck's sake move on, it's getting boring. Anyway are we getting a curry tonight? Kundan or the Raj?'

I don't care I am not coming! she is seething. 'Oh, the Kundan then,' she says as she turns off her phone for the last time and simultaneously and equally finally, her commitment to their relationship.

As this, the final conversation of their lives as a couple together is taking place, and because she is desperate to avoid him spotting her through the window, she has wandered into the market place. Hugh, seeing that she was on the phone and having no idea as to the import of her discourse waves from a distance.

She can't engage in any banter so she wheels away into the middle of the market square and pretends to browse the books on Derek's' second hand stall, as so many do when they are plucking up the courage to treat themselves to a doughnut as big as a car tyre or a samosa the size of a pillow. No-one does it the other way around. No-one browses Hugh's comestibles whilst ogling "The Thermal Conductivity of Concrete, Volume 3" or a first edition autobiography of Roy Jenkins.

When the call ends, she runs up to the rear entrance and a second before she burst into the pub to confront him, she pulls up short when sees saw Adrian sitting opposite Roberto.

Her heart stops momentarily. She falls over a table and grazes her forehead on a stone sill but runs away before anyone sees her. Confused, angry and momentarily stunned, she trips again as she flees up into the market square.

She goes into Wellington's and buys some cotton wool for her forehead, then stumbles around the corner to McDonald's and cleans her wound in the basin of the toilets. She has nowhere to go. The rectory is a building site, and she has already decided she will never go there again, most certainly not until she has a full understanding of what the fuck is going on.

Where is Pete? Where the fuck is he?

In the Falcon, the conversation is violent but delivered in a hushed and urgently precise manner.

'Get it over with,' demands Roberto.

'Look I didn't want to come here, I wouldn't ha-'

'Just come out with it.'

'I urgently need ten thousand pounds. My family - ' Adrian stutters and is easily halted.

'I don't give a fuck what you want or why you want it. Why do you think I might?'

'You have to help me, you have no choice.'

'Look you piece of shit, I might have helped you lot a year or two ago. Now, if I wanted to, which I don't, I can't. I've just mortgaged the next twenty years of my life; do I look like I have ten grand to spare? I ride around Cambridge on a fucking bicycle like a fucking student. I don't even have a car.' He says, leaving out any mention of his recent business expansion.

The truth is that he could raise the money easily, but he has a much larger problem with this unwanted visitor.

'So imagine I give you ten grand. You go away and sort out whatever fuck up you've created for yourself. Then, I don't hear from you for a couple of years, and you inevitably fuck up again because you're a moron; otherwise you wouldn't be here in the first place. By then I've put all this shit behind me, and you come back again to crap all over my life. Why do you think there is any chance that I would risk that?' demanded Roberto furiously.

'I assure you that you will never hear from me again, I wouldn't ask for help but I have no choice, my – '

'Leave it there. I am not interested at all. You northern in-breds have used that "Won't hear from me again" shite once too often. That line has lost its sparkle!' he spits.

'Do you want me to tell anyone where Peel Plaice chippy gets its table salt then?' Adrian shoots back almost petulantly.

'Get the fuck out of here you scumbag. Fuck off. I'm giving you nothing.'

'Okay, okay.' Adrian has to play his ace. 'That was Hazel in the shop this morning wasn't it?'

Roberto stops in his tracks and says quietly 'What?'

Adrian, sensing a power-shift, continues 'I know who she is. I'm a detective and Pete is, was, my pal in the force. You know that.'

Roberto sits back in his chair and speaks more slowly.

'So why should that mean you know Hazel?'

'You don't need to know that. You just don't want me to speak to her before I leave Cambridge, I know that for sure. She would leave you in a heartbeat if she knew what I know.'

Roberto needs time to think. 'Okay sit there. What do you drink?'

'Jim Beam. But I'm watching you. I'm not drinking anything that you have handled. Remember, I was compelled to see the results of your experiments.'

'Don't give me that you parasite, your colleague asked for it and you helped to deliver it. You guys are up to your neck in this shit way more than I am. You're paid to keep crime off the streets and you crossed over the line. Don't come here threatening me. I'm merely the gun shop owner. You and your pal decided to buy the gun and fire it.'

'We thought it would knock over two or three of them. If we had known that twenty four...'

'Shut the fuck up you idiot, this is not the fucking deaf home. In any event you should have thought of that you *imbecile*. What did you think they were going to do with 22 portions of fish and chips? Get your own fucking drink.' Roberto throws a £20 note across the table. 'I'm assuming that you can't afford to buy a drink South of Doncaster.'

On the way back to the table, his chance comes when Adrian is called back to pick up his change. Roberto has practiced this move in his mind and he only needs a fraction of a second to deliver a squirt from the syringe in his pocket and slide it up his sleeve. Adrian is sure he has swivelled around too quickly to have allowed time for him to try anything, but he is wrong.

When Adrian becomes drowsy as they leave, Roberto sits him down on a bench outside in the narrow courtyard. In the height of summer this would have been packed with revellers, but this chilly autumn evening everyone is inside. With one eye on the rear window of the pub, he smashes his elbow into Adrian's face three times rendering him unable to rise from his seat. He then runs back into the pub and orders two double Jim beams and nods toward the slumped figure outside.

'He's tired, poor lad.' Roberto stands with his back to the pub window holding Adrian's nose and head back while pouring the drinks into him with soothing words. 'Drink this mate, this will sort you out.'

He leaves him on the bench once he has managed to get as much of the liquid as possible down the recently aggressive foe. With Adrian now a delirious wreck with a broken nose, it isn't much. Adrian chokes and dribbles but in his semi-conscious state swallows enough of it to make the enterprise seem worth another shot or two. Roberto runs over to the 7/11 on Market Street to buy another bottle.

He rings Hugh on his mobile 'Hi pal. Sorry to bother you. Can I borrow the van this evening to collect a fireplace I bought on the market and run it down to the rectory?'

'Sure, but be quick,' says Hugh. 'I need to be in bed before nine so get the keys and leave them under the mat when you come back. I'll be asleep when you drop it off so don't wake me.'

Hugh has perfected the art of grabbing the rest he needs to continue his superhuman lifestyle and the slightest interruption to his sleep pattern could throw him out for days.

Roberto drags the ex-cop across the short stretch of market square cobbles and pushes him down the steps to the subterranean WC's where Hugh had detained the car dealer's hapless apprentice and wannabe assassin some time ago.

He peddles furiously over to Hugh's, picks up the van, throws the bike in the back and returns to the pub; blocking the yard entrance by reversing the van into the narrow alley.

He clambers through the back of the van exiting by the rear doors as there is no room between the van and the walls. The throng around the bar are jostling to attract the barman's attention and no one notices Roberto dragging Adrian up the steps and into the back of the van onto a pile of empty cardboard bread trays.

He drives flat-out seven miles south to a disused quarry near Barrington. Hazel had pointed it out to him one day when they had to restore an old floor in the rectory with a limestone substance called 'clunch', a type of limestone building material used in south Cambridgeshire for the authentic restoration of period property. Hazel had been taken out there a week earlier by Kim and they had come back with a white lime mushy paste all over their boots and jeans.

Hazel had driven him there later to show him on a diversion from a rectory meeting. The provenance of materials and the historically geographical inertia of the supply chain was a part of her life and study now. Roberto was not so interested, but had gone along to feign willingness and appear to be supportive.

He had noticed that the quarry was now mostly closed, awaiting re-development. He was astonished by the scale of the place. It had been active since 1900 and until recently had also been a significant cement works. The removal of limestone had left a crater that would accommodate half of Cambridge and was home to several large lagoons, most of which were inaccessible in the van.

He finds one which he can get near without getting stuck and drags the body into the water piling rocks on and punching it down into the slime. In doing so he becomes completely covered in a sticky white paste. He very nearly sinks into the lagoon himself and only just manages to pull himself out by grabbing a steel pipe. He is choking and resembles a dripping white zombie.

He stands and catches his breath watching the bubbles escaping from the unconscious body as it sinks slowly into the lime.

There is no-one around. He has struck lucky. Two months later the quarry is reconnected to a rail branch line and it begins to take spoil from a new rail tunnel being dug in London.

Two and a half million cubic metres of excavated spoil is soon to be deposited in the quarry crater, brought out of London via Willesden freight terminal by train at night. Once again fortune favours the criminally insane. No one in the north knows of any link between Adrian and Roberto or Cambridge. Adrian, in the grip of a desperate venture to rescue his hotel hadn't had the presence of mind to leave a paper trail as Pete had done eighteen months before.

Roberto finds a hose pipe next to an outbuilding and turns it on himself, dousing his stinging eyes. It takes a long time to wash the white paste off his body and his clothes are ruined.

He has no choice but to remove all of them and carefully empty the contents of his pockets into a crisp packet he finds on the floor of the van. He pulls a roll of bin-liners from beneath the seat and drives back to Cambridge driving through every puddle he can find to clean the wheels of the van, wearing one bin-liner, with his clothes and shoes in another. It is dark by now. He hopes he was still in time to meet Hazel in the Kundan, if she is still talking to him.

He first has to park the van against the side of the doorway to the flat. Luckily Hazel isn't in. He dives into the cellar and hides the bin-liner under the stone floor with his hidden chemicals. He darts upstairs, in such a hurry that he doesn't look around. He quickly throws on a tracksuit, returns the van to Hugh's house and cycles back home. The whole episode lasts just over an hour from start to finish. He is now completely exhausted, sweating and breathless, feeling like he'd run a half marathon.

He was used to maintaining a comfortable distance when dispensing lethal mixtures but this was the first time he has been up close and personal with a victim and he doesn't like it one bit. This is a very different experience and one he has no intention of repeating. Luck has been on his side again. He knows it can't last.

He showers, collapses on the bed and picks up his mobile to call Hazel before realising that he is now very late and she hasn't rung. He calls but her phone is dead.

He looks around the room and for the first time since his return becomes aware most of her clothes and possessions are missing. Some paperwork for the rectory restoration lies in the waste bin with the keys.

The words *"Bastard"* and *"Liar"* have been carved deeply into the timber surface of the kitchen table. She had used the router she had bought to practice rebating when gamely intending to make her own bedroom furniture.

Despite the circumstances and the fact that it was the first time she had used it, she was quite pleased with the result. She had only intended to write 'Bastard' but it went well and she, bizarrely found herself enjoying the precision tool cutting into the glossy new timber table top. Immersed in the moment and thinking it may be her only chance to use it, when she finished the "d", she continued.

Roberto collapses to the floor and holds his head in his hands.

A couple of grand in a brown envelope to that dickhead every couple of months wouldn't have broken the bank. How much does she know? He had to assume the worst and find her to neutralise her by persuading her or worse.

I'm losing it here. Clumsy, messy, fucked in the head... where is she? He feels like his skull might explode.

The guilty can't avoid carrying the burden of what they have done. They will always make five out of two and two. Paranoia and tendency to judge others by their own moral code, often brings the evil and guilty to the wrong conclusion and leads to their downfall. Carrying the knowledge of their deeds is a 24/7 job.

Roberto is not the only manic person rushing around Cambridge in a borrowed van that evening. His pharmacy business had hired a small one to set up the new shop and knowing that Steph had the keys, Hazel told her that she was moving some stuff to the rectory but took it to a store room at St James College in the infrequently used laundry behind her office.

The door didn't lock and all she could do was to leave a note.

"Hazel's stuff. Please leave till Monday, Thanks x."

26 Transience and Passion

Hazel returns the van to Steph and cycles furiously north-west out of Cambridge without stopping until her body can no longer push the pedal for another rotation. It is dark and she is crying as she falls exhausted at the side of the A1. She is a very healthy woman, tall and strong, but her spirit is broken.

Roberto must find and stop her to contain the situation. He doesn't know how much Hazel has unravelled. She may know he is a killer or just that he has been selling drugs to schoolboys. What will he do if it is the latter? Can he save the relationship? If it is the former he will have to stop her somehow, anyhow. All he knows is that he isn't going to jail.

Hazel sleeps in an empty wagon container in a field at the side of the A1 which is used as an advertisement hoarding. *"Jesus is our Saviour,"* it reads. She hadn't noticed, but wouldn't have agreed with its message if she had.

The drumming of the nearby traffic and the biting cold doesn't stop her from sleeping but she awakes at dawn, freezing, with an old man's face six inches from hers. She smells his breath on her face before opening her eyes and her disorientation at the moment of awakening makes her default to defence and flight instantly.

She automatically springs to her feet knocking him over. Her instinct is to repel and survive. He is on the floor on his back in a moment. She leaps over him and is out of the container and on her bike in a second, pedalling as fast as she can. The farm labourer who had entered the trailer to collect his tools meant her no harm, but she couldn't wait around to find that out. After ten minutes of fevered flight as furious as the day before, she calms down and pushes her bike to a café where she digs into a huge, unhealthy breakfast.

She returns east of the Great North Road when she realises that it is no place for a bicycle ride and takes the narrow lanes, getting lost and at one point inadvertently heading south again for half an hour. It doesn't matter. She is confused and alone but vitally far away from Roberto. She hasn't got a clue where she is or where she is heading so he will have no chance of finding her.

For the first time in her life she reads a tabloid newspaper. She is having lunch in the Stibbington Diner, a 24 hour truck-stop.

She amuses herself by looking at the pictures and wondering how such trivia about untalented, vacuous, minor so-called celebrities can be presented as news. She has no idea who any of the people are or what they have done to earn their fame. Looking around at the wagon drivers and travellers she has time to consider how vulnerable, isolated and alone she is. Rather than be cowed by this, instead she feels a rush of excitement, a thrill that for the first time, her destination, her next move, is in her own hands. Not planned, steered, organised or financed by the men in her life.

She has credit cards and some cash with her. Like Roberto she had cleaned out most of her savings to put into the deposit and restoration of the rectory, but she does have enough money left to survive for a while.

Returning to Cambridge is not an option. She borrows a mobile phone from a truck driver and rings her boss at the college. She gets the estate's unit office manager.

'Please can you tell Professor Wright that I've been called away urgently? It's a family crisis and I need a couple of days to sort it out. Could you arrange to put my possessions, which I've left in the laundry into a safe store? And please, I would very much appreciate it if you could ask him not to alert my father as I will be meeting him soon. I'm really sorry. I will explain as soon as possible.'

When his PA rings her back five minutes later the truck driver passes her the phone with a smile.

'It's for you, love.'

'Oh sorry, thank you very much.'

'No problem love, but my secretarial services will have to close in five minutes. I have to be in Leeds by two o'clock.'

'Tim says he will only go as far as to say that he expects you to turn up for a meeting within a week to explain yourself and to discuss your future to avoid disciplinary action. He asked me to impress upon you that this is the one and only time he can tolerate such disappointing behaviour.'

In fact Professor Wright had said that it was curious behaviour, but fine for now. Things were quiet and it would afford him the chance to extend his own weekend in The Cotswolds.

The PA chose not to share that part of his message with Hazel. Her boss's attitude was far more relaxed and accommodating towards the young and attractive new assistant than he ever had been towards her and she resented it.

Until now Roberto had dealt with most of the financial burden. They enjoyed a high standard of living, spending far too much on meals out, drink, clothing and travel. The recreational drugs they occasionally dabbled with appeared from nowhere via Roberto's new friends in Petersfield. She had saved the money that Hugh gave her for helping on the stall, but now she had a full-time job, she looked forward to independence.

She has no idea where she is headed or where to go.

Handing back the phone, she says 'Thanks. Much appreciated. Sorry did you just say you were on your way to Leeds? Do you take passengers?'

'No sorry love, it's against company policy to carry passengers. We're not insured for it. History shows that our loads are under threat from scumbags.'

'Can't persuade you to break the rules then?' she pouts, dangerously goading a man who could have taken advantage of her vulnerability.

'Nope you can't. Anyway, if you don't fancy waking up dead, wrapped up in a carpet in a layby, I wouldn't go around asking strangers for lifts. There are nutters everywhere on the roads. You know that surely?'

Unused to being told 'no', she wonders what is happening to her power over men and presses on.

"With a word you can get you what you came for," she was once told by her Byronic boyfriend.

'Not even for me?' she smiles as seductively as the surroundings would allow.

'No, look I've told you. Piss off now will ya? You're younger than my daughter, and you're pushing me here. I'm not going to give you a lift to Leeds. Just go away if you know what's good for you. Go on, fuck off!'

Taken aback by the ferocity of this rejection and ashamed of herself for trying, she peddles off across the motorway bridge and eventually arrives in Peterborough. She takes the flat country lanes through sleepy villages. After donating her bike to a bemused charity shop worker and walking away without saying a word, tired, but increasingly determined, she takes the east coast mainline train north. As Leeds had been mentioned, it becomes for no other reason, the only plan she has. She will go to Leeds.

Roberto rings her mobile a hundred times, arrogantly assuming that she will turn it back on in time, once she has calmed down. It lies in the mud on the bed of the Cam not two hundred yards from where he is petulantly jabbing the redial button.

Meanwhile, Hazel arrives in Leeds cold, dishevelled, lonely and scared, but also unexpectedly empowered and excited by the adventure.

The train journey has given her time to think. For the first time she begins to run over her time with Roberto: The death of her ex-boyfriend, the partying, falling out with her dad, the whirlwind of working in the shop from Mrs Pickle's regime through to the sale to Wellington's.

She remembers the change in the old lady's mood from vicious battle axe to bedridden, compliant cabbage. Her own mood swings and Roberto's admission that he had medicated her to manage her. The rollercoaster ride of life with him had offered no time for analytical contemplation, but now she felt ashamed not to have questioned anything. Her estrangement from her father now troubled her. What was behind Pete's persistent questions and obvious interest in their life? Her discovery of the strange wooden box was odd, and Rob's violent reaction to finding her looking into his personal effects, worrying.

The train soon arrives in Leeds and she treats herself to a night in the Callings Boutique Hotel. It is a very cool, expensive, but restorative retreat tucked away in a discreet corner of the city on the edge of the River Aire. A short walk through cobbled lanes between wharves and warehouses from the shopping district and theatre, but sheltered from noise and intrusion by the tall brick buildings along the bank-side.

During the early days of her relationship with Roberto they had stayed there on her birthday. He had taken her to see Ray LaMontagne at Leeds University refectory and she has not forgotten the thickest towels, the sexiest staff, the superb bathrooms and bedrooms and the fabulous food. She remembers how much in love she was then and yearns for all of that right now, but not with him.

In the bathroom mirror she recoils in shock at her appearance.

She is covered in mud and the cut above her forehead must have been disturbed in the night. It has bled and congealed in her hair. Why hadn't anyone mentioned it?

When she had checked into the hotel, she noticed the reserved politeness of the sultry receptionist who betrayed her concern by frowning as she said. 'Can I help you?' It was markedly different in tone to the cheerful 'Have a very good evening, Sir,' she had just offered to the American businessman leaving as Hazel had entered.

The phrase 'Can I help you?' just four words, can be used in many ways. This particular one loaded with inquiring but firm expectation of an explanatory response had a huge dollop of concerned and defensive surprise and razor sharp edge attached to its tone. It would suit the Duke of Devonshire in his silk pyjamas knocking on the door of a gypsy caravan attached to a rusty Ford Transit he had woken to find in the middle of the Chatsworth lawn.

Rather than a genuine offer of assistance, in this context, 'Can I help you?' actually means 'What the fuck are *you* doing on my land? Your explanation had better be good, because my wife has called the police!'

The tone of the greeting she received made her feel diminished in the gaze of the attractive woman. Her aura had surprisingly given Hazel a momentary shiver.

She now felt bad for misjudging the situation and the receptionist, incorrectly. She mused that the girl must have been working hard not to say *'Please leave,'* or *'What the fuck happened to you?'*

Hazel looked haunted and drained but didn't need to look like a tramp as well. She can sort this easily.

After a long bath and sleep, her legs stiff and her back aching with a searing pain from all the furious cycling, she sleeps for ten hours and shops for clothes the next day in the Corn Exchange, the Victorian Arcade and Harvey Nichols. Pleased with her new look and her flight from Roberto's grasp; her new adventure now feels more exciting. The distance between them allows her time to reflect and begin to reinvent herself.

She drops into Fernando's in the Victorian Arcade and has her blonde mane removed by a flamboyant stylist. Her new gamine boyish appearance gives her a huge thrill. She has never before sported short hair but then *New hair, fresh start, new life,* she tells herself.

It gives her a lift to feel that she looks good and feels refreshed. Although only skin-deep, physical beauty blesses the fortunate few with an easier ride through life than the majority. She wasn't aware of ever deliberately trading on it but couldn't deny that it had helped her occasionally, and now she needed everything she had to survive.

Hazel knew that she was considered by some to be 'hot'. To her own shame tinged with amusement, she sometimes felt it too – like now. Emboldened by what she sees, the raging self-doubt, about her ability to survive is diminished by the pumping adrenaline from the need to ensure her survival alone. She carried a conflicting basket of feelings around at the best of times. But never anything like this.

She desperately needs her father now. She can't ring him for help as easily as she could have done a year ago. There's something about the edge she got from knowing her survival was entirely dependent on her own decisions for the first time in her life.

Her ability to deal with it empowers her. It gives her a slightly horny, alive feeling. She knows Rob will be looking for her. She is however, pleased with the success of her escape so far. She feels like a hungry leopard, a dangerous and sleek animal. Maybe she now has to hunt to survive.

Dr Anderson is in Tuscany arranging the sale of his farm. His dream of a retirement in the sun reading and writing and growing fruit is now no longer at the forefront of his mind.

The loss his wife and estrangement from his daughter have floored him and he now contemplates his impending retirement with dread rather than excitement.

Of course, if he knew his beloved daughter was in trouble and needed him he would be there instantly but he has no idea. The last time they spoke, she was excitedly engaged in setting up her new life with her chosen man. He should have been happy for her because she was clearly excited about her new adventure. For that of course he was grateful, but his reservations about Roberto never went away. If anything they hardened.

A lifetime dealing with the education and improvement of the progeny of the elite, managing their ambitious but always intelligent and resourceful parents made him a very good judge of character.

Nothing he had learned about Roberto gave him confidence that the man would not one day hurt his daughter. That day had come and he had no idea.

Back in the hotel foyer wearing new jogging bottoms and T-shirt, Hazel presents herself at reception. It took a couple of trips up the cobbles into the shopping streets to get herself sorted, each time passing reception in a more fitting state. She smiles when the receptionist takes an audible intake of breath at the sight of this vision before her, unrecognisable as the tramp who had stumbled in yesterday.

'Right! Where do I go to get some action?' asks Hazel, smiling broadly.

'Anywhere you want to, looking like that!' replies the girl behind the counter standing up and turning to reaching a street map from a shelf. Hazel can't help but notice the dark-haired young girl is wearing a tight black skirt and thin white blouse, through which her black lacy bra failed to restrain her pert nipples. In the fleeting glance that decorum allowed, Hazel notices that they seemed to be reacting to her rather positively, or was it her hungry imagination?

No ring and a sensational figure, the afternoon sunshine through the window overlooking the river renders her blouse irrelevant for the purpose of disguising her profile.

In one second a brain electrified by the thrill of escape, supercharged by the imperative to survive can take in, process, record, file away and produce a response without its owner's sentient involvement.

The numskulls in all departments within her brain are tired from working overtime and are now pulling the levers of control independently of one another. There is no time for them to convene a meeting to plan a rational course of action.

'*What the fuck is happening? Stop it, focus*!' shout Hazel's sensible behaviour monitor to all other departments.

The vision operatives behind her eyes are sending messages of joy and abandonment to the hormonal department downstairs in level 7 and forward planning and health and safety were gagged; tied up in their office with the door nailed shut by the irresponsible clowns in the department of fun.

The girl passes Hazel the map and points out some venues for music, film, food and dancing.

'Where do you recommend?' asks Hazel.

'Depends what you want really, what are you into?'

'Oh, I've had a very, very tough week and I need to relax and think for a few days. I need to lay low for a bit and de-stress. I could do with a wild one then a rest to regenerate I guess.'

'Yeah, I noticed you were looking like you had a challenging day when you came in.'

'Ah yes, I thought you were about to call the police, and when I saw myself in the mirror I can understand why.'

'You sure scrub up well though, don't you? I hardly recognised you when you walked in just now compared to the bag lady that came in yesterday.'

'Your flattery will take you a long way, you know,' says Hazel, as she wanders towards the lift knowing that she's being followed by interested and interesting eyes.

As the lift doors close she can't resist checking herself out from front and rear in the full height mirrors to consider how she appears to her new friend. She saunters back to her room, her heart racing.

Men are causing mayhem in her life. She's alone now with no one to trust.

'Hey, room service. Any chance of some whisky, room 5?'

'I know which room you're in.'

'So what's keeping you? Bring two glasses.'

The girl arrives with one double in one glass.

'Where's yours?'

'Can't drink on duty. Got work to do.'

'Look, I'll be direct with you. I'm in town for a couple of days. I'm alone and in trouble. I need help. I'm scared that my ex will be trying to find me.'

'Can't blame them for that.'

'I can't let him catch up but for now I want to play out. Where do I go?'

'Meet me in the Steel Embrace at seven. It's on your map.'

'Wow. Thank you, that's very kind of you.'

'Don't mention it. I need a drink myself. I have to get back to work now.'

'What's your name?'

'Carla.'

'Thanks Carla, I'm Hazel.'

'I know your name. I have your card details, remember?' She says with a wink as she leaves the room. Hazel lies back on the bed and finishes her whisky.

Dressed in her new jeans, CHL leather boots (they had to be) and long-sleeved black T-shirt over her brand new Carine Gilson lingerie. It's the whole deal. She'll face her new future from a position of strength and renewed confidence, she tells herself.

The Steel Embrace is a bar and restaurant underneath an elaborate brick Victorian hotel. She walks down the stairs and finds Carla on an old leather sofa in an alcove decorated with rock music memorabilia.

'Sorry. Work uniform, I live half an hour out of town, no time to change.'

'Don't apologise. You look fantastic.'

'So do you!'

'I'm just getting used to the new hair, it's weird. I've had long locks since I was five. I keep raising my hand to sweep it from my face and there's nothing there.'

'It suits you.'

'Not too male then?'

'Absolutely not. You look fabulous. Tell me what is your crisis? You have cash, beauty, an ex-boyfriend chasing you, great clothes. All quality problems from what I can see.'

'You are kind. The truth is, I can't be specific, not because I'm attempting to be secretive but because I only have questions, not answers. All I know is that ten years ago I had a clear vision of my future. Now half the people I care about are either dead, betrayed me, or disappeared.'

'Including you, it seems. I mean, clearly you are not dead, but you appear to have disappeared.'

'Disappeared? Can't you see me?'

'No, no disappeared from wherever you were before here I mean... In a hurry it seems. You have no luggage and looked like a drowned rat when you came in. Then this morning, after sleeping till noon, you go out; four trips in and out and you're back with a couple of grand's worth of shopping, a new hairdo and crucially no luggage to carry it all away with. This is all the behaviour of someone on the run to my expert eyes.'

'Wow, its Sherlock Holmes disguised as Penelope Cruz! Been keeping tabs on me have you? I have a new tattoo as well. You missed that didn't you, while you were spying on me!'

'Never! Show me!' pleads Carla.

Hazel rolls up her sleeve and the gauze bandage beneath to show an African looking pattern down her right forearm.

'It's raw and sore. What do you think Miss Observant?'

'Looks painful, but will suit you when it calms down. Lovely actually. What do you mean have I been keeping tabs on you? We're a bit quiet and we don't often get people like you in the hotel alone.'

'What do you mean people like me alone?'

'Wounded, frightened, beautiful gazelles I mean. What happened to your forehead anyway? Your ex?'

'No. I fell over while spying on him and smacked my head on a stone. Does it still show?'

'Not as much as yesterday, but a massive scar will go with the tattoo anyway,' grins Carla 'Why were you spying on him? I can't believe he was stupid enough to be with another woman.'

'No. A bloke.'

'A bloke?'

'Yes, a copper.'

'Interesting. What's going on?'

'I wish I knew.'

'So your ex is seeing a copper on the sly.'

'Yes, but not like that. I don't think for a minute they're shagging. He's a Yorkshire copper; it's still illegal up here, isn't it? No, seriously, I don't know what they've been up to, but after years of trying to find out who he really was, we hit a crossroads. It dawned on me way too late that I was being lied to, only because I came across them arguing. They were almost coming to blows and I was supposed to believe that this bloke I kind of knew from Yorkshire was a Cambridge drug addict. It made me wonder about the connection between them. I don't know what it is but I've got a feeling that it's something dark.

'Things happened around us that I didn't question before but should have done. All of a sudden, nothing seemed to make sense anymore. It's kind of like everything was a bit weird but I didn't notice. I feel stupid now that I didn't question a lot of things earlier. As things started to come undone, he showed a short fuse which only got worse when I asked more questions.' She revisits her recent travails partly for the benefit of her new pal, but it's also the first time she says it out loud. As she does, she tries to make sense of it all. Hazel's delivery is now once more embellished by the manic arm movements and animated facial activity that have disappeared of late.

'What gives you that feeling? And anyway, don't get the idea that convention rules in the north, it's not the 1950's anymore, despite what the food and the dress of most of the populace might lead you to believe.'

'Oh believe me I know that. I grew up 60 odd miles north of here. West Fell.'

'Where?'

'West Fell, North of Swaledale.'

Hazel finds herself moving nearer to Carla as she speaks and notices that Carla doesn't back away. Both are running detection programs to assess every potential body-language hint: the occasional hand on a wrist when making a point, wide eyes and holding a glance, the smile and speedy eye over bodies. Neither have a plan for where this could go.

'Never heard of it. I'm from Colchester. As soon as I leave the south east I'm lost'

'Ha, anyway the thing is, I became very close to one of the coppers, they were linked to some very serious events. Do you remember the travellers who were poisoned for instance? Well they were involved in that, as investigating coppers you understand. My favourite one left the force and disappeared. The other one, who is still sniffing about and arguing with my bloke, was in the papers recently and he's resigned now as well. Anyway there's clearly some serious shit going down between them, none of which I can really explain until I get the facts straight myself. But I can't stick around being lied to by everyone, so here I am! ...What are you drinking? I have a bottle of Malbec on the way.'

'Cool, but I'll just have the one, I have to get a bus,' Carla says, checking her phone for the time.

'Don't go yet. I need the company. Let's have dinner.'

Hazel doesn't want to be alone tonight.

'There's no big rush but I do have to get back. I have a bloke coming to give me a price for some tiling at eight thirty. I don't have enough cash to go eating out on a school night anyway.'

'I'll get it for you. Is the food any good here, or do you know anywhere?'

'Ok, but we'll have to be quick. Let's eat here then we don't have to neck this wine too quickly.' They order and chat while they enjoy the wine.

Hazel knocks it back at twice the speed of Carla and when the meal comes she quickly waves the empty wine bottle at the waiter mouthing '*same again*' deliberately, giving Carla no time to object.

'Look I do have to go.' says Carla, 'No more for me.'

'Please stay. Why don't you put off the tiler bloke until tomorrow and stay in town with me.'

'Look, I don't know who you think I am, but I can't just book into luxury boutique hotels when I have the whim to get away.' It comes out more harshly than she intends.

'Sorry I didn't mean that to wound.'

Hazel quickly comes back to earth.

'No, I'm sorry, I am being selfish. I'm just confused. But don't be fooled, I only have enough money to stay here for a couple of days and that shopping trip I just did represents more expenditure on myself than I've indulged in for the whole of the last five years. I've just spent more on three triangles of lace than I have spent on all the jeans I've ever bought. Don't think I go swanning around like that every day.'

'It's my good fortune that you did. I don't often get mysterious babes turning up out of the blue and offering me dinner.'

'I can't understand why not,' smiles Hazel. 'Do you have a significant other at home?'

'I wish, I've only been in Leeds for two months. I'm starting at Yorkshire Television in February. My rental came to an end, so I thought I would up sticks and take any job till then. My partner left to travel the world and I would have gone too if this job didn't come up. Three triangles of lace, what can you mean?'

'Oh, you must miss him then.'

I hope you don't, thinks Hazel.

'Her.'

'Oh, sorry,' Hazel is excited that her hunch about Carla is spot on.

I'm not sorry at all I am happy that you are free, she thinks to herself.

'Don't be sorry, we had come to a dead end anyway.' Carla replies sadly.

'What's the job?'

'Art direction on a period TV drama.'

'Wow, well done you.'

'Thanks. It's my first leg up from assistant to senior so I'm keen to get on.'

'What does that involve then?'

'Mostly fighting your corner between the designer and producer and trying to retain some artistic, visual creative integrity... Corralling the props guys, the painters, the chippys and costume department. Fighting to see if between us, we can weave a tapestry which is faithful to the script and can be done on a tight budget, usually with no time to spare. That's the gist of it really. Everything you see on the screen except the actors, the speech and the music passes through our hands in some way or another. At the same time covering for the middle aged male designer who is fuck-knows-where, when he's needed. Usually somewhere he shouldn't be with the new intern. Who most times, just happens to be a ridiculously hot chick.'

'Ooh, who knew it was so sexist in that world. I imagined it to be very inclusive and collaborative.' Hazel cosies up to her new pal, checking her out whenever Carla's gaze is elsewhere.

'It is all that too, but basically there is a complicated hierarchy. You're usually doing your boss's job for him while he humps a teenager in a hotel on location on expenses somewhere, but then returns only just in time to take all the credit. Or that's how it usually pans out.'

'Ooh, you jealous then?'

'Fuck off you!' says Carla, hurt and slapping Hazel's arm.

'AAAAArrrgggh!!! My fucking Tatt!' yells Hazel, 'You bitch!' then 'Sorry!' to the waitress who comes to see what the noise was then 'Sorry' to Carla for calling her a bitch.

'No, I'm sorry I will have to be more careful handling you!'

'Anyway, no. Film and telly is still a bit of a blokey world. The hardest part of the job is to get it done on time when everyone is on the fucking phone all day arranging to shag each other, sniff coke or get pissed whilst recovering from last night's debauchery.'

'It sounds exciting though, no?'

'It can be, but mostly very high pressure, long hours and very uncertain career-wise. Digital this and that, which I don't understand enough of will soon be able to recreate any situation you care to mention without all the traditional craft skills. A spotty youth in a cupboard with a laptop somewhere will be able to replace a hundred crew so it will be a case of adapt or die. Plus almost everyone is self-employed on a contract for a specific shoot, so relationships are crucial because as soon as it's done everyone disperses on to the next job and the spotty youth you shouted at one moment, is tomorrow's hot producer or director. Anyway I'm rambling. What are you looking at?'

'You.'

'Why?'

'I like to.'

By the time they finish their food, the second bottle has gone and time has slipped away as it does when you meet someone a bit special.

'Fuck, fuck! I forgot the fucking tile bloke. It's nine already. Shit! Oh no!' wails Carla. 'Look what you made me do!'

'Don't worry; he probably didn't turn up anyway. What now? More wine, then a club?' encourages Hazel, relaxing into a wine fuelled seductive wanton frame of mind.

'Nooooo. I'm on duty at seven in the morning. I *must* go.'

'Look I have an idea. Why don't you stay with me?' says Hazel holding her arm and looking pleadingly Carla's eyes.

'What do you mean stay with you? Where?' Carla removes Hazel's hand from hers.

'Owwww!! My tatt! Please, could I settle up with you?' she says to the passing waitress. 'We have to go now… My date is pulling out on me.'

'I'm not your fucking date you presumptuous madam!'

'You can stay in my hotel room, silly,' retorts Hazel, holding aloft Carla's ring-less hand and pointing to the empty finger. 'Don't you fancy it? You checked me in remember? It would save you rushing back home, only to have to get up before dawn to be back in town for 7.'

She draws circles on the palm of Carla's hand causing sensuous tingling from the gentle touch of her fingertips.

'Of course I remember. But are you crazy? How do I get past reception?' Carla pulls her hand free.

'But you *are* the receptionist,' says Hazel innocently, less confidently, wide eyed and now under the influence of far too much wine.

'You really are confused just now aren't you? I'm the receptionist when I am on duty. But as soon as I'm off duty, someone else is.'

'So?'

'So I leave work at six, then return pissed with a guest and disappear upstairs. What do you think will happen to me in the morning?'

'You would be smiling all day? They would give you a pay rise?'

'I would be collecting my P45 on the way out more likely! Playing out of hours with the guests on the premises is definitely not allowed, no matter how hot they are!'

'But you're the receptionist in the morning so you wouldn't grass on yourself would you? And what *do you* think I mean?'

'The night staff hand over to me in the morning. What will they think when I come downstairs doing the walk of shame instead of through the front door moaning about the weather and the buses like I do every day?... *I think you mean you want me in your bed*.' Carla whispers as Hazel settles the bill with her rapidly depleting card.

They stagger up the stairs and in to the street. It's now dark and cold and neither are wearing warm clothing.

'Look!' says Hazel, trying but failing to walk in a straight line as they head towards the bus stop, 'I've got a cunning plan. I'll go in first and cause a scene over my room card and you could sneak upstairs. ... And yes, I do want you in my bed if you don't mind!'

'But we've only just met, what if you are a strangler?' Carla raises an eyebrow, now intrigued and feeling a shiver of excitement.

Hazel stands up to her full height and pushes her athletic frame into a glamorous pose, shouting to some passing revellers, 'Oi! You there! Yes you! Donkey-jacket-beardy man. Do I look like a strangler?'

'No. I suppose you could be, but I'm willing to chance it,' replies the donkey-jacket-beardy man to much amusement from his pals.

'See!' Shouts Hazel '*He* would chance it.'

'Oh fuck. Shut up you tart. You'll get us into trouble.'

Hazel stops and became instantly serious.

'I'm already in trouble, don't you get it?'

She has no choice but to toughen up to survive. How spoilt and privileged she had been, and how unprepared she now was to tackle life without men she could trust.

Sure, life had been wild back in West Fell but it was amongst friends where she felt safe and although she rejected his attempts to rein her in at the time, she was still close enough to her father to be rescued by him. The village was a safe playground where she tested the boundaries knowing she could go home. She was now utterly alone, cavorting drunk around the streets of a strange city.

Tonight she wants to be held tightly and comforted. The bravado, the tattoo and the new short hair are a part of her new posture but she still harbours conflicting feelings of vulnerability. Hedonism seems the only option. She is out of her depth and more fragile than she will admit, yet she tells herself: *Don't fuck me around evil world, I'll fight back.*

'Look, ok I will come back with you. It's my job after all to look after guests and you are a danger to yourself in this state, but don't get me sacked then fuck off in the morning.'

'Don't worry I'll put in a good word for you if you look after me.' She cackles at her own wit as you only do when seriously under the influence.

In fact it's a piece of cake getting in to the hotel. Hazel asks for another bottle of Malbec which the night receptionist has to get from behind the bar.

Hazel lets Carla in while he fetches the wine. She slips upstairs and waits at the door to room 5.

'Fancy meeting you here,' purrs Hazel grabbing her by the shoulders and dropping her head to kiss her gently on the lips.'

'Come to check your mattress madam,' Carla succumbs to subservient roleplay as Hazel's breathing becomes heavier. She keeps contact with Carla's lips whilst taking the key card out of her back pocket.

Inside the cosy room they both become more coy and reserved than they imagined they might. Nothing a little more wine wouldn't fix.

'May I take a shower madam?' asks Carla, 'I need to test that for work purposes too,' she lamely jokes.

'Be my guest.'

'I need a coat hanger.'

'Why what are you going to do to me?' Hazel sniggers.

'My blouse has to be ironed for work in the morning. It's already creased to fuck.'

'Let me do it while you have a shower.'

'No way, you're far too pissed, you'll burn a hole in it.'

'Here allow me,' Hazel stands up in front of Carla, a full head taller. She unbuttons Carla's diaphanous blouse as carefully as a drunk can whilst kissing her neck and removes it from her shoulders, revealing Carla's black lace bra and the fabulous breasts she has been admiring all evening.

Hazel wonders if her slender, athletic frame is less inviting to Carla than her fuller, shapely figure is to Hazel but she needn't fear. Electrified by its perfection, Carla intends to explore every inch of it.

Hazel envelopes her in her arms and kisses her lips. As their tongues meet, Hazel unclips Carla's bra and caresses her breasts.

~ 340 ~

'You're not really from Colchester are you?'

Carla unbuttons Hazel's jeans and slides her hand inside making Hazel whimper as she thrusts herself against Carla's palm, imperceptibly widening her gait to help Carla's fingers.

'I am. My mother is Spanish though.'

'So fucking inviting,' whispers Carla as her fingers slide inside, making Hazel groan with pleasure.

They are entwined for several minutes drifting towards rapture until Carla suddenly whispers 'wait' and pulls away. She wriggles free from Hazel and removes her arms from her blouse, hanging it on the back of a chair and drops her bra on the floor. Carla leaves the room and spends some time in the bathroom while Hazel helps herself to some more wine. Becoming impatient with desire, she can wait no longer and removes all but her expensive new lace knickers to join Carla in the shower. 'Saving water!' whispers Hazel.

'What kept you?' Asks Carla turning her head back and leaning on the wall to gaze at her and drink in the moment. Hazel gently stoops slightly to kiss Carla's full and soft lips, whilst her hand runs light and free over Carla's rounded buttocks. Hazel lifts Carla up, gently pushing her up the wet shower wall to her height and further keeping her elevated with her arm under Carla's perfect bottom with her legs wrapped around Hazel's back whilst she kisses her breasts and takes turns to bring each nipple to her lips briefly, to burying her tongue in Carla's mouth.

Hazel then lets her petite frame slide gently back to her feet without parting from her flesh. Carla's left hand slides into the front of Hazel's knickers again to tease away all the world's problems.

'What you got these on for? They won't take them back if you shrink them.' Their electrified, excited nipples trace a gentle path across each other's alert and receptive skin like the ends of gentle fingers teasing a sleeping partner awake. They entwine and explore each other gently, then with more feverish urgency, employing their tongues, lips and fingers; leaving nothing undiscovered in an escalation of unbridled passion until even the confines of the generous shower is restricting their movements.

Leading her to the bedroom and lifting Carla on to the middle of the sumptuous bed Hazel winces when Carla's elbow digs into her tattoo. She grits her teeth until the searing pain passes, unwilling to let any torment whatsoever, physical or mental, intrude on her moment. She begins to explore all of her new friend beginning with her erect, dark welcoming nipples. Again, one at a time on her lips, in her mouth and the tip of her tongue. Carla shivers with ecstasy as Hazel pours Baileys from the mini bar over her breasts and licks slowly away. She parts Carla's legs and buries her face between them, feasting like a hungry leopard while Carla grabs fistfuls of her short hair and encourages her head into her crotch. She holds it there whilst Hazel's tongue teases her to delirium. Once fulfilled, Carla returns the favour for longer and with equal hunger until Hazel yells with the primeval violence of a feral and haunted beast.

In Carla's arms Hazel finds all the comfort, passion and excitement she needs to forget the last 24 hours and they enjoy each other more wantonly with increasing abandon and careless excess, disturbing furniture and wrecking the bed until a knock on the door stops them dead.

Hazel leaps from the bed like a starving tiger awakened by an abandoned fawn, knocking Carla on to the floor. She grabs the mini bedside table and holds it aloft behind her back by one of its legs scattering everything it has on it across the room as she opens the door on its chain.

Her senses are tingling. Her crushing fear and the instant switch from a pinnacle of erotic fulfilment to instinctive self-protection give her no time to take breath.

'I am very sorry to disturb your fun, but would you be kind enough to tone it down a little? Enjoyable as it is to hear you so obviously having such a wonderful time,' says a cultured and calm American voice, 'I do need some sleep this evening and I can hear everything through these walls.'

'Sorry, so sorry,' Hazels mumbles, her face already crimson from the stimulation she was enjoying.

'Don't be, I was enjoying it myself for sure, but jeez, guys, don't you need some sleep? I have an important meeting tomorrow which requires some considerable preparation, believe it or not my workstation is wobbling around and I can't concentrate.'

'We will be quiet... apologies, sorry sorry.'

Hazel closes the door and helps Carla back into bed.

'Are you ok? Sorry, I was up before I had time to think. Owwww my fucking tatt!' She yells again, immediately forgetting her promise. She put her hand over her mouth and stands still and silent expecting the American to come back. He doesn't. There is silence for a minute.

'Oooh no come here. You were my magnificent saviour!'

An intelligent mind is the sexiest; jeopardy and fear combined with loneliness and yearning sharpens the senses. The need for temporary escape brought two hungry brains together to explore the outer limits of physical and spiritual ecstasy.

Eventually they drift off to a slumber but what seems like moments later dawn comes with a bang.

The morning light rises over the river, the exhausted lovers awake from their short sleep by a thunderclap and the sound of rain hammering on the sliding window. Hazel gets up and throws the curtains wide, opens the window to the Juliette balcony over the grey water and leans out.

Standing naked in the daylight she stretches to full height and holds the top of the door frame whilst the storm outside lashes her body with freezing rain. She turns to check that Carla is there and it wasn't a dream.

The water refreshes her and she stays there allowing it to rinse her and tighten her skin with goosebumps.

'Hey come back in. It's getting cold in here. I have to go to work in half an hour. I don't want to waste a second.' Hazel shuts the window and turns to see Carla in higher definition than through yesterday's wine goggles. She wants her all over again.

They continue from where they were politely interrupted by the light-sleeping American, Carla's passion ramped up by the memory of Hazel's protective instinct and electrified by the sudden thrill of wrapping her arms and legs around Hazel's freezing wet skin.

Hazel rolls her over and pushes her upper body above Carla's with her arms locked straight so she can admire her. Cold rain drips from her nose and chin on to Carla's breasts.

'You really are a life saver.' Her tongue slides across Carla's toned smooth torso collecting the cold rain drops as the tiger in her awakes once more. She was scared and lonely when she arrived. Now she feels able to take on the world once more.

They make love more gently and in silence after their interruption, the fear of awakening their neighbour, adding a new and conspiratorially exciting dimension.

Carla is back at work at 7am exhausted, but not regretting a moment. No-one notices that she had come downstairs into the lobby rather than through the front door or that she isn't soaking wet despite the horrendous storm outside.

Hazel is asleep before Carla reaches the lift.

She sends some breakfast and coffee to Hazel's room at 10am and checks on her when she doesn't come out before noon. She finds her sitting cross legged on the bed struggling to set up a mobile phone. 'Fucking things, I haven't a clue.'

'I can get Jake downstairs to set it up for you if you want, it will probably need charging.'

'Thanks babe, come here.'

'No way! If I get in there, I won't get out again. Listen, I have to know. Are you checking out or are you staying? You booked one night and you've overshot checkout time by an hour already. I told the crew to leave your room till last, but they're done. Sorry to ask but I also need to know if it's available. The hotel is busy tonight, so they need to know if they can book it out.'

Hazel looks confused. It reminds her that she doesn't have any idea what to do next. 'I'll stay one more night and get a plan together.'

'I guess you can come to mine for a spell if you have no options. But we'll have to talk first.'

'Will you come and see me before you leave this evening please. Say I'm asking about car hire or something. Here, my phone; it would be great if you could get it working. I need to make some calls.' says Hazel, just a tiny bit hurt that Carla won't join her again, but grateful for her offer.

'Sure, catch you later.' Carla blows Hazel a kiss with a grin that ignites her beautiful face and lights up the room.

'Oh! – Hey! – wait Carla. I told you! I said you would be smiling all day!'

Hazel asks to borrow a laptop and uses it to search for Adrian and any trace of Pete or the Manford family. She has to start somewhere. By the evening, she has gathered some addresses in the Ilkley and Grassington areas, a working mobile, a new wardrobe, a tattoo and a new holdall. She has a plan.

She rings her aunt, her only other living relative and tells her she's fine.

She hasn't seen her for two or three years but recent events remind her that she has no one else in the country to care for her now her dad is in Italy.

'I'm no longer with Rob or in Cambridge for the time being.'

'I'm worried about you dear. Roberto phoned several times and then turned up out of the blue at midnight yesterday looking for you.'

'At your house in the Lake District? At midnight? Shit! I mean, good heavens. Don't worry, it's just a tiff, I need to let him stew for a bit.'

'Be careful dear. I wouldn't rush back to him if I were you. Take some time before you make your next decision. You know you have a bed here whenever you wish.'

'Thanks, I love you. I'll be in touch soon. Let me know if you hear from Dad, this is my new number, but of course don't let Roberto have it if he shows up again.'

Her aunt had been comprehensively briefed by her brother and shared his view of Roberto.

This was chilling news. Roberto was looking for her and worked out that she would probably have gone to her aunt. She nearly had done. Her aunt's Lake District home was on her mind as a refuge.

The truth was that she would have headed straight there if she had formed a plan sooner and had thought it through. She hadn't got that far. It was just good luck that she rang first after randomly ending up in Leeds. Her indecision and lack of a strategy had saved her from Rob's grasp but now she must be very careful.

Carla comes to see her. Hazel is looking worried.

'What's up?'

'Oh nothing. My ex has been pestering my aunt looking for me. I need to make myself scarce for a while.'

'Ok, here's a plan.' Carla says, seizing the moment. 'You come home with me tomorrow evening. Check out at 11am tomorrow and wait for me at Leeds station in the pub near the north entrance. I'll see you there at six. You can amuse yourself in town up and down the Victorian Arcades or check out the Henry Moores.'

'They make great hiding places.'

'What do?'

'Never mind. Thank you. I promise I won't overstay my welcome.'

Hazel is sitting on the bed and Carla sits to her right. They kiss and Hazel lies back on the bed, hooked her long legs around Carla, using their strength to pull her closer.

'No. No! Put me down, I have to work and I'm skanky.'

'You are not skanky, you smell of passion. Stay with me tonight my saviour.'

'I can't. I got away with it once, but I can't risk it again. Besides, I'm all manky and need a change of clothing. I will have to tidy up at home to make room for you.'

'Don't make any big efforts on my behalf. I'm very, very grateful to you. Come and see me in the morning then? Bring me breakfast?' asks Hazel excitedly.

'I think that might be possible, but only if you don't get me into trouble.'

'You are so professional.'

'Not really. I'm going to lose my job if you don't leave soon...That American checked out this morning and left you this.'

It was a business card. On the back it said. *"Thanks for the unforgettable night"*

'Oooh! Awkward!' Hazel is embarrassed. 'At least he didn't know it was you in my room.'

'He did! The first thing he said at breakfast this morning was, 'How's your friend's tattoo?'

'Oh dear!'

'Yes! "Oh dear!!" Anyway I've deleted your extras from your bill. Would a professional do that? You can't afford to pay it can you? It costs a fortune to stay here.'

'Yes, don't worry, it's worth every penny. I've never been looked after better in my life and I can afford it, unless I empty the bar this evening because you've abandoned me.'

Carla smiles and kisses Hazel goodbye, slipping from her grasp and keeping her distance by the door, ready to escape.

I will have to speak to Dr Benj when he gets back from Italy. Hazel starts wonder when she'll see her dad again. *I don't want to contact him now because he will try to sort everything out or go to the police or something dramatic. I have to learn on my own what the fuck is happening first.*

She didn't know that Roberto had already thought of that and had rung her father in Italy. He told Dr Anderson that she had left Cambridge and he wanted her address so he could send her some urgent papers.

'How can you not know where she's gone?' Her father demands to know.

'We had a minor tiff. She'll be fine I'm sure,' Roberto replies as calmly as he can.

When her father can't reach Hazel on the phone and draws a blank through his contacts at St James, he's on the next plane home and takes a taxi from Stansted to Cambridge to confront Roberto.

After a blazing row, he gives Roberto two hours to inform him of his daughter's whereabouts before he involves the police.

Dr Anderson had rung St James, from the airport in Italy. He tries to appear relaxed in case it turns out to be a minor tiff as Roberto had said and she returns unscathed, she wouldn't want him to have caused a stir. So he merely leaves more messages for her to get in touch.

After all it's her first real job and having helped from behind the scenes to get her a start, the last thing he wanted to do was to step in and threaten her employment. It was one thing to help her into the post but having done so, she was on her own. It's now up to her to prove herself. It was important to both of them that she found her own feet. It is this strongly held belief that prevents him from asking the right questions. He merely leaves a message for her to ring him. If he had asked to speak to her immediately, it would have become clear that she was unavailable.

He instinctively knows that there is something wrong. He can't breathe properly again until he hears his daughter's voice.

Whilst in Leeds Hazel is unaware that her father is looking for her.

He contacts his sister and learns more before he boards a plane. He doesn't even tell his sister that he is coming back. He implores her to ring as soon as she hears from Hazel, but he knows that if Hazel has left Roberto, she would more than likely seek refuge at her Lake District home. If his sister knew where Hazel was, he didn't trust her not to let the cat out of the bag if Roberto paid her a visit.

He now knows his long held mistrust of Roberto is entirely justified: the man can offer no explanation for Hazel's absence. He won't overreact until he knows more, but he's certain that Roberto is not being entirely honest with him and he hopes that this will precipitate the end of her infatuation.

He can't sleep so he walks the streets of Cambridge, to no avail. He buys a pastry from Hugh as he set up his stall. They had not been introduced until that moment. He was just any other customer as far as Hugh was concerned until he shows him a photograph of Hazel.

'I'm looking for my daughter. Are you here every day?' Dr Anderson has no idea that she had worked for him on the stall.

'Oh! Of course I know Hazel. She is my greatest asset. Very pleased to meet you. She hasn't worked on the stall for a few weeks and I haven't seen her for a little while though.'

'Which stall?' Dr Anderson is puzzled.

Hugh swept his hand across the array of bread in front of them. 'This one of course.'

'My good God has it come to this?'

'Come to what? What do you mean?' replies Hugh, affronted and confused. 'Why don't you ask Roberto in the chemists? You do know him surely?'

'We have met, but she is not with him at the moment and that is the only positive thing I can say.'

She hadn't mentioned her part-time job knowing her father would be disdainful. She was right. He knew very well that Oxbridge colleges demand the total undivided attention of their students. Most of them worked in holiday time, but working in the university towns during term time was mostly frowned upon. In his eyes it was further evidence of her typically irresponsible and unprofessional approach, but he couldn't take away her degree. Now she was in full-time work in a field connected to her studies, whilst she took her post graduate degree. There was nothing he could do about it. He was too late to intervene anyway. Her safety was his only concern now.

Children go their own way and do what they need to do whilst making their own mistakes and hopefully learning from them as they go. Parents tend to proceed with trepidation, their decisions tempered by past mistakes. Most of us make our bravest and most adventurous decisions, as well as our most stupid, when young.

For an academic snob like Dr Anderson, working on a bread stall by choice rather than necessity constituted time wasted. Valuable time, which could have been better spent on research, education or travelling., not to mention exercising, playing or listening to music - just about anything else but indolence or demeaning, poorly paid toil. He would never know the pure feeling of contentment gained from providing a useful service and earning some money honestly whilst engaging interesting people from all walks of life. Here in Cambridge that meant retired media moguls and archbishops, renowned writers and academics, students and party-animals on their way home.

Hugh also looked after council workers on their way to work, world leaders and pop stars passing through town, tramps and addicts, tourists from the east and west and just ordinary Cambridge residents. Each day was an education and a pleasure to Hugh.

The closeted world created within the walls of large public schools and the Oxbridge colleges can create people aloof and ignorant of the pleasure of social interaction with a wider community and Dr Anderson was a good example. It was his loss that he had not learnt this lesson despite benefitting from the best education the world could offer.

Hazel loved her time working on the stall as much as she did her studies and in another life would have been happy doing just that. Events beyond her control would mean that she would never find solace in Cambridge again.

27

A Snarling Hound Snapping at Fleeing Heels

Hazel is on a mission of her own, fleeing from Roberto but also hunting for the truth and searching for Pete.

Pete is in Malaysia, en-route to Australia hiding from his own demons and misdeeds, he is also running away from Hazel.

Adrian was dead and gone. As the first trainloads of London earth are deposited over the area where he lay, Roberto's life begins to implode. His fight to retain his new life in Cambridge is now over. He signs the pharmacy business over to Steph for a pound. She quickly closes the second shop and consolidates the business back in the Fitzwilliam Street premises.

Learning from Mrs Pickles, Roberto retains the leasehold from the college that owns the property and, in contravention of the lease agreement barring subletting, he takes a sky high rent from Steph. As she inherited a very good business for free, the young, keen entrepreneur knows it will be hard work but accepts that it is a cracking deal. Her work ethic will ensure the continued success of the enterprise. Roberto fails to inform Steph of the clause in his purchase of the business which prevents its sale without first offering it to the previous owner. He decides he will deal with that problem later if it arises.

He lays off the builders at the rectory permanently and asks them to remove their equipment, but can't put it on the market without Hazel's signature. It is another reason to find her quickly.

He could either rebuild her trust a second time, or not. If he could, he may be able to persuade her not to involve the police for long enough to get their money back out of the rectory. If not, he may have to take more profound action. He did believe that he loved her, but she would have to accept him for what he was or he would have to silence her and feast on her memory.

He doesn't know where to begin to find her, but he knows she will contact her father as soon as she can.

Dr Anderson arriving in Cambridge searching for Hazel has saved Roberto the chore of tracking him down but also presented a more pressing problem, one he must urgently address.

In the Falcon, he ruminated. He is now an isolated figure whose demeanour alienated him from his friends in the pub. Where once he held court and kept pace with the academics and the football fans, he has become a loner; a miserable sod largely ignored.

It would be easy to remove Dr Anderson with poison but that wouldn't help to find Hazel. Roberto did resent him as a potential blockage to his relationship with her but the sands are shifting and it could be too late now for that to matter. Now he just wants to get to her before it is too late. Perhaps he can use Dr Anderson to smoke her out. After an hour of focused concentration he has an idea. He needs to take control of the doctor's mobile. Hazel would ring it for sure. He would incapacitate her father, not kill him; but with possession of his mobile, he would be able to track her down.

Roberto rings him, taking care to do it from a 'pay-as-you-go' mobile and says 'I have news. Hazel has been in touch at last. She'll be up at the rectory at 5pm and wants you to be there as well.'

'Where is she? Where has she been? I want to talk to her. Immediately! Why didn't she phone me herself?' Dr Anderson thunders.

'I can't help you I'm afraid, I tried to phone her back but it was a call-box. I can pick you up and we can travel up there together.'

'Alright. But only because I don't know where the house is,' the doctor continues, lowering his voice and slowing his delivery. 'I don't trust you. Whatever the outcome, I do not want you in my life. My daughter's decisions are her own, but I will be making my opinions known to her. I have resisted the urge to tell her my view of you for too long, which is not one you will be pleased to hear. I have resolved to do what I can to help her to make the correct decisions for her future. It is my most earnest hope that this will include her ridding you from her life forever.'

Beginning to panic for his own self-preservation, Roberto tries to put himself into the mind of someone contrite.

'I'm so sorry Dr Anderson. I know mistakes have been made but I do love your daughter and I am anxious to put things right if there is any way I can.'

'Well that may or may not be the case,' replies Dr Anderson angrily. 'Furthermore your illegal supply of stimulants to my school has created problems that go far beyond anything you can imagine and you have me to thank for the misguided decision I made not to involve the police to protect my school and more importantly my daughter. If she is harmed in any way I will immediately reverse that decision, which I don't need to add is one I now bitterly regret. I am warning you, once I have spoken to my daughter, I hope this is the last I ever hear of you. If it is not, I assure you that you will regret not respecting what I am telling you now.'

Seeing he is losing ground, Roberto tries to show defeat in the hope of giving enough ground to bring Dr Anderson round to his idea.

'By the sound of what she had to say about me just now I don't think you need worry. It seems she now shares your view. We are meeting to decide what to do about the house and she made it perfectly clear that she was looking to end our relationship.'

It worked.

'If true, that is the most profoundly comforting news. Pick me up at 4.30 at the Corpus Clock.' He rings off not waiting for Roberto's response.

This gives Roberto another idea. He arrives in the market square 10 minutes early in the van he borrows from Steph.

He says to Hugh 'Hey mate, Hazel is coming to meet me, give me some samosas, quick.'

'You found her then?'

'Oh, yeah. She was just freaking out about the new job, the house, falling out with her dad etc. You know how it is.'

'He hasn't fallen out with you over it then?'

'Oh yeah. He's fine. Just dealing with his own guilt about the way she was brought up and taking it out on me. Some of your samosas would cheer them up I reckon.'

'Here,' said Hugh throwing some into a bag, 'Have them.'

'You are a star, thanks,' says Rob.

'Are any of these veggie ones?'

'Yeah, I know he only eats rabbit food. He had some yesterday.'

'He was here?' Roberto is stunned to hear that Hugh had met him.

'Yes. When I was setting up first thing he'd been walking the streets looking for her since Sunday. He's a bit of a toffee nosed twat isn't he?'

'Yes, He's no fan of mine. Can't think why.'

He'll be hungry then hopefully, thinks Roberto.

'Which are the vegetable ones?'

'Green spot on them. Orange spot chicken. Red spot chicken tikka.

'Colour coded food eh? Perfect'.

Purple for poisoned ones then perhaps.

He has ten minutes to put the chemicals in the samosas, which if he knew what he was doing, would knock out Dr Anderson but not kill him. It is the same phial he had used to incapacitate Adrian. Roberto knows that Hazel's father is a vegetarian so the green spot ones were laced with the clear liquid he prepared in the cellar. For now he is still living above the shop until he moves on to the rectory, when Steph would take over the whole building. He blesses the fact that the cellar can be accessed from the side alley and manages to come in and out without Steph being disturbed in the shop. He has more than enough time.

Dr Anderson arrives dressed for bad weather on a grouse shoot, with his phone in his leather gloved hand. As they drive to the rectory, Roberto tries several times to lighten the mood, to no avail.

He does ascertain that Dr Anderson has checked out of the don's accommodation at St James that he'd been using. He plans to take his daughter to Yorkshire that evening if she will come.

On the way Roberto offers Dr Anderson a samosa.

'Hugh from the bread stall asked me to give you these.'

'Not at the moment thank you.'

'I can warm them up on the wood stove when we get there.'

'No, thank you.'

They drive south east out of Cambridge for half an hour out into the remote village of Newton Bridge. The rectory holds a commanding position at the top of the lane which leads to the church and beyond, up to ancient oak woodland. Its position, faded grandeur and quiet location made their choice so easy.

Roberto and Hazel had walked the wood several times and it was fundamental to their decision to mortgage themselves forever to get their hands on the rectory.

Her father is impressed by their choice, but wishes she had done it with another man. In fact any man other than the one she had chosen.

Dr Anderson explores the garden deep in thought mostly to keep away from Roberto, who stays inside and gets the wood burner going, putting the samosas in a tray on the top.

He cracks open a bottle of red wine and pours three glasses.

Dr Anderson comes in after twenty minutes and warms himself by the fire.

'You said she would be here by 5?'

'Yes, what time is it now?'

'5.15 precisely. How is she travelling here?'

'She is getting a lift from a friend she said.'

'Which friend?'

'I don't know, it is probably Kim the designer. Samosa?'

'No thank you.'

Roberto takes one and pretends to take a bite as he leaves the room.

'I'll take a walk down to the junction at the bottom of the lane and see if she is coming. Back soon. Help yourself if you get peckish.'

His breezy and friendly attempts to engage Dr Anderson in a conversation are falling on stony ground. There is to be no rapprochement. He gives up and wanders down the lane throwing his samosa over a hedge, where it poisons voles and badgers for weeks, and heads to the pub for a hard drink.

He figures that with him out of the way and Dr Anderson left alone, he might get hungry. He is right.

When he returns half an hour later, one of the samosas is missing and the venerable Dr Benjamin Anderson EdD MBE is fast asleep in the old armchair Roberto had prepared earlier for this moment.

He leaps into action, pockets his mobile phone, bundles his limp body into the cellar and locks him in. He takes the wine and the samosas down there and checks that there was no way out.

He takes the keys for the house that the builder keeps on a ledge over the front door and puts them in his pocket. He shuts all the windows and doors and yanks the gates together, dragging brambles and weeds with them as they meet in the middle for the first time in twenty years.

Dr Anderson would sleep for the rest of the day. He would not remember how he got down there and he would then have to escape.

The wine and samosas will keep him alive for four or five days at least if he consumed them sparingly, should he not be rescued. Roberto had given him a very strong tranquiliser. He had no intention of killing him. He hadn't yet thought what he would do when this was over, but he would work something out to explain what had happened.

By then, Roberto hopes he would have dealt with the whole situation and been on his way, one way or another. He imagines that he will be able to tip someone off who could rescue him, or return himself; but not before he catches up with Hazel. He has to deal with one problem at a time. He has no idea how he will extricate himself from this rapidly deteriorating situation. Come what may; he knows he must stay in control.

It doesn't work out that way. Roberto thinks he will find Hazel within twenty four hours and then be back to deal with her dad. He doesn't give Hazel enough credit. Her determination to keep ahead of him doesn't help her father.

The cellar has no windows and the rectory is far enough away from the sleepy village for no one to hear him shouting.

Roberto returns to Cambridge and heads straight for the Falcon.

Steph is in there with a middle aged woman.

'Hi this is Patricia. She's going to work in the shop. Hugh said you were meeting Hazel. How did it go?'

'Hi, Patricia. Pleased to meet you. She didn't show up unfortunately. Neither did her dad. I wonder if they found each-other and are having some family time. She must have been up there at some point as she'd left a note.' He lies knowing, that if she had rung or texted, there would be a record of it.

'Oh shame, where is she?'

His mood changes in a flash. He is a coiled spring. The pressure of working out what to do to keep pace pushes him to breaking point. He leans in towards Steph and in a hushed, but threatening tone he spits out a sentence that reveals more about his collapsing world and inability to stay ahead of events than he intends.

'Look, I don't fucking know. I wish I did know where she was. If you hear from her before I do, you fucking tell me immediately right? And in the meantime, get off my fucking back.'

Steph recoils and unnecessarily apologises to him.

'Ok ok, sorry. I can see why you're edgy, but don't take it out on me.'

She has never, in all the time she has worked with him heard him raise his voice. This was dramatically out of character for such a cold and detached man who rarely spoke to her at work.

Patricia doesn't know what to make of it.

'Don't worry, you won't have to work with him,' Steph says quietly.

'Pleased to hear it,' replies Pat, 'What's his problem?'

'I don't know, but I've just learnt something I didn't know about him. He must be under a mountain of stress to behave like *that* in public.'

He storms out of the Falcon and sits on a bench on Parker's Piece. The old man is sorted for now but he doesn't know what to do next. He has to find Hazel. He doesn't want her to leave him. Locking her father in the cellar of their future home was not going to be forgiven. Events are spinning out of control. All he can do is to try to stay a step ahead. He is beginning to doubt his own judgement and question his ability to come out of the other side of this without losing everything, including his mind.

Where can she be? He asks himself.

Playing with her father's mobile, he establishes that the call register shows a missed call from a number not assigned a name in his phone's directory. It has not left a message. He correctly guesses that it might be Hazel. He has nothing to lose so he transfers the number to a pay as you go and calls her. She picks up immediately but he cancels the call as soon as he hears her voice.

Shit shit, I need to sharpen up. He only just managed to stop himself from speaking. She would have known then that he had seen her father. He curses his stupidity. *Text her when you are close!* He tells himself.

He takes the train to London and looks up a few of her school and college friends without success.

He has to change tack. He buys a Ducati Monster from a dealer in Stevenage and some black leathers and helmet with some cash from the underground store. It is a very fast sports-bike on which he can appear anywhere, anytime without being recognised.

As soon as she makes contact he can be on the bike and with her before she knows what's happening.

Unlike the Filton, he can get the bike easily up the track to his wood and hide it in the woodshed. The helmet will also prevent his identification on CCTV. He removes the rear number plate from an old moped he comes across in a farmyard near his woodland and fixes it to the rear of the bike. If he gets caught out on a speed camera, it should keep the police off his case at least for long enough for him to work out a plan.

Basing himself at his rural retreat, he makes several trips around the south calling everywhere he thinks she might be. By now her old uni pals also know she is missing.

'No don't contact her,' he explains 'Give her time, but if she contacts you, don't mention I've been in touch as that might piss her off even more. Instead let me know of any news so I can make it up to her. Thanks.'

This desperate approach merely raises suspicion. No one has seen or heard from her but if they had they wouldn't have told him. His dismissive and silent demeanour has earned him no allies.

Exhausting all possibilities south of Peterborough he returns to the Lake District arriving in Hawkshead at dusk. He waits in the wooded hillside above her aunt's cottage and comes down to the house at night.

He hides in the garden, watches the house and asks in the village shop in the morning. No sign of her having been around at all. Her aunt seems to be busy with the usual pottering about of the retired. If Hazel had been here, he feels sure that he would have seen them together or in the house.

He gives up and goes south east to West Fell. The last thing he wants to do is show up there, particularly without Hazel as it will only result in more questions to answer but he has to consider the possibility that she might stay there with friends, most probably Natasha or around the school.

There are more people there he wants to avoid than meet, but he knows that if she has been there recently, the whole town will know.

He calls on Mark Deacon on the pretext of catching up with the vehicle renovation work and after a brief chat, he knows without asking that she hasn't been seen around. Mark has no news of anything untoward about the whereabouts of Dr Anderson either so he decides to leave while he is ahead of events.

It is time to head back to take stock and lie low, but first he remembers being asked to provide £10k to rescue Adrian's Grassington Hotel which he believes is in this neck of the woods. It is an easy place to start; there can only be one or two hotels in the town and his relatives might reveal some leads he could follow to find her.

Receivers had taken over the hotel and it was for sale, but still open and run by bean counters in order to honour the existing bookings.

'Is this who you're looking for sir?' asks the receptionist handing over a card Hazel left for Adrian two hours earlier. She had written her new mobile number.

'You've just missed her.'

Roberto stares at it, smiling.

'Did she say where she was going by any chance?'

'No, but she came here from Skipton. A cab dropped her off and she went back in a local one that we ordered for her.'

'Do you have a number for the taxi?'

'Sure, it's Andrew Hall. He's the only cab driver in the village.'

He thanks the receptionist and phones immediately. Andrew is an owner-driver.

'Can I get a cab from Grassington Square to Leeds please?' he asks, in order to open a conversation and explore the possibilities.

'Eh? What's all the excitement about going to Leeds all of a sudden? Depends when, squire. I'm in Leeds right now. Just brought a fare all the way from Grassington after doing 'nowt all morning. Won't be back for an hour and 'alf. Shame you didn't ring earlier, you could have shared the fare.'

'Shame. Tell me was she tall and athletic with long blond hair?'

'No why? Who's asking?'

'Oh, it's my wife. We were supposed to be meeting for her birthday weekend in the dales, but I got held up at work. She's not best pleased with me and I'm desperate to catch up with her and make it up to her. So if you see her when you get back to Grassington, please could you give me ring? I'll give you cash if you can get me in touch with her, I'm so upset.'

Fortunately for Roberto Andrew Hall, like many taxi drivers prides himself in his avuncular nature and satisfies his natural curiosity by asking gentle probing questions so he can amuse himself by painting a picture of his customer's lives. During the long ride to Leeds he had hidden his inquiries behind jovial small talk and found out a great deal that Hazel was happy to impart to pass the time, never imagining for a moment that his next customer would be the monster she was fleeing.

'Well good luck to you. You'll have to be quick before someone else looks after her. She's had her hair cut short because she wants a fresh start way away from you presumably and she looks like dynamite to me pal so you'd better hurry up.'

Bingo, fucking Bingo! he can't contain his pleasure at catching up with her at last. 'Where did you drop her please, I need to catch up with her urgently.'

'Well I am very sorry sir, but under the circumstances and in view of what she told me I-'

'I tell you what Mr Fucking Nosy Parker, forget it. I have changed my mind.'

He had what he needed to rope her in.

What form of words would her father use on a text message? He considers his next move for half an hour in the Forester's Arms at the top of Grassington Square.

He has to act quickly in case she is travelling that day. *She may already be on the GNER out of Leeds already. But where to? South probably.*

He discreetly charges her father's phone through a socket next to the bar whilst he reads the Guardian and sips a single malt.

'Darling daughter I have spoken to Robert. I must see you as soon as possible. If you are still in Leeds let's meet please. Can't speak on the phone. He is with me now. Meet me tomorrow. 6pm. Leeds. Footbridge at the Royal Armouries. Where we met last year.'

Roberto *does* know how to send a text - Dr Anderson would use all of a word. He wouldn't use text shorthand and would use punctuation, and he had heard her father use the phrase, '*My darling daughter*'

To avoid his ex-wife and other ghosts in Ilkley, he goes east from Grassington to Pateley Bridge and then stays overnight in Harrogate.

He is getting close. They both know parts of Leeds from their stays at The Callings and Roberto recalls that Hazel had had lunch with her father and had visited the armouries one afternoon.

Roberto turns up at the hotel and hangs around just in case. He doesn't go inside and discounts the possibility that Hazel could be staying there as she was scathing about the cost of the place when they stayed there previously. Now paying for herself, he imagines that she won't consider it.

In fact, although not in residence and now living with Carla, she is at that moment in the hotel lounge having a coffee and keeping warm whilst waiting for the time to walk down to the river bridge.

She is ten feet away from him hiding behind a pillar from where she can admire Carla as she works. Carla has made her promise to behave and not reveal their relationship on pain of death, so Hazel amuses herself by teasing her from across the room: unbuttoning her blouse, carelessly tousling her hair and fanning herself for that unkempt look on the front of a glossy magazine while blowing kisses. Carla cannot make eye contact and do her job efficiently. She stares at the desk and deals with her customers diligently, scolding Hazel from afar with hand signals and wide eyed looks of incredulity when possible.

When the time comes, Hazel leaves Carla a generous tip with a note on a napkin: "Can't wait till I see you later. Off to meet my dad. xx"

Roberto sees Hazel from the balcony of a pub on the opposite side of the river on the Calls Wharf. He leaves his drink, runs up the stairs onto the street and down the cobbled path between the towering, brick warehouses. He is then on to the bridge and sprints to within twenty feet of her before she turns and sees him.

She shrieks and runs in the other direction, across the paved area around the Armouries Museum. She sprints across the open carpark, gaining space between her and Roberto who is running as fast as he can, shouting.

'Hazel, we need to talk, I love you!'

His mistake is to lure her to an area of open spaces, river crossings and canal towpaths. Hazel is long limbed and athletic; Roberto is fit enough, but no match.

If she had continued out on to the industrial areas of Greengates and the top end of the M1, she would have easily been able to lose him, but she makes a huge error and heads for the multi-storey car park hoping to find some people to save her.

During the day it would have been the best move, but at this time of the evening, there are few people around and tragically the doors into the shopping area are locked. Roberto catches up with her on the third floor trying desperately to open a fire escape. He stands fifty feet away from her while catching his breath.

'Hazel, I just want to talk to you.'

She is terrified and angry and fights back.

'Where's my father? What have you done? What is happening?' She berates him venomously.

He tries to calm her, but she is furious, scared, shaking and wide-eyed.

'I don't know where your father is, why would I?'

'You're using his phone. Keep away from me; he's supposed to be here. Why are you here? I don't trust you.'

Roberto steps forward holding out his hands.

'Look Hazel can't we just go for a drink and talk about this?'

'I don't want to talk to you about anything unless you tell me where my father is. How did you know I would be here if you hadn't seen him? Where is he? Was it you who sent that text? *What have you done to him?'* she screams.

'Look, Hazel I can explain everything.'

He moves again towards her, but she takes the initiative and lunges at him with her foot.

She catches him hard in the groin and he steps backwards giving her room to follow up with a knee to his stomach and a punch to the side of his head which gives her fist an eye-watering stabbing pain. She knees him in the face as he bends in pain, knocking him over and runs past him and back down the ramp.

He rises from the floor and follows, but he knows he can't keep up. He watches her sprint over the bridge and into the town knowing pursuit is pointless. She is going like a train, her long strides putting yards between them like a long jumper's run up. She propels herself through the centre of Leeds, dodging between the traffic on the roads when the footpaths were too congested. She runs the distance between the river by the armouries to Leeds station in four minutes. Even if he had known which way she was going, he knows he has no chance of catching her.

From the station she leaps breathlessly on a train without knowing its destination and gets off at the first stop. From there she catches a cab straight to Carla's flat.

He knows he will have to find her quickly before this unravels any further and involves the police.

He wonders about going back the rectory to release her father. *But then what? He may have already escaped or been rescued, in which case the police would be looking for me.* In any case, how would he explain her father's incarceration?

Panicking and turning over his diminishing options, he begins to lose his ability to think rationally. *Do I have to silence her too? I love her, but I am not going to jail.*

Is he capable of killing someone he loves to secure his freedom? If she and her father disappear as well as Adrian, he will be arrested within days. In so many ways it has gone too far.

If he had the time to step back and think, nothing was stopping him leaving the country but he hadn't yet completely given up the possibility that he could put all this right.

If I disappear too, how can they be sure I am the perpetrator not a victim? One of the coppers could have gone off the rails.

Hazel knows now that there is something far more sinister going on than she has imagined: everyone is either disappearing or dead.

She decides that the time has come to contact Pete at work or his employers. She rings Bradford police and is put though to a detective who asks her a lot of questions about why she wants to speak to him. She says she had met him socially and was puzzled as to his whereabouts.

'So are we, to say the least.' Pete's colleague agrees. 'I'm travelling but can I come in on Monday for a chat?' asks Hazel.

'Yes, that would be appreciated. Pete left the force for a career break six months ago and we've heard he's sailing somewhere, but not contactable. Adrian is no longer in the force and is missing following the collapse of his family hotel business. We want to speak to both of them urgently. It's very strange and concerning, it's been ages since we or their families have heard from either of them which is very out of character, we would normally expect at least the odd joke or abusive text message. Would you let us know as soon as you see either of them, if you track them down before we do?'

'Be glad to help if I can, but I am not sure I know anything useful.' She honestly replies.

She remembers that Pete had mentioned his mother still lived in Ilkley and so she takes the short train trip from Leeds station to call and see her.

Half an hour in the library looking through telephone directories throws up three Manfords in the Town, P, A.E and Mrs E.A.C.

Pete's mother lives in a tidy flat in the basement of a large terraced house just opposite the Grove shopping street.

'Come in dear. I'll put the kettle on,' the kindly white-haired old lady welcomes her. 'Do sit down in there. Would you like a slice of lemon cake?' she asks, pointing to the living room.

'Oh, no thank you. I don't want you to go to any trouble.'

Pete's mother brings a piece anyway and insists she eats it. After the terror of the past few days, Hazel soon relaxes in the reassuring company of this lovely lady.

'You look tired dear. Are you alright?'

She hadn't even asked who Hazel was and she was making her feel at home and worrying about her.

Hazel explains to Mrs Manford that the past few days have been very difficult and she doesn't understand what's going on but insists that she has to find Pete quite urgently.

Pete's mum is used to his job throwing up random visits and this is nothing exceptional. Still bright as a button she first assumes that Hazel's arrival is connected to his police work.

'I don't really know quite where he is, my dear. He was on a ship with his friend Berty going to India - or was it Australia? I can't remember. He is at sea you see, so he can't ring me.' Mrs Manford chuckles at her own unintentional rhyme.

'Anyway, you have your tea and I will see if I can find a number.'

'Thank you so much Mrs Manford. You are so kind.'

'Oh don't be silly dear. It's nice to have visitors, and anyway I am not Mrs Manford, I'm Ann, ok?'

'Yes of course. Thank you.'

Ann flicks through a large box file with handwritten notes containing phone numbers.

'It's in here somewhere,' she mumbles to herself.

'You don't have a computer then?' Hazel ventures.

'My daughters want me to get a computer, but what do I want one of those fiddly things for? They cost a fortune and the batteries never work, my son says. I have used this system since I was a librarian. My father used the same cards and he became an archivist. Neither of us ever needed a computer then to do our work and I don't need one of the bloody things now. I'm too old to learn and I'm very happy without, thank you dear.' She is kind, but firm.

A large black cat jumps up on to Hazel's lap giving her a fright.

'Oh, sorry! Get down Jacob, you beastly awful creature. He's lovely really but he has no manners. He doesn't belong to me; he lives across the road with a nice gentleman who goes out to work. Jacob comes over every day to keep me company. It's a very good arrangement; I get the Jacob's company, but I don't have to feed him or pay any vet's fees. I simply phone his owner and he comes and takes him away. Cats don't have owners they have staff you know. I'm Jacob's daytime carer and he is my gentleman caller!' she smiles.

Hazel imagines how great it would be if this lovely woman was her grandma rather than the austere cold hatchet-faced old cow she had to go and visit as a child who claimed to be her father's mother, but was so unpleasant, judgemental and snobbish that Hazel could not imagine how she could ever have nurtured a family.

Ann invites Hazel to her favourite restaurant Monkman's so she has more time to chat. Hazel declines several times but resistance is futile.

Hazel finds Ann's company so engaging and comfortable that she is soon pouring out her heart and telling her she is in trouble. She doesn't say that she is on the run from her ex and fearing for her life, but tells her she needs to stay away from her boyfriend until she had decided what to do.

'I understand, my dear. Why don't you stay over and give the blighter time to think what he has lost? I will sleep on the couch and you can have my bed. It will be fine; I will lock Jacob out so he doesn't pester you in the morning if you want to lie in. That will do the trick and by tomorrow, he will be begging you to come back. What is it? Is there someone else, my dear?'

'Something like that yes. That's very kind of you, but I couldn't possibly take you up on that, you don't know me. I could be a fugitive or something.' Hazel laughs nervously.

'Oh don't be silly, it's no problem. Any friend of my Peter's is alright by me.'

'The truth is Ann, until my life is sorted out. I don't know where to go next.'

'I tell you what, I've had a thought. I don't know why I didn't think if it before. One of my daughters has a flat around the corner and she is working in Belgium at the moment. I'll give her a ring and you can stay there.'

'I can't believe that you're so kind.'

'Oh for goodness sake, shut up and just enjoy yourself my dear.' Ann insists but with a smile. 'Just call it our little adventure!'

'I'll just get the key and show you where everything is. It used to be our family home until all four of them moved out and Fred died. I have a daughter who does education policy in London. She's doing very well but I don't understand it. Then I moved round here to be near the shops. My oldest daughter took it on and has done a lovely job sorting the place out with the help of her younger brother. She's abroad all the time. I think you know

Peter quite well, don't you?' she says with an understanding and sympathetic look.

'Well not very well, but he has been kind to me and I really could do with speaking to him soon if I can.'

'It's been very difficult for him since that awful business in Menston. I won't pry my dear, but if he has any of the sense we gave him, he shouldn't be meddling around in boats whilst a lovely friend like you is in need of help. He should jolly well get himself back as soon as he can. I will tell him that if he remembers to let me know where he is this side of Christmas.'

Hazel starts to cry and hugs the kindly old lady. It is the first time she has felt safe for weeks.

As Ann opens the front door to goes back to her flat, Hazel says,

'I'm sorry but could you do me one last favour.'

'Yes dear, what is it?'

'No-one must know I'm here just yet. Not even Peter for a couple of days. I don't want him to inadvertently tell my ex that I am here. I need some space.'

'My lips are sealed. It's our little secret dear. Anyway Peter hasn't rung home for weeks. If I know him he is swanning around the globe having a jolly old time. I don't expect to speak to him for a few weeks. He needed to get away from that awful business at his work. He's taken on more troubles than a little tacker like him should ever have had to deal with and he's better off away from it if you ask me. I do miss him though'.

The next day Hazel awakes to the sound of birdsong and looks out of the rear bedroom window. There is a wood at the bottom of the garden and she looks out over the idyllic semi-rural paradise where Pete built dens and bridges over the stream with his older brother who went on to specialise in the restoration of rural buildings. There are pictures of the family around the house, pictures of a happy, outdoor life. They were lucky to have such a warm and kind mother who cared for strangers without inquiring into their lives. Her own mother had been capable of being harsh, critical and unkind. She had rarely praised Hazel or bolstered her confidence, quite the opposite. It was only now she was gone that Hazel forgave her and understood that her mother was someone who simply wasn't equipped to cope with life, and parenthood in particular. Perhaps she resented Hazel and her carefree world.

It's too late now, she thinks as she wanders around the large Victorian house overlooking the beautiful, steep-sided valley and the moors beyond. She decides that she could be very happy if she were ever part of this family.

When she tidies up and heads towards the front door, she sees a note with her name on it.

Her heart stopped for a moment.

No one knows I'm here. How can this be for me? She freezes and shakes with fear as she reads the note. It was from Ann.

"I have spoken to my daughter. She is on her way to a conference in Bulgaria and won't be back for a week. I told her I needed to put up a friend in need and she said it's no problem; make yourself at home, Ann"

'Actually think I will,' Hazel accepts.

She stays for almost a fortnight and takes walks up the mossy paths through Heber's Ghyll woods, a Victorian landscaped dell, adorned with moss-strewn boulders, a steep stream cascading over the rocks, meandering paths and quaint, wooden footbridges. She ventures on to Ilkley Moor, through Middleton Woods, up the Dales Way footpath along the side of the River Wharfe to Addingham and then to Bolton Abbey. She passes the hotel where she and Pete had stayed, circling each other all night, so close but a world apart. She finds the medieval ruined stone priory on the bank of the river and sleeps in the sunshine. On the way back she lunches in the Devonshire Arms and wistfully wonders how different things could be now, had she been more assertive in consummating her last visit there with Pete.

It's so nice that no-one knows where she is. She decides not to speak to Carla until she can sort her head out and find some answers. She finds Carla's love invigorating but the balance seems wrong somehow. Carla is in deep for the long term and Hazel is just taking each day as it comes. Rather than deal with yet another dilemma, she simply texts to say she is fine but needs to sort some things out before she returns and ignores her texts and calls after they became hysterical. The peaceful wooded paths along the river offer the perfect place to reflect and try to plan a way forward.

Despite the succour she gains from spending time in Wharfedale, it solves none of her problems. Her hope that it will lead to discovering Pete's whereabouts is not coming to fruition. She had hoped he would contact his family while she hung around and she still has no idea where her father is. Italian police have checked the farm in Tuscany and although he has been seen there recently no one in the village knows when he left.

When no answers come she eventually decides it's time to move on. She takes some flowers round to Ann's flat and finding her out, correctly surmises as it is lunchtime that she would be in Monkman's. Ann is there at her favourite table.

'Thank you so much, you have saved my life. We must keep in touch but I have to go now.'

'Well you know where to find me dear, I don't go far these days.'

Ann takes her hands and pulls her close. 'Now listen to me young lady. You come and stay whenever you need to and that's an order!'

'Thank you so much, I will never forget you. Please, if you hear from Peter, ask him to ring me as soon as he can. I have left my number on a note through your door.'

'I will, don't you worry.'

After three meetings with Bradford police a picture is beginning to emerge from their hard work.

All roads lead back to Roberto as she had begun to suspect. He is now a wanted man. She can't work out what has been going on and nor can the police, but it is enough to know that they can never be together again.

But what about Pete? Will I ever see him again? Has he just used me to get to Roberto? Will I want to see him?

...And then what about Carla? It's been a refreshing and exciting experience. As two intelligent and independent women we understand each other well. Carla has become my saviour and insatiable lover. But now that's not enough for her...

Hazel finds herself sinking deeper into another impossible situation. She is in no position mentally or emotionally, to commit to a long-term relationship.

What they have is born of need for rescue and it has flourished in the heat generated by the exceptional circumstances. Their physical relationship had flared up into a wildfire in no time at all, but is now beginning to dwindle. It is not helped by Carla's fury when Hazel returns to her flat.

'Why did you not tell me where you went?'

'I couldn't, I really couldn't. '

'So you just show up again weeks later and expect me to look after you? Is that it? How do I know you won't do that again? I can't have a relationship on that basis. Why did you turn your phone off? Don't *ever* do that. That's no way to treat me.'

'I can't predict what will happen, Carla; my life is out of control, please bear with me while I try and sort it out,' pleads Hazel.

Now Carla had left the Callings to begin her work at YTV, it is all consuming. The only time they have together is when she is exhausted. Hazel has her own demons and as she isn't working, they begin to behave like a 1950's man and wife. Hazel doesn't mind housework, and even tries her hand at the tiling she had prevented from being professionally executed with impressive results.

Hazel reads more than at any time in her life outside of her education. She needs to see people and stretch her mind. She spends a lot of time on the internet trying to find traces of Pete but her relationship with Carla is heading into choppy waters. Now she wonders how much of it was born of her predicament.

They begin to argue when Carla becomes more serious and begins to make long-term plans. As Hazel pulls away, Carla senses it and tries to convince her to settle down, become 'a couple'. It becomes clear they are on a different page, petty arguments spring from insecurity, threatens and eventually chips away at what they have. Hazel feels guilty for using Carla for comfort and safety and thoughtlessly leading her on.

She lives day to day in torment over her lost friends and family and her indecision to deal with her predicament. This pressure boils over when Carla begins to give her ultimatums about where their relationship is going. It doesn't help that Carla is now either working or exhausted. It seems she wants her lover to be housebound and always available when she returns late into the evening wanting to download the minutiae of each challenging day.

Hazel drifts on, hoping that someone else will make the decisions for her.

Their parting is messy and painful. Carla becomes hysterical when Hazel tries to explain and it ends in a fight when Carla tries to stop her from leaving.

'What do you want from me?' Carla asks when she declines the idea of a foreign holiday.

'You aren't going to be here in July are you? That's why you won't come away with me.'

'The truth is, I just don't know'

'How can you not know?' Carla demands.

Hazel is finding it frightening now. She is reacting like a trapped rat in a barn running from here to there, attacking anyone who gets close. When the final scene comes, she has to overpower Carla to get out of her flat. It becomes physical.

Carla tries to block her path to the front door. Hazel, panics by being restrained and carrying only a tiny back pack, eventually pulls Carla away from the door leaving her in tears.

'How dare you keep me by force? Let me go.'

She hates herself for causing Carla so much pain but can't give her the reassurance she needs.

'I will call you when I have sorted my life out.'

'Please don't,' Carla weeps.

After two weeks looking for Hazel and drawing a blank, on his way to his forest cabin Roberto decides he must visit the rectory to cover his tracks. He arrives at midnight. He builds up speed on the outskirts of the village then quickly turns off the engine of his Ducati and coasts down the lane through the village silently passing the last few houses before the open fields that separate the rectory from the other cottages. No one has been there since his last visit. The gate is still closed as he had left it and there is some mail in the box on the gate.

He wheels the bike into the garden and rests it behind the high ivy-covered brick wall. It is almost a certainty that no-one will travel down the lane this late. It meanders across fields to the nearby woods that isn't even used by dog walkers during the day as the public footpath ends at a hostile sign from the nearby estate just beyond the rectory. *"Do not enter, regular vermin control, danger of accidental injury. You have been warned."*

There are several public footpaths along the river which have much more inviting options other than risking the ire of the landowners from Newton Hall.

No-one heard Dr Anderson scream for help. It took six days to die a terrible, lonely and painful death.

In the cold cellar he had experienced a kaleidoscope of torments. He went through rage, determination to escape, making enough noise to attract attention, through depression, starvation and finally quiet acceptance when he knew no-one was going to come to help him. He died hallucinating and engulfed in madness.

Removing the emaciated and rotting corpse of Dr Anderson was quite easily the most horrendous, unpleasant and nauseating thing that Roberto ever had to do.

The skin on the doctor's once noble frame was detached from his skeleton and moving the body, it slipped and slithered like a plastic bag of melted butter. The chemicals Roberto had used to poison him promoted an accelerated decomposition which had reduced his body to a maggot farm. The poor man's features were moving to parts of his frame that they didn't belong.

He tries to distance himself from responsibility for this despicable crime by reminding himself that Dr Anderson hated him, never trusted him and would have prevented him from long-term happiness with his daughter. If he concentrates hard enough he can make the experience belong to someone else. He wasn't involved. He enables himself to become detached as he drags the rotting and collapsing corpse out of the house. He lays the body on a plastic sheet of damp proofing material and drags it across the garden trying not to look at it.

He persuades himself that he is an unwilling bystander witnessing an awful event rather than the perpetrator.

He strives to project these thoughts to unrelated random events and memories to avoid being in the present doing this terrible work.

Later when alone, in hotels and anonymous guest houses, even in his private sylvan paradise, the horror of what he has done will revisit him. There is no escape.

A couple of months earlier he had murdered Adrian. The sight of his limp and vacant face withered by the lime in the quarry haunts him. In the darkest hours of the night he can't escape his deeds, but by day through the distractions of ordinary life and alcohol he often forgets what he has done. Now, to get through the horrendous task of lifeless human body removal without equipment or expertise, he must make himself believe that this is not him doing this dreadful deed.

He can barely stop himself from vomiting as he shoves the remains of this upstanding and eminent man into a body bag fashioned from a laundry carrier he bought for the purpose. The stench is fetid and unendurable and the physical effort shocks him. He doesn't want physical contact with the corpse. He doesn't really want him to be dead. He had just got in the way but that doesn't matter now. No-one will give him credit for that. The ease of the process which was originally an experiment to see if a couple of annoying toe-rags could be cleanly removed and the lack of any negative consequences has led to this.

Roberto resents DC Manford's interference which has taken over his life and now he has to do these despicable things to avoid detection.

It is now entirely about damage limitation. The naked aggression of an animal fighting for survival. He has no control of where this is all going and his ego tells him that he is the only person qualified to ensure his own safety. He hates being interfered with by anyone, not least a copper with more than one reason to see his downfall.

Using a head torch to light the way, he drags the body to the bottom of the garden. An open pit has been dug by the builders to accommodate a fibreglass septic tank. The bottom of the 4 metre hole had filled with white sludge created by rainwater mixed with soft chalk. He hopes that the body will disappear when he shoves it over the edge. The water isn't deep enough, so he takes a ladder from the scaffolding at the rear of the house and goes down into the bottom. He steps off the ladder and onto the soft ground. Immediately he sinks up to his waist and is stuck for half an hour clinging to the base of the ladder.

Is this where I die too? he thinks. *I deserve this.*

He manages to eventually drag himself out of the mire gripping the rungs of the ladder until his fingers bleed; he hauls himself free and stands on Dr Anderson who sinks out of sight. Roberto is exhausted by the time he scrambles to the surface. He only narrowly manages to avoid joining his once potential father in-law in a joint grave. By now the ladder has sunk into the mud at the bottom of the hole by about a metre. It's stuck, but he has to retrieve it otherwise the builders will dig it out when they come to remove the scaffolding. There is a serious danger that they could drag the remains of Dr Anderson to the surface. He waits until his breathing subsides and gets to work again. After an hour of struggling around in the dark, he attaches a scaffold plank to a stack of concrete blocks, forming a fulcrum by pushing the plank through the rungs of the ladder which protrude above the surface of the earth.

He stands on the far end of the plank and manages to lever the ladder out of the mud. As this happens a large section of the side of the trench falls into the hole, removing any possibility of the body rising to the surface.

Good, he lets out a relieved breath.

He has no choice but to leave it to chance that the builders won't clean out the bottom of the hole before dropping the huge onion shaped tank into the ground.

He knows that the tank is due to be lowered into the hole to rest on a base of clean gravel. Fuelled by adrenaline, he is able to tip half a dozen wheelbarrows full of the gravel down into the hole. With luck the builders will simply complete the job if or when they are re-engaged. Hopefully the passage of time will mean they won't remember exactly what stage they had got to at the point they were stood down.

Recent rain has caused some of the earth which formed the sides of the hole to collapse, and he is able, by attacking the sides at the top of the hole with a shovel to make some more fall in.

He lays down on the wet grass completely shattered. He knows there is no longer a possibility that he can rescue the situation and return to any kind of normality.

He returns down into the cellar and confronts the scene left by Dr Anderson's incarceration. He had clearly tried to escape. There were scratch marks on the window frame and some blood. Roberto wonders about burning the house down to remove the evidence. He doesn't care now if the whole building disappears, but perhaps there is another way.

He lights a fire in the cellar and lets it burn until it becomes a huge blaze. There is little to burn. Some rubbish from the building project and timber shelving, old rags, some chairs but in spite of that it still turns into a large smoky conflagration. He throws diesel from the builder's hut over the areas where he thinks the professor might have left traces and retreats up the stairs. He cares not what happens next but to his satisfaction it seems to remain contained in the cellar. The stone floor and steps and the vaulted brick ceilings prevent its spread to the rest of the house. He opens the door at the top of the stairs which turn the stairwell into a funnel. He lets the smoke out of the back door, confident that the remote location and darkness will prevent any interference.

After an hour or so, the smoke subsides to the point where he can return to the building.

He dampens the staircase by running a hose down the stairs for half an hour. *Well maybe that will do, maybe it won't. It will be a while before anyone comes looking for the old man here.*

Roberto doesn't eat for two days.

28

I Will Walk the Earth for You, to let you Feel my Love

While her father is being buried in a muddy pit, Hazel is back in Ilkley trying to track down Berty's family. She thinks they may know something of Pete's whereabouts.

She learns that Berty's father was once a blacksmith and also ran a pub in Burnsall. His mother was a friend of Hannah Hauxwell, the legendary recluse from lower Birk Hatt Farm in Grisedale. These nuggets of dales folklore help her to track down Berty's wife Liz who now unhelpfully lives in Sri Lanka. Their children still live in the area.

She eventually finds one of their daughters running a café. Hazel strikes lucky as Liz, Berty's wife is in town on a rare visit.

They meet for lunch in Victoria's, the famous Ilkley tearoom where a coffee and cake can cost more than a regular three-course meal. Ann joins them briefly, but has to go after a quick drink because she has arranged to meet a new friend in Monkman's for lunch; a woman who she had recently met on a bus. Ann collects new friends every day.

Around them in Victoria's, rich retired ladies gossip about their holidays on the Amalfi coast while oily coiffured travelling salesmen like Harry Pippin man-spread towards each other blowing smoke up each-other's egos in the hope of pecuniary advantage. Parasitic reptiles in expensive suits, smelling of aftershave, sporting unrealistic tans and selling their dreams of imaginary riches, sip tea and pretend to admire each other's car logo key rings.

Hazel plies Liz with tea and 'fat rascals', unfeasibly large and frighteningly delicious buns, which loosen her already animated tongue further. Liz is a force of nature, speaking at a hundred miles an hour with tales of Berty's exploits.

'He's on the way to Thailand. Or in fact could be there already. He rang a fortnight back and mentioned that Pete was on board. I think Peter was planning to come ashore in Thailand and head home, but I'm not too sure. I'll ask when he calls next and pass on a message if he's still on board. But to be honest love, that could be this afternoon or it could be in three months' time,' says Liz as she grabs another fat rascal.

'Please could you ask him to ring his mother as soon as possible and tell her where he can be contacted?' pleads Hazel. 'I have an urgent reason to speak to him and I'm prepared to travel anywhere in the world to see him, I'll be on the next plane if I can find him.'

'Oh I see, it's like that is it? How far gone are you, love? I warn you; once he gets a taste of life at sea you won't see him for years. Berty went for a month and that was nearly ten years ago. If you want my advice, I wouldn't rely on any man. Bring it up yourself.'

'Oh, no! It's not like that, thankfully. It's all a big mess, but I am not pregnant.'

Liz gives Hazel a complicated set of instructions including numbers and codes which might connect her to the boat's satellite phone and the number of the owner's office in New York. She grabs the remaining two rascals and put them in her bag as they leave.

Using these useful leads, Hazel eventually obtains a crackling and intermittent connection to the boat and briefly speaks to Berty.

'He has been onboard… left the boat in Thailand to fly home a month ago. Told me not to tell you.' He says, casually betraying his promise. 'Is it raining there?'

She decides to find out precisely what Ann knows about Pete's whereabouts. She feels sure he will have kept in touch with his mother.

Back in Ann's flat, after a few sherries, she lets slip that he might be in Australia or could at least be thinking of heading there. She says that Liz had told her about the HM Bark Endeavour taking part in the Sydney Harbour Bridge anniversary flotilla and how Berty and Pete had spoken enviously about the possibility of joining in with the Conquistador if the owner could be sufficiently distracted to allow them the time.

It was clear that Berty wasn't going to make it, but perhaps Pete might be making his way there as he had said he would love to given the chance?

It's an impossibly long shot, but just like Amelia Earhart halfway across the Atlantic with a dodgy stomach and only an empty baked bean can on the cockpit floor, Hazel has nothing else to go on.

The next day Hazel books a flight to Sydney. What better way of putting space between her and Roberto than to fly to other side of the world? Even if Pete isn't there.

She still hasn't heard from her father, so she leaves a message on his work answering service, which she knows he can access from Italy. She measures the tone carefully hoping it shows concern, but not panic.

'Hi Dad. Very worried about you. Give me a call very soon. This is my new number. I'm fine. It's over with Rob. Don't want to see him at the moment if ever. Love you.'

They haven't been in contact for weeks now. There is no mobile signal in Tuscany at his farm. Roberto had contacted him via the school that had passed on a message when he last checked in with his secretary. The school was by then extremely concerned about her father's whereabouts. They knew he was in Italy and often didn't hear from him for up to a week when he was on leave, but he would never leave it this long. They

~ 383 ~

eventually involved the North Yorkshire police who didn't exactly rush to raise the alarm, but eventually arranged an address check and after eventually getting a response from Italy, he was traced to his flight into Stansted. They at last alerted the media and had several high level meetings with their West Yorkshire colleagues. Although less than twenty miles away, the North and West Yorkshire forces were slow to co-operate. They are run as separate fiefdoms and although fully briefed about the missing policemen, they were less concerned about Dr Anderson until now.

Hazel has avoided contact with the school for fear of reigniting old scandals which might embarrass her father. It was their English reserve that prevented Hazel and her father from doing what was required to contact each other but by the time the police begin to join some of the dots, she has slipped out of the country.

She arrives in Sydney in time for the celebrations to mark the 75th anniversary of the Harbour Bridge but the Endeavour isn't in the harbour. It is booked to return during a firework display at the head of a flotilla after a trip to the Hobart Wooden Boat Festival. It had been at sea for eleven days.

Keen to be on board the Endeavour, Pete had indeed joined it in Tasmania as part of the 'mainmast watch.' He knows how to scout a subject; previously it would have been a scumbag on the run, but now it's a ship.

He was collecting glasses in a harbour-side bar during the festival and whilst enjoying a romantic tryst with a backpacker, spots the magnificent wooden ship. It is lit up whilst moored in Devonport Bay. Its master, Joe Motson comes ashore for an evening and invites him to join them for a trip home to Sydney, retracing Cook's route.

Excited at the prospect of a once in a lifetime adventure, he is not able to resist sharing it with Berty who was still in Thailand, waiting for his boss to arrive for his delayed fishing trip.

In a rare phone conversation with Liz, and despite Pete's entreaties to keep the information to himself, Berty shares this news with his wife after she tells him of the beautiful girl who was searching for Pete.

'I wondered why he didn't want anyone to know he was with us. He was obviously running away from something but that's nothing new. Half my crew are on the run from this or that. Makes a change from divorce and debt. A pregnant beauty chasing him eh? The dirty scoundrel. Was she married?'

'I don't think so and she denied being pregnant too, but I didn't buy that. She's a very nice girl but seemed to be carrying a very heavy burden of some sort. You behave yourself. Berty when do we see you?'

'Don't know, love. I think I might get home for Christmas this year because the boss is in Tahiti looking at a villa in December, but you know how it is. Anything could happen. It's too far off to say at the moment. Bye love. Speak soon.'

Pete spends a fortnight on the Endeavour sleeping in a hammock, climbing the rigging, learning to navigate by the stars. The crew are a mixed bunch of adventurers, some running away from experiences and others running towards them. It is one of those unique moments so vibrant that most on board quickly form friendships that will endure for the rest of their lives. They share an experience so special only those on board will understand.

There are prolonged periods when Pete is able to temporarily forget his recent life, but try as he might, Hazel is never far from his thoughts.

They arrive in Sydney early from the narrow gateway formed by the Sydney Heads cliffs to the protected waters of the largest natural harbour in the world; they slip in as the sun rises behind them meeting a flotilla of small ships, mustered as far as the eye can see to greet them. The bridge is closed to traffic and lined with waving families.

The ship is carefully moored and after an hour of tying up and frenetic sail-craft, the crew venture ashore to join the reverie.

Hazel is there waiting in the shadows for the crew to come ashore. She sees him first strutting confidently down the gangplank with half a dozen other crew members who make a beeline for the nearest bar.

She intends to step out to greet him as he leaves the boat, but seeing him in the flesh after so long holding an image of him in her memories makes her step back, feeling unwelcome. She very quickly feels out of place and overwhelmed with doubt, unexpectedly unsure if she is doing the right thing. She can still leave without saying anything and return to England. But no, she has to. How else can she make sense of her life?

For fuck's sake, Hazel! When are you going to learn how to make a decision? She scolds herself and stays out of view so she can follow him. She wants to pick a moment when he is alone, but the chance doesn't come.

She watches him, not wanting him to leave her sight whilst she summons the courage to approach him, the evening air cools and she wishes she had brought more layers. The bar is teeming with drunken revellers. She can see him drinking and laughing with the crew. He looks much younger than she remembered. He has lost weight and caught the sun.

With a lump in her throat, she pushes through the crowd, pokes him in the back and says 'What do you have to do to get drink round here?'

Pete almost falls over with genuine shock, delight and fear. He doesn't know what to think, but he feels like he's just been shot.

'Hazel! How the ffff-?!'

'Shhh. Take me somewhere quiet!' she yells in his ear.

They throw their arms around each other and yell with joy.

They drink a couple of beers with the crew and make their excuses.

All the bars around the harbour are packed to overflowing and everyone is partying like only Australians can, loud, cheerful and friendly.

'See you tomorrow, Brian. Behave yourself!'

'Brian? Who is Brian?' asks Hazel.

'Me.' replies Pete sheepishly. Brian Armitage!'

'What's that about?' Hazel quizzes, becoming tired of constantly asking questions and not getting answers.

'Tell you later,' stalls Pete as usual. 'Anyway, how long have you been in Oz? And how the fuck did you know where to find me? I just can't believe you're here! No-one and I mean no-one knows I was on that boat today. It's so wonderful to see you!'

He holds her and looks into her eyes.

'Is it really you? I cannot ever explain how blown away I am to see you, I thought I had traversed the world to make this moment impossible. Not because I didn't want you but because I do and I can't ever have you.' He hugs her again to prove it's real.

They walk away from the party and head along the shore putting distance between themselves and the noise and lights. They talk and talk.

'Why did you disappear? Where's my father? Where's Adrian?' Pete can't answer her. What he does know he still can't tell her.

'I met your mum, she's amazing Pete, you must let her know where you are! She put me up in your sister's house and was so kind.'

'She knows where I am, bless her. I knew I could trust her. She has never let me down. I bet she dragged you into Monkman's!'

He wonders about Roberto. 'Where is he? Do you still love him?'

She in turn demands of Pete that he tell her what is going on. She had travelled across the world and spent months tracking him down. She wants answers.

They go back to her room where she had left a bottle of wine. She demands he come with her and explain while they drink.

'First I have to tell the crew where I'm going, even if I'm not going back to the boat. I owe them that. I can't leave them not knowing where I went. If I don't see them again I won't have their contact details and I can't do that. You don't mess with maritime etiquette. Besides, my bag's still on board.'

'I'm coming with you. I'm not letting you out of my sight now. Give me your mobile number before we go out in case I lose you.'

'I don't have one. Come on then.' He set off for the door.

She takes hold of his arm and turns him round to look him in the eye.

'Come on, of course you do. Why don't you want me to have your number?'

'I'm telling you I don't; I don't want to speak to anyone so it's just one more thing I don't have to think about charging up and avoiding getting wet on the boat.'

'You're not on the boat now, so get one and give me the number, will you? I haven't come all this way to find to let you slip away again.'

'Ok, ok I will if you get off my arm and come on.'

They return through the throng of revellers and find the crew an hour later by which time they are engaged in the serious business of drinking through a massive Sydney party night. They climb aboard and Pete shows her the boat and his hammock.

'Why couldn't you take me with you? This boat is magical.'

'You wouldn't have come. You know that.' says Pete as he emerges from the hold carrying a tiny rucksack.

'Where's the rest of your stuff?' She asks, puzzled.

'That's it, that's all there is.'

'But it's tiny and it's not even full,' she probes the limp bag.

'Hey! What's that on your arm?' He notices, pushing up her sleeve and examining her tattoo.

'You? With a tattoo?... Hazel Anderson with a tattoo!' he mocks. 'What did your dad say?'

'Don't you like it?' She asks quietly.

He pauses and looks at it for a moment, then faces her and says.

'You are the most amazing, interesting and exciting woman who ever set foot on planet Earth. I love you now and I've loved you for years.'

'Why didn't you tell me that in West Fell?' She has tears rolling down her cheeks.

'You were happily attached. I was unworthy of you. I needed you to show me you wanted me and you didn't. And because I was pissed all the time...'

'Ok, ok enough. Enough! Come back to my place and tell me where my father is.'

'How do I know where he is? How long ago did you lose him? How can you not know where he is?'

Pete is suddenly very concerned. If he had disappeared he could think of one person who would almost certainly know what happened.

Back at her room, they are not even half way through the wine when they end up in the bedroom. The reticence of their previous two similar encounters in Bolton Abbey and Cambridge had gone and they devoured each other. Their encounter is just right. It is beautiful, passionate, and tender; an outpouring of years of passionate yearning, years of denial. They make love for an hour, and then another.

It is perfect. Pete is fit, tanned and lithe; and for the first time feels worthy of this moment. Back in England and full of pies, fish and chips, beer, guilt and insecurity, he had felt his body was undeserving of hers and his mind, heart and soul unworthy of her love but the months travelling and the time on the boat have turned him in to a different man altogether.

Her journey to him makes their consummation perfection.

Pete doesn't tell her anything about the murders and his use of Roberto to deal with his problems. He doesn't tell her that the man she loved was guilty of killing her ex-boyfriend. He realises, however, that he won't be able to avoid this forensic questioning from her any longer and the impossibility of the situation hasn't changed.

If he tells her, she is implicated unless she immediately alerts the police. It is the one thing he acknowledges that Roberto had done to save her. Despite his despicable behaviour, he had saved Hazel from going down with his ship. Pete can't do to her now what Roberto had successfully avoided for so long. He can't change the past, no matter how much he regrets it, but he too must protect her now.

Hazel drifts off to sleep in Pete's arms and when she wakes in the morning, she is alone.

She rushes down to the port and up the rope bridge on to the Endeavour and pleads with the crew. The captain stands up from his morning coffee.

'Where is Pete please?'

'Who?'

'Brian, I mean Brian, where is he?'

'Sorry love, he's left for good. The ship is now in its permanent berth and there's no need for crew until the next voyage. I have no idea when that might be. He was going to stick around to help decommission the vessel but he turned up this morning and said something urgent had turned up. We're well crewed so I let him go.'

She screams and cries and curses him for abandoning her as she runs back down to shore.

'I always thought he didn't look like a Brian,' chuckled the captain.

She doesn't know that he is watching her from a distance with tears pouring down his face. He is inconsolable as he watches her walk disconsolately back towards her room. Both of their hearts are broken. He had left her a note which she hasn't yet found.

"Sorry my love, but I can't allow what we have done to drag you down with us. I cannot be with you. Throw this note away and forget me. I will always love you but our lives have to be apart. Tell no-one you have seen me. Tell Commander Walker at Wakefield what you know about your dad's disappearance as soon as you get home. I can't help. Yours forever Pete .x"

'No! No! No! You bastard!' she wails pointlessly throwing a chair at the wall and kicking her rucksack across the room, heartbroken and in utter despair.

Later in the day she trawls the rail station, the bus stops, and the cafés around the port desperately trying to find him.

Pete hitchhikes out of Sydney towards Adelaide at dawn, quickly picking up a ride at a truck stop. His opening line to the driver of a road train, 'Wherever you're going, mate.'

He ends up in the Blue Mountains after a week of drifting, calling to stay at a farm he had heard about which takes in travellers and asks no questions. It is run by a man who had been in prison for selling cheap wine that he bought in bulk when his crop failed. He had discovered that he could make a very good living from re-labelling supermarket wine with his own vineyard labels rather than going through the bothersome business of actually growing any grapes of his own.

When the 'bottling plant' is raided for the second time, Pete makes a rapid getaway and decides it's time to leave Australia. He had only gone that way because he thought Hazel might expect him to do the opposite. He has no plan, no direction. No idea what to do with the rest of his life.

Hazel ends the day asleep on a park bench with two empty bottles of wine on the floor beside her. She has given up on life.

29 No Rest for the Wicked

At the Rectory Roberto hoses what he can of the mud off his motorcycle leathers and instead of heading for the woods near Baldock, rides north back into Cambridge. On the way, he remembers the business card that a Ligerian man had given him with some vague prospect of a job with the maniac Manoosma. At the time he couldn't imagine anything he would like to contemplate less. But now it seems like a golden opportunity.

Just one thing on his mind now: *I have to get away from here!* He must keep moving.

He makes one last visit to the flat above the pharmacy. It is still dark outside when he free wheels the bike the last two hundred yards coming to a halt silently at the end of Fitzwilliam Street.

He quickly packs a few vital possessions into a small rucksack: passport, bank details and some clothes. He is out of the flat for the last time before dawn breaks. He puts the keys to the flat through the letterbox for Steph to find with a note saying *'On the move now for a while. Might be back soon, good luck.'*

He rides south and briefly calls at his cabin. He cleans out the safe box of the last few hundred pounds, wraps the guns up in plastic and buries them in a steel box away from the building. He turns off the water and calor gas tank, checks the shutters are locked and changes the padlock on the top gate to his land. He doesn't know when or if he will ever return, but he knows it will always be there.

He had bought it through an offshore shell company created for the purpose. His name appeared on no documents relating to its ownership. It came with 18 acres of forest and 50 acres of valuable pasture which he had leased permanently to the farmer who shared part of the access track. Roberto let him have the lease free of charge on one condition: that he respected his privacy and never divulged the existence of the cabin or his identity to anyone. He told the grateful farmer that he was a deep-sea diver in the oil business to explain his absences.

Roberto returns to the A1 at Baldock. At junction 7 he swings off and skirts around Stevenage, arriving at Coasters café in Knebworth. He had been there with Hugh who used to live in the area. The owner is just setting up for the day and lets him sit and have a coffee and read the paper while he fires up the stove.

Roberto's appetite has returned. The brain can file away whatever we force it to witness. It just needs some time to lock it away. He orders a large breakfast and is taken aback by the scale and quality of what is put before him.

'You should charge more for this,' he tells the cheerful owner. 'This is restaurant-quality food.' Roberto is very hungry after his nocturnal adventure and enjoys his breakfast but can't finish it.

'Nice day for a ride. Where are you heading?' The owner asks.

'Oh just took a day off; going into London to see friends.' he lies. He does think a few days in London might be the only place he can stop and think. In truth he is waiting for a polite time to phone Ramalia. They are an hour ahead and it is still a little early to call.

After another coffee and a thorough perusal of the papers, he decides it is time to chance it before the café gets busy.

'Do you mind if I use your phone? My mobile is on the blink.' He lies. 'I'll pay for the call, it's abroad.'

'Sure. Help yourself. Abroad you say? Where to?'

'France.' he lies again.

'Yeah, No problem.'

After the call which goes better than he could have hoped for, he gives the café owner a twenty pound note.

'Keep the change,' he says, 'It will cover the call.'

'We don't get itemised bills here so I'll never know if I owe you or you owe me'.

Perfect thinks Roberto, but says 'Forget it. Have a pint on me if you are up on the deal. It doesn't matter. You've helped me out.'

He later arrives at the newly opened Ligerian Embassy, a far more discreet and compact operation than its previous grand HQ in Pall Mall, which was closed down after UK government ejected all its staff and cut diplomatic ties in the wake of a string of unacceptable adventures perpetrated by the Manoosma family.

After twenty odd years of isolation following a carefully targeted strike on his compound by the Americans, Manoosma has behaved himself as far as the Western world is concerned. The strike was designed to show him what could come his way if he exported any more of his random acts of terror. Prompted by his sons, he has recently put out a tentative hand of friendship towards the West.

He offered compensation for the victims of previous incidents and joined in name but not deed, with the pointlessly branded 'war on terror'. Tony Blair had recently made a trip to the desert. A handshake had been arranged between the dangerously deluded tyrant and Mr Manoosma. They reopened an office in London which was being used as a stepping stone to normalise diplomatic relations. Manoosma was cynically attempting to purchase a respectable place in world affairs and with it the removal of sanctions. He gave not the slightest toss about the atrocities he and his gang had perpetrated and neither did Mr Manoosma. For a time it worked. We fickle British allowed them to re-establish links in London, do large oil deals, purchase luxury goods and sponsor universities. The *'War on terror'*, whatever that meant, was sold as a worldwide coalition. In fact it consisted only of the UK, the US, Spain and hilariously, Albania. Some other tiny and unknown outposts that were clearly dependent on US aid and who would live to regret it had also joined in. The Germans wisely sat on the fence and the French kept quiet as usual and let everyone else do the heavy lifting while they carried on selling arms to all sides 'probably'. Don't imagine that Bin Laden lost any sleep on hearing that Albania was mobilised against him.

When Roberto arrives at the Bureau he finds that it is primarily being used to facilitate the lifestyles of Manoosma's sons and associates on their grand tour. Posturing and arrogant, they spend Ligerian oil money on themselves and the shadowy figures who keep them in power, making contacts and attempting to put deals together to secure their family's grip whilst their father descends into complete madness. Or that's what we are told anyway.

Roberto's timing is perfect. Musa is in town and will meet him for lunch.

He presents himself at the office and meets a surprisingly polite and urbane man who speaks English very well. He demonstrates a detailed interest and understanding of a host of subjects: global economics, English football, and even Filton cars.

'We have one of those back at home,' he says, 'We have every car. We buy through intermediaries as they are very strange about who they will sell to.'

'Tell me about it,' says Roberto 'I had to get fake references and show bank statements before I could buy one.'

'We have much in common my friend Roberto. More than you know.'

No not really thinks Roberto. *Nothing whatsoever in fact.* But politely he says 'Yes, we do.'

They chat as they walk to a waiting limousine which is driven by a bearded, be-suited silent man wearing dark glasses.

As the meal in Kensington Place wears on, they get down to details.

The traffic on Kensington Church Street and the pedestrians outside seem to belong in another world providing moving wallpaper to gaze at whilst attentive staff deliver anything they require.

Musa is extraordinarily candid and surprisingly insightful.

'The sons of successful powerful world leaders are no different to the sons of any other dominant fathers. They both grow up in a huge shadow which protects them but at the same time keeps them in the dark and saves them from the tedium of real learning or education, despite access to expensive tutelage.

'However, intelligence is how you understand, process and utilise information, not merely the quantity presented. So how to progress as adults in our own right? This is more a case of chance rather than inherited wisdom. So it often follows that they rarely possess the intelligence, guile and hunger necessary to continue the franchise conceived and curated by their father's Godlike efforts, much beyond the lifespan of their parents. They rarely have the confidence to imagine, dream and to plan the future.

'I and my brothers are aware of this danger. Although our respect for our father is absolute and sacred, we are trying to engage with the world beyond our borders and beyond our father's lifetime. We hope this way we can use our country's wealth to continue the work of our father to look after our people.

'The world is a different place than when our father liberated Ligeria. Now we must engage with the world. No country can survive in isolation. Although we wish him to be there to impart his wisdom for many years to come.'

Roberto decides that his best chance of benefitting from this unexpected turn of events is to listen in rapt and respectful silence, and so he nods earnestly and allows Musa to continue.

'Our respect and love for our father has no equal and is eternal, but the challenges he has faced, and now faces more than ever, leave him a troubled man.

It is our task to ensure his benevolent legacy continues beyond his life on Earth. But unfortunately, first we must silence the voices of rebellion within our borders.'

Roberto agrees with this assessment, but doubts Musa's ability to take forward his family's dynasty without being overrun by either his subjects or one or two of his more feral siblings, whose deranged exploits have been extensively documented by the media.

Musa's thoughts go further, showing that he is not a one-dimensional clone of his father.

'Often the result of a union between a psychopath and a handpicked cowering beauty, not necessarily blessed with a sparkling intellect, their children are usually spoilt, ignorant, lazy people,' continues Musa autobiographically.

'Whilst they can often inherit mental problems from their parents, they can rarely boast the back-story of valiant struggle and victorious revolution which drove their father to take on all detractors and make it to the exalted position of unchallenged leader. Blood is spilt often and indiscriminately by these dangerously deluded and cosseted young men.

'I understand this is not entirely dissimilar to my brothers and myself,' he candidly confesses, 'I think I am not the only one of my family to spot the danger but the lone one who is doing anything about it and planning to avoid its pitfalls.'

'You are a very insightful man Musa I am impressed by your handle on your situation.'

'Don't be surprised my friend, you English have the best schools but don't have a monopoly on intellect as you assume.'

Roberto can't imagine Ligeria passing into the hands of Manoosma's children, some of whom he had heard displayed the stupidity and arrogance of those who had no knowledge of a life outside a dictator's compound. Or is that how it really is?

He thinks of Baby Doc Duvalier and the lethal family of Saddam Hussain and wonders what a son of Hitler might have been like.

Just like this chap probably, dangerously arrogant and untouchable and probably more so by having the sense to exploit the benefits of an expensive education.

Roberto winces at the clumsy attempts of Musa and his entourage to seduce the waitress and feels sorry for her to have to endure blatant sexual harassment in order to keep her job. In Ligeria no doubt she would have been forced to accept his revolting advances and lunges or she might have faced execution.

Here in London, judging Musa to be a whole lot more enlightened than he is, Roberto is bold enough to try and explain to him that he should control himself a little.

'Musa my friend, we try to be more respectful to women in our country, please leave her alone. Perhaps visit a lap dancing club where we could pester and maul the women who are experienced at dealing with red-blooded men with cash.'

At this gentle suggestion, the mood turns temporarily sour. Musa bristles at the impertinence.

'Who are you to tell the son of the leader of Ligeria what he could do or say? I could buy this restaurant now,' he says. 'I could buy this street and not notice the cost. I can do anything I want to do. Who are you? You are no one. Who is she? No one.

'If you are going to work for my family you will not ever challenge me or try to correct me. If you don't understand this, there is no point in our continuing this conversation and I must ask you to leave now before my staff removes you.'

Roberto realises this is the kind of speech Musa has learnt from watching his father. Although he does not feel particularly threatened, he knows that in Musa's homeland it will carry a whole lot of very real menace and so he apologises in order to keep his interview on track whilst making a mental note to always carry some insurance in his pocket.

The arrogant bully before him can no doubt buy the street as he boasts, and clearly has more to offer than the apparent trappings of his birth right, but Roberto can let that pass, because he could poison the man in front of him and kill him in ten seconds with an untraceable substance and take out the whole street for fun if he so wishes. No-one would ever know what happened. He could do the same for his staff, all the other diners and half of Kensington before anyone works out how it is done.

This knowledge gives Roberto a degree of comfort which enables him to deal with it. In any case he needs a way out of the chaos he has created. But he knows his survival will depend on how he handles this new delicate opportunity and it all comes down to relationships and trust.

Their security detail has gone ahead and asked for some privacy, so they are given a room at the end of the restaurant reserved for private parties.

Roberto is amused to notice that a conversation must have taken place between the restaurant staff. The attractive waitress is now serving at the opposite end of the building and been replaced by an apparently overtly gay man who is either very camp by nature or a great actor having a laugh, he can't work out which.

Roberto sees no reason to delay.

'I'm in serious trouble and need to get out of the UK immediately. If you need my expertise, your timing is perfect.'

Job interviews seldom include a line like that, but his scant knowledge of Ligeria tells him that he was not dealing with any normal employer.

'They tell me that you have detailed knowledge of pharmaceutical products and how to use them to make people well.'

'You are well informed.'

'So if you know how to make people well, you must know how to make them unwell, Roberto.'

'Yes I suppose I do. It's not why we are there, but you are right.'

'My father has many, many people who he wants to make well. He has built many hospitals for the poor and our country loves him for it. He has used the oil to build schools and hospitals, not as you have done in the UK, where you have used your oil to hide the failures of your governments and to pay people not to work, to stay at home and be fat. Yet you are borrowing billions from foreign banks and governments, including ours, to build your hospitals.' Musa raises his hands and employs a quizzical face to emphasise his point

Fair enough, thinks Rob.

'Our glorious leader, my father, is loved by his people for this. He shares the riches of our oil to make the country good for all Ligerians. He freed us from the greed and tyranny of the Italians and previous rulers. We can use your knowledge to make more people well and to look after the old.'

'So where can I help?'

'We need more experts in our hospitals. We need someone who can keep our childrens well.

'But we have many enemies at home and abroad and we don't want them to prosper. We think that there might be a very important role for you. I need to put something to you delicately.' says Musa, leaning forward and speaking more quietly.

'My father has many enemies, Roberto.' he hisses. 'He wants to change and become friends with the West but there are strong forces at home that resists this.

'We have offered our help to heal the mistakes of the past between our countries and we now do much business here in London. I have personally given two millions of dollars to a university here. There are many traitors who wish to harm my father and sometimes we must protect ourselves from these traitors. We know that you can help us with this. We have been keeping our closest eyes open on you and we think you are the man we need to assist our laboratories and help my father to calm those who wish him harm.'

'Calm them?'

'Yes. Make them calm and not angry against my father.'

'How calm exactly do you want them to be?'

'It depends on the strength of the threat they pose to us. Some we wish to be just a little calmer and some we wish to become so calm that they do not move at all,' he smirks.

'I think you understand me, no? You will come to Ramalia and meet my father, Roberto. He has to look you in the eye and shake your hand before he will know if he can trust you. When can you come? Our father knows you. He knows all about you from many years.'

'I hardly think he does, how could he?' Roberto says, dismissing at once the ridiculous notion that the Ligerian leader could have the tiniest knowledge of his existence.

'You have to understand something very important and on which your life may depend.' hisses Musa again, quietly conveying as much menace as he could muster.

'Don't you *ever* question me, or my family in *any* regard if you wish to work for us. Are you 100% and totally clear on this vitally important point? And please consider your answer before giving it to me.'

'Well, yes I understand and yes, I am available. Ready right now if you want. Sooner the better for me in fact.'

'I am returning home tomorrow. Can you come with me?'

'Certainly I can, if I can get a ticket at such short notice.'

Musa laughs out loud. 'You don't need a ticket my friend. I am your ticket. Meet me here tomorrow at nine o'clock and we go to Ramalia.'

'Wow! Fantastic!' Roberto is barely able to believe his luck.

Never one to dwell on how good fortune came his way, he embraces it and as he realises he has no escape or reason to go back, he can now relax. He checks into the RavIna Gorangi, for what he hopes will be the last time.

He is given the room that Hazel had once christened 'the suicide suite,' due to the vast sliding sash window that opened wide enough to fly a helicopter in. It was regularly fully slid back during the day to reduce the smell of urine from the hand washing basin. She suspected it was used by men to save a walk down the corridor to the communal bathroom at night. In fact it also had no waste trap and so vented drain stenches directly into the room. Instead of fixing it for twenty quid, the window would be left open each day between guests and the curtains would regularly be flying around in the wind. It always looked to Hazel like someone had recently dived out onto the street below.

Today, just back from Australia, Hazel decides to see if there is a room available there too. She has only enough cash for one night, which was given to her in Oz by a sympathetic consular official.

Hazel is given a single room on the top floor.

As she climbs up the wide turning staircase which pitches perilously from the supporting wall into the middle of the stairwell, she clings on to the very low handrail and feels queasy as she peers down to tiled lobby floor. She catches a glimpse of the leather-clad leg and arm of a man leaving the tiny lift and heading for the door carrying a crash helmet and shivers for no apparent reason.

Warming up in Stringfellows, just because it was there, Roberto somehow then ends up at a house party of the underground movement 'The Twisted Sisters Of The Night'

It is hosted in a penthouse flat on the top floor of a Georgian stucco terrace in the middle of Holland Park, a five minute walk from where his Hazel is trying ignore the television set in the room next to hers and get some sleep.

The party is in the private residence of an internet entrepreneur. An orgy of some considerable decadence takes place. The only rules are; no shoes in the flat and no talking on the way in or out to avoid trouble with the neighbours. The night passes in a haze of coke and alcohol and morning comes before Roberto can guess whether he is a flag or a balloon.

At dawn for the second time in twenty for hours he finds himself waiting for a café to open.

I am definitely far too old for this now. He thinks, yearning for water, coffee and breakfast.

Roberto stands outside the hotel and considers returning inside for his breakfast. Then he remembers the last one he had been given at this establishment. Breakfast is not something that regular customers of the budget hotel would ever risk.

Although it's an interesting London hotel, it's not everyone's first choice, due to the epochs that passed between the change of bed sheets and the vintage of the cornflakes, which were dished out daily into the bowls set on the tables. If untouched, they were surreptitiously returned to the jumbo box by the parsimonious Serbian manager in between shaving in the kitchen sink and sneezing over the scrambled eggs before serving them in his vest. The hotel catered primarily for those on a very tight budget, Serbs who had just arrived in the UK, Polish builders, and student travellers. The only breakfast option was shouted from the kitchen door by the manager. 'Fried or scrambled?'

Roberto can afford better, but its location, safe, free parking and reliable availability counts more favourably than its shortcomings.

Hazel is in the dining room disconsolately pushing her scrambled eggs around when she hears a voice she thinks she recognises: 'Please can I settle my account? And I would like to leave my motorcycle in the car park, I have an important meeting. I will collect it later this morning.'

'No it is not possible; you must book a room to leave your vehicle. The car park is very small and we need space for new residents.'

Hazel's blood becomes as cold as the coffee in front of her and she is frozen in fear. When she hears the front door bang followed by silence she breathes again.

A few moments later from the rear window of the dining room she sees the leather clad crash-helmeted biker mount a red Ducati that has been in the car park all night. It slips away out of sight. She can hear it revving at the junction of the narrow side street whilst Roberto awaits the traffic lights to join the busy road on Holland Park Avenue. The rumble from the V-twin rattles the draughty sash windows as it pulled away.

She thinks no more about it. She doesn't know anyone who has a motorbike.

If Roberto had not gone out for the night, and Hazel not slept in, they most probably would have met on the stairs or in the corridor.

Hazel has been repatriated without ceremony from Australia the day before. After coming into town by train from Heathrow and not sure where she should go next, she was asleep two floors up from the room that Roberto had taken, but not used.

She knows the place from her time with him and didn't like it too much, even then. She had said 'Braving the attention of the old Yugoslav men in the bar makes me feel like a prostitute, please can we stay somewhere else?'

Now out of options, she can only chance it and pay for one night and then sleep at a friend's house the next day, if she could only remember the name of the street. Or get on a northbound national express coach sooner perhaps. She is confused, broken, abandoned and feeling sick.

Due to his hangover and his preoccupation with meeting Musa on time, Roberto would not have even recognised Hazel. Such was her dishevelled and neglected appearance and the hollowed red hunted eyes she had developed recently.

When she checks out in the afternoon the bike is back in the car park where it will stay for a fortnight until it is stolen.

Roberto had rushed to Daunt Books in Marylebone and bought 'Deer-Law and Liabilities' by Parkes and Thornley and 'Mediaeval Parks of Hertfordshire' by Anne Rowe. If he is going away he will use some time to study deer keeping. He fancies a quiet life in the woods near his hideout and knows of one estate nearby who have a position free for someone to manage their deer herd.

He could perhaps slip back to the UK sometime and yet again start anew. It is forward thinking to the extreme and will probably lead to nothing, but thinking ahead has served him well so far. From there he rushes to a bike dealership in Shepherds Bush to try and sell his Ducati, but the salesman isn't in and the mechanic asks him to come back an hour later.

He has no more time, so he returns it to the hotel car park, books a room for a week and walks away leaving the keys, leathers and helmet in the room. He had paid for the bike in cash and not changed the ownership on the log book. He books the room to buy time in case he doesn't actually get away to Ligeria, in which case he will have a plan B in place. He counts on the fact that if he does get away, it will be a while until anyone alerts the police to his disappearance.

He knows that once the room is booked, the owners will not visit it until he checks out. There was never any room service, only a cursory clean between occupants at best.

Hazel will never know, but this time, good fortune and his degenerate tendencies have worked in her favour and perhaps saved her life.

Roberto walks to the Ligerian Embassy and presents himself promptly at 9am. He is shown into a sumptuous back office by a secretary who was perhaps chosen for her pulchritudinous quality rather than her secretarial skills. Who knows, she could easily have been the most efficient PA in the business and it could be happy bonus that she is a dark-haired beauty.

'Musa will be along soon,' she purrs. It is an hour before he arrives. Musa is in the same shape as him by the look of it. Juggling phone calls and signing papers, he only briefly acknowledges Roberto.

'What time is our flight?' he asks, more to make small talk than as a real question.

'Be quiet, I am busy,' barks Musa in a tone which he had kept well-hidden the day before. 'The plane goes when I say it goes,' he adds.

The PA brings Roberto the uniform of a pilot and shows him into a room where he can change.

'Wear this.' She says and stays to watch him change.

She checks the contents of his pockets and has a quick rummage through his leather man bag, his only luggage.

'Do I have to fly the plane?' jokes Roberto, checking himself in a full length mirror.

'Only if the real pilot dies on the way,' she replies.

'Does that happen often?'

'Anything can happen,' was the succinct reply.

He gives up his attempts at levity.

The uniform fits perfectly and once in the car, Musa relaxes and the urbane mood of the day before returns.

'I am sorry to be abrupt with you earlier my friend, but it was a busy night and I had things I had to do before we left. My life is sometimes too complicated.'

'So you can fly a jet, Roberto? This is very impressive, where did you learn?' says Musa.

'Er no not really' –

'Not really? Not really?' Shouts Musa ' What can you mean *not really*. Have I been misinformed?'

'Well it seems so. You do know that I am a pharmacist?'

Musa and his bodyguards burst into hysterical laughter.

'Your face!' shrieks Musa, unable to contain his amusement.

Roberto doesn't know how to react, caught between embarrassment and the need to keep a subservient position.

'You thought you would have to fly the plane. That is so funny, you believed me, no? I know your humour here. You fell in that didn't you, eh? You did, didn't you?'

'Fell for it, not in it,' Roberto corrects lamely trying to reclaim some dignity whilst forgetting not to challenge Musa.

'Err yes I did, the uniform, etc'. He says weakly.

'The uniform is serious; you are the co-pilot ok? It is simpler that way. You don't have to do anything once we are in the air. Just look like you know what you are doing. We gave the co-pilot the day off. It prevents the meddling of the customs people and the questions. Always too many questions! You must understand, in my country our family need to answer NO questions. Here in the UK everyone is the boss. Even the women and Mr Blair's ladyboy men like Mr Mendleshon'.

'Er, we can't use those descriptions here now.'

'What? What? There you go again telling me what I can't do, Roberto. You *have* to learn.'

'We can't imagine how you get anything done here. So it is hard for us to be slow and polite and wait for everyone to be happy before we can get on and do anything. It is very frustrating for us.

'It takes you twenty years to build a road. Nineteen years to make sure everyone is happy, which is impossible, then one year to build the road. You English are all totally mad.

'You wait for the traffic lights, wait for the queues, wait for the permission to land, wait for the taxi, wait for the opening times, wait for the table to be available, wait for the postman, wait for planning permission, wait for the bank to open, wait for the builder to turn up, and on and on. It makes us very very angry!

'You even have to wait for your degree from the University, even when you have given them 2 millions of dollars. You still have to wait for the committee of the women and the ladyboy men to decide if you can have your degree that you have paid for. You should learn from Italy. It is so much better in Italy. My brother is a very good footballer and we buy the team and he plays for Perugia. They don't have to wait in Italy. Especially now my father is a friend of Mr Berlusconi. You pay the money and they say thanks to you, we need the money and now we have the money, so now you can play for us, thank you very much.'

'You should get your Tony Blair to sort it out. He came to see my father you know. They did many good deals to sort out the past and be friends and to buy oil and we give him millions of pounds to say sorry for the past. He is very good friend of my father. We can do deals together. My father tells him to get rid of the women who tell him what to do and the ladyboy men who want to get married to other men. He should just have real men around him so he can be a strong leader. Mr Tony Blair. He is coming to see my father again later this year.'

'Really? Is he?'

'Yes, you see, my father is sending this plane for him. We would like to make billions of dollars available for investment in your country and Mr Blair will work with us when he retires. By the way my friend, you must learn that you agree with *all* of *everything* we do. Not *most* of it. And don't ever complain. No one may complain. When you learn this you will be fine, Roberto. You will do very, very well.'

'I agree with 'm*ost*' of that.'

'That's very funny, you are a funny man.'

Their limousine sweeps into the military airstrip at Biggin Hill. They are allowed though security barriers on presentation of some papers and it comes to rest at the side of a small business jet.

Looking at the huge military refuelling and heavy transport planes which dwarf their tiny craft, Roberto asks 'How do we get permission to fly out of here?'

'Shhhhhh, my friend you don't need to know. My father is a very good friend of Mr Tony Blair, how often do you need me to remind you and don't ask questions that a pilot wouldn't ask you stupid man.'

'Oh yes, of course, sorry.'

The flight is smooth and relaxing. Behind the eight luxury seats is a small freight area which contains a covered pallet. It is something heavy and valuable and Musa's staff spend a lot of time loading it and fussing around it. Roberto instinctively knows not to ask what it is but he hears Musa tell someone over the radio in English 'There's a delivery arriving by sea next week and a single ton hidden in there; it's all we could get, but without it none of us would be here'.

Roberto never discovers what it is, but he soon forgets as there are a great many mysterious things going on, most of which he can sense he is best not knowing about.

They are in Ramalia before dark and met by a stretch limousine and people carrier which is used to take away the carefully unloaded secret cargo. He is taken to Manoosma's compound in the evening.

Why do despots always have a compound? Roberto wonders. *Normal people have houses, Royals have palaces. Megalomaniacs used to be identifiable by their weird facial hair; Hitler, Stalin, Saddam Hussain. Now the internationally recognised sign of an out-of-control nutjob is the size of his 'compound'.*

By that measure Manoosma is Premier League. His compound is the size of a town, a heavily guarded military installation. The home of a despot who needs protection from the people he has subjugated, rather than the sumptuous palace of a king who is comfortable in his position and loved by his loyal subjects.

The inner sanctum is as lavish as it is tacky. Roberto finds himself in an astonishing new world. Being presented to Manoosma is a strange experience. This man he knows only from the news as a threat to world peace who possibly funded the IRA and blew innocent passenger planes out of the sky is now in front of him, surrounded by Amazonian female bodyguards like a Bond villain. He isn't stroking a cat, and his interpreter translates.

'He asks "How can we trust you?" He wishes you to know that you are welcome and he has much work for you to do. You will be protected and well paid but you must never betray the Ligerian people.'

'You will have an office and a laboratory and you will report to the head of the army, his cousin. You will be taken to a hotel today and tomorrow you will be shown where you will live. You will start your work on Monday. There is much work to be done, many many traitors who must not be allowed to continue.'

After a pause, Roberto asks 'To continue what?'

'To continue alive,' comes the short reply.

At this point, Manoosma beckons to Roberto.

He draws him close to his face and looks him in the eyes from 50mm. He stares and doesn't move or speak for what seems like a year. It may have only been a minute or two at the most but the socially inappropriate and awkward silence is unbearable and his breath is like a blast from the arse of a diseased wildebeest that had dined on roadkill curry and gherkins for a decade.

Roberto desperately wants to recoil but can't prise himself from the grip of the madman and doesn't dare try. His eyes are tired and old but strangely familiar, his skin moist and oily and his lank, black hair is greasy and matted. Despite his expensive looking African robes and gold Swiss trophy watch, he stinks like an incontinent tramp.

Manoosma murmurs something repeatedly to Roberto which he can't understand, kisses him on both cheeks and nods, smiling a sinister smile he imagines paternal.

It sounded like 'Roberto, Roberto Yaa Bunay ya Roberto,' and some other mumbling he couldn't catch. It was all he could do not to recoil in horror.

He has to rely on Musa's translation.

If the translation was accurate it was chilling.

'Welcome my son, I knew one day you would come to me. We have been looking after you. Work hard and never betray me'.

He turns to Musa and says something else.

'What else did he say?' Roberto doesn't want to miss anything.

'He told me to look after my brother.'

What the fuck did that mean? Roberto is scared to ask. *Surely not?*

Roberto is confused and later takes Musa to one side and asked 'Did he really call me his son?'

'We are all his children. He is our father and the father of the country.' explains Musa dismissively as he walks out of the room.

'I hope he didn't mean that literally?' Roberto thinks back to the meetings that led to him getting the wooden box contract and the large payment for work later that enabled him to buy his car.

Could they have been keeping a watchful eye on me? But why? He had often wondered how such a peculiar job had come his way.

Roberto resolves to find out one day if Manoosma had spent time in Italy when he was a history student or perhaps in the army…Could he possibly have chanced across his wanton mother in London?

History shows many a despotic international nutjob benefiting from a solid English education and using it to help them take control of their homelands for evil purposes. So why not him too?

Having little or no option, Roberto decides to try to make the best of his time in Ligeria and see what fate might bring. Whatever awaits him cannot be as bad as a long jail-term... could it?

After days of intense scrutiny and distrust from his minders, who initially don't take their eyes off him for a moment, they begin to relax, apparently aware that he is in no position to escape.

Eventually they fall victim to the curse of the bodyguard and the security team, namely that you do your job well day after day, year after year and nothing happens. No-one escapes, nothing is stolen, no-one gets shot on your watch and you never get a moment's thanks or acknowledgement, but let slip for a moment when something does, and you're finished.

Roberto works hard to win their trust. Eventually their concentration begins to slide. When they leave him alone and he doesn't show signs of absconding he wins more freedom.

On a visit into Ramalia, they leave him in a coffee house whilst they disappear to a brothel. He notices an internet connection behind a room divider that his security has missed. Roberto is not allowed anywhere near the web in the compound unsupervised so he quickly takes the opportunity to research escape routes out of the country.

He is comfortable and secure from being sent to jail in the UK, but he is very uncomfortable with the motivations of his hosts and decides that a sensible move would be to work out how to disappear if it becomes necessary.

He can't risk airports or main roads, but it seems there are possibilities of escaping by sea. There are many cargo ships coming in and out. His scant knowledge of the Mediterranean doesn't help. He jots down a few numbers and prints off a map of the ports. His ignorance of the geography of the area is total, but half an hour on the internet is enough to tell him that rather than travel the large distances to the east where there were many choices, if it becomes necessary, he can flee to the west and head for the tiny ports of Abu Kammash and Zuara. There, he imagines he might be able to get a boat ride to Tunisia.

He rules out escaping by land to the south. He could never survive in the desert and wouldn't have a clue where to go if it doesn't work out here, but something tells him that a bit of knowledge of the geography might one day save his skin.

He never once gives a moment's thought to his victims but is determined to make sure he doesn't become one himself.

He is given a new laboratory, staff, a pool of cars to choose from and an apartment with domestic assistants. He finds the constant presence of soldiers and secret service staff suffocating. He knows he is always under scrutiny. He understands that, despite the strange meeting with Manoosma who he rarely sees again, he is an outsider to the rest of the family. They know he has the knowledge to eliminate anyone. He is never allowed near food or to be alone with any of the Manoosma family, whose sons are particularly suspicious of him. Paranoia is in their blood.

The family are in a spin of frenetic activity. They are trying to restore their international reputation or rather establish one for the first time, and had made pronouncements about their wish to be included in the western controlled worldwide' War on Terror'. It was a bit like Hitler offering advice on conflict resolution but worse.

Despite the undoubted good he had done for many sections of Ligerian society with the country's oil wealth, their father had taken power and kept it by brutally removing any opposition.

Roberto now has a key role at the centre of this inhumanity.

Manoosma's sons travel abroad constantly to spread goodwill with mixed results. A startling number of western businessmen begin to show up to try and do deals now that sanctions are lifted. As well as his laboratory work, Roberto finds himself being asked to read business documents and try and help Manoosma's translators interpret the nuances of business discourse.

Amongst the older generation there are still a few who speak Italian as a result of colonial occupation. Roberto has a basic knowledge of Italian, and Latin from his medical studies but no Arabic.

After being told he will be their translator in business meetings with visiting western businessmen, he asks to see Manoosma.

His request is denied, but he is given a chance to plead with Musa not to put him out in public view. He explains that if he is photographed or recorded and if word gets back to England, there will be an inquiry into his identity and he will quickly then become the story and threaten the family's quest to re-enter the fold.   Roberto explains that for him to be in any way effective, it is essential that no-one in the west ever discovers that he is present in Ligeria at all, let alone welcomed by the family.

To his immense relief and gratitude, the message comes back from Manoosma that he understands and agrees with his assessment; however he will still be required to help with documents.

Perhaps there is a lot more to the man than the western media and politicians lead us to believe. We are all ruled by the power of nightmares whichever side of the fence we are on.

An intensive Arabic course is arranged for Roberto and he attends regular lessons timed to fit into his rapidly increasing workload. His assigned tutor is a student and yet another distant Manoosma cousin.

Very soon his new mission becomes clear. He first takes over the state pharmaceutical service and is asked to re-organise it, root and branch. This is a huge task completely beyond his capability to deliver, but he pays lip service to it in order to satisfy his new employers. It does them some good to appear to care about the hospitals and health care service which they have largely created with oil money. It is something they can genuinely take some pride from, but lately corruption, sanctions and lack of resources are bringing it close to collapse.

The flip side is the other programs they have in mind. Roberto is consulted on how to carry out mass poisoning, and tasked to work with water engineers to perfect a valve attached to a small copper tank which is to be plumbed into domestic water supply pipes. The evil device is designed to inject carefully calibrated quantities of poison into water mains in controlled doses, at intervals decided by a complicated circuit board, through injectors and one-way valves.

Larger versions are trialled which are intended for large diameter urban supply pipes. Roberto works hard to avoid knowing where and when they are deployed and by who. He doesn't want to know.

He refines strategies to drug, incapacitate, murder, and even dissolve body parts. Although now a seasoned murderer, it is far more unpleasant than he finds palatable. Despite being responsible for many horrors in England, he retains a distaste and revulsion for what he sees when forced to confront the results of his work. Without his own motivations and control, he doesn't like being forced to engage in other people's profoundly unacceptable activities.

The family are clearly struggling to maintain their grip on power and the patriarch's behaviour is becoming more eccentric by the day.

One day Roberto on his way to the compound from his lab, comes across Manoosma giving an interview whilst sitting in a golf buggy and holding an umbrella out of its tiny window whilst minions train hose pipes over him.

'This cannot become any more bizarre,' Roberto says out loud, confident there are no English speakers nearby.

Manoosma sees him and beckons to him to come. When he is satisfied that the cameras are not rolling, Roberto steps forward.

'You translator son-' he says jabbing a finger at the interviewer.

Roberto quickly replies, 'I am sorry leader, er father; I have to deliver these urgent chemicals otherwise they will not be operative.'

He runs away into the building and makes himself scarce, resolving to give the increasingly unhinged and isolated leader a wider birth.

He feels a not dissimilar shift of motivation that someone who turns a hobby into a way of paying a mortgage suffers. Like musicians who, after decades of performing for pleasure, find themselves having to spend the rest of their lives travelling the world performing a small number of hits they wrote years ago in order to pay the gas bill.

Murder is now Roberto's full time job and it strips away all the fun – if you can call it that. Many people die; so many of the lunatic's imagined traitors, enemies, employees, members of the ruling family and his political machine are brutally massacred.

A whole town is poisoned when they resist a new factory scheme which is vital for the Manoosmas. A hospital is used as cover to deal with people who they wish to incapacitate and to drive fear through the community to frighten and discourage opposition.

Roberto's expertise is used to eliminate political and business opponents and remove political activists who attempt to organise opposition.

Musa or his staff would burst in to his laboratory with demands, 'Come, you are needed now!'

Irrespective of what he is involved with at the time, the urgent request can be anything from a poison to put in someone's wine, a plan to wipe out a village, or an opinion about which film they should watch.

Even he is shocked to the core when asked to help to research the possibility of controlling and distributing viruses which he knows cannot be controlled once released. He pretends to co-operate but swaps samples and uses placebos. He is in no position to take a moral position on who will be eliminated but he is aware of the mayhem that infecting people with a disease that can't then be controlled can unleash.

Luckily the leader now has many problems to grapple with and no time for Roberto.

Musa tries to persuade him to continue when it doesn't at first work by insisting that it is part of an attempt to find a cure. Roberto can't quite work out what he thinks of Musa.

In a different world he might have been a force for good, but, he thinks, *he is caught in an impossible situation. If he distances himself too much from his father or earns his disapproval, he could easily be killed.* Roberto sees signs that Musa is looking ahead to a time after his father and wonders if he can find redemption as a unifying leader.

He has too much blood on his hands for sure, and a dangerous temper but so have many other successful world leaders. Roberto knows he is in no position to judge.

He has access to all the benefits of an insider at the court of one of the world's most successful despots. He lives a life of considerable luxury and can enjoy pretty much whatever he wants, provided he continues to co-operate fully with the work and doesn't try to leave the compound unaccompanied. His time in Ligeria enables his trail back home to go cold.

Roberto continues to work hard realising there was no escape from his new post, but history is on the turn and as the Ligerian revolution takes hold. During the Arab spring, his luxury lifestyle gradually comes to a halt. Travel outside the compound becomes impossible and gradually the whole family and its grip on the nation collapses. It is every man and woman for themselves.

Manoosma's reign comes to an end and the family disperse into the North African desert, leaving carnage and the fertile environment for an explosion of extremist religious terrorism and factionist splinter-groups between Manoosma loyalists, Ramalia-based moderates and the many elements of extremist Islamic cultists.

It is eventually no longer safe to travel. Roberto remains within the dwindling inner circle until the last moment when Manoosma is dragged like a sewer rat from a drain by revolutionaries and murdered. He loses power the same way as he acquired it: he lived and died by the sword.

Musa and his brothers do what they can to hold back the tide, but eventually surrender to the inevitable and flee.

30 The Beginning

Back in England with no idea what to do next, Hazel is asked to come and speak to West Yorkshire detectives still keen to confirm the whereabouts of two of their detectives and examine any potential connection between theirs and her father's apparent disappearance.

Pete's boss and a younger DS sit her down and ask her to tell them informally what she knows.

'You were a good friend of DC Manford we hear, do you know where he is?' asks the older man whilst the younger one observes her intently.

'Sorry no, I haven't seen him since he came to West Fell in the summer of, ooh was it 2004 or 5, I don't know him very well,' she lies to protect him, not knowing what she was protecting him from.

'And your partner, where is he now?'

'I wish I could tell you. And I wish you would tell me what it is you think he has done? We are no longer together and will never be an item again if he reappears. But I am completely in the dark about what it is he has done.' she is able to be honest this time.

'Why are you not together, what happened? Did he harm you?'

'No, I found myself unable to trust him because I became aware that he was avoiding telling me something, but I have no idea what.'

The younger man intervenes more harshly.

'Ms Anderson, can you tell me why so many people around you have died or disappeared in the past few years? Including both of your last two boyfriends and your father and if what I'm hearing, possibly your latest boyfriend too? What are you doing to them?'

Hazel open-mouthed with shock at the idea she was now under question, feels naive in the extreme, not to have considered all this in the round and how it might look from the outside.

'Steady on Dave, Ms Anderson is here to help us and is not under caution.'

'Look guys, no one is keener than me to get to the bottom of all this and I am devastated about my father's disappearance; it is completely out of character for him and he was so close to retirement. He's been struggling since my mum died and I desperately hope he's just wandered off to find some peace, but it's just not him, all this, not him at all. I am very worried.'

'There, that's another one right there! Even your mother has died too. Do you think it odd that this is interesting to us and I have to say, no one in my family or friendship group has died in the past ten years. If I had lost as many as you I would begin to think I was toxic or --'

'Dave! Dave for heaven's sake, NO! Please come outside with me now! That is unacceptable....I am so sorry Ms Anderson.'

The men leave her in the room whilst they argue in the corridor.

As soon as they are away, the younger one winks at this colleague and whispers 'make it loud.' They shout at each other for her benefit.

Eventually the older man re-enters the room.

'Thank you so much for coming in. I apologise again for my partner. He is a good copper and never lets go of a hunch; but his bedside manner needs some work,' he smiles.

'We do need to explore this in more detail you understand, but no-one is suggesting you are guilty of anything.'

'He fucking was,' she replies pointing a thumb at the door.

'Well instead of having him drilling down like a jack hammer, would you mind if we went through the last three or four years of your life and try and see if we can get any indication of where we should start to unravel all this?'

'Of course, I am only keen to understand myself.' Hazel really is.

After an hour when she becomes tired and her head begins to spin she asks if that could be enough for the time being. Playing good cop, he offers her a fatherly contact if ever she needs someone to talk to.

'Please keep in touch and let me know if anything new comes up. We are here for you anytime if you feel threatened or afraid.'

Having been interrogated, Hazel is stunned by the fact that she had never seen it from a distance and just coped with every event as if unconnected. She is still unaware that Roberto had been medicating her but it dawns on her far too late and for the first time that she knows nothing about him or his past, save everything he had told her. But what of that is true? She realises he had given her a narrative that she never had cause to disbelieve but she has no points of reference.

The bond of trust broken, she now needs corroboration before she will believe anything. She had met his ex-wife and kids once, so helpfully directed the police to them.

As she gets up to leave the interview room, she suddenly feels sick and rushes into the toilets before throwing up lavishly.

Hazel has not felt well since she returned from Australia. Roberto and Pete had both saved her from being implicated; but she is floored by the continued search for her father and the realisation that she had been naive in the extreme not to dig deeper.

She chances across a dog-eared copy of 'Somebody's Husband, Somebody's Son' by Gordon Burn on a second hand bookstall on the South Bank while walking along the Thames before she heads back north. She buys it thinking it might help her understand how to look for signs.

It does her no good. She gives up half way through and bins it, as it gradually makes her feel ill to have thought she could have found answers from the life of Sonia Surzma. Instead,

Hazel learns that few people have ever quite believed that the Yorkshire Ripper's wife knew nothing of the evil work of her husband. Decades later it still seems inconceivable, yet she had missed it all. This gives Hazel no comfort.

She doesn't know why, but she didn't tell her interrogators about meeting Pete in Australia, insisting that she couldn't find him. Her instinct to protect him was immediate but irrational.

Feeling poorly for several days, Hazel sees a doctor who confirms she is pregnant.

Oh! She is numb inside but now her actions to protect Pete make more sense. Perhaps her body knows more than she does. She decides to allow events to take their course and see if he comes forward explain himself.

She finds herself unable to sleep, feeling sick all the time, especially in the mornings.

The news of her pregnancy brings her both overwhelming joy and deep sadness that she can't share this news with her parents. The unanswered questions about her father's disappearance haunt her every day and night.

Hazel hopes the fact that she can only be bearing Peter's child would have brought her father the same joy.

After the night in the Balkan hotel where had she narrowly avoided meeting Roberto, she had travelled north to Hawkshead to stay with her Aunt Irene.

Her aunt does her best to provide a loving home but the long Lake District winter does nothing to lift Hazel's spirits. She is left alone to contemplate her recent behaviour still unaware of the extent that she has been manipulated. It brings on a period of dramatic, hysterical and mental decline driven by guilt, confusion and too much time for lonely introspection. No longer the carefree hedonistic and lithe adventurer, she is losing the will to continue.

She misses her mother massively and knows that her mother's struggles would have made her the perfect partner to help her through her current predicament. They could have bonded and it would have helped her mother heal, but all Hazel has now is a destructive cocktail of guilt and confusion.

She loses all hope of any chance of happiness in the future. Her fear never leaves but gradually subsides. She spends her time reading, often doesn't get out of bed and stops using a mirror. She begins to dislike her body and loose her confidence.

Her mood swings and erratic behaviour test her Aunt's patience so she takes long walks beyond the village to the edge of Esthwaite, the large and lonely dark sheet of water south of the village. Cold, deep and far away from the summer tourists on private land, it is a wildlife haven.

Whilst walking its banks she comes across a new dark green fibreglass open Canadian canoe. Looking around and seeing no movement, she borrows it and drifts out to the middle of the lake, hundreds of metres out, where she lies back beneath the edges of the boat.

Staring up at the sky, a good distance from where she launched, invisible and alone she falls into a deep and troubled sleep.

A terrible nightmare unfolds where her unborn child is ripped from her body by a shrieking monster in a hooded cloak with a slashing sabre. Her mother screams at her that she has ruined everyone's lives. 'You killed me! You killed your father and your child!' She sees her father drifting backwards away from her into flames pleading quietly and politely 'Why can't you save me, my darling daughter?'

Sweeping in and out of view, Mally, Mrs Pickles, Pete all fall over into the fire with arms outstretched and the monster comes back towards her this time with Roberto's face staring impassively, his eyes red and not moving, staring beyond her whilst he slashes a sword towards her, holding accusingly aloft, her child.

'Is this another life you will destroy?' he calmly asks as the black boiling swamps of hell surround her. She sinks beneath whilst Roberto slashes at her face and tosses the baby he has ripped from her into a burning cauldron. As he comes towards her again, thrusting his blade closer and closer until she feels a rush of air as it passes from her skin she knows the next swing will bring the blade deep across her face.

She suddenly throws herself sideways into the freezing water, in that moment not knowing if the vivid and horrifying drama unfolding is a dream or a horrific reality; one she had caused. She must end her torment. She has no intention of saving herself and in her anguish forgets her baby. The water is chillingly cold and shakes her into an electrified, awaken state.

Confused by months of lack of sleep, her mind has been dulled by sleeping pills and suddenly overwhelmed by the weight of the water dragging her down, she submits.

She becomes calm and makes no attempt to swim to the surface. She swallows the ice-cold water in gulps, wanting it all to end here and now. She loses consciousness and drifts downwards.

A resident of on the lake shore is reading in a 1930's revolving timber summerhouse on the shore whilst her husband paints the woodwork on the exterior. Their garden enjoys a swathe of perfectly maintained grass that falls down to the water's edge and she just happens to look up at the right moment to see Hazel slip into the water.

If she had moved her head up from her book two seconds later or earlier, she would have seen nothing and Hazel would have been lost, perhaps never found. Without a trace of any belongings in the boat, it would have been assumed that it had floated away by itself in the wind.

'Christ almighty David! Someone just fell from that boat. I saw someone enter the water!' The elderly lady yells at her husband, causing him to rush to the shore.

There is a fishing boat used by the neighbour next door just 50 metres away. The couple were in their garden and their handyman, Matt Birch are gathering leaves from the lawn. With extraordinary luck he is a strong swimmer and a member of the local cave and fell rescue organisation.

'Get in that boat!' shouts Matt to the pensioner who throws away his paintbrush and leaps in.

Matt rows out to where the empty canoe is drifting, strips off his shirt and jeans and dives three times. 'There! Where the bubbles are coming up!' points the old man watching from the boat. Eventually Matt finds her metres below the surface almost too deep to reach. He drags Hazel to the surface and into the boat, unconscious.

It takes all of their combined strength to get her in without capsizing the sturdy wooden rowing boat, no small mercy as the older gentleman tells Matt later that he couldn't swim! Strong and experienced as he was, Matt couldn't have righted the boat and got either of them back in on his own.

He performs CPR on Hazel and after what seems like eternity, she springs to life ejecting a torrent of water from her choking mouth. By the time they row ashore, an ambulance called by the observant lady is only ten minutes away.

Hazel awakes in intensive care and there is a huge fuss around her for hours, her pregnancy the cause of extreme concern. After an agonising wait, the news that she has not lost her baby is the precise moment her life changes forever.

No one event in her entire existence could be more of a damascene turning point. The shock of near death, and her and her baby's survival is her salvation.

The next few days are a blur. Hazel sleeps for hours and drifts into a comatose dream-state; sedated to enable control of her condition. When she regains consciousness something feels very different. Her stomach aches but isn't the same. She is now the mother of a tiny premature boy the size of a mouse, born three weeks early by caesarean section and without her knowledge or involvement. She cries out and there he is; tiny and pink, waving miniscule hands smaller than her thumb and complaining loudly in need of his mother.

'I have never been involved in a closer call than that,' the doctor tells her 'You will both be very fragile for some weeks.'

She doesn't have to be told that her destiny is now to protect her baby.

Hazel begins to heal from that moment. Just staring at her baby as he sleeps begins to cure her. She can never again be so selfish and thoughtless.

They are kept under observation for weeks as they both became stronger. When she eventually returns to her aunt's with her tiny baby she begins to renew her childhood interests in art, poetry and music; she grows closer to her aunt taking a real interest in her as a person. She learns much about her father's childhood that explains his detachment.

As she grows in strength, her vibrant and inquisitive mind returns. Resilient and enhanced by maturity and experience, but still held back by memory loss, inability to sleep and constant concern about her father, which continues to haunt her. Moving on completely to a new life proves impossible.

Matt Birch becomes an ardent admirer and good friend. He often calls and is very kind to her. It becomes clear that he has feelings for her and despite her feeble attempts not to encourage him, before long he proclaims his love.

'I'm flattered Matt,' she tells him. 'But the timing is all wrong. I hope you understand. I've still got so many questions to find answers for before I can even think about a relationship.'

It's hard for Hazel to resist Matt. Not so long ago she would have torn his shirt off his back and devoured him whole, but now she has her son and her recovery for his sake to consider and her recent heartbreak is still too raw.

'It's my destiny to meet the right people at the wrong time or meet the right people and not know when it's the right time and this may be no different, but I just have to stay single for now for many reasons.'

Despite knowing how dangerous it is to play with people's feelings, she can't help occasionally teasing him and mildly flirting with him. On his birthday she buys him a tankard and fills it with condoms, saying 'That should keep you in stock for a few days, you must be a very busy boy!'

'Is it true you were naked when you rescued me and gave me CPR, my hero?'

'Don't tease me; I won't be responsible for my actions.'

'Just my luck to be unconscious and miss that treat! Do you rescue people from the caves and the fells like that? I might have to go and explore Gaping Ghyll and get a bit lost!' she continues.

'Stop it Hazel. You're playing with fire you know!' he must behave.

Old habits die hard and as time goes on Hazel knows she is being unfair to Matt. She is wiser now, and knows it could all end in tears – she's seen it before.

The day comes for her to bring clarity and finality to their burgeoning relationship as they meet by chance on the Hawkshead Ferry. She is on her way to the doctor's to see if he can help her with insomnia; Matt is on the way to deliver some logs to a customer near Bowness.

The short journey across the lake on the tiny ancient line-dragged ferry gives her an ideal time-limited opportunity to talk to him and the chance to leave the scene as soon as the ferry docked. She doesn't plan it this way but it was the perfect place to deliver bad news.

'Hi, Matt! Fancy seeing you here... You're not stalking me are you? Look I have been meaning to have a word, you know we get on great and I couldn't think of a nicer man to be with, particularly just now, well no I don't mean just now', she gabbles as the far shore approaches.

'You see the thing is, I really have to be alone just now. I am so sorry; there is no chance for us just now, perhaps one day; no, not one day, that's not fair. I mean, well I don't know what I mean, but I do really fancy you and love that you care for me, but things are just so, so fucking difficult ...'

'Hazel, its fine, I understand. There are too many unfinished threads. We can still be friends can we? Promise?'

'Of course, of course,' she hugs him tightly immediately regretting her decision as she grips his massive, safe arms and wraps them around her. He surprises her by taking rejection well, or at least hiding his real feelings perhaps to make it easier for her.

She seriously wonders what the hell she was doing rejecting this fine specimen, an honourable strong and gentle man.

Am I just a total fucking idiot? She asks herself immediately fancying him all over again.

The first time she has managed to make an adult decision and it may well be the wrong one. She had sailed through life letting fate or other people decide her destiny up to that point, a strategy that had delivered wildly mixed outcomes. This one is down to her.

'Look after yourself Hazel,' Matt smiles and returns to his truck, driving away with wave.

She watches as his truck bounces up the ramp on to the quayside waiting for her turn to drive ashore. By the time her car hits tarmac she has changed her mind and back again.

Matt is a gentle soul. He is hurt but keeps in touch and true to his word, remains a genuine friend. In truth he decides to give her time and space, hoping beyond hope that she might one day change her mind. Like Pete, he needs it to be her decision and not his persuasion.

The healthy boy she named Matt – Little Matt or 'Matty'.

Hazel takes to motherhood well and enjoys it very much. Her mother's curse of depression does not take root as she feared. Her anguish is caused by extreme events, grief and loss, rather than chemical imbalance or inherited problems.

No greater joy has ever been known to her than seeing the smiling face of her son. He gives her a reason to be, a reason to get up and take on life.

She settles into Lake District life, takes a part time PA role with a well-known film producer, director and screenwriter whose reputation for shocking gothic epics sustained his hedonistic and flamboyant excesses into old age. His success in the film world saved him from the tiresome business of adulthood. His ruddy faced and portly fizzog is topped off with a rampant mane of unruly grey locks.

He is working in the Lakes on a long-term writing and film development project and lives nearby in a stylish 1970's experimental house which he rents from a friend. It is in its own small valley in an elevated position with vast Lakeland vistas overlooking Hawkshead and beyond.

In time, working for him and seeing up close the very best and worst excesses of a creative maverick, she becomes able to temporarily forget the past and finds herself able to concentrate on her new career. Her new boss works through the night when he feels like it, then stays in bed for weeks when he doesn't. He is an unashamed drinker, womaniser and occasional genius who takes life on like a wounded rhino charging through a busy china market.

'Hazel darling, without you I am lost; before you I was a failure, you are my saviour!' he exaggerates perchance to flatter and deceive.

'Come and stay in my villa on the Cote d'azur, come to Cannes for the festival.'

The work is not particularly taxing and the hours suit her new life as a single mother. It is never dull; one moment arranging travel to and from London for his girlfriends and business associates and the next sitting in on script read-through and plot development meetings where she is encouraged to participate and contribute, or wandering to the property's immaculate kitchen-garden to collect organic vegetables from the list of perfectly ready specimens indicated on a blackboard by the gardener who came with the house.

She doesn't have to cook, the purple faced roué reminiscent of a gin-soaked octopus has brought his personal chef with him, a middle aged Portugese lady who takes no prisoners.

Spotting potential trouble from his wandering hands and lecherous mind, Hazel keeps her boss in check by explaining some ground rules.

One morning when he staggers into the kitchen in his dressing gown, which he deliberately fails to tie up sufficiently to disguise his pink and sweaty body, she takes her chance to let him know which way up the world is. Channelling her father she lectures:

'Look I'm up for anything and don't mind being a part of an unstructured work environment, but you have to know and understand that no matter how hard you try I'm not up for any hanky-panky.'

He feigns shock and protests his innocence, 'My dear, what *do* you think of me?' but accepts her strident lecture with the chastened innocence of an overgrown public schoolboy who has been caught scrumping apples.

She also finds herself shouting at him when he attempts use her to deceive his third wife over his rabid pursuit of an actress who was chasing a role. She resolutely refuses to be a part of his deception and promises to resign if he asks again. When he succumbs and refocuses on his work without damage to their working relationship, she knows she has called it right. He isn't really outraged by her stance, and doesn't sack her for insulting him.

In a fair world he would be locked up for harassment but they work well together and with a greater respect and understanding after that hiccup.

Hazel is not about to make the same mistake as she did back in the West Fell pharmacy where she had thrown herself at the mercy of a demon. This overweight and lecherous old man lives every moment of his life in the moment hiding nothing, neither metaphorically nor physically.

His pathetic attempts at seduction she finds comical and she sees his pink body so many times she has to engineer a faux resignation to insist that he dress before she arrives for work.

She can see him coming a mile off; her new boss is old enough to be her father, probably grandfather and is not ageing well.

Hazel's aunt looks after Little Matt while she works, which is a godsend. Hazel is penniless now and has to work. Her father's estate, including a healthy pension, considerable savings, some stocks and shares and the proceeds of the Tuscany farm are stuck in probate hell until he can be pronounced dead, which could take another three years at least. Without a body it is all in the hands of lawyers and police. The same applies to her small stake in the rectory, but that's an impossible situation to resolve as she isn't related to Roberto and his whereabouts are unknown.

Hazel has no interest in any of it. If it means her father has gone it has no value, and she'd rather not think about it.

She has had no contact with Pete since the night in Sydney so it's unlikely he knows he is a father.

Hazel sadly concludes that Roberto has probably got to her father but the police have not managed to find a single piece of evidence to prove this, or pin down Pete, Roberto or Adrian's whereabouts.

This all changes when an envelope with Pete's scrawled message, still legible is handed in by the receivers of Adrian's hotel. It was left there carelessly by the inebriated DC.

'Fucking hell!' his colleague exclaims when its contents are examined.

'The boss needs to see this urgently!'

It contains Pete's insurance documents detailing his suspicions about Roberto that he had entrusted with Adrian when he first went to Cambridge to recruit him.

His colleagues unravel Pete's notes and quickly realise he had been hot on Roberto's tail.

'So, that's what he was up to in West Fell...'

The meticulous detail in the notes implicated Roberto in several unexplained deaths in Bradford and West Fell and lead to his Cambridge pharmacy and the rectory being searched.

'He really was married to the job. He should have brought this to me from the outset. What the hell was he doing keeping it to himself? We could have brought this guy in long ago.' His boss has to admit that he should have taken more note of what Pete was capable of.

Rumours are that Pete is in Australia, but searches and investigations deliver no results. Retracing his footsteps, the trail goes cold after Thailand. Berty tells the police that he had seen Pete's air ticket home, but checks reveal that no one had turned up for the flight.

Hugh is interviewed at length but there is no evidence that Dr Anderson had in fact met up with Roberto, although it is assumed to have happened. The cellar fire is assumed to be relevant but no forensic evidence can be found. The drainage work has been completed and filled in by the contractors before they were stood down, so when the septic tank is removed and re-excavated at the request of the police, the contractors assure the detectives that they had dug down further than the original excavation. Nothing is found. The remains of the skeleton are missed by millimetres.

Roberto remains missing, perhaps dead. The consensus is that hopefully someone they suspected so evil and possessed of his expertise would know that the game is up and may well have done the decent thing by now.

Adrian also on the missing person's list, now lies beneath a million cubic metres of excavated spoil and will never be found. He was last seen in Cambridge by Hazel, but she had no idea what happened after she had seen him in the Falcon with Roberto.

Without a shred of hard evidence, in time the investigations become less intense and eventually everyone moves on. They have no choice. No-one forgets, but the whole episode remains a mystery. Theories are as plentiful as raindrops but no-one can get close to the truth.

They have never admitted it to her, but the police hope that her stay with her aunt may eventually smoke out one or more of the people they seek. The detective in charge of the investigation has a sneaking suspicion that Hazel knows more than she has told them and therefore justifies taking a risk with her safety. If not for this hunch, they would have helped her to assume a new identity but instead they tap her phone and follow her around, possibly exposing her to danger.

On the off-chance that Roberto might reappear, a police officer is positioned, firstly in her aunt's annex, then in an empty holiday let in Hawkshead for the first three months, but budget constraints and the complete lack of any clues as to Roberto's whereabouts eventually water down her protection to increased home security, some electronic alarms linked to Windermere police station and occasional updates with her assigned contact.

Her aunt's house is fitted with CCTV and panic alarms but nothing ever happens.

Now back on form, with gradually renewed self-confidence, Hazel attracts interest once more but until she learns what had happened to Pete she keeps her distance and whenever a new relationship looks like it might develop beyond the frivolous she backs away.

She keeps in touch with Pete's mother Ann who claims she hasn't heard anything from him. She did in fact have one letter that she hid from everyone. It was short but told her what she needed to know.

It's now over three years since anyone has spoken to or had word of him.

Ann guesses that Hazel and Pete had enjoyed a special relationship, but she didn't know they had been together in Australia and assumed that her child was Roberto's. That is until, on a visit to her brother Des, a retired boffin from the nuclear sub-base in Barrow-in-Furness, she comes to meet Hazel for tea in Bowness. She is introduced to Little Matt and knows in an instant that he is her grandchild. Hazel knows she knows. They simply exchange a glance, embrace and say nothing.

Ann resolves to treat the beautiful little imp as family from then on.

'Liz told me that you were expecting. I'm so happy it turned out so well.'

'How could she have known that?' asks Hazel, puzzled 'I didn't tell anyone and I certainly wasn't when I met her.'

Ann smiles as she gazes at the child. She concludes that this must mean that Liz or Berty had seen her or heard from her son. It didn't, it emanated from Liz's hasty and inaccurate conclusion when she had met Hazel in Ilkley, that Hazel was looking for Pete because she was carrying his child.

Wily Ann sits Little Matt on her knee, and looking into his blue eyes sees her son looking back. She says 'Do you know I have a naughty cat called Jacob. Would you like to come and see him?'

'Yes please,' the toddler replies quietly, unused to meeting strangers.

'What colour is he?'

'Black with little white stripe like a tie and he likes little boys.'

'Mummy. I want to see Jaycat.'

Ann smiles contentedly. She knows that any grandson of hers is bound to have the Manford stubborn streak and that pester power would mean Hazel will have to bring him to Ilkley one day.

A week later Little Matt trips and falls whilst toddling along the edge of the lake, still talking about going to see Jaycat and carrying the toy cat that Hazel has bought him, hoping against hope that it will suffice.

He damages his tiny shoulder and seems unable to move his arm without pain. Frightened he may have broken a bone, Hazel takes him to the doctor at the Kendal health centre.

'It's just bruising my dear. He will heal naturally with absolutely no need for anything but rest and some very mild painkillers. If he continues to show signs of discomfort after a few days, by all means bring him back, but I'm sure he will be fine.'

Hazel had been advised by the police to use the Kendal Pharmacy and ones in Windermere and Bowness in rotation in order to keep herself safe. The Kendal one they could monitor from their divisional headquarters more easily, but as the years pass, their initial close scrutiny of staff appointments on her behalf are eventually forgotten.

Her doctor prescribes something for Matty to take to reduce his pain and help him sleep and she goes to the on-site pharmacy. She has a repeat prescription to collect for herself as well. Still occasionally having trouble sleeping and although her doses have reduced to the point where she is looking forward to leaving it all behind, she is not quite there yet and still needs something to help her nod off occasionally to keep away from alcohol.

She approaches the counter and waits her turn in the queue. There are two women working the front desk, one is middle aged and serious who is distributing the prescriptions under her own steam, very ponderously and methodically. The other is very young and unsure of herself, but dealing with the customers as quickly and efficiently as she can.

The chemist twice refers to a colleague in the rear office and asks the man who has his back to the counter if he can come out to the front desk to help her. He remains impassively staring at the wall ignoring her requests.

She and the older woman press on with raised eyebrows feeling that it would be unprofessional to publicly fall out with their colleague.

'Don't worry Karin,' the older one hisses 'I'll speak to the manager about him and request that he's not re-hired after this week. He's only covering for Colin. He's off with his bad back again.'

'Good. That horrible beard is revolting. I know they are all the rage down in London, but he just looks like a git. He has such smart and expensive looking clothes but he needs a shave. He looks like Father Christmas!' In time the queue subsides and Hazel, who has her hands full restraining Little Matt, arrives at the front of the queue.

'Busy day for you lot,' she says breezily.

The girl smiles and studies the two prescriptions carefully.

'I'll have to ask my colleague about this one.' She enters the rear office to consult the pharmacist.

At that moment Hazel is distracted by Matty who has decided to hobble across the floor to investigate an interesting coffee table adorned with magazines and leaflets. The door to the rear office closes quietly when the assistant comes out; pushed from within as if fitted with a closing device, but in fact gently propelled by the occupant of the inner sanctum by the tip of a highly polished Charles Tyrwhitt brogue.

The assistant returns and comments to the other receptionist just beyond earshot of Hazel who is rescuing her son. 'I don't like working with that new locum, he just silently gawps at you when you ask him a question without speaking. V*ery* creepy.'

She asks Hazel 'Is it ok if you wait a few minutes or perhaps come back later as the pharmacist is a little behind with his list. We've been so short staffed recently; I do apologise.'

'Don't worry, I know exactly how it works,' Hazel says without elaborating but experiencing a mild shiver of unpleasant memories. Unwelcome and still hurtful thoughts speed through her mind, but she is used to this now. Extensive therapy and her own moment of rebirth after her near-drowning have taught her to dismiss negative and paranoid feelings.

'We have the power within ourselves to choose whether we look up or down, to allow ourselves to be happy or sad, to see light or shade,' her therapist had said.

Alright for you, you smug twat she thought. *Try going through what I have and see how cheerful you can tell yourself to be.*

It did begin to help eventually though, and she can now almost say she is content. If she hadn't been through the last five years, she would not have had her son, who was now tugging a pile of magazines towards himself, about to upend the coffee table.

'Hey! Come here tiger. Leave that lady alone. I'm so sorry... he is so full of energy.' She grabs him whilst apologising to the sour-faced woman who is directing the kind of stare that only English women direct towards other English mothers; a disdainful look which says *"Call yourself a mother? Control your little brat."*

In a flash she forgets her shiver and her thoughts move on to imagining elbowing the old woman in the face as she swings her child around.

'Here we go, let's have a look at these elephants.'

As exquisite and peerless a joy as motherhood is, she is having difficulty adapting to the constant vigilance required to restrain and protect her inquisitive three year old. As a single parent, there is rarely a moment off and she finds herself unable to hold on to any thought for more than a second or two. At any moment and without a pause for thought her child would do something potentially harmful, heartbreakingly cute or spectacularly antisocial, often involving some vaguely warm fluid being lavishly spread from all parts of his tiny body.

Thankfully, the worst of that period of full-on 24/7 attention was receding a little for Hazel, but out in public areas and becoming more mobile, Matty is now presenting a fresh set of challenges. Her feisty child's break for freedom distracts Hazel and takes her attention away from the counter.

Eventually the assistant emerges with a paper bag.

'Here we are dear, sorry for the delay.'

The back-office door remains closed.

'Hey no problem at all, thanks.'

Hazel puts the package on the dashboard of her car, quickly straps Little Matt in and sets off for home deep in thought.

'Hey Matty boy, can Mummy have a rampant affair with Big Uncle Matt please?' she asks her son. 'Just nod for yes.'

He is already asleep.

She wonders if it's time for her to ditch the sleeping pills. Aware of the possibility that she could now be using them as a prop and could perhaps let nature take its course. Her mother had become addicted to sleeping pills at the end of her life and she knows the danger of becoming dependant on chemicals.

A tumble with hero Matt might help her sleep, but it was time to grow up and stop taking whatever she wanted. She respects him far too much to do that to him. She also knows well how restorative the Lakeland Fells are, how long-distance walking can cure depression, aid restful sleep, allow time for reflection and contemplation, time to consider new adventures and intellectual challenges and inspire all manner of artistic and creative endeavour.

'The NHS should prescribe time in the mountains and hills instead of mountains of pills and time to be ill,' her Aunt Irene regularly tells her. She is a disciple of Wainwright and had retired to the Lakes with her late husband to spend as much time on the fells as she could.

'No substitute for rampant sexual exploration,' she would have said if it were not her aunt talking.

Hazel knows the excitement and joy of new love. Maybe she could do with some chemical attraction instead of a chemical cosh?

Maybe I will take them, but if I do I'm going to make them my last. Or maybe I won't. See how tired I feel later she thinks, as the Hawkshead ferry comes in to dock and she drives aboard.

She agonises about whether or not to ditch the pills or just use this one last prescription. Her own indecision infuriates her.

The ferry docks and as she drives up the ramp she has to swerve around a backpacker who emerges from the pedestrian gate and strays onto the vehicle ramp. He is wearing black, his face covered by a hood and scarf leaving just a slit for his eyes. She waves an apology, even though it's not her fault.

Where is he heading at this time? She wonders. *It's a long walk to anywhere along narrow dark lanes with no footpath up the side of the fell from the ferry.*

But she's not minded to offer anyone a lift these days.

The drive from the ferry back to her aunt's usually takes about 15 minutes and during that journey as she gazes at the bag, she resolves not to take them, then again decides to, back and forth as the packet slides in front of her across the dashboard and back again as she rounds the bends through Far and Near Sawrey.

Her phone rings and reaching across to pick it up as it is sliding away from her she rounds a narrow left hand bend with dry stone walls each side.

'Hero Matt' she reads, taking her eyes off the road for a moment.

Her heart jumps and as she picks up the handset a horn blasts. She notices too late that the road is blocked by a tractor. She drops the phone and applies the brakes as hard as she can.

Everything in the car including her precious son who wasn't strapped in adequately shoots past her and hits the dashboard. Her tyres screech as the tractor approaches and she screams as the car comes to rest against the front wheels of the tractor stopping just in time to crumple the front bumper but nothing else.

'My baby, my baby!' she cries as she removes her seatbelt and runs around to the passenger door. He is out of sight under the foot well and silent.

She picks him up and removes his hood which has slipped forwards to cover his head, to revealing the giggling face of an unharmed baby who had enjoyed the drama and unexpected flight across the car.

Once she has got rid of the angry farmer and resumed her journey her hands stop shaking. She has to admit she had been thinking about Matt too much recently and is confused by his apparently calm acceptance of her rejection.

She now wishes he had fought harder to persuade her or even fought at all.

She knows this route well now despite just coming close to disaster, familiarity the main cause of her lack of concentration. She knows that the phone signal is weak here and that when she turns the next corner she will lose signal completely until she goes to work the next day. She slows down to find a layby to call him from a safe place but there is nowhere and a car behind her that had already been inconvenienced by having to wait for her to sort out her near miss, hoots at her to clear the narrow lane so she drives on home.

Make your mind up, you silly Moo, she tells herself.

The rather odd, silent, bearded, but well-dressed Kendal health centre locum with a crumpled forgery of a DP9 form in his pocket doesn't turn up for work the next day.

Some random dates

1511 Establishment of St James College Cambridge
1525 Establishment of West Fell school, Cumbria
1546 West Fell School is rescued and protected from Henry VIII's commission by its strong links to St James College Cambridge
1551 Ottoman colonisation of Ligeria
1693 John Harrison is born Foulby nr Wakefield
1728 James Cook is born
1764 The Earl of Pembroke is launched, Later renamed the HM Bark Endeavour, the vessel which Cook used to discover Australia and New Zealand
1776 Captain James Cook dies
1803 Birth of Titus salt
1806 Birth of Jacob Behrens
1815 Birth of Samuel Cunliffe Lister
1853 Salts Mill on outskirts of Bradford opens, the World's largest Alpaca weaving shed
1873 Completion of Lister's Mill, Manningham Bradford, the world's largest silk mill employing 11,000 men, women and children
1876 Death of Sir Titus Salt
1889 Death of Sir Jacob Behrens
1893 First national meeting of the independent Labour party. Little Germany, Bradford
1906 Death of Samuel Cunliffe Lister
1910 Italian Colonisation of Ligeria begins
1932 March Sydney Harbour bridge is opened
1942 Birth of Munmar Mohamed Abu Minyar Manoosma in Qusf Abu Hadi. Ligeria
1946 Birth of Benjamin Cornell Anderson
1947 Italy loses control of Ligeria

1960 Audrey Peckitt, a romantic idealistic English student is partying in Rome. She meets a Ligerian history student from Alreef who regales her with stories of struggle and a coming new dawn for his homeland. He gives her a copy of Nasser's 'Philosophy of revolution'.
Chalk and cheese doesn't even begin to describe their differences, but the excitement and courage of youth overrules their misgivings. A brief and frenetic encounter sweeps them to rapture before they begin to argue; he aggressive, passionate and idealistic, she peace loving and vague. After a violent row which requires the police to separate them, he returns home to join the military.
1969 Muammar Mohamed Abu Minyar Manoosma seizes power in Ramalia
1980 Hazel Anderson is born in Cambridge
1983 Sir Ernest Hall and Johnathan Silver purchase and begin to restore Dean Clough Mill Halifax
1987 Jonathan Silver buys and saves Salts Mill
1988 Dr Benjamin Anderson EdD later MBE is appointed head of West Fell School, Cumbria
1997 Death of Jonathan Silver
2000 Urban Splash buy and save Lister's Manningham Mills
2001 July Bradford riots
2003 Manoosma accepts responsibility for downing an American passenger plane and pays compensation
2004 Feb the first of only 7 hand built British Filton fighter T cars is produced
2004 March Tony Blair shakes hands with Manoosma and oil companies sign deals worth £550 million for exploration off the Ligerian coast
2004 May Ligerian football association presents its bid to hold the 2010 world cup.

2004 Feb A man calling himself himself Roberto Antonelli arrives in Bradford to work as a locum pharmacist at a small independent shop near Thornton Rd, Bradford.

2005 Oct Roberto Antonelli and Hazel Anderson move to Cambridge

2007 Replica of HMB Endeavour takes part in celebrations to mark the 75th anniversary of the completion of the Sydney harbour bridge.

2011 Oct Sirte Ligeria. Manoosma is dragged from a drain and executed

2011 June Hazel Anderson takes her three year old son to collect a prescription.

2013 December Ecovril Publishing receive a manuscript from the home of a reclusive neighbour

2014 A man known as 'Wocko The Woodman' unexpectedly disappears from the North Hertfordshire estate where he occasionally helps out managing a deer herd, playing music and writing poetry.

Little is known of him except for the fact that his remote cottage was often empty, sometimes for years at a time.

He would explain these absences when pushed by saying he had been working away

2015 Due to the vision, resilience, hard work and investment made by some inspirational and impressive people, many parts of Bradford are at long last now indeed bouncing back, but the police force is still in dire need of rescue and the NHS has to be carefully watched and nursed.

Roberto Atonelli, DS Peter Manford, Dr Benjamin Anderson and Adrian Collingbridge are all still missing without trace.

Hazel Anderson? Well we know, but we just cannot say.

Thank you page

Without many good and patient people this would not be a book.
We would like to say a huge thank you to everyone who helped
even if they are not mentioned here.

But Especially-
WGR whoever and wherever you are
Peter D
Jim
Derek Salt of the Earth's Crust
Henry
Rosina
Christina
James
Elliott
Paul
Victoria
Becky
Sophie
LWW
Julian Prendeghast
Captain Kev
Mum and all family

But especially the totally fantastic Chau without whom nothing
would get done.
You are my rock, my saviour and the reason the living is
worthwhile.

Design and artwork CNL